THE DIARY OF AN UNWILLING VIRGIN

THE DIARY OF AN UNWILLING VIRGIN

ADAM PEARSON

APEX PUBLISHING LTD

First published in 2005 by
Apex Publishing Ltd
PO Box 7086, Clacton on Sea, Essex, CO15 5WN, England

www.apexpublishing.co.uk

British Library Cataloguing-in-Publication Data
A catalogue record for this book
is available from the British Library

ISBN 1-904444-43-1

Typeset in 10pt Times New Roman

Production Manager: Chris Cowlin

Cover Design: Adam Pearson
(Parts of the Southampton Football Club logo have been used on the front cover design, the logo was kindly supplied by Southampton Football Club)
Southampton Football Club have in NO way endorsed this book.

Printed and bound in Great Britain

To my Mum, for giving me life.

To Janet and Basil, for giving me my wife.

To Alicia and Debbie, for making my life worth living.

To Joanne, for your inspiration.

I would also like to dedicate this book to my precious God daughters, Karen Suzanne Spurgeon and Chloé May Pengelly.

ACKNOWLEDGMENTS

I would like to thank Garry Smith for being the first person to read the manuscript. His positive remarks were a driving force towards publication.

Fiona Burnett's encouragement helped me believe that publication was a course I should take and her input on the cover design helped as well.

Apex Publishing Ltd have been a great help and I am very grateful to them for giving me this chance.

I would especially like to thank everybody at the world's best radio station for their help and support - 107.8FM The Saint.

Finally, without the support of my family this project would not have been possible.

WARNING

Some people may find some of the material in this diary offensive or controversial. My answer to that is that this is my personal diary and you shouldn't be reading it anyway, so hands off!

Any similarities between characters in this diary and real life people, are obvious, but as these writings are for my eyes only it's tough shit!

INTRODUCTION

My name is Troy Brown. I am fifteen years old. I have a mop of mousy blond hair, which won't style into anything, which I find most annoying. I'd love to have a haircut like Duncan of Blue or Charlie from Busted, or indeed anybody else that would make girls fancy me.

My Nan Brown gave me this diary for Christmas, continuing the tradition of giving me naff presents, so I thought I'd make use of it.

I live in Cowes on the Isle of Wight. (I use the word 'on' instead of 'in' as proof that I am an islander, as only a true islander would use that term.)

Cowes is a dying town that only comes to life for one month a year; a month in which all sorts of shops open when the only shops we have for the rest of the year are a couple of supermarkets, two DIY stores, a couple of banks, Woolworths, Boots and lots of yachting stores.

I love this town, but it is fast becoming a large residential unit, which will soon rely entirely on the capital town on the island, which is five miles away, Newport, for all shopping needs.

I live with my mum, Alison, who has long, wavy blonde hair and is quite good looking for her age. I have just overtaken her in height. A few of my mates have claimed that they fancy her! Which I think is sick even though I fancy my own aunt.

I also live with my dad, Kevin, who is slightly overweight and balding at the age of thirty-six. He farts a lot, moans a lot, eats a lot and is obsessed with Southampton Football Club, as am I.

My dog completes our family group. He is a big-boned Yorkshire Terrier called Griz, short for Grizwald. We live in a house, funnily enough! Our house is in a road called Baring Road. It is quite a nice neighbourhood and our house is a detached bungalow with a big front and back garden with a golf course behind it.

All the houses on our side of the road have a stone front wall which, I was told, used to be the boundary wall of Lord Baring's estate, many years ago.

1 January 2003, Wednesday

This morning I was the first one up as Mum and Dad were suffering the ill effects from last night's festivities. I fixed myself some toast and Marmite and settled down in front of the TV. There wasn't much on but I just flicked around the Sky channels for a while.

This went on for an hour or so until my dad staggered into the front room, still wearing most of the Dolly Parton costume he had worn last night. In fact it was all of the costume minus the wig and the fake tits. The make-up that my mum had put on him had originally been applied to specific regions of his face. Now it had all migrated to populate the whole of it.

'Get us a drink, son,' he slurred.

'What do you want? Tea or coffee?' I replied, getting wearily out of my seat.

'Naah! None of that malarkey, mate! Get us a can of lager out of the fridge.'

Drunken sod!

An hour of stereophonic flatulence followed before we set sail, on the Red Jet, to Southampton.

The Red Jet is the most expensive water journey in the world and my dad and I make the trip every time our beloved Saints play at home. Dad foots the bill for me. We have season tickets.

Normally the trip is event free, but on this occasion the two cans of lager that Dad had consumed for breakfast, had, combined with the rocky motion of the Red Jet ferry, made Dad ask the steward for a sick bag. He didn't waste it. Nor did he waste the other two he was supplied with - highly embarrassing as my dad makes a hell of a racket when he retches.

Dad tried to persuade me to agree to join him in a taxi up to St Mary's, but I insisted that we travelled by foot. I told him the fresh air would do him some good. The real reason was that I didn't want him throwing up in the taxi.

This seemed to do the trick, as he seemed to perk up when we got to the ground.

We were playing Tottenham Hotspur in the Premiership, our second closest rivals behind Portsmouth, after they poached our manager, Glenn Hoddle, a couple of seasons ago.

Revenge is sweet as we won one-nil. We virtually floated back to the ferry terminal and got home at around six fifteen.

Mum had our traditional post-match meal ready for us, which is steak and chips. Wonderful!

My mate, Ed, a good-looking lad who wouldn't look out of place in a boy band with his floppy brown hair and his bright blue eyes, phoned during tea.

He asked me if I'd like to go round to his house for a session of games on his X-Box. So, once I'd eaten my cherry cheesecake pudding, I was off.

Ed lives about five minutes away from my house, down Egypt Hill. His Dad always has the most up-to-date electronic equipment. This Christmas he had acquired a DVD recorder! Ed has got one of those Nokia mobile phones that take pictures! Such a gimmick! He took one of me as I arrived at his front door, but you couldn't see anything as it was too dark.

We played a few games, which he won - hardly surprising as he has had so much practice. He always wins in everything he does. It's sickening. He supports Manchester United as well.

After three hours of getting trounced by him and annoyed by his thirteen-year-old little sister, Zoe, I gave up and went home.

When I got in, the front room stunk of Dad's farts so I just went to bed.

2 January 2003, Thursday

Dad was happy this morning. His cheering awakened me. Last March his Nan had passed away and it had taken all this time for probate to be sorted out. The cheque he had been waiting for, his third of her estate, had finally dropped onto the doormat. Twenty-three thousand, four hundred and seventy pounds and seventy-two pence.

'That's it!' he beamed. 'Tonight we are going car hunting!' And he hugged my mum and then me.

He then ran around the house celebrating, Alan Shearer style. It was bloody funny!

My mum had to emphasise that he drive carefully to work, reminding him who would inherit the money if he were to kill himself in the car.

My dad drives a crappy old Vauxhall Astra, so anything would be better than that!

After breakfast, Mum and I walked Griz down to town to get some holiday brochures. We stopped off at Tiffins Café for a cup of tea so that we could browse through them.

A lot of things go through your mind when you have a windfall. I was daydreaming for most of the day but I eventually realised that it wasn't me who had received the money, it was my dad, and this fact was gradually sinking in with Mum as the day went on.

By the time Dad got home from work in the latter part of the afternoon, she had worked herself up to breaking point, and when he came through the front door carrying a digital camera for me and a diamond-encrusted bracelet for her, she flew.

They rowed on for the next two hours or so, in which time I played with my fantastic new digital camera.

Nice one, Dad!

When Mum had eventually calmed down it was well past teatime, so Dad said he'd go out and get a Chinese takeaway. This started her off again!

'YOU'RE GOING TO SPEND ALL THE F***ING MONEY BEFORE THE CHEQUE'S EVEN CLEARED AT THIS RATE!'

Mum only swears when she's really cross. So she swears quite often. Her rages are usually related to money, mess or laziness, of which there is an abundance in our house.

Dad stormed out.

'Now he's going to crash the bloody car!' Mum whined before bursting into tears.

Fortunately, by the time Dad arrived back with the meal, she had got it all out of her system and Dad persuaded her to go out with him to the Cricket Club.

So I was left home alone. Well, I would have been if I hadn't gone round to Ed's to show him my camera. Of course he then had to show me his, which was a combined stills and video camera.

Flash bastard! No pun intended.

I got back home at midnight and planned on going straight to bed. However, I was put off by some disgusting noises coming from my parents' bedroom, so I decided to watch *Sky Sports News* for a while.

3 January 2003, Friday

When I got up this morning Dad had left my pocket money in the usual place plus a bonus of ten pounds. That meant I had twenty pounds for the week.

I phoned Ed to see what he was up to and he suggested that we should go to the cinema. Our mate Spud was at Ed's house when I got there.

Spud is sixteen years old and a stocky lad, who isn't particularly nice looking as far as my mates and I are concerned. He has a similar bad hair problem to me, so he sticks to a grade one all over. He calls it a low maintenance haircut, but he has the most beautiful girlfriend in the world - Lara Matthews.

God, she's lovely! She's fourteen (going on fifteen), slim, with shoulder length, dark brown hair, jewel-like brown eyes and perfect, unblemished skin and hands. She smells good. She IS female perfection.

How he pulled her we'll never know. The lucky bastard!

Ed said that he'd give Meat a call to see if he'd like to come along. Meat is tall and muscular with dark shiny hair and eyes. He also has a bum fluff moustache which we all take the piss out of - behind his back, of course.

Meat's real name is Nathan Edge, but we gave him the nickname Meat and Veg, which was shortened to Meat.

We caught the bus up to Newport and decided to watch *The Lord of the Rings - The Two Towers*. The bad thing was that the cinema had run out of popcorn! How useless is that? A cinema without popcorn!

The film was quite good. I did start to nod off during one of the many long battle scenes though.

That killed a couple of hours and I went to meet Dad at work, ready for our car-hunting trip. He finishes work at two on Fridays but otherwise he finishes at four-thirty. Mum was already there.

We went to the Volkswagen garage and test-drove this excellent, brand new Polo GTi. Dad and I were well taken with it. I think Mum liked it as well. She didn't say much but she smiled a lot.

We were buzzing with excitement when we got home. Mum cooked us dinner while Dad and I browsed through the various Volkswagen brochures that we had collected.

I took one of them round to Ed's house. Even he was impressed, despite the fact that his dad drives a Mercedes.

We played on his X-Box until I actually won a game and he got all stroppy about it. Then Spud turned up, unannounced, very excited.

It is Lara's fifteenth birthday on Monday and she told him she wants to lose her virginity to him that night! He was literally quivering with anticipation and who wouldn't be? He is SOOO lucky!

When I got home I found it very difficult getting to sleep. I can't help thinking that Lara is making a BIG mistake having sex so young. She's so pretty. She could have the choice of any lad at school. I hope it doesn't spoil her. I hope she doesn't get pregnant. Unless it's by me of course!

4 January 2003, Saturday

Dad awakened me this morning. I was right in the middle of a fantastic dream in which I was making love to Lara.

He was in a hurry because he wanted to get up to the Dell Supporters Club in time for the kick-off of the Manchester United versus Portsmouth FA Cup match which was being shown live on the big screen at twelve-thirty. Our match against Tottenham, again, wasn't due to kick off until five forty-five as it was being shown live on BBC1.

When we got up there, at eleven o'clock, there was only one other, bald headed, bloke sat in the best seat, all on his own. It stayed like that throughout the game so the atmosphere was a bit flat, despite the pleasure of watching Pompey get stuffed four-one.

We had lunch in the club - sausages and mashed potato with onion gravy. Lovely!

We stayed in the club for most of the afternoon. It gradually filled up as the day went on, as we watched the development of the other FA Cup third-round ties on *Sky Sports News*. After the final results had come in we went into the stadium.

The match was fantastic! We won four-nil. Dad and I were sat right behind the Spurs dug-out and could see the expressions of pain and misery on Spurs' coaches, Glenn Hoddle and John Gorman's, faces. Exquisite!

When we arrived home at around eight forty-five, Mum told me that Spud had been trying to get hold of me so I gave him a call and he asked me to go round to his house urgently. So I got on my bike and rode all the way down to his house, which is down where the old railway station used to be, in Arctic Road.

When I got there he quickly beckoned me to his room. After I'd sat on his bed and he'd checked that there was no one in earshot he said, 'I've done it, fella!'

'Done what?'

'Had my first shag!'

'First shag?'

'First this year!'

I sat there, with my jaw open.

'But I thought Lara said it would be Monday night?'

Then he dropped the bombshell.

'It wasn't with Lara. It was with Katie Wallace!'

I was gobsmacked. Katie was known as the school bike and, although not ugly, was nothing compared to Lara. Why couldn't he wait just two more days?

'I haven't told anyone, just you. I had to tell someone! Isn't it brilliant?'

I pretended to be impressed and envious while he proceeded to tell me the gory details of his sexual encounter.

When he had eventually finished, about two hours later, I got a chance to ask, 'Why couldn't you wait just two more days?'

'Come on fella! It was handed to me on a plate! It's not guaranteed that Lara will go through with it. This way I get the best of both worlds!'

Hiding my disgust, I made my excuses and went home.

When I got home, Dad was sat there with his feet up watching *Match of the Day*.

I stayed up and watched with him, but my mind was elsewhere - thinking about the dreadful mistake Lara was about to make.

5 January 2003, Sunday

Mum and Dad decided to go to Newport to peruse the sales. I tagged along but while they looked in Next, MK1 and New Look I went off to HMV to look at the CDs and DVDs on offer.

I was just looking at the buy-one-get-one-free DVDs when I felt a tap on my shoulder. I turned round and my heart leapt. It was Lara beaming at me!

'Hi, Troy. What are you up to?'

'Not a lot! You?'

'No. I was thinking of going for a bite to eat at McDonald's. Would you like to join me? We can have a chat.'

My heart lifted. I don't know if I managed to conceal my delight as I said, 'Okay then.'

It was lovely to have a legitimate excuse to gaze into her sparkling brown eyes. To look at her beautiful, soft hands and try to think of an excuse to touch them. To think that Spud could touch her whenever he liked and probably took that fact for granted.

She spent most of the time talking about Spud. I just kept quiet, trying to stop myself from telling her what Spud had been up to.

She told me I was a good listener. But to be honest she could talk about anything just so long as I could spend all my time with her.

When we'd finished we went off to find either her Dad or my parents, depending on whom we found first. We found mine in Dorothy Perkins.

To my delight Lara asked me to accompany her back home on the bus. Dad gave me the bus fare with a wink.

When we arrived at her house, which is about ten minutes' walk from mine, I expected to say goodbye to her on her doorstep but she invited me in. Oh joy!

Her mum's lovely. She reminded me of Mrs Potts from *Beauty and the Beast*. Then I thought about Spud and Lara and that reminded me of *Beauty and the Beast* as well. Her mum gave me a cup of tea and some biscuits and we went to her - gulp - bedroom!

I was just in ecstasy. We talked about the forthcoming return to school for a while. Then she started going on about Spud and her birthday and I, weak that I am, gave in and told her.

She seemed to take it quite well. She thanked me, from the bottom of her heart, and promised that she wouldn't let Spud know that it was me who'd blabbed.

Teatime came oh too quickly and I left, with a guilty feeling in my stomach. This feeling was softened by the warm feeling of pleasure I experienced when I thought of the company I had had today.

Mum and Dad were in when I got home. They presented me with my own pay-as-you-go mobile phone. How excellent is that? I was the only one of our group of friends who didn't have one.

So you can guess what I was doing for the early evening until I was interrupted by the sound of the doorbell.

I opened the door and was shocked to discover Spud standing there with a face like thunder.

'What's up?' I asked, tentatively.

'Aren't you going to invite me in?' Spud grunted.

I stepped aside and Spud made his way through to my bedroom, after waving at my parents through the glazed partition between the hallway and the living room. I followed him, gingerly.

'Lara's blown me out!' he moaned when I'd shut my bedroom door behind me.

'What? She's finished with you?'

'Naah, ya nob! She's made out she doesn't feel well and doesn't want to see me.'

I sat down on my bed feeling greatly relieved. I thought that he had come round to hit me. I thought that Lara had implicated me. But, thankfully, she hadn't.

He tried to persuade me to go out with him but I told him I was tired and wanted to get an early night for school tomorrow. So he left in a bit of a huff.

I wrote out Lara's birthday card and went to bed.

6 January 2003, Monday

This morning one of the most embarrassing things that has ever happened to me occurred. When you wake up in the morning with a full bladder, you often have an erection. My mates and I call it a piss-hard-on adventure. It is more commonly known as 'morning glory'. Now, my inconsiderate mother burst in on me this morning and ripped off my bedclothes. I was fast asleep lying on my back with my willy poking out of the top of my underpants.

Mum obviously looked, and tried to conceal a laugh as she said, 'Come on Troy, school today.'

I quickly flipped onto my front. Mum shut the door and my alarm went off!

I got washed and dressed and went into the kitchen where Mum and Dad had obviously been sniggering to themselves at my expense. I wondered when the first double entendre would rear its ugly head and Dad, predictably, obliged when he called out, 'Don't have too *hard* a day at school, son!' as he left for work.

Mum tried to hide her amusement as I glared at her.

'It's nothing to be ashamed of, love!' she said as she tucked into a digestive biscuit and looked up at me through her eyebrows while reading the horoscope in the paper.

I kept silent, hoping that the subject would now be dropped.

'You'll make some girl very happy one day.'

'MUM!' I scolded as I stormed out of the kitchen with my toast and tea, which I consumed in my bedroom.

The doorbell rescued me at eight-thirty as Ed called to accompany me to school.

I am in year eleven at Cowes High School and this is the stage of term that people have usually decided whether they are going to go to year twelve or not. I rather think not. I want to get a job and some independence, but we'll see what happens after the exams.

I saw Lara as we queued for Maths and I gave her birthday card to her before she went on to her first lesson. She was walking with Katie Wallace, the adulteress!

At break time, Lara came up to me and thanked me for the card and then told me she was going to dump Spud! Mixed feelings of relief and anxiety over Spud's reaction came over me. What if she told Spud it was me who let the cat out of the bag?

When we arrived at our Geography lesson, Spud was stunned about the news but obviously had no idea it was me. He said that he'd asked Katie why she'd told Lara and Katie had said that she was Lara's friend and didn't want to lose her and that she'd regretted it ever since it had happened.

I felt relieved.

At lunchtime I thanked Lara for not saying anything and she said I could go round to her house in the evening to help her celebrate her birthday. I accepted joyously.

After lunch we had English in which we had a debate about cars. This was class joker Jason Dwyer's idea.

I put forward my case on why the Ford Ka was such a naff car and everyone was well impressed. Most people agreed with me that the fact it was such a popular car was amazing. Well most of the boys did, anyway.

Miss Webb, our English teacher, told me that I'd make a good politician. I wouldn't even consider that option. I couldn't give a toss about politics and religion. All they ever seem to do is cause wars and arguments. Look at the problems we've had with Catholics and Protestants, and Muslim extremists and George W. Bush. I could write a thesis.

Things were obviously going well today, after the poor start, and I scored a fine hat-trick in the football match we had in the final lesson of the day, Games.

On the way home, Spud poured his heart out about Lara, but he seemed more annoyed about the money he'd spent on the CD he'd bought her for her birthday. I told him he could get his money back if he still had the receipt. That soon cheered him up.

'What are you up to tonight, fella?'

I had to think fast.

'Oh, erm, I'd better get on with that Geography essay on cloud formations.'

'But that doesn't have to be in until next week!'

'I thought I'd get it done, out of the way.'

'Whatever!'

Off the hook I went home, watched some telly until Dad came in, then we had dinner.

Dad told us that he'd be picking up the new car on Friday afternoon.

After tea I had a long bath and got ready to go round to Lara's. I think I overdid the Lynx because Dad said that I stunk like I'd sprayed the whole lot on me.

I felt a bit out of place at Lara's, as, apart from her two brothers, I was the only lad there. Lara's two best friends were there, Kylie Williams and Kelly Brent. Both of them are really nice-looking girls, but they had nothing on Lara. They all giggled incessantly for the whole evening. She wasn't as much fun as when she's on her own. I spent most of the evening chatting to her mum but having said that, it was still nice to be in the same room as her for an evening.

We did go to Lara's room for a while, but when they started trying to put make-up on me I decided it was time to go.

When I got back home, Dad started lecturing me on how to treat girls.

'Don't jump into bed with them on the first night and always take a condom with you.'

'I do know, Dad. I'm fifteen years old not five!'

7 January 2003, Tuesday

I was awakened this morning with a knock on the door from Mum. Once again my alarm went off moments later. What is the point?

Mum handed me an envelope with my name on it, which she had found amongst the morning mail.

It was from Lara. It read as follows:

Dear Troy

I just wanted to write to you
to thank you for being such a
wonderful friend to me.
If it wasn't for you I would
have made a BIG mistake.
You are a wonderful person.

Lots of love
Lara
xxx

I put the note in my bedside cabinet.

Ed called round for me, as usual, this morning. Apparently Spud is ill with a sickness bug. I hope he hasn't given it to me!

The first wisps of snow were blowing around in the bitterly cold wind.

I did see Lara at a distance during break. She smiled and waved.

I received a text from Spud, during break. It read: 'I DON'T FEEL V WELL. RUNS & CHUNDER'.

How pleasant! Now I'm going to be paranoid about the slightest stomach rumble.

Out of the art room window we could see the year-ten girls playing hockey and Lara was among them - perfect legs. Mr Vibert, our Art teacher, told me off for looking out of the window.

At lunchtime me and Ed went down to the icafé and had a chat with the owner, Vernon. He regularly enthrals us with his tales of women and football. Then it was time for us to go back for Geology.

After Geology we had Maths. There were some roadworks outside and Miss Wainwright, who was standing in for Mr Quick, our cantankerous regular Maths teacher, apologised for the noise saying, 'We'll try and work over the din of that machine gun.'

'It's not a machine gun, Miss.' I said. 'It's a road drill.'

She sent me out of the classroom! I had to spend an hour in the corridor. After the lesson had finished, I apologised and said that I didn't mean to be cheeky but it fell on deaf ears. She's put me in detention tomorrow afternoon. I explained to her that I was supposed to be playing in our school football match against Sandown High but she just said, 'Tough!'

I met up with Ed at the bike sheds and we walked home together. He asked me what I was doing tonight and I said that I wasn't sure.

I wanted to see whether I could see Lara or not before making a decison. So when I got home I texted her: 'WHAT R U DOIN 2NITE?'

She texted back: 'CING KYLIE U?'

Plan B was now in force so I texted her: 'CING HEAD CASE 2 WATCH FOOTY ON TV.'

Head Case was Ed's old nickname. His name, funnily enough, is Edward Case. We don't use this nickname very often, as he hates it.

So after tea and Geology homework I went round to Ed's and we watched Manchester United versus Blackburn Rovers in the Worthington Cup semi-final first leg, which was a one-one draw.

During the match the doorbell went and I didn't think anything of it until I prepared to leave. Dad was in Ed's dad's study looking at his computer. I got a lift home with him.

8 January 2003, Wednesday

I had to go to school by myself this morning as Ed sent me a text saying he now had the bug. When I got to school I discovered that Lara was off as well.

Spud was still rough so I had to hang around with Jason Dwyer and Jason Ince during break and lunch. Both the Jasons had a fiver on whether Dwyer could get off with Katie Wallace before half-term. I chipped in with a fiver that he wouldn't. So that's easy money for me then!

On the subject of Katie Wallace, she came up to me at lunchtime and started chatting about Spud. She was asking me if Spud had said whether he liked her or not. I told her that he hadn't said anything to me.

It seems to me that Katie really likes Spud, but I don't think the feeling is mutual.

That is the first time that I have ever spoken to her. She seems quite nice.

Our first lesson of the day was PE and Mr Castle asked me if I was fit for the game this afternoon. I told him I had detention and he said he couldn't afford for me to be unavailable for the match, as the bug had taken out so many players. He said he'd try and sort things out for me.

Miss Wainwright called me out of my Geography lesson in the afternoon to say, 'Mr Castle has pleaded your case for parole and we have decided that if you score a hat-trick this afternoon you will have the detention revoked.'

'Thanks, Miss,' I said in a surprised voice, even though I wasn't. There was a rumour that Miss Wainwright and Mr Castle had a thing for each other.

I was allowed to leave Geography an hour early to get changed and ready for the two-thirty kick-off.

With Spud and Ed out of the team, we were having to blood new players. Jason Dwyer and Tom Sibley came into the starting line-up.

Tom was very pensive, as he had only come back to school this morning after having had his protruding ears pinned back.

He still got stick, though. Jason Dwyer said, 'If we win we'll have to remember not to mistake him for the trophy, like we used to do.'

The operation had definitely improved his looks. I heard a couple of girls say that they hadn't realised how sexy he was.

I wonder what cosmetic surgery I could have done that would make me popular with the girls or, more specifically, Lara.

It was nil-nil at half-time and Tom was obviously trying to protect his ears as he avoided heading the ball at all costs and Mr Castle substituted him. He brought on that well-known hothead, Jason Ince, who was as quiet as a mouse off the pitch, but a psycho on it and, true to form, in the first minute of the second half he had hacked out their forward and been sent off. The resulting penalty hit the post but as I was running in to clear it, it bobbled up off a divot, hit my knee and went in the roof of the net.

This wound me up and from the kick-off I received the ball and ran past what seemed like twenty players before slotting the ball past their keeper at the near post. The celebration run wore me out.

Our other centre back got sent off about five minutes from time, which meant I had to drop back and defend and try to hold out for a draw.

In injury time, the player I was marking was put through on goal but I had him for pace. I slid in with my tackle but unfortunately the ball spooned up into the air and over our goalkeeper, who had come off his line to close the attacker down, and bounced into the empty net.

There was no coming back from that and the double jeopardy for me was that I had detention on Friday afternoon, so I would miss the arrival of our new car.

I stayed at home this evening and watched television. With all my friends going down with the bug it was like waiting on death row for the first symptoms to arrive.

Dad and I watched Sheffield Wednesday beat Liverpool two-one in the other Worthington Cup semi-final first leg.

9 January 2003, Thursday

So far so good as far as escaping the bug is concerned. I had another lonely trip to school this morning and when I got there our form teacher Miss Steele was off and Miss Wainwright took registration.

The year hardnut, Terry Smith, was back after his six-week suspension for headbutting a year-twelve prefect after he'd been told off by the prefect for smoking in the toilets. Terry was quite intimidating, even to the teachers, when he was in a bad mood, but I always got on quite well with him, ever since I beat him in an arm wrestle at Solent Middle School.

We had a free lesson in Biology, with Mrs Bowen being off.

At break time Terry just went up to Katie Wallace and put his hand down the front of her skirt, took it out again and said, 'Yep! She's got pubes!'

'Get lost!' said Katie with a big smile on her face. Me, Tom and Jason Ince were in stitches of laughter.

At lunchtime we all went down to the icafé where Terry and Katie were spotted flirting outside the bank. Well Katie was doing all of the flirting, anyway.

I wish I could pull a girl that quickly and easily. Mind you, it *was* Katie Wallace.

I sent a text to Spud to warn him about Terry and Katie.

History was so boring this afternoon that I was nearly nodding off. The bell was such a relief.

Ed phoned me this afternoon saying that he felt much better and asked if I would like to go round to his. I would have loved to but didn't want to take the risk, so I declined his offer. Then I got a text from Lara asking me if I'd like to go for a walk with her and her dogs. I thought that I would be less likely to catch anything from her in the fresh air so I agreed.

She called round for me and we walked along the seafront. At one point I took the dog leads and she took hold of my arm. If only I could have frozen that moment. But it was over all too quickly.

I told her about Terry and Katie and that everyone thought that Katie was a bit of a tart.

Lara defended her by saying that she had a hard time at home and that she was just vulnerable. Katie lives with her cantankerous old grandmother and doesn't get much love at home, so she seems to go after it in any way, shape or form that she can.

I began to feel a bit sorry for her.

Lara invited me in but I turned her down, making out I had History homework to do when really I didn't want to get anywhere near any germs that might still be present in her house. As I left she kissed me on the cheek. Normally I would have absolutely loved it, but all I could think of were the germs. She saw that I looked uncomfortable and apologised. I went away calling myself an idiot under my breath.

When I got home Dad asked me if I'd had a nice time.

I said that I had and he asked, 'Have you asked her out yet?' I replied that we were only friends.

He said, 'Yeah, right! I can tell you are smitten!'

I stayed silent for a while and then pointed out that I had absolutely no chance with her. He said, 'How do you know until you've tried?'

10 January 2003, Friday

I lay awake for hours, pondering whether to ask Lara out or not. I didn't want to lose her friendship, but I didn't want to miss out if I had any chance of having her as my girlfriend. I decided that I would ask her but I would have to pick my moment.

At breakfast I was watching some news article on GMTV about some siege that had ended. The police officer being interviewed said that the gunman refused to give himself up alive. At that point Mum changed channels. I expect he continued to say, so we shot him.

Ed called round this morning. I told him that it would look a bit suspicious if Spud didn't turn up at school today, as he was the first to go down with the bug, so he texted Spud to let him know that he was going in. Spud didn't reply.

As Miss Wainwright was doing registration, an out-of-breath Spud came bursting through the door, apologising profusely.

Miss Wainwright used a typical old teacher-to-late-pupil cliché to greet him.

As we filed out of the room a few minutes later, Spud told me and Ed that Tom was having his sixteenth birthday party tonight and that he'd sorted out some bottles of cider to take, courtesy of Tom's older brother, Karl. All we had to do was pay two pounds for each bottle.

At break time Spud, me and Ed met up with Lara, Kylie, Kelly and Katie to tell them about the party. Spud kept very quiet in what was obviously an uncomfortable situation for him.

When Terry turned up, Katie latched on to him like a limpet. He didn't look very comfortable with this and at lunchtime I spotted Katie crying on her own behind the school minibus.

'What's the matter?' I asked her.

'Terry doesn't want me,' she sobbed.

'Don't worry. Still come out tonight, we'll cheer you up.'

She carried on crying but did agree to come.

I made sure it was all right with Terry later and he said he couldn't give a toss and that Katie was like a giant octopus.

In detention I caught up with the work I had missed because of being sent out. It was dark when I left.

When I arrived home I assumed that one of Mum's friends had turned up because a Ford Ka was parked in our drive. I thought that Dad would be furious not to be able to drive his new car straight into his own driveway.

When I got into the house, there was just Mum and Dad sat beaming at me from their usual chairs.

'Well, what do you think of her then?' asked Dad.

I paused for a while, trying to work out who Dad was referring to. I assumed he meant Mum as she was the only female I could see.

'She's not bad for her age.' I changed the subject. 'I thought you were getting the new car today.'

Dad looked at me with exasperation.

'I'm talking about the new car, dung head!'

I hoped it wasn't true but I had to ask, despite realising.

'You bought a Ford Ka?'

'Yes,' said Dad, ironically.

Scenarios of chronic piss-taking from everyone at school started to form in my mind as I tried not to look disappointed.

'I thought we were going to get the Polo GTi.'

'I got a very good deal for this one, mate. Your mum made me realise that this way we'd have nearly four grand extra in the bank. You'll grow to like it. It's much better than the bloody Astra!'

Dad was right with the last thing he said, but I now had to prepare myself for some serious stick.

Ed and Spud called round at seven and we met up with Lara, Kylie, Katie and Kelly on the corner of Woodvale Road and made the ten-minute walk to Place Road Stores where we me up with Karl.

I had my ten pounds pocket money, so I ordered two bottles of cider and chipped in for a communal bottle of vodka. There were so many bottles to carry that we all struggled with carrier bags and began drinking the cider to lighten the load.

The party was pretty good even though Tom's parents had promised to come home at eleven o'clock, which would signal the end of the party.

Karl acted as bouncer. He was wearing a Fulham shirt. I pulled his leg about this fact.

'Why do you support them?'

'My dad showed me a video of George Best and Rodney Marsh playing for them and taking the piss out of the opposition, Hereford I think, and I just started listening out for their results and began supporting them.'

'Does your dad support Fulham, then?'

'No, he supports Manchester United.'

'Oh. How often does he go to see them play?'

'He's never seen them play, apart from on the telly, of course.'

I raised my eyebrows and thought to myself, typical Man U supporter. 'Have you ever seen Fulham play?'

'Yes, I saw the one-all draw at The Dell, last season.'

'At The Dell? That's good, considering it had been knocked down for months by then.'

'Saint Mary's then! Sorry, I can't get used to saying it.'

'I suppose you call your current ground Craven Cottage, do you?'

'No, we are ground-sharing with QPR at the moment.'

'Yes, I know.'

'Why did you say Craven Cottage, then?'

'Never mind.'

Katie got very drunk very quickly and eventually she was lying on the living room floor, semi-conscious. Every lad, that didn't have a girl with them at the party took it upon himself to snog and grope her while she was in this state. They all had a hand down her knickers and, even in my drunken state, I thought that this was bang out of order. I was tempted, I admit, for reasons of curiosity, but I couldn't bring myself to do it.

A bit later the girls had dragged Katie upstairs to the toilet where she was sick.

It felt like the night had only just begun when Tom's parents arrived home and everyone left.

Me, Tom, Spud, Lara, Kelly, Ed, Meat and Kylie all went down to the chalets in Gurnard to drink the vodka.

Somehow I ended up falling down the embankment and banging my head. In my semi-conscious state I recall Lara coming over to see if I was all right and everyone else laughing. Then I sat up and shouted, 'GUESS WHAT?' They at once shouted, 'WHAT?'

'MY DAD'S JUST BOUGHT A FORD KA.'

This was followed by deep laughter from the boys and 'What's wrong with that?' et cetera from the girls.

With plenty of Dutch courage inside me, I slung my arm around Lara as we propped each other up on the way back up the steep incline of Woodvale Road.

'I love you, Lara.,' I half-slurred and half-dribbled into her ear.

'I love you too, mate,' she slurred in reply.

Even in my drunken state I recognised the platonic nature of her response.

We sat on the curb outside Lara's house for a while, and Meat and I pretended to fish in the gutter.

Eventually me and Ed gave up and left them all to it.

I started to feel very sick and disoriented when we reached our drive and threw up.

After I'd got into bed the room started spinning and when the text alert went off on my phone I had to leave it.

11 January 2003, Saturday

I was sick first thing this morning and my parents sadistically cooked a fry-up for breakfast, which helped me bring up more bile.

My dad was moaning about the vomit that he had just washed off the side of the car when I managed to collapse into one of the chairs in the living room. I remember vomiting but I hadn't realised where. I couldn't admit it to him.

Mum fixed me a pint of orange squash, which tasted strange. This was followed, over the next hour, by a couple more pints, each one tasting better than its predecessor.

When I felt that I could stand without instantly retching, I went into my room to get my mobile and read the text I couldn't read last night. It was from Lara: 'YES ID LUV 2 GO OWT WIV U :).'

My heart jumped into my throat. I could not, for the life of me, remember plucking up the courage to ask her but that didn't matter. I went into the bathroom to freshen up, suddenly feeling perfectly fine.

It took me about an hour before I felt that I looked and smelt all right, and I went out on my way to Lara's house. It was eleven-thirty when I left.

Lara looked surprised and tired as she invited me in. I went to kiss her but she didn't seem to notice. She led me into her living room where I was shocked to find Tom lounging on her settee. 'All right?' I said in an inquisitive manner as I sat in the chair opposite. Then, to confuse me even further, Lara came into the room carrying a glass of juice. She put the glass down and lounged on the settee, wrapping her arms around Tom.

Lara noticed the confused expression on my face and said, 'Me and Tom got together last night after you lot left.'

I then realised that she must have sent the text to me by mistake, as I was also under 'T' in the address book on her mobile phone. I imagined my head changing into the head of a jackass like in a Tex Avery cartoon. Then I had to watch them two smooching while making awful small talk for, I decided (so as not to make my visit look strange), an hour.

When I got home, Mum and Dad had gone out in the car so I had the house to myself. I went to bed and switched on the radio to listen to the Middlesbrough versus Southampton match, which was a two-two draw despite Saints being two-nil up halfway though the second half.

Mum and Dad brought home a Megabucket from KFC, which was most welcome as my appetite had returned with a vengeance.

Dad asked me what I had planned for tomorrow and I said that I had nothing planned and he asked me to go out with him and Mum for a drive in the new car. I felt obliged to go so agreed to do so.

When *Blind Date* came on the TV I decided to go round to Ed's. I timed it rather well, as his family were just about to sit down and watch the DVD of *Bend It Like Beckham*.

I told Ed about Lara and Tom and he said, 'You were a bit slow there, weren't you? You'll not make that mistake again.'

I bet I will.

12 January 2003, Sunday

I had a bit of a lie-in this morning before our big trip out in the new car. We set off at eleven-thirty so that we would arrive at the Eight Bells Inn for lunch. The Eight Bells is very popular and we wanted to make sure we got a table.

I ordered half a chicken and chips. Mum ordered lasagne and chips and Dad went for roast beef and yorkshire pudding.

Mum's meal and mine turned up at the same time, but there was a new man at the bar and he made a mistake with the computerised till, which didn't register Dad's meal.

The good thing, though, was that he got his meal for free. However, he did have to wait ten minutes while it was prepared and Mum and I continued our meals.

The car is quite nippy and Dad was right when he said it was much better than the Astra. I'll have to get used to it anyway as I will probably have to learn to drive in it.

After lunch we went into Newport so that Mum could look around the clothes shops.

I went to HMV but this time I didn't bump into Lara. I expect she was smooching with Tom somewhere, lucky sod.

I bought the Girls Aloud CD single in HMV and went looking for Mum and Dad in Boots, as that was where they said they were when I phoned them.

The security alarm went off as I walked into Boots. I looked around and nobody seemed to be leaving with anything. Then I met Mum by the One-Hour Photo Centre and she asked me to hold the bag she had just been given containing the camera she had just bought. Then she told me to wait there while she fetched Dad from Hursts DIY shop. So I browsed around and got a text from Mum telling me to meet them both at the car.

So, slightly irritated by being messed around, I headed for the front of the shop and as I went through the door the alarm sounded and a security guard grabbed me by the shoulder. He grabbed the bag with the camera in it and shook his head, 'Come with me, son.' He said as he led me to this office upstairs.

I tried to explain that it was my mum's shopping, but they wouldn't believe me because I didn't have the receipt. I said, 'What about the bag?'

'That's an old trick,' the security bloke replied.

My phone rang and I was about to answer it when the store manager snatched it out of my hand.

'To whom am I speaking?' he said. Then he paused. 'Oh I am the manager of Boots. We have your son here on suspicion of shop-lifting. He tried to leave the store with a camera.'

Then an uneasy expression appeared on the man's face. 'Okay Mrs Brown, we'll see you in a few minutes.'

Several minutes later my mum came into the room in a rage, waving the receipt at the security guard.

'How dare you treat my son like a criminal?' she ranted. 'I want a refund on this camera! I'll get one from Argos.'

The manager was very creepy and apologetic but you don't mess with Mum when her gander's up. She got her refund.

As we left the shop the alarm went off yet again. It turned out that the CD I'd bought from HMV was setting it off.

'If you'd taken me with you when you left Boots, none of that would have happened,' I said to Mum as we walked back to the car, which was parked in Currys' car park.

'Sorry, love,' said Mum.

We went to Argos but they didn't have her camera in stock.

Then we went to see my Grandad Brown. My Nan and Grandad Brown divorced ten years ago but are beginning to strike up a new friendship as they head into their mid-sixties.

Grandad took early retirement last September. He is a large man with a gravelly voice but, although he can be ferocious, he is mainly as soft as a teddy bear. He's just like his son, my dad, in a lot of ways flatulence, mainly. They seem to have their own way of communicating while they are together. 'Smelly thunder from down under,' Grandad calls it. That phrase never fails to have my dad in stitches of laughter.

When the methane levels reach danger point we usually have to leave.

We then went round to my Nan's in Pan Estate.

Pan Estate has a reputation for being a rough area. That's how Nan got her house so cheap. But she's never had any trouble since she moved there and her place is really nice.

We had tea and toasted teacakes while we were there. Nan, in contrast to Grandad, is very small in stature but has a larger than life personality to make up for it. She's always the life and soul of any social gathering.

We left at seven, as Mum wanted to get back in time for *Coronation Street.*

When we got home, Dad got me to help him take some boxes into the house. They turned out to contain a bloody superb computer, printer and scanner.

'Call it a late Christmas present,' Dad said with almost a tear in his eye as he saw the expression of sheer delight on my face.

I gave him a kiss on the cheek and Mum a huge hug.

'This will help you with your Computer Studies homework.' she said.

Dad and I set up the computer. He'd made sure it was a better spec that Ed's. That's why he was around there the other night.

Before we knew it, it was one a.m. What a topsy-turvy day!

13 January 2003, Monday

I could hardly wait for Ed to call round this morning. I quickly invited him in to show him the computer. He was well impressed but added, 'We are going to be upgrading ours soon.'

He'll have to wait a few months, though, if he wants to upgrade to something better, as you can't buy better than this.

Ed told me that the rest of his family, apart from his little sister Zoe, had gone down with the bug, and when we met Meat and Spud they said that their parents had also succumbed.

Tom said his parents were all right but Karl was ill and was worried that he wasn't going to be well enough to take his driving test on Wednesday.

When Miss Steele, our form teacher, did the register, it transpired that Terry was off sick as well. This bug is rife. I bet I catch it and miss the Liverpool game on Saturday. That would be typical of my luck.

Me, Meat, Ed and Spud met up with Lara and her friends at lunchtime. We all went down to see Vernon at the iCafé, but Ricky Kinsella, the town drunk, was sat on the seat opposite, whisky in hand, abusing everyone. This didn't bother me but the girls were a bit freaked out so we all went back to school.

In the English lesson debate this afternoon I had to put forward the case in favour of cloning. I said that clones are represented as complete copies of people in literature and on the media, personalities and all. I said that this was impossible, as identical twins are naturally occurring clones and their personalities are different. I said that couples in which one person is infertile could clone one or the other parent in order to have a baby. This was not well received by the debaters and when I defended myself by saying that each family should be allowed to have a maximum of two cloned children, one of each sex, I was laughed out of the debate.

I thought I'd put up a good case but Miss Webb said that she took back her remark of last week, saying I'd just committed political suicide.

It was a stupid theme anyway. I didn't ask to be selected for it.

After we'd finished games in the afternoon we were walking back to the changing rooms when Lara called out of the art room window, 'Nice legs, Troy!'

The feeling is mutual, although I don't think she was being serious as I heard laughing in the background after she'd called out. She also blew a kiss at Tom and shouted, 'Tom, show us your six pack!'

Tom blushed but duly obliged, to whoops of delight from the girls in the art room.

Mr Castle said that technically I shouldn't have had to do detention last week because Miss Wainwright said I could get off if I scored a hat-trick, and I did, in an unorthodox way.

I couldn't wait to get home and play on the computer. Dad has set up the phone line for unlimited Internet access as well.

I had my tea while playing on the computer. Ed and Meat came round to mess around on the Web and we had the TV on while Pompey lost to Sheffield United. Excellent!

Ed showed me some good chat rooms, especially for teenagers. We got chatting to this girl, Daisy, who is fifteen and seems really nice.

Spud was supposed to be coming round but apparently he's got a new girlfriend. What a surprise!

The lads were kicked out at eleven o'clock by Mum. Though she did it politely, it was embarrassing. I went to bed soon afterwards - knackered!

14 January 2003, Tuesday

When Ed and I got to school, we met up with Spud who was telling all about his new girlfriend who is an older woman and doesn't mind the fact that he is only sixteen. She has her own house and he spent a whole afternoon in bed with her when he was meant to be off sick. So he never did have the bug! He wouldn't tell us her name. Apparently, she is still married.

At break time there was a scrap between Terry and his usual best mate, Jason Ince. Mr Castle broke it up. Ince seemed to come off the worst.

In Art, Tom Sibley was mucking around, making clay penises and breasts while he thought Mr Vibert was out of the room. Unfortunately, for both of them, Mr Vibert crept up behind Tom and grabbed his ear. He obviously had forgotten about his recent operation. Tom let out a squeal of pain and blood started to trickle down his neck.

Mr Vibert looked horrified. 'Sorry Sibley!' he said in his posh voice.

Tom showed Mr Vibert the blood, which had transferred to his hand.

'Come on, I'll take you to the medical room.' He put his arm around Tom as he led him out of the room and shouted over his shoulder, 'The rest of you get on with your work, QUIETLY!'

Five minutes later Miss Wainwright, who had been teaching in the class next door, came in and told us off for all the noise we were making.

Mr Vibert came back about fifteen minutes after that and said that Tom had been taken to Casualty. Everyone went quiet for a few moments, and then murmuring began as we all wondered if Mr Vibert would get into trouble.

Tom sent Lara a text message at lunchtime to say that the wound had reopened and that he would not be in for the rest of the day. Lara said that she was going to bunk off for the afternoon to be with him.

Me, Ed, Meat, Jason Dwyer and Spud The Stud, as we were now calling him, went down to the icafé. It was quieter than yesterday as Ricky Kinsella was crashed out on his seat.

Vernon tried to bribe me out of my season ticket for Saturday's match against Liverpool as he is a Liverpool supporter. The match had sold out and he offered me fifty quid. I declined.

After a very boring Geology lesson, it was Maths and the return of Mr Quick.

Quicky is a tubby, balding Welsh tyrant who runs his lessons as if they were torture chambers, and you will suffer unless you are pretty with big tits, like Hayley Knight.

Every lesson is an episode in comedy involving Jason Dwyer, who Quick hates because he is the only one in the class who is not scared of him.

I can't write down the whole lesson word for word but I will try to include a funny moment from the day's lesson:

Episode One of Maths:

'What's the answer to this one then Jay-sern Dwyer?'

'I don't know, sir.'

'IT'S ON THE BOARD! Just goes to show ewe weren't listening were ewe?'

‘Pardon, sir?’
‘Get out.’

We walked home and the lads were discussing an evening out, hanging around the town, as it had warmed up a bit outside. I declined because I wanted to get back to the chat room and chat to Daisy.

She didn’t appear in the room until around eight o’clock and we chatted for two hours. She lives in Eastleigh so we might be able to meet up one day.

I asked her to e-mail me her picture and I e-mailed mine to her, but by the time I had packed up, at about ten-thirty, I hadn’t received a reply

15 January 2003, Wednesday

I am absolutely gutted! I found out, on the way to school, that Ed, Tom and Meat had met up with Lara, Kylie, Kelly and Katie. They went down to Gurnard Bay at night and skinny-dipped. The girls were completely naked as Ed described, ‘Tits, pubes an’ all.’

I can’t believe I missed seeing Lara naked. I am so disappointed. Why do I always miss out on things like this?

My mind was on it all day and I couldn’t concentrate, or miss the secret winks and smiles between all the skinny-dippers at break and lunchtime.

Apparently, Mr Vibert wasn’t in school today. Everybody, except Tom, thinks he’s been suspended. Tom says that he will stick up for Mr Vibert if he is in trouble, which I think is good of him.

We found out that the release date for the next Harry Potter book, *The Order of the Phoenix*, has been confirmed as June the twenty-first. I phoned up Ottakers bookshop and they hadn’t heard the news, but the lady I spoke to put my name down and said that I would be top of her list. She would try to get me a first edition. Try? I would be desperately disappointed not to get a first edition after being top of the list!

We had an away match at Medina High School this afternoon and were virtually back to full strength, which is probably why we won three-nil. I scored two and Meat, our big centre back, got one as well.

The lads were planning another night out on the town with the girls.

I wasn’t going to miss out this time.

When I got home from school I checked my e-mail and I had got one from Daisy. Her picture is fantastic. She is really pretty.

At seven, Ed, Meat, Jason D, Tom, Lara, Kylie and Kelly called round and we walked down the town. We spent an hour or so in the icafé. Vernon said that one of his football manager friends had watched our match this afternoon and was revelling about one of our players who scored two goals. That was me! He asked me if I minded if he gave the bloke my phone number. I said that I didn't.

He also told me a rather amusing joke: An Englishman, a Scotsman and an Irishman walk into three separate bars. The Englishman walks into a wine bar, drinks a bottle of Dom Perignon and ends up in bed with the barmaid. The Scotsman goes into his local pub, drinks eight wee drams of whisky and ends up in bed with a prostitute. The Irishman walks into a steel bar and ends up in hospital with a gashed head and concussion.

After a while we headed off for the seafront. We had just got past Egypt Point on our way towards Gurnard when this car came screaming along the Esplanade. It screeched to a halt beside us.

'Who's that idiot in the RS Turbo?' asked Meat.

'Oh, yeah,' said Tom, ' I forgot to tell you Karl passed his test this afternoon.'

Karl leant out of his window, 'Anyone want a ride?'

Tom and Lara climbed in, followed by Kylie and Kelly.

They sped off at high speed, and revs, after turning round at the junction to Egypt Hill and the Esplanade. You could see curtains at the nearby old people's flats twitching as they roared away.

This left me, Meat, Ed and Jason.

As we were at the foot of Egypt Hill we decided to go to Ed's house. We went on Ed's computer and found Daisy in a chat room. She said that she only wanted to chat to me when I mentioned that all my mates were with me. So I rushed home and chatted with her for an hour or so before going to bed.

I can't believe I missed out on the skinny-dipping again!

16 January 2003, Thursday

I was reading in the paper this morning that TV presenter Matthew Kelly has been arrested after being accused of child abuse by two people. A few years ago Southampton football club's then manager, Dave Jones, was accused of abusing over twelve children but was found to be innocent. I think that trial by media is awful. To be accused of sexually abusing children and to be innocent of the charge must be the worst situation to be in. In this country you are supposed to be innocent until proven guilty.

Meat and Jason called round this morning and we met up with Tom at the school gates. He said they had had a great time tearing around in Karl's car last night.

'He's a bloody good driver! You'll never guess what speed we got up to along Forest Road? One-twenty! It was wicked!'

Jason Ince and Terry had obviously patched up their differences today because they were acting like they had been the best of mates for years, laughing and joking and slapping each other's back. Weird!

At break time, Lara and Tom got told off for kissing behind the bushes at the bottom of the field. Apparently, Mr Castle caught them and things had progressed past the kissing stage and on to the next, but Tom said that it was only a passionate grope. Lara was in tears because she was told that her parents would have to be informed. Tom got detention because when Mr Castle started on about teenage pregnancy he said, 'We have just had a Biology lesson, sir!'

At lunchtime, me, Spud, Ed, the Jasons, Tom, Lara, Kylie, Kelly and, for a change, Terry went down to the icafé.

Ricky Kinsella was back to his abusive self and this gave Terry the chance to give him some verbal back. They were standing, like two stags ready to lock antlers, exchanging threats and snarling at each other.

Jason Ince was just about to go over to pull Terry away (he'd been watching with great amusement, with the rest of us) when Kinsella made a drunken lunge at Terry. Terry avoided it easily but somehow lost his footing and fell over. Kinsella just fell on top of Terry and started wrestling with him.

Someone had obviously called the police near the start of the argument because you wouldn't normally see a policeman in Cowes. It was the two officers that had responded to the call that prised Kinsella off Terry, who then put on the hard-done-by-victim act.

After Terry had given his details, Kinsella was dragged, handcuffed, into a police car and driven away.

Ricky Kinsella has a long history of time in and out of prison for similar incidents.

Well, that made the lunch break go quicker than normal, as it was oh too soon that we were back at our desks for an afternoon of History.

Spud is being very cagey about his new girlfriend. Nobody has seen her yet and we are thinking of setting up a surveillance plan to get a glimpse of her.

Lara walked home with Ed and me. She said that she wasn't seeing Tom tonight and asked me if I'd like to go round to her house for a chat. I felt a bit embarrassed being asked in front of Ed and tried to sound unenthusiastic as I said, 'Yeah, all right then.'

It must have been good acting, as Lara said, 'You don't have to if you don't want to!'

'No, no!' I blurted quickly, 'I do. Honestly, I do.'

Ed just smirked at me.

When I got home, Mum was all worried. Griz, the dog, wasn't very well. He had a swollen arse. Dad said that he looked like a baboon. He was scooting around the carpet on his backside. Mum calls this action, 'tobogganing'.

I went with Dad to take him to the vet. On the way, Dad was moaning because the view at every other junction seemed to be obscured by a variety of white vans. We nearly had a collision at one junction when a white Ford RS Turbo went past at very high speed and Dad only just avoided hitting it. I recognised the car as being Karl's, but Dad was seething so much that I thought it best not to mention it.

When we took Griz in to see the vet it turned out that the scent gland in his anus was impacted (blocked). The smell that came out when the vet relieved the problem was horrendous.

'He'll need a bath when you get him home. He'll stink,' the vet observed.

Stating the obvious or what?

After he had been bathed I thought I'd take Griz round to Lara's so we could walk all our dogs together. Unfortunately, he was in a bad mood and got very snappy with Lara's big, fat Labrador cross, Loo Loo, and I had to take him home. Lara came with me, without her dogs. She held my arm as we walked. That was nice. I walked as slowly as I could so that I could savour the moment, but we reached my house very quickly.

When we went in, my dad was out and Mum was giggling on the phone to someone, so I took Lara to my room and showed her my CDs. Then we perused some old photograph albums containing pictures of me when I was little. Lara snuggled up to me to look. I tried to draw out the exhibition for as long as I could.

Lara said that I was very sweet as a child. Then she put her arm around my shoulder and said, 'You still are!'

I couldn't think of anything to say and got all tongue-tied. Then I fumbled round for some other old albums, which we looked at. It was just wonderful to spend this time with her. But the time was cut short when Mum knocked on my bedroom door saying I had a visitor. It was Tom. He said that he had finished helping his dad decorate their living room and had decided to go to Lara's, and Lara's mum had directed him to my house.

Lara was positively delighted to see Tom. I had to go back through my photo albums for Tom's benefit. This time he had the benefit of even closer contact with her, and the exhibition of our old family snaps just wasn't as enjoyable.

After we had finished looking at the pictures the subject turned to Spud. Tom and Lara were planning to spy on him on Saturday to try to get a glimpse of the mystery girl, so I agreed to lend them my digital camera.

After listening to their plans of espionage, into which they have enlisted Meat and Ed, I saw them off at my front door and went to bed. I look forward to getting reports on their findings.

17 January 2003, Friday

Spud was getting more and more wound up as the day went on as we teased him about his girlfriend. At one stage he even grabbed Meat's V-neck jumper. I think he shocked himself because he soon let go but he didn't say anything.

At lunchtime everyone else went down to town but I made my excuses so that I could find Spud and have a chat with him. I went around the school looking for him but couldn't find him anywhere.

Katie Wallace said she'd seen him heading towards the golf club so I gave up.

However, I did meet up with him as we left at the end of the day, and I took a diversion home via his house so that we could chat.

He said that he couldn't handle the piss-taking about this girl because he felt differently about her. He said that he was in love with her.

He said that he'd been seeing her since New Year's Eve. So he was three-timing Lara at one point! I wonder if his new girlfriend knows about his fling with Katie?

He must love her, though. He just doesn't want to talk about his sexual exploits with her as he has done in the past.

It's like Spud has grown up overnight, the boring git!

I didn't get home until half past four. Mum and Dad must have had a row because Dad was sulking in front of the television and Mum was sulking in her room. I went on the computer and chatted with Daisy for a couple of hours. She was getting very saucy and erotic with the things she was saying. I never realised that typing suggestive things on a keyboard could turn you on. Eventually I had to go to bed. I was so tired.

18 January 2003, Saturday

When I checked my e-mail this morning I got the following message:

> *Dear Troy,*
>
> *You were fantastic last night. I really REALLY want to meet you.*
> *Please e-mail back soon so that we can arrange a meeting.*
> *If you want me.*
> *I want you.*
>
> *All my love*
> *Daisy*

I sent a message back to her saying that I wanted to meet her too.

I went to see Ed this morning to tell him the news. He said he wanted to come along, secretly, to get a glimpse of her. That will be a laugh.

I went home for a steak and chips lunch, for a change. Dad was washing the car. When I got in, Mum was on the phone. I heard her say something with the phrase 'it's late' in it. I didn't catch any more of what she said, but to make conversation I asked her what was late and she went berserk. She told me off for eavesdropping!

It turns out that she had ordered some clothes from her catalogue well before Christmas and they were well overdue. Fair enough, but what an overreaction, though.

After lunch, Dad and I made our way to St Mary's Stadium to watch Southampton's terrible performance against Liverpool. Our seats were near the front and we got absolutely soaked in the swirling rain.

Before the game, which we lost one-nil, as usual, we went into The Dell Supporters Club where Dad met former Saints and Liverpool midfielder, Jimmy Case.

Dad was a right idiot, acting as though he'd known Case all his life.

Case must be used to people like Dad because he did a great job of humouring him. We got our programmes signed, but that ended up being a pointless act because the rain soaked everything we had.

When we got home I couldn't get on the computer quick enough to see what Daisy had written.

I had no e-mails, but I got in touch with her in our usual chat room and we had a private chat and arranged a meeting before the Millwall game next week. I'm going to go with Ed to that game, so I phoned him up this evening and Dad helped me buy the tickets online.

Daisy will meet me by the rock at the entrance to Asda, the rock that has Asda's low-price promise on it or something. This week is going to go so slowly.

19 January 2003, Sunday

This morning Mum and Dad announced that next weekend Grandad Brown would be staying here to look after me while they went away to Paris for a dirty weekend.

I must say I am very surprised that Dad is prepared to miss a home game for Mum. I bet she was well impressed.

We went around in the car to pick up Grandad and Nan to bring them round to our house so that Mum could cook us all a big roast.

It was nice to see Nan and Grandad getting on so well and it seems that they are finding a new friendship. Obviously, they can't live together, but they still enjoy each other's company, in small quantities.

When Mum and Dad decided it was time to take Nan and Grandad home, I decided to go to Lara's to see if there were any developments in 'Spud Watch'.

Lara and Tom said that they had followed him for two hours but didn't see him with any girls. They gave me my camera back. I must say I was a bit disappointed. I was expecting to hear some interesting news.

We all went out and walked to Ed's house. Meat was there and we had a chat about various things before heading off for a walk along the Esplanade.

Lara had phoned Kelly and Kylie and we met them by the chalets in Gurnard. It was dark by now and the place was deserted. After a session of stone-skimming, Meat suggested skinny-dipping. I have never been so excited in all my life, especially when the girls all agreed with enthusiasm.

Everybody started to take their coats off, so I busied myself with getting all my clothes off as quickly as I could. Soon I had slipped off my underpants. It was very cold. I could hear sniggering and looked round to get my first ever look at naked women in the flesh.

To my horror and infinite embarrassment, they were all standing there huddled together, watching me fully clothed! When they saw the shock on my face and when I'd hidden my bits with my hands, they all burst into laughter. Then, to add to my misery, an old woman walking her dog came along and said, 'You'll catch your death skinny-dipping at this time of year, young man.

Your friends seem to have more sense than you do.'

I hurriedly got my clothes back on. It was difficult to be annoyed with them all because it was very funny. I swear I'll get them back somehow, though.

20 January 2003, Monday

I woke up this morning with a sore throat and sinuses. I've caught a cold. I gradually felt worse as the day went on.

Mr Vibert was back at school today. He was off with the bug last week and hadn't got into trouble for pulling Tom's ear.

At break time I had to put up with the girls from last night wiggling their little fingers at me and giggling.

At lunchtime I bought some cold and flu tablets from Boots and was feeling a little better by the time our English lesson started.

Jason Dwyer asked a question that we all wished we'd had the bottle to ask, 'Miss, why can't we discuss something interesting like sexual habits?'

'I hardly think that would be an appropriate subject for an English lesson. Perhaps you should ask Mrs Bowen if she would include it in her curriculum.'

'That's a shame. We could have had a mass debate.'

She ignored the time-honoured pun after saying, 'Be quiet, Jason.'

We debated asylum seekers and whether we should let any more into the country or let any that are currently here stay.

Until the recent terrorist plots involving immigrants, I have been quite happy with the country letting in people worse off than us, but if they come here to try to kill innocent people, I'm not sure we can afford to let anybody in now. It's very scary.

Most people in the class agreed with me.

When we left the school building to head home, I stumbled across a heated row between Lara and Spud. They quickly stopped when they saw me, though, and Spud stormed off.

'What's the matter with him?' I asked Lara.

'Oh, nothing! He's just in a mood because we keep hassling him about his girlfriend.'

A similar thing happened when I got home. Mum and Dad were in a heated conversation, which stopped abruptly as soon as I entered.

'Talking about me are you?' I asked.

'Don't be so paranoid!' Dad said.

'What are you doing home from work?' I asked him.

'Nothing much on, at the moment, so I took a half day.' Dad quickly changed the subject. 'One of your mates called round at lunchtime.'

'Oh, yeah!' I said, a bit confused. 'Who?'

'Stuart Hudd.'

Stuart Hudd is Spud's real name. It comes from his initials, S. P. Hudd.

Why on earth would he call for me at lunchtime when he knew I was at school. Then Mum cleared up the puzzle.

'It was me he came to see, actually. His mum asked if she could take some old magazines off my hands for the clinic waiting room. I thought I had a load but I must have chucked all of them out. I'm afraid he had a wasted trip.'

'I thought you said he'd called for Troy?' said Dad.

'No, I said that he was one of Troy's friends, Kevin. That's one of your problems. You NEVER LISTEN!'

And with that she went to the kitchen.

Dad looked at me. I knew what he was going to say. It was one of his catchphrases.

'Women! I love 'em! Especially when they haven't got any clothes on!'

We laughed in a loud, laddish way and Mum poked a disapproving expression around the kitchen door.

Dad told me, over dinner, that he had sorted out my work experience at his firm. I'm there for a week as from Monday. At least it's a week off school. Dad said that he and Mum would be back from their dirty weekend on Sunday evening.

I got a phone call from this bloke, Dennis, from Osborne Coburg Football Club. He asked me if I'd be interested in training with them, with a view to playing for them. He'd seen me play against Medina High School last week. I agreed to go to training on Wednesday evening. I asked if I could bring a couple of mates along with me, and he said that would be fine.

Mum said that Dad should go along and try to get fit. It looks as though he will be coming as well. It should be a laugh.

My cold was making me feel terrible by the evening and even the cold and flu tablets didn't seem to work so I made myself a hot water bottle and went to bed early.

21 January 2003, Tuesday

I woke up feeling absolutely terrible this morning, so I decided not to go into school.

After Dad had gone to work, Mum made me comfortable on the sofa with my quilt, a hot water bottle, the paper, the remote control and a cup of Lemsip.

I had to watch the daytime TV shows like *Trisha* and *This Morning*..

I dozed off and was awakened by Mum at lunchtime with some more Lemsip and a cheese and pickle sandwich. She went out and left me alone, during which time I went online and surfed the porn sites that I could access - the ones that accepted that I was eighteen just because I clicked on the button that said, 'Click here if you are 18 or over.'

Mum was out for an hour, and a half but I saw her coming up the garden path and was easily able to shut down the computer and settle back under the duvet before she came in.

She looked a bit worried when she entered. She had been to an appointment at the doctor's.

'What's the matter?' I asked

'Oh, nothing major, dear. Women's problems.'

As soon as she'd said that I realised that it was a subject I didn't want to delve into. We'd only recently studied the menopause in Biology. Mum is thirty-four so she must be heading for it soon. That's probably why she was worried. It's probably sinking in that she is getting old.

Dad arrived a bit later than normal. He had gone into Newport to buy himself some new trainers. We sat and watched *The Weakest Link* together while Mum prepared the dinner, which was savoury rice stir-fried with bacon, sausage and mushrooms. It's our favourite.

Lara came to see me this evening, which was wonderful of her. She brought me her dad's favourite cold remedy, which had been collected in a plastic Coca-Cola bottle. It turned out to be sherry. She only stayed for half an hour. She was getting bored of the Liverpool versus Sheffield Wednesday match that Dad and I were watching. It was the second leg of the Worthington Cup, Semi-Final, and Liverpool won two-nil.

22 January 2003, Wednesday

I felt a little better this morning. Lara's dad's special remedy must have done the trick. However, I thought it would be best to stay at home for another day, just to make sure.

So it was another morning of daytime television.

Spud came round at lunchtime, acting a bit more cheerful than he has been recently. Mum wasn't pleased to see him, though. She complained that I was supposed to be at home resting, but Spud persuaded her to let him in and he helped her prepare my lunch while I listened to one of the CDs he'd brought round for me to listen to on my CD Walkman.

Spud and kitchens obviously don't go together too well, as he emerged from the kitchen several minutes later, scrubbing a stain with a damp cloth. Some margarine had got onto his trousers. It looked like he'd wet himself until Mum lent him her hairdryer to dry it off. You could see that she found the whole thing very amusing. Even though Spud was blushing, he too saw the funny side of it.

He also had lunch and went back to school, leaving me the collection of CDs.

Dad arrived at the normal time and I obviously couldn't go to football training but Dad still went. Mum also went out, so I was home alone for a couple of hours. A couple of hours of illicit Internet surfing went very quickly before Dad limped back in at eight-thirty. He could hardly walk.

'Did you get injured?' I asked him.

'No, I'm just knackered.'

We watched the Blackburn versus Manchester United Worthington Cup Semi-Final, second leg, which was interrupted when he collapsed on the floor with cramp. I had to bend his foot up while he groaned and winced in agony. It was hilarious.

After the match had finished and United had won three-one, he struggled off for a bath. Then Mum arrived, all rosy cheeked from the fresh evening air.

She sat with me for a few minutes until we heard screaming from the bathroom. We quickly ran to see what was wrong only to find that Dad had got cramp in his other leg. His head was nearly underwater and his leg was up in the air. Mum pulled his foot back, chortling, much to Dad's relief of pain and annoyance at her amusement.

After that hilarity I found Daisy in a chat room tonight and made sure it was still all right for us to meet on Saturday. She was as excited as I am. She told me to make sure that I brought something with me.

Does she mean a present or a condom? She must mean a present. I will have to buy a bunch of flowers or something.

23 January 2003, Thursday

Back to school today and Spud was in a right mood. He demanded his CDs back, saying he'd only lent them to me while I was ill. I said that if he was that desperate for them I'd pop home at lunchtime and get them. He said not to bother, he'd go and get them himself.

We all agreed, the lads and me, that he must have had a row with his girlfriend.

At lunchtime we discussed Spud's moodiness with Lara who had had a chat with him at break time. We'd guessed right. Apparently his girlfriend is going away this weekend and he doesn't want her to go. He finished with her but now regrets it. It all sounds like too much hassle for a sixteen-year-old to cope with, especially leading up to his GCSEs.

Also during lunchtime, Ed came up to me and told me that Katie Wallace had asked him out. He'd told her that he'd think about it and then asked me for my advice.

I told him that she was a nice girl who was a bit vulnerable. He might as well give it a try, especially as he thinks she's nice looking.

At home time they were walking, arms around each other, until we went our separate ways at the junction of Crossfield Avenue and Baring Road. They had a very long snog, and I knew that I wouldn't be seeing Ed this evening.

When I got home Mum, was in the midst of packing for their weekend away. So I helped her for a while until Dad came home.

After tea, Meat phoned me. It seems that only him and me were without female company and he'd been invited out for a burn in Karl Sibley's car, so I agreed to go out with them.

Karl called round for me at seven. He drives like Colin McRae. You get quite a buzz from the speed and acceleration of his RS Turbo. It was brilliant! We cruised, at high speed, around the island, via Freshwater, Military Road, Ventnor, Sandown and Ryde.

At Ryde we stopped off at the icafé and played on a few machines for an hour or so and then we went bowling at LA Bowl. I won. So that was an advantage of not having Ed there.

Karl had to stick to the speed limit as we passed the crematorium. Meat had spotted a police car waiting. It followed us until we arrived at the dual carriageway in Newport.

I was home at just past eleven. Mum and Dad had gone to bed, so I did as well.

24 January 2003, Friday

I had to say my goodbyes to Mum and Dad this morning before going to school. They were booked on an eleven-fifty flight from Southampton Airport. Before I left for school I had to put up with a lecture.

Dad had heard Karl accelerating away last night and he told me to be careful because Karl was an 'accident waiting to happen'. I assured him that Karl was a good driver.

'Good driving is safe driving. You cannot drive at high speed on this island. It is suicide,' he preached.

Ed called for me as usual. He had enjoyed his evening with Katie and seemed glad to have taken my advice, but when we got to school a few people started giving him stick, asking him if he'd shagged her yet. He tried to ignore them but I could tell that it was getting to him. At least he'll have the weekend to spend with her, apart from our trip to Southampton that is.

If all things go well for me with Daisy, Meat will be the only one of us without a girlfriend.

Tom was off today with the stomach bug, which is still claiming victims.

At lunchtime, Terry and Jason Ince joined us at the icafé. Terry was hoping to get a chance to wind up Ricky Kinsella. When Kinsella saw Terry he walked off with a barrage of heckles ringing in his drunken ears.

Vernon said that his mate was disappointed that I didn't turn up to training on Wednesday, as they could have done with me for their game tomorrow. I told him that I couldn't have played anyway as I was going to Southampton. Vernon advised me to give up watching Saints in favour of playing. I said I'd never do that.

Lara was chatting to Meat a lot during the lunch break. I hope this doesn't mean she fancies him.

When I got home this afternoon, Grandad was there waiting for me. He cooked my dinner for me - baked beans on toast. I miss Mum already.

I went on the computer to see if I could catch Daisy in a chat room. I didn't, but she did send me a saucy e-mail.

'I can't wait to run my hands all over your body,' she wrote.

I bided my time and went back online when *Emmerdale* started, and she was there. I asked her if we could have a chat over the phone, but she said that she wanted to speak to me, for the first time, in person.

We arranged to meet at eleven o'clock.

Meat phoned me this evening. Lara told him, at lunchtime, that Kylie fancies him. He's going to ask her out tomorrow. Now I am desperate that things work out between Daisy and me.

Grandad went home at about ten o'clock. I thought he was supposed to be staying with me. This left me no time to organise a party or anything, so I spent the night alone in the house.

25 January 2003, Saturday

I had to make my own breakfast and tidy up this morning. I had a bath before heading down to Ed's house. We caught the ten-thirty Red Jet and got the free bus to Asda.

Ed went into Asda and waited, out of sight, to get a glimpse of Daisy. We devised a safety plan, in case I wanted to get out of the situation. I had his number selected on my phone and all I had to do was press the 'send' button if I needed Ed to come and rescue me.

So I waited by the stone, as arranged, next to this smelly, scruffy, bald bloke for about five minutes. Then that bloke turned to me and asked, 'Are you Troy?'

'Yes,' I replied, a bit shocked.

'Hello. I'm Daisy's father. She asked me to come and fetch you and take you to our house.'

I didn't feel comfortable with this and tried to talk myself out of the situation.

'I can't really. I've got to go to the Saints versus Millwall game.'

'I can give you a lift to that. Kick-off's not 'til three!'

It was time to press the send button on my phone and, just as Daisy's dad grabbed my arm to escort me to his car, Ed arrived and pretended he'd just bumped into me.

'Hello, Troy, mate. You goin' to the match?'

'Yeah.'

Ed grabbed my other arm. 'Come on then, we can meet the players in the car park if we go now.'

He then shepherded me away. I called out to Daisy's dad, who looked very annoyed, 'Tell Daisy that I'll talk to her tonight, online.'

So then Ed and I walked to St Mary's Stadium. We had a burger outside the ground before going in.

Southampton were terrible in the match and we got more entertainment watching a punch-up in one of the executive boxes behind us. We drew one-one after a very late equaliser by Kevin Davies.

When I got home, Grandad was there and there was no traditional postmatch steak and chips. Instead we had chip-shop fish and chips.

I went online to try to chat with Daisy, but every time I tried to talk to her she must have pressed her *ignore* button. So I've blown it with her, and when Ed and Meat called round this evening with girlfriends on their arms I didn't want to play gooseberry.

So I had a boring Saturday night in. Grandad did stay tonight, though. I wonder why he couldn't stay last night?

26 January 2003, Sunday

Grandad cooked a fry-up this morning. It was virtually deep-fried. I've never seen so much fat in a frying pan. The smoke alarm kept going off, which must have annoyed the neighbours on a Sunday morning.

Tom phoned to see if I'd like to cheer him on in a football match at Northwood Recreation Ground. I had nothing else to do, so I skateboarded up there. He must have phoned everyone up, as they were all there. Meat and Kylie and Ed and Katie, were paying more attention to each other than to the match, but Lara stood next to me to watch. The bonus of this was that when Lara got cold she hugged my arm.

Tom played quite well, although his team, Northwood, lost two-nil. We all went our separate ways afterwards. Lara waited outside the dressing room for Tom and the rest of them went for a gang smooch somewhere.

When I got home, Grandad was in the middle of cooking lunch - cheese on toast with tinned spaghetti on top. Yum yum not!

Grandad had received a phone call from Dad saying that they should be on the five-thirty Red Jet, so he suggested we went up to the cricket club to play pool. So that's what we did, and I thrashed him six-nil. He blamed his back. He made out that he had difficulty stretching over the table for long pots. I said he was just crap.

So at six we picked up Mum and Dad from the Red Jet. They weren't speaking to each other. We stopped off at the Chinese takeaway on the way home and had dinner while Dad enthusiastically relived their weekend minus the gory details. He was particularly impressed with Paris St Germain's stadium, as they had watched Paris St Germain beat Marseilles two-one in the Coupe de France. Mum was obviously not as impressed. She did cheer up, though, when a bunch of flowers arrived for her halfway through the meal. She couldn't understand why they were anonymous though. Dad said that he had forgotten to write out a card.

He looked at me and winked, so I winked back. That was a good move of his.

They had brought me back some sweets, a Paris St Germain shirt and a model of the Eiffel Tower. Grandad also got a model of the Eiffel Tower and a programme from the Marseilles match. While Mum cleared up dinner, Dad and I discussed Southampton's hopes, or lack of them, of reaching the next round of the FA Cup. He was delighted when I told him that the replay against Millwall was being shown live on Sky.

We also discussed the forthcoming week at work and he described a few of his workmates. These descriptions went over my head a bit. I'll find out for myself tomorrow.

After Grandad left, I texted a few of my friends to see if any of them weren't seeing their sweethearts tonight.

Spud was the only one who texted back and he came round at about quarter to eight. But all he wanted to do was watch television with us. He sat next to Mum on the settee and guzzled tea and made small talk with Dad about the time he'd been to see Paris St Germain play. After *Dream Team* finished, Mum decided to go to bed and he took the hint.

Soon Dad was snoring in his chair so I went online, but Daisy continued to ignore me so I sent her an apologetic e-mail.

27 January 2003, Monday

Mum woke me up an hour earlier than normal, at seven a.m. Dad and I ate breakfast together, which only normally happens on Sundays.

Dad works at a company called MP Graphics. They are a reprographic company and produce films, plates and digital files for printers.

When I arrived, Derek, one of the bosses, showed me around. He asked me what I was interested in and I said computing so he put me with Dad for the morning. Dad does something called repro for which he uses a programme called Adobe Illustrator to do something called trapping of something he called artwork files so that they are in a fit state to be sent to the printers.

The day dragged. Derek kept coming up behind me and saying. 'Any good?' I don't know what he meant by this. He even did it when I was sat down having my tea break. There was this other bloke called Nigel who always farted loudly every time he walked through the room.

There is a young lad there that I get on with quite well . His name is Stan, which is quite an old-fashioned name for a seventeen-year-old. He's a really good laugh. He drives a red RS Turbo - exactly like Karl's, only it's red. He drives in a similar fashion as well, as he overtook Dad in the car park when we left at four-thirty, which set Dad off swearing.

It was nice to have dinner on the table as we came through the door. After I'd finished my meal I went to Ed's. He said that school was rubbish. More people had gone down with the bug. His sister Zoe started annoying us so we decided to take a walk to Lara's house.

Tom, Meat and Kylie were there. Ed had hoped that Katie would be there and when she wasn't he left to go round to her house. He came back, though, an hour later. He was all grumpy because her Nan wasn't very well and wouldn't let her go out or let anyone in.

We had quite a good laugh at Lara's, especially when we played Twister. I had a legitimate excuse to put my head between Lara's petite thighs, although when she lost her balance and fell on my head it really hurt as my nose got squashed against the floor. It was nice to get the sympathy but the fact that my eyes were watering was a bit embarrassing.

When I got home at around ten, Spud was walking down our garden path. 'Oh, there you are!' he said. 'I've been looking for you lot everywhere!'

I asked him why he hadn't tried phoning me, and he said that his mobile was playing up. After I'd told him what we'd been up to and he had a moan for a while, he left and I went in. It was far too late to do anything anyway.

Dad was out and Mum was in the bathroom, so I went to bed.

28 January 2003, Tuesday

Dad got me up this morning, as Mum was feeling very ill. She has got the bug. It's really knocking on my door now. At least catching it at the start of the week will mean I should be well enough to go to the Manchester United game on Saturday.

At work today I helped Stan pack away loads of files. It was really boring, but we had a laugh talking about how tough people always talk with stiff lips and look at you in a menacing way to try to intimidate you, and the way they always say, 'Come on then!' and 'Fancy your chances?' when they feel the chance of a fight is coming. So we pretended to be tough nuts with each other, then had a great laugh pinging elastic bands at each other.

After we had finished I did some repro exercises on the computer, which is an Apple Macintosh. I use a PC at home, so it took me a bit of time to get used to this alternative operating system.

I got an invite to Lara's by text during the day, so I was eager to finish my dinner and get freshened up as soon as possible.

Even though she was feeling bad, Mum still cooked us our dinner.

Lara wanted to talk about her feelings for Tom. She thinks that if you go out with a lad for more than six weeks you should think about sleeping with him. I think Katie Wallace thinks it should be six minutes. That made me wonder if she and Ed had done it yet.

Although I am very envious of Tom, he is a great lad, so it wasn't difficult for me to agree with all the nice things Lara was saying about him, even though I wished that it were me she was referring to.

We also got onto my problem of not having a girlfriend and she said she'd be getting to work on that for me. I am intrigued.

I got home at about half past eight and Mum and Dad had gone to bed. Very strange! I watched the Chelsea versus Leeds match on my own before going to bed myself. I was really tired tonight. This work lark seems to be really taking it out of me.

29 January 2003, Wednesday

Mum was still ill this morning but Dad and I, so far, haven't caught the germ. Dad let Mum lie in and sorted the breakfast out for us.

At work, me, Stan and this right idiot called Mark had to throw lots of old files away into this skip. Mark keeps on making funny noises and repeats your name with an annoying, squeaky voice, adding an extra bit that he makes up himself because he thinks it's funny. My name, for instance, is Troy Tempestuous and Stan's is Stan Collyflower. I think that we showed considerable restraint in not punching him.

One time, during our file clearout, Mark got called away to the phone, so me and Stan decided to wait for him, behind the door, holding big cardboard tubes as if they were baseball bats.

When we heard him approaching, we put on our toughest, most intimidating expressions and menacingly slapped the cardboard tubes into the palms of our hands. Unfortunately it was Derek, the boss, who greeted us and promptly summoned Stan away.

He was gone for about twenty minutes, so I was stuck with that prat, Mark. I feared the worst, but Stan said that Derek didn't even mention it. He wanted to discuss the design of a website with him.

After we had finished, I was put with Stan to help him design this website for Derek. It was for Derek's sailing club, so I suggested we took some digital pictures in Cowes. Derek allowed us to go out for a couple of hours to take the pictures.

Stan does drive exactly like Karl - fast and furious! So we got to Cowes Parade in ten minutes. We spent five minutes taking pictures, then went off into the town and popped into Tiffins for a cup of tea and a chocolate muffin.

While we were sitting there, I was gazing out of the window and I saw Spud with his girlfriend, and she *is* old. She is quite dumpy with a bad, dyed perm. She must be around my mum's age. He didn't see me but I'll mention it to him when I next catch him in a good mood.

I wonder why he wasn't at school today.

After our hour and a half of skiving, we went back to work and started setting up the website, but it was soon time to go home.

Mum, the trouper that she is, once again had dinner ready for us, despite the fact that she was still feeling very poorly.

Dad and I went to Osborne Coburg's football training tonight. It was very hard work and I can see why Dad was so worn out last week.

I played well and Dennis asked me to play on Saturday, but I had to decline because Dad and I are going to watch Saints play Manchester United.

When we got home, Spud was waiting for me in the front room, having made himself very much at home. He was sat there with his feet up on the pouffe, remote control in one hand and a cup of tea in the other.

He was watching the Liverpool versus Arsenal game. Mum was there with him. She said that he'd called round half an hour ago and she'd told him that he might as well wait for me to come back from training.

All he was after was a ticket for Saturday's match, but the match had sold out ages ago. He stayed until the end of the match.

As he was leaving, I saw him off at our front door and told him I'd seen him with his girlfriend today. He pretended that he didn't know what I was talking about and then said, 'Oh, yes! I bunked off school today to see her. Don't tell anyone, fella! Or we'll both be for it!' Then he looked at me with a deadly serious expression on his face. 'I mean it! Don't tell anyone! If it gets out, I'll know who it came from, won't I?'

How can I keep it to myself?! I've got to tell Lara. I trust her.

30 January 2003, Thursday

Mum was a bit better this morning and she made breakfast for us.

It's a miracle we haven't gone down with this thing as Stan was off work today with it. I wish Mark had caught it, then I could have had a day without constant chicken impressions and quotes of Troy Tempestuous.

I spent the whole day creating Derek's website. He was well impressed. I even sorted out a domain name for him. He slipped a ten-pound note into my hand just before me and Dad left.

It was pay day today and we went down to town, in the sleety snow, so that Dad could draw out his wages. We popped into Sainsbury's so that he could buy Mum a bunch of flowers. Pay day was also the day on which, once a month, we have a KFC dinner, so we picked one up at the drive-through on

the way home.
Mum didn't eat much of it. She still hasn't got her appetite back.
Tom and Lara came around tonight. They have fixed me up with a blind date tomorrow night. I'm meeting this girl tomorrow evening at Cineworld in Newport. It's nice of them to do this for me but it's a shame they arranged it for Newport. I'll have to blag a lift or get the bus.
I couldn't tell Lara about Spud because Tom was there.They did tell me, though, that Spud is in trouble at school for skiving.
They decided to go down to Ed's house so I joined them. As we left and said goodbye through the glazed partition, it looked as though Mum was crying and Dad was holding her sympathetically. She must have been moved by the fact that Dad had bought her flowers again.
Like the weather, things were a bit icy between Katie and Ed. It might have been because Zoe was pestering them, though. We just sat in Ed's living room watching television for an hour or so, then Lara and Tom left. Katie decided to go with them. I stayed with Ed for a while.
Ed's a bit frustrated with Katie because she hasn't agreed to have sex with him yet. She says that she really loves him and wants the first time with him to be special so he'll have to wait, but he's annoyed because she didn't wait when she did it with Spud. I asked him if he wanted to go out with her for her or sex and he said that he didn't know.
I successfully stopped myself from telling him about Spud's girlfriend despite a terrible urge to do so.
Once again Mum and Dad had gone to bed when I got home.
I went online to try to find Daisy but when I found her, in her usual chat room, she continued to ignore me. That's it, I give up with her.

31 January 2003, Friday

I woke up this morning with a huge volcano of a zit on my nose. Just my luck!
Mum was still under the weather this morning. She said that she would be seeing the doctor today. I hope she's not got something serious.
It was my last day at work today and I spent the day finishing setting up Derek's website and, even if I say so myself, it is rather good.
Derek is absolutely delighted with it and he told me to come and see him once I'd finished school, in the summer, to see about the possibility of me working there. I am so chuffed. It means I won't have to go into year twelve.
I told this to my careers lady, Mrs Dawson, when she came to check up on me.

Yesterday I wished that Mark, the prat, had the bug. Today my wish came true, so it was an enjoyable day, especially because they close up at two on Fridays.

After we had arrived home there were a couple of hours until dinner so I went down Woodvale Road and loitered around Lara's house until I saw her walking down the hill. Fortunately, she was on her own so I was able to talk to her. We went into her house and her boudoir, as she called it.

I was finally able to tell her about Spud's girlfriend. She asked me if I was sure it was his girlfriend.

'It must have been!' I said. 'He told me to keep shtum about it.'

'Did you agree to keep it secret?' she asked.

'Yes.'

'Well why are you telling me, then!' she snorted. 'Remind me not to tell you anything in confidence, won't you!'

She was annoyed with me! I was so shocked I didn't know what to do or where to look. I could feel my face glowing red.

I tried changing the subject but it was no good and I left, feeling more awkward and stupid than I have ever felt.

I was, obviously, quiet and miserable when I got home. My parents tried to prise the reason for my grumpiness out of me but I was too ashamed to tell them. Lara was right, after all. I should have kept it to myself, as Spud had asked me to.

I couldn't even sound pleased when Mum told me that all she had was some sort of virus.

I couldn't eat much of my dinner, even though it was our favourite savoury rice dish. I just kept thinking of Lara. I decided to go and sulk in my room.

At about half-past five I got a phone call from Lara. She apologised for being stroppy with me and said that she didn't mean anything that she had said. She was tired and irritable because it was her time-of-the-month. I was so relieved, but that relief turned to horror when she asked me if I was nervous about tonight.

'What about tonight?' I said

'The blind date!'

I was supposed to be meeting her at six o'clock and I hadn't even started getting ready. I quickly said my goodbyes and had the quickest shower and change of clothes I have ever had.

I asked Dad for a lift to Newport. Disaster! He'd drunk two cans of lager. So I phoned up Karl and begged him and, thank goodness, he agreed to take me.

We arrived just in time. Lara had told me that the girl would be wearing a green scarf. As we arrived, Karl spotted Kelly by the entrance.

'Things might get confusing!' he said. 'Kelly's wearing a green scarf. Let's hope not too many girls are wearing green scarves. Otherwise you might have difficulty in finding your date.'

I got out of the car and walked over to Kelly.

'Hi, Kel,' I said.

'Hello, Troy,' she replied in a surprised, yet friendly voice. 'What are you doing here?'

'I'm on a blind date,' I said.

'Oh! So am I.'

Then the penny dropped and we both laughed.

We weren't sure that we wanted to be on a blind date with each other but decided that we might as well make the most of it.

We watched *Catch Me If you Can*, the new film with Leonardo Di Caprio and Tom Hanks. It was quite good. Nothing happened between us. I couldn't pluck up courage to make the first move and I was very conscious of the throbbing zit on my nose.

After the film we chatted and walked to the bus station and caught the bus together, back to Cowes. I did enjoy Kelly's company but I'm pretty sure she doesn't fancy me, even though I'd be more than happy to go out with her.

I didn't have to walk her home as her house is only yards from the bus stop at the Round House. I didn't get a kiss either as we said goodbye. She did thank me, though, and she said that she had had a nice time.

I had just about got to my house when I met up with a distraught Katie.

I asked her what was the matter.

'Ed's dumped me!' she sobbed.

I invited her in for a chat. We went to my room where she bawled her eyes out, but she said that she couldn't tell me the reason why Ed had finished with her. I put my arm around her to comfort her. I held her as she cried for quite a while and then the door opened. I looked around expecting to see Mum or Dad but it was Ed.

'YOU SLAG!' he snarled.

We jumped up and tried to explain but he just wouldn't listen. He said that our friendship was over and that he never wanted to see either of us again. Then he stormed out of the house, past a stunned Dad.

I didn't know what to do. I couldn't go after him because I had Katie, who was now in floods of tears, with me.

Dad came to the rescue. He called Katie a taxi and said he'd look after her while I went off to try and find Ed.

I searched everywhere I could think of but I just couldn't find him. He'd turned his mobile off as well. In the end I had to give up and go home.

I got in after midnight. Dad had waited up for me.

'What are you playing at?' he asked.

'It's not what you think.' I said.

I was too tired to explain so I went to bed, totally and utterly dejected.

1 February 2003, Saturday

I didn't get much sleep last night and this morning I wanted to find out what had happened to Ed but I couldn't bring myself to phone him.

I decided that I would skateboard down to Katie's house to see if she had heard anything, but when I got there I was turned away by her Nan.

Then I went to Meat's house.

He said, 'What are you up to with Ed's bird?'

'I met her along my road. She was crying her eyes out so I took her into my house to comfort her as a friend. I was sat on my bed with my arm around her comforting her and Ed walked in. He put two and two together and made seventy-three!'

'I told him he should have given you a chance to explain.'

From that I knew Ed must be all right. 'When did you speak to him?' I asked.

'He phoned me about an hour ago.'

I then left and went to Lara's to see if she had any ideas about what I should do.

She said that I should just go round and see Ed. But it was him who was jumping to conclusions so I thought he should come to see me.

That was how I left it as me and Dad went over to Southampton for the Saints versus Manchester United game. Which, surprise surprise, we lost.

I was listening to the other results on the radio as we walked back to the ferry terminal and it was announced, on the news, that the space shuttle Columbia had broken up on re-entry. The wreckage is spread over several American states.

Dad then went on about the time when the space shuttle blew up just after launch before I was born.

We watched it all on the news while we ate our steak and chips. There were huge chunks of debris all over the place, mainly in Texas, and some body parts have been found. How awful!

As Mum and Dad cleared the table there was a knock at the front door. It was Ed and Katie. 'Sorry, mate!' he said.

'Thank God for that!' I said as I invited them in.

They have patched up their differences and Ed says that he understands that I only see Katie as a friend. That said, though, I will think twice about helping her in future.

Ed told me that a few people had made arrangements to go round to Tom's house and play Trivial Pursuit while his parents were out at the cricket club.

So we walked round to Tom's where we found Lara, Karl, Karl's mate Stevie, Kelly, Kylie, Meat, Jason Dwyer and Jason Ince.

After about two hours of play, some players started getting bored and Jason Dwyer decided to tell us that his party piece was the fact that he could fit all six Trivial Pursuit cakes into his foreskin. Unfortunately someone asked him to prove it and he did, to a mixed chorus of laughter and screams. The girls hid their eyes but I noticed that most of them were peeking through the gaps in their fingers.

Kelly had been in the toilet during this time and when somebody mentioned party pieces in connection with Trivial Persuit cakes she, without waiting for the outcome of the story, showed us her party piece. She can fit all six cakes into her mouth. She returned to the toilet when Jason said that he had just had a blow job by Proxie.

Obviously that put an end to the game, as nobody wanted to touch the pieces after that.

We left the board and everything out, in the hope that Tom and Karl's mum would clear it up, and then we went for a walk down the seafront.

Once again the suggestion of skinny-dipping came up. This time I refused to take anything off. Katie and Ed stripped down to their underwear and went in. I must say, Katie has got a fantastic figure. They didn't stay in the sea for long, and after they came out of the water they ran up Egypt Hill to Ed's house to warm up and dry off.

It was getting on for half past ten so I decided to go home and watch *The Premiership*.

Dad told me that on the local news there was a report that a fifteen-year-old boy has gone missing in Southampton. They are kicking up a big fuss over it but I expect he has run away to London. He's hardly going to end up dead, like all those young girls that keep disappearing. Girls are far more vulnerable than boys.

2 February 2003, Sunday

I had a long lie-in this morning. It was lovely. I didn't get up until eleven o'clock so I missed breakfast.

Grandad Brown arrived at half past with Nan Brown, ready for lunch. There was a lot of talk between Dad and Grandad about the space shuttle, the impending war with Iraq and whether Arsenal or Manchester United would win this year's Premiership title.

After we had finished our apple pie pudding, Dad tapped the side of his wine glass with the handle of his knife. The glass broke.

'Shit! Oh well, that got everyone's attention,' he said. He grabbed Mum's hand and they both looked very nervous.

'We have a bit of an announcement to make.'

Grandad interrupted, 'You want me to look after the house again.'

'No.'

'You've won the Lottery.'

'No!'

'You've decided to renew your marriage vows,' said Nan.

'NO!' said an irritated Dad. 'Will you shut up, this is hard enough as it is!'

'You're not sending me away to boarding school, are you?' I, unwisely, joked.

Mum glared at me, 'Troy!'

'Oh, come on you two!' chortled Nan. 'What can it be? It's not as if you're pregnant or anything.'

A look of horror came over Mum and Dad's faces.

'Well, actually.' said Mum.

A look of shock came over Nan and Grandad's faces.

I was waiting for them to say, no, of course not, but they didn't.

Nan and Grandad jumped out of their seats and hugged, kissed and congratulated Mum and Dad.

'Well it's about bloody time,' laughed an obviously delighted Grandad.

Nan was in tears of joy.

'Are you then?' I asked, hoping I had completely misunderstood.

'Yes, love,' said a beaming Mum. 'You're going to have a little brother or sister.'

I just sat there for a while, speechless.

'Aren't you going to say anything, Troy?' asked Grandad.

I tried to sound enthusiastic. 'Congratulations.' I failed to do so.

I helped Mum do the washing-up. She told me that everything would be all right.

I said, 'Are you sure you are pregnant?'

'Of course I am.'

'Why do you want another baby?'

'Well, it wasn't planned. It's taken us a while to get used to the idea but, now we have, your father and I are looking forward to it.'

'When's it due?'

'September the twenty-fifth.'

I gave Mum a hug. She looked like she needed one.

'Don't tell anybody yet, Troy. It's unlucky to make it common news until I'm about three months gone. Okay?'

I agreed to keep it quiet. I'm hardly going to want to broadcast that sort of news, am I?

At least, with it not being due until September, it gives me plenty of time to find somewhere else to live. There's no way I'm going to live here with a screaming brat around.

I can't believe they can be so stupid and they are the ones that keep telling me to be careful and take precautions and I haven't even had sex yet!

Ed phoned tonight but I pretended that I didn't feel well.

I went online tonight and searched the Internet on having babies late in life.

God, I didn't think people even had sex when they got to their age! I can't help thinking how disgusting the whole thing is.

On the news tonight they had the parents of that missing boy pleading for him to come home.

If he's on the streets, he's hardly going to be watching television is he?

The father broke down. I think this might be suspicious as, in the past, kids have been murdered by their father or stepfather who has gone on to make an emotional plea in front of the cameras, despite knowing full well what has happened to the child.

3 February 2003, Monday

Things aren't going too well for me at the moment. I found out this morning that the reason Ed wanted to see me last night was that he wanted to tell me something.

On Saturday night, after their skinny-dip, he and Katie went back to his house where they went to his room, dried off and one thing led to another, as they say.

It looks as though I'm going to be the last virgin on the Isle of Wight soon.

Jason Dwyer brought a copy of *FHM* to school with him. I was flicking through it at break time and looking at a picture of Myleene Klass - or to put it more frankly, drooling over the picture - when Kylie and Kelly came up and called me a pervert.

I argued, 'How can it be perverted to like looking at attractive members of the opposite sex with little or no clothes on? Surely it's only natural, otherwise men wouldn't want to shag women and therefore there would be no people.'

Which reminded me of my parents' predicament.

In our English lesson this afternoon we debated whether we should go to war, alongside the USA, against Iraq. We all agreed that there should be no war without United Nations approval, otherwise it makes a mockery of the UN.

We all feel totally helpless. This government was elected democratically but will undemocratically go to war with the say-so of an American warmonger.

I had a chat with Kelly as we walked out of the school gates. She said that she wouldn't mind going to the pictures with me again one day (as friends). I said, 'Okay, how about on Saturday?' And, amazingly, she agreed.

At least this time I can prepare myself a bit better. I've got her phone number now so that will make life easier as regards fine-tuning the arrangements.

When I got home, Mum was rooting through one of the spare bedrooms for my old baby things. She had found my old cot, hanging mobile with Winnie the Pooh characters on it, blankets and an old book which was called *Baby's Firsts*. I had a look in this to see what my first words were, but all that was written in it was my name and date of birth. There was a cutting from the *Isle of Wight County Press* that had been folded into the book. It read:

Brown (née Stenning)
Kevin and Alison are
overjoyed to announce the
arrival of Troy. A baby boy
born at 16:05 hrs on 22 June

After dinner, Dad and Mum decided to make another announcement. Because of Mum's pregnancy they have decided to have a UK holiday this year.

They have booked a luxury caravan on a site near Blackpool for two weeks at the end of July. How exotic not!

I said I'd go with them I've got nothing better to do, even though we'll be away over Cowes Week.

All my mates were seeing their partners tonight, which left me feeling a bit like a one-pound coin in a pocket full of two-pound coins.

I sat with Mum and Dad watching television, including a programme about Michael Jackson in which he swears blind that he has only ever had cosmetic surgery on his nose.

Yes and George W. Bush has been nominated for the Nobel Peace Prize NOT!

4 February 2003, Tuesday

There is a bizarre rumour going around school, which I first heard at break time, just after Terry had had a massive scrap with Ed.

I didn't see the fight, just the aftermath. Ed came out of it worse. He had a fat lip, bleeding nose and a black eye. Terry just had a bloody hole in his trousers at the knee.

I found out later, when Ed came back to class after a visit to the medical room, that it was all because Terry had called Katie a slag.

The rumour is that Terry is gay. He is the hardest boy at the school and if he hears this story somebody else will be receiving a pasting.

The evidence for this is that he spends all his time with Jason Ince, who is almost as hard as Terry.

Whoever started this rumour had better have made sure that they have covered their tracks.

Terry was lucky as the fight was broken up by Spud before any teachers got wind of it. Apparently Ed told the lady in the medical room that he hurt himself playing football at break time.

If Terry had been caught he would have probably been expelled.

Lara has had her dark brown hair cut into a shortish bob. She used to have her hair just below her shoulders. It is very straight and shiny. She looks absolutely stunning with her new look. My eyes were sore with staring at her.

I said to Tom, 'Lara looks nice with her new hairstyle.'

Tom grunted, 'I don't like it! I told her not to get it cut.'

'Surely it's up to Lara how she wears her hair?'

'Yeah, like it's up to me whether I go out with her or not.'

Oh dear. Well, if he does finish with her, she can cry on my shoulder any time.

This afternoon it was Episode Two of Maths:

'P, Q and Z plus R is equal to what then, Te-roy Brown?'

'24?'

'NO!'

'Ed-ward Case?'

'Yes sir?'

'What's the answer?'
'What's the answer to what, sir?'
'PQZ PLUS R ewe fhat head!'
'I don't know, sir.'
'Haaaylee?'
'Twenty-seven sir.'
'Yes. It's on the board, see? Well done Hayley!'
'Jason Dwyer get out.'
'What for sir?'
'For pick-en ewer noose in class.'
'What's wrong with that?'
'Ewer scoopen what remaining brains ewe've got left onto ewe-er littal finger. So there's not enough brains left to learn anythen so, shut ewer feece and GEETT OOUUT!'

When I got home, Mum told me that she had been to the dentist and he told her that he was retiring. The thing is that there are no dentists available on the island. They are fully booked up. That includes private ones. So we are going to have to find a dentist on the mainland.

Lara came round tonight. She'd had a row with Tom so she'd come round for a moan. They, unfortunately, are still seeing each other, for the moment.

I took some pictures of her with my digital camera and, after she left, I uploaded them onto my computer. They came out really well and I spent ages just gazing at her image on my monitor. She is the most completely beautiful thing I have ever seen. If only she could be mine.

On the news, the police have found the dead body of that missing boy weighted down with bricks in the River Itchen. They are looking at the boy's computer for any evidence that he might have met his assailant in a chat room.

I'm sorry, but you don't arrange to meet strange men in chat rooms do you? At least I played safe and made sure I was meeting a girl. I made her e-mail me her picture. I wish she had turned up.

Mum told me that Nanny and Grandad Stenning are coming down from Penarth, in South Wales, for the weekend. So that means plenty of pocket money this week.

Grandad Brown and Grandad Stenning always like to compete in the 'who's-the-most-generous-grandparent' competition, whenever they are together.

They don't know that Mum is pregnant yet, so we are going to have to go through the same announcement routine as we did on Sunday.

5 February 2003, Wednesday

There was a lot of tension at school today. Terry and Ed were still giving each other dirty looks and Lara and Tom weren't talking to each other.

Jason Ince came up to Ed and told him to keep out of Terry's way. 'If you know what's good for you.'

Ed said that they should keep out of each other's way.

Spud was full of himself today. He's got a new girlfriend and this time it's not such a secret. He's going out with Emma Hewings from year twelve. Apparently he pulled her at the Chicago Rock Café on Saturday night. How they both got in there, under age, mystifies me. They got in with Karl Sibley and his mate Stevie. Neither of them are over eighteen either. Some people are so jammy.

Emma is a stunner as well, but it's very unusual for a seventeen-year-old girl to go out with a sixteen-year-old boy.

Emma drives a Mini Metro to school, so there is an added bonus for Spud, to go along with the obvious sexual one.

He was back to his old self in bragging about every gory detail of their sexual experiences.

At lunchtime a few of us went down to the icafé to see Vernon. Ricky Kinsella was asleep on his bench. Just before it was time to return to school, Terry blagged an ice cream from Vernon and plonked it, cone upwards, on Kinsella's head. He didn't move and we ran away as fast as we could. This seemed to *cool* the tension between Terry and Ed for a while.

When we felt that we were at a safe distance, we slowed down to a walk and I, fed up with all these evenings without any mates around, suggested a footy night, watching the Millwall versus Southampton FA Cup replay on Sky Sports.

Ed and Meat agreed, but Tom said that he wanted to go to Osborne Coburg training and Spud made his obvious excuses.

When Dad got home I asked him if it would be all right if the lads come round to watch the football and he was delighted. This meant that he thought that I was including him in the lads night in. I didn't have the heart to tell him that he wasn't invited, so I had to accept that he'd be there.

I phoned Ed to see if he could get his dad to persuade my dad to watch the match down at Bar One but that plan backfired when Dad invited Ed's dad around as well.

The good thing was that the dads made sure that there were plenty of cans of lager available and didn't mind us drinking them as well.

The Saints won two-one after extra time and the extra half an hour of drinking took its toll on Ed and Meat who were more than a bit tipsy, even though the dads had put a limit of two cans each.

After we had had a good laugh at Liverpool's defeat by Crystal Palace and Blackburn's inability to score any penalties in their shoot-out against Sunderland, all our guests left.

6 February 2003, Thursday

School gets more and more boring as the term goes on. The lessons are spent watching the clock, which stutters through every second as if it is a major effort to move the second hand to the next little dash.

Then break time and lunchtime came and the clock seemed to make up for its lack of energy before returning to slow motion until home time.

Kelly and I walked together down to the icafé at lunchtime and we discussed our forthcoming trip to the cinema. I said that I would buy the *County Press* tomorrow and then we could see what time the films were on.

Ricky Kinsella was sat, as usual, on his bench, rather subdued. He seemed to have a red, blotchy mark on his forehead. We speculated as to whether it had been left there by Terry's ice cream yesterday.

We had a chat with Vernon about cosmetic surgery. The actress, Leslie Ash has recently had her lips ruined by a plastic surgeon. Vernon made me laugh when he said that she reminded him of a halibut after an allergic reaction to lipstick.

'The lengths women go to in their quest to look like Rio Ferdinand (Manchester United defender with an extremely prominent top lip) is beyond me,' he said.

We all laughed loudly. Kinsella thought that we were laughing at him and started getting abusive so, without Terry there for back-up, we all left.

The afternoon went even slower than the morning. The bell that signified the end of the day seemed to have an extra glorious semi-tone to it.

For once, Ed didn't go off with Katie and we walked home together.

At home, Mum and I had a chat about various things - school, the inheritance money, the car - and after I told her about Spud and his new girlfriend she started getting a bit upset. I asked her what the matter was and she said that it was her hormones that were extra active at the moment. I expect the fact that I was talking about young love reminded her about how old she is.

Hormones have a lot to answer for. They give me zits and make pregnant women oversensitive.

She went off to her bedroom for a while, probably to grizzle, and I switched on the television and watched *Sky Sports News* until Dad arrived.

The phone rang, as it always seems to do, during dinner. It was Dennis, the manager at Osborne Coburg. He told me that they were short of players for Saturday's Reserves game against Newchurch so I agreed to go along and play. Dad also agreed.

There was nothing worth watching on the whole of satellite and terrestrial television, which is just as well because it gave me an opportunity to get on with some homework.

7 February 2003, Friday

I got up early this morning so that I could skateboard down to the Parade shop and get the *County Press*. I had breakfast when I got back and I browsed through the Entertainment page while munching on a slice of toast and Marmite.

On *GMTV* they said that the police have arrested a man in connection with the murder of that boy in Southampton. They found the man's IP address on the boy's computer and the company that runs the chat room has some record that the two of them were communicating in a teen chat room.

I don't understand why the boy would go off with a man he met in a teen chat room, unless the boy was gay or something.

They are now looking at the man's computer for any evidence.

As Ed and I walked to school, he told me that the girls are having a sleepover at one of Lara's friends' who lives in Ventnor. So we decided to arrange our own, and when we spoke to Spud he said that his parents were away on Saturday night so we could stay there. Then Meat and Tom were roped in.

I asked Kelly if we could cancel our cinema trip until next week. She said that was fine as she wanted to go to the girls' sleepover.

At lunchtime, on our way down to the icafé, Ed and I caught a glimpse of Daisy's dad's picture on someone's television screen as we walked past a house that had no net curtains.

We were intrigued and when we got to the icafé we asked Vernon to switch on his television. Unfortunately the picture wasn't displayed again.

When I got home, I was greeted by some slobbery kisses from Nan Stenning, and a bear hug from Grandad Stenning before being presented with the gift of a box of Ferrero Rochet.

I can't stand Ferrero Rochet but I heartily thanked them nevertheless.

After dinner, came the dreaded announcement, which was followed, oh too quickly, by far too many more slobbery kisses and bear hugs, then an apology from Grandad to Mum after he realised that perhaps it wasn't a good idea giving her a bear hug in her present condition.

After dinner I helped Mum dry up and told her about spending tomorrow night at Spud's. She started what I call 'whisper shouting' at me. Whisper shouting is exactly the same as normal shouting, with the same aggression and gestations, but the shouter only whispers. This tends to happen when whoever wants to shout doesn't want to be heard shouting. I have always found it a rather bizarre phenomenon.

She calmed down after I told her that it was strictly a lads-only night in.

Mum persuaded me to spend the evening with all of them to make up for the fact that I was not spending tomorrow evening with them.

We went to the cricket club this evening, where Grandad got drunk and I spent nearly the whole time up there watching Nan squander a small fortune on the fruit machine. At one stage she won twenty-five pounds, only to put it all back in again.

We had to get a taxi home, and me and Dad had to carry Grandad into the house.

8 February 2003, Saturday

After breakfast, Dad, Grandad and I watched *Soccer AM* on Sky Sports. Grandad was reading *The Sun* and on the front page was a picture of Daisy's dad.

I found out, to my horror, that he has been accused of the murder of that young lad found in the River Itchen a few days ago. It said: 'Police examining Marsh's computer found illegal images of young boys and e-mails that appeared to have been sent by boys that Marsh had met in chat rooms. He had evidently been masquerading as a girl called Daisy.'

The bloke is called Trevor Marsh and I was that close to becoming his victim. The thought sent shivers down my spine.

I went to Ed's house. He had already heard and was as shocked as I was. He suggested that we went to the police, but I said that we should think about it for a while.

This afternoon Dad and I turned out for Osborne Coburg Reserves against Newchurch Reserves. Dad was substitute and I played up front. Our players, except for me, were awful. They could hardly string two passes together. In the first half I was passing the ball all over the park and our players kept on losing the thing. So in the second half I was a bit more selfish and I was rewarded with a goal when I ghosted past their centre back and slotted the ball under the diving goalkeeper.

We lost four-one and Dad came on for the last ten minutes. He didn't get a touch.

The one thing that annoyed me a little is that Dennis, the Reserves manager, calls everyone by his first name but puts 'ee' or 'zee' on the end and my name was Troyzee. Dad's was Kevee.

I was voted man of the match as I was told on my way out of the changing room.

The steak and chips dinner this afternoon was especially nice.

Ed called at about seven and we walked around to Spud's.

We had our own little party, drank seven bottles of cider between us, and set up our sleeping bags in his front room. I was lucky enough to get the sofa. Spud and Meat were on the floor and Ed and Tom had a chair each.

Tom had this stupid idea of having a penis measuring competition. We had to put our erect willies into an empty toilet roll and mark, with a biro, where it came to.

I couldn't get it up, so my mark was the lowest. Meat had a problem getting rid of his so he disappeared to the bathroom with Spud's Kylie Minogue calendar for a while.

I explained that I couldn't get it up and Spud said that I could borrow one of his dad's Viagra tablets. They took the piss for most of the night.

One thing that was funny, though, was that Spud got out his dad's dictaphone and whenever anyone felt a fart coming on they recorded it.

9 February 2003, Sunday

I have never had such a laugh over breakfast before. We all piled into Spud's kitchen for tea and toast and listened over and over again to the Fart Symphony, as Tom called it, on the dictaphone. We also added a few more to it during the morning.

At ten o'clock it was time to set off home, as Tom had to play football.

I had a quick bath before Grandad and Nan Brown arrived to help us take the grandparents Stenning to the Bargeman's Rest for lunch.

Today is my dad's thirty-seventh birthday. I gave him his card and he was as happy as he always has been whenever I have given him a card, right from when I was little.

After lunch Nan and Grandad Brown went on their way and we went back to Cowes to help Nan and Grandad Stenning prepare for their departure.

Dad and Mum took them down to the Red Jet as I couldn't fit into the car with all of them and their luggage.

I went to Ed's where he had transferred the Fart Symphony to CD. We had a great laugh listening to it with his little sister, Zoe.

I had to go at teatime because he was seeing Katie tonight. So I was left to my own devices once again.

I stayed in and watched television with Mum and Dad.

10 February 2003, Monday

Me, Meat and Ed met up with Spud at the school gates and, fortunately, he had the Dictaphone with him and the rest of the year could get a laugh out of the tape.

Spud said that he was off on a two-week holiday to Turkey on Friday, the lucky git. His Uncle Ray lives out there.

He asked me if he could borrow my digital camera so that he could take some pictures of topless sunbathers. I said that he could but I couldn't let Dad know because he'd go mad.

At lunchtime, once again, we went down to the icafé where Vernon added to our montage of flatulence. Lara asked Spud when he was going to stop being so vulgar. He said, 'When I get to record a girl fart!'

'That won't *ever* happen,' she sneered to rapturous laughter from all the lads.

Ricky Kinsella was quiet for a while, probably making sure that Terry Smith wasn't with us. Just before we headed back to school, Spud went and sat next to him for a chat. After he got up and joined us on our way, Kinsella started shouting, 'Poof, Queer! I'll 'ave 'im next time I see 'im!'

I asked Spud what he had said and he told me, 'I just let Mr Kinsella know that little rumour about Terry. He seemed to take exception to it for some reason.'

'Have you got a death wish or something?' I said.

'I couldn't give a toss, fella! I'm off to Turkey next week. That's all I care about at the moment.'

Let's just hope Terry doesn't find out until after Friday, otherwise Spud might find himself mashed.

In English, we had a discussion about reality television shows. It was quite heated as you either love them or hate them. I, personally, love shows like *Big Brother* because you can't predict what is going to happen. It's also good that ordinary people can be entertaining. Real life has far more impact as entertainment than fictional drama.

After *Big Brother* was mentioned we started discussing George Orwell's vision of 1984 and all the CCTV cameras that are about nowadays. A couple of people said that CCTV cameras were an invasion of privacy. I said that they were only an invasion of privacy to a crook that wants to commit a crime or has already done so.

When I got home, Dad was there. He was shell-shocked as he had been told at work that MP Graphics' controlling firm, The Diamond Group, had put forward a proposal to close the Isle of Wight site.

The Diamond Group have their headquarters in Manchester and have sites all over the country. These sites have been bought because they had large repro contracts that The Diamond Group wanted.

MP Graphics' contract was the Atkinsons Supermarkets packaging contract but they have lost half the contract to another supplier.

Half of the workforce is going to be offered jobs at a site in Fareham.

Dad is worried that there will not be a position for a Mac Operator there. Mum and I told him to keep positive, but he seems to think that when they close the site down on March the thirty-first he'll be out of a job.

I had a phone call from Lara this evening. She asked me to go around to her house for a chat.

She's had another row with Tom and she's thinking of finishing with him. She asked me what I thought she should do and I so wanted to tell her to finish with him but Tom is my mate, so, through partially gritted teeth, I told her to sleep on it and see how they both felt tomorrow.

The problem is that Tom wants to sleep with her. I can't blame him for that. Lara doesn't feel as if she is ready yet. I hope she continues to feel that way.

I can't deny that, secretly, I want them to split up, but I can't have any influence over it this time. Not unless I find out that Tom has been up to mischief, like Spud was.

I went home when I saw her clock read ten o'clock, but as a I walked up the road and checked my own watch I saw that the time was actually nine forty-five. I could have spent fifteen more minutes with her. I was so disappointed.

11 February 2003, Tuesday

Dad was a bit apprehensive about going to work this morning, and I was the same about going to school.

The fact that Dad's firm is closing down means that the possibility of me having to go into year twelve has increased.

Ed called, as usual, this morning. He told me that Jason Dwyer asked Kelly out last night and she said yes. So there goes my cinema trip!

Why can't I get a girlfriend? I am so depressed over the fact that I am forever single. Am I that ugly?

This news played on my mind all day, and when I saw Lara and Tom snogging at lunchtime it rubbed salt into the wound.

Just to make things worse, Lara came up to me and thanked me for stopping her from finishing with Tom last night.

'You are such a fantastic friend,' she said. I struggled to look pleased.

The rest of them went down to the icafé but I decided to stay at school and sulk.

The only thing to break the day was Episode Three of Maths:

'Right! Come, shut up and sit down Jason Dwyer get out.'

'But I haven't done anything yet, sir.'

'It's that word, yet, see? It implies that ewe are plan-en to disrupt my lesson. Call it crime prevention.'

The end of day bell was like an instant end to torture.

When I got home, Dad was already there. They had all been sent home early.

He said that he had been offered a job at Greetings R Us in Freshwater but said that he'd rather stay with The Diamond Group if he can.

All the couples, which now include Jason and Kelly, went to the cinema tonight. They invited me but I would have felt too out of place.

I don't ever remember feeling as depressed as this before, except perhaps for the time when Southampton were three-nil up at half-time against Tranmere and went on to lose four-three live on TV.

12 February 2003, Wednesday

I had a heart-to-heart with Ed on the way to school this morning. He told me not to let it get me down because women aren't attracted to miserable gits. I said that was rubbish because Mum was attracted to Dad. He said, 'Do you have any evidence that they are still having sex?'

I changed the subject to tonight's England game.

We met Spud at the school gates and he said that he was down at the icafé last night and a legless Ricky Kinsella was rambling on about queers and poofs so much so that he was removed by the police for being drunk and disorderly.

So at lunchtime we all trooped downtown for a bit of Kinsella baiting. When we arrived he glared over at us looking for Terry, who wasn't with us.

Kinsella wasn't as drunk as normal, so we kept our teasing down to a minimum as he was perfectly capable of staggering over and punching one of us.

Dad was at home, again, when I arrived back. He was feeling a bit more hopeful about staying employed and is going to Fareham tomorrow to see the Diamond Kingsland site.

We both went to football training tonight to burn off some tension and frustration. It worked.

When we got home we switched on the England versus Australia match and were horrified to see that England were losing two-nil and James Beattie had been taken off at half-time along with the rest of the first choice squad.

England ended up losing three-one. As if it's not enough that they thrash us at cricket, now they can gloat about this as well. It would be wonderful to be able to beat the Aussies at something.

13 February 2003, Thursday

Ed called round this morning as usual. As we walked to school we discussed the weird thing that the schools on the mainland break up for half-term tomorrow but we on the island have to wait until next Friday.

In Biology this morning we did blood tests. My blood group is AB. So at least I am not O for ordinary.

Spud is leaving tomorrow for his holiday and I forgot to bring my camera to school, so at lunchtime we both went to my house to get it.

We cut across the golf course, dodging stray tee shots on the way. A ball rolled to a stop just in front of us. We looked around for the striker of the ball but there was no one in sight, so Spud picked up the ball and threw it into the nearest bunker, then we ran off.

Mum was in a right mood when she saw us. I pretended I was showing Spud my football programme collection. Spud slipped my camera into his bag and we headed back across the golf course.

These two women were searching for a ball. Spud said, ''ave you lost your ball, luv?'

'Yes I have. Excuse me, but are you members?'

''E is,' he said rolling his eyes in my direction.'

The woman looked me up and down with a disgusted expression on her face and her nostrils flared.

I smiled as charmingly as I could. 'There's a ball over there in that bunker. Is that yours?'

The woman left to investigate and we made our way across the golf course as quickly as possible.

The boredom of the History lesson this afternoon broke all records and I actually did nod off.

When I got home from school, Mum said that the police had been round and wanted me to give a statement regarding the e-mails I had received from and sent to that murdering pervert, Trevor Marsh.

So after Dad got home we went up to Newport Police Station, where I told the officers what had happened when I met up with Marsh a few weeks ago.

After we had finished they thanked me and I felt like a really good citizen, but as soon as we got home Mum and Dad tore into me saying I was lucky to be alive and they grounded me from using the Internet for one month.

That is so unfair as I have been shocked enough by what happened to know not to do it again.

After they had finished ranting at me we sat down to dinner and Dad told us that he had been over to Fareham to check out the facilities at Diamond Kingsland. He said that he was well impressed. They are a growing company and the only profit-making part of the Diamond Group. So he is quite hopeful, especially since they have promised to pay the travelling expenses of all island-based employees.

'A Red Funnel season ticket means free travel to all home football matches!' he said.

Ed invited me round to his house tonight, even though Katie was with him. We chatted in his room for an hour or so, mainly about my lack of a love life.

14 February 2003, Friday

The postman arrived this morning with a Valentine card for Mum! I have never received a serious one and, although I hoped for a pleasant surprise, I knew I wouldn't get one this year either.

I thought about sending one to Lara, but decided that it would be a waste of time since she is seeing Tom at the moment.

Ed arrived as usual and had to ask if I'd got any cards, just so that I could ask him.

'I got two' he said, 'though one of them was from my sister!'

We met Meat at the school gates and he had got two as well. Lara had received six. I wish I'd sent her one now.

At lunchtime we went down to see Vernon, and Ed asked him if he'd got any cards. He reached under his counter and produced a huge pile of them.

'Been saving them up over the years?' joked Meat.

'No, mate. Here are last year's cards.' And he reached back under his counter and produced an equally large wad of cards.

Feeling totally left out, I called across to Ricky Kinsella. 'Got any Valentines today, Ricky?'

To my disgust and dismay he reached into his coat and waved a pink envelope at me. Then he winked.

I don't believe it. Even a drunken tramp like him can get one. Even if it was a joke, someone had thought of him.

That put me in a bad mood for the rest of the day.

Jason and Kelly asked me, as we left school for the weekend, if I would like to go to the cinema with them. 'No thanks,' I grunted, ungratefully.

After I had sulked at home for a while and cheered up a bit, I regretted my hasty reaction and thought how nice it was for them to ask me, so I phoned Kelly and asked her if I could change my mind.

'You can change your mind if you want, but it won't make any difference because we've changed our minds as well.'

So that was it, I thought, until just as *Coronation Street* started my text alert went off and it was a message from Lara: 'CAN U CUM 2 MY HOUSE. PLEASE.'

So I quickly grabbed my coat and skateboard and sped round to her house.

She was very upset. She had split up with Tom because he got a card from another girl and had also sent that girl a card in return. He also objected to the eight cards that Lara ended up with.

It has really finished this time because Tom has decided to go off with the other girl.

I know it is horrible, but I really enjoyed hugging Lara to comfort her. I've never got so close to a girl before. I so wanted to kiss her but there was never going to be a chance of that happening because her face was buried in my shoulder.

After a while she stopped crying and we sat together on her bed. I got to hold her precious hand. My hand became clammy but she didn't complain. I wish I could have stayed there all night, but all too quickly it was time to go.

She asked me if I could go round and keep her company tomorrow afternoon, but I had to turn her down because I'm going to the FA Cup game. She made out that she understood, but I could see in her eyes that she was very disappointed.

I could smell her perfume on me as I lay in my bed tonight, and when I shut my eyes I could see her exquisite face shining at me.

15 February 2003, Saturday

After breakfast this morning, I sat with Dad for a while and we watched *Soccer AM* together. My phone rang. It was Tom.

He said that he was sorry it had had to end with Lara but he had fallen for this other girl, big time.

She goes to Medina High School, so I am yet to see what she looks like but she'd have to be amazing to be better than Lara.

I told him that I would look after Lara and he said, 'Thanks, mate. I do still care about her, you will tell her that, won't you? I hope we can still be friends after everyone has got over everything.'

As I travelled over to Southampton with Dad, he told me that he'd been to check out the job offer at Greetings R Us in Freshwater but he hadn't told Mum yet because he was a bit dubious that a job there wouldn't be a secure one. So he is going to see what happens with his application to work at Diamond Kingsland.

It was bitterly cold as we got off the ferry in Southampton and the cold air smothered us as we walked down the pier. We jumped on the bus that the club lays on, which was nice and warm.

When we got into the stadium it wasn't so cold and we were able to enjoy our two-nil victory over Norwich, feeling fairly comfortable in our seats.

Southampton are now in the FA Cup quarter finals. This is a rare thing for us. I so hope we can get drawn at home in the next round, as I don't know if Dad will fork out for an away trip bearing in mind his current uncertain work situation.

We caught the bus back to the ferry. We normally walk back but the bus got us to the terminal really quickly so we will probably use it in future.

After dinner I phoned Lara to see if I could go and see her, but she said that she was staying the night at Rachel's. That's her Ventnor friend.

I am so disappointed. I was really looking forward to seeing her.

So, once again, I stayed in on a Saturday night. How sad is that? I tried to stay up and watch *Match of the Day* but it was on so late that I fell asleep and was woken up by the theme music as the programme ended.

16 February 2003, Sunday

This morning Ed phoned me during breakfast and suggested that we go up to the park to watch Tom play football. I declined at first but changed my mind when he said that Tom's new girlfriend might be there.

We both skateboarded up to the recreation ground and they were putting up the goal nets as we arrived.

She was there. Tom pointed her out to us and then, as he walked to the changing room, introduced us to her.

She is blonde and very pretty (though not nearly as nice as Lara). Her name is Donna. It seemed weird seeing them kiss, when only days ago he was snogging Lara.

As we watched the game she was very enthusiastically cheering Tom on. When she called out, 'Oi, ref that was never offside!' when Tom was put clean through on goal and the linesman (who is supplied by the visiting team) incorrectly flagged, I asked her if she watched a lot of football.

'I've got a season ticket at Fratton Park,' she said.

I felt a cold shiver go down my spine. She is a Pompey supporter. I felt an uncontrollable urge to take the piss.

'So you don't know anything about football then?' I teased.

'Why, who do you support then?'

'The south coast's only Premiership club.'

A scowl came over her face and suddenly she wasn't very nice looking.

'Scummer!' she snapped. 'Next season you won't be the only south coast club in the Premiership because we'll be there and we are going to stuff you.'

'I doubt that,' I retorted, 'as most of your players will be drawing their pension next season.'

'We'll see!' she huffed and then she walked off and watched the match from the opposite side of the pitch.

'What's Fratton Park backwards?' I called after her. She didn't answer. 'Crap not arf!'

It's very shallow, I know, to take a dislike to someone because they support Portsmouth but it's as good a reason as any and Lara will appreciate it.

At half-time Tom waved at Donna and walked over to us and asked us what we thought of her.

'She seems nice,' said Ed.

'Charming girl!' I said, sarcastically.

'I'm glad you like her,' beamed Tom as he left for their half-time team talk.

Me and Donna passed several glares at each other during the second half, but when the final whistle sounded me and Ed skated off, to avoid any more unfriendly behaviour. We did bid Tom a farewell wave before we left.

I arrived home just as Mum and Dad got back from Tesco. I helped Dad lug shopping bags into the house.

I couldn't wait to tell Lara about Donna, so I sent a text to her asking her to let me know when she was back home.

She sent a text straight back saying that she was at home, so I skated over to her house as quickly as I could.

I told Lara that Donna was ugly and rude and that Tom was a complete idiot to go off with her.

I stayed there for the rest of the afternoon and played Monopoly with her and her two brothers. I was just on the verge of winning when her younger brother, Lee, got in a mood and flipped the table over, sending all the game pieces everywhere.

I went home soon afterwards, where I had a salad dinner with Mum and Dad.

I stayed in this evening to watch Wolverhampton Wanderers knock Rochdale out of the FA Cup. The match was shown on BBC2.

Dad went to bed but I wasn't tired so I stayed up and watched a biography programme about Ozzy Osbourne.

He reminds me of Ricky Kinsella a bit.

17 February 2003, Monday

The last week before half-term began in the usual mind-numbingly boring fashion. Tom and Lara steered clear of each other until lunchtime when we were casually enjoying some of Vernon's football anecdotes at the icafé.

Lara came up and ordered an ice cream and promptly shoved it into Tom's face.

We tried not to laugh but it was really funny. Even Tom had to laugh until he noticed Ricky Kinsella chortling over at his bench. He shouted over at him, 'Piss off you drunken sod!'

Kinsella was too drunk to get up and reap some sort of punishment so he had to resort to verbal insults which were so slurred that we couldn't decipher them.

In English this afternoon we discussed great world leaders. I put forward the case for Nelson Mandela who is by far the greatest leader of his country the world has ever known. To spend all those years incarcerated by white men and yet have no grudges against whites shows incredible strength of character.

When I got home Dad was there. He said that he had an interview for a position in Fareham tomorrow, so he is very nervous and apprehensive.

Tom, unusually, invited me round to his house this evening, to watch the Leicester versus Portsmouth match on Sky.

He didn't let me know that Donna was going to be there.

Things started quite well when Leicester scored and I was able to take the piss out of her but, apart from that, Leicester were awful and Pompey played very well and deserved the equaliser they scored in the second half and I couldn't deny it. Donna loved seeing me looking hacked off and I left as soon as the match finished.

It is horrible to have to admit it, but Portsmouth will be in the Premiership next season. It will bring extra tension to our season, especially if they are ever above us in the league.

18 February 2003, Tuesday

When I got up this morning I was astonished to see Dad washing the car. It was bitterly cold. I asked Mum what he was up to and she said that he was very restless last night and was doing it to take his mind off things.

When I saw Tom at school I asked him why he had put me and Donna together last night. I wondered whether he wanted to see if we would end up scrapping.

He told me that Donna said that she doesn't like me. I said that the feeling is mutual.

'And all because of football!' he said. 'It's pathetic.'

Terry and Jason Ince insisted on coming down to the icafé at lunchtime. We were expecting a confrontation but Kinsella wasn't there.

Vernon said that he was there last night but hadn't turned up at all this morning. Terry said that he'd probably been arrested.

So that was partly a relief and partly a disappointment as Terry and Kinsella usually provide good entertainment when they are together.

This afternoon it was Episode Four of Maths:

'Can anyone tell me the formula for pye?'
'Pastry, gravy, meat and veg, sir.'
'Fancy ewe-er-self as a cook then do ewe Jay-sern Dwyer?'
'No, I thought it was a trick question.'
'This is a maths lesson ewe faht head.'
'No I didn't sir.'
'GEETT OUT!'

At home time Ed went off into town so I headed for home on my own. I saw Lara ahead, also walking on her own, so I caught up with her. She was a bit miserable.
'You told me that that Donna tart was ugly!' she said.
'Yeah?'
'Well I saw her with Tom yesterday afternoon and she's really pretty!'
'Well that's your opinion,' I said. 'She's not a very nice person and, for me, that makes her ugly.'
That seemed to make Lara feel better and I walked her home before going home myself.
Dad was in. He had had his interview but they said that they would decide later this week. So the poor bloke has to continue to suffer.
After dinner I went to Lara's house. We had a great laugh.
First of all we had a chat about sex. She said that she wouldn't just give her virginity away. It would have to be a special moment and with a special person. I said that it would be nice if it were like that but I wouldn't mind giving mine away at any time.
After that we played tickling games and play fighting which was great because it gave me an excuse to put my hands all over her body.
After we stopped for a rest she turned to me and said, 'I love you, Troy. You really know how to cheer me up.'
I was dumbfounded. I wanted to say something cool but turned into a jabbering fool. All I could say was 'Hmmph!'
She hugged me and I hugged her back. My heart was pounding so hard that I felt that it was bouncing around my ribcage.
I didn't want to let go but all too soon she pulled away.
I composed myself and felt that it was now or never.
'W-will y-you go out with me?' I stuttered.
Lara looked very surprised. 'Oh, that's so sweet,' she said. 'When I said I loved you, I meant as a friend.'

My hopes and dreams shrivelled away with one sentence. 'You're such a good friend it would spoil things if we got together. Don't you think?'

I nodded and tried to stretch a reassuring smile across my scarlet face.

She put her arm around me. 'Thanks, though. That's really cheered me up.'

It didn't cheer me up, though. It had the completely opposite effect and soon afterwards I left.

I took the long route home, via the seafront. While there was hope of going out with her I felt alive but now.

What am I going to do?

19 February 2003, Wednesday

I couldn't face school today so I pretended to be ill. I must have looked bad because Mum commented that I didn't look well.

I stayed in bed until Mum came into my room and told me that she was taking a walk to town.

I got up and lounged around in front of the television. At lunchtime Lara phoned me. She asked me what was the matter and I lied to her and said that I felt sick. I suppose it was only a white lie because I do feel sick but not physically, just mentally.

Mum came back from her shopping trip and said that I looked much better. She made me a corned beef sandwich for lunch. I forced it down.

Soon it was teatime but Dad hadn't turned up. Mum tried to ring his mobile but it was switched off.

He turned up at six o'clock, an hour and a half late. He had had another interview very late and had forgotten to switch his phone back on.

He said that it was awful having to watch his workmates leave. Some people were going up for their interviews and being told that there wasn't a position for them and that they could leave straight away. Dad has got a position to apply for, but seven people are applying for five jobs. They will all find out tomorrow whether they are successful or not. So that means another sleepless night for Dad.

I wouldn't be surprised to get up and find him mowing the lawn or something.

Mum told Dad that it would do him good to go to football training and I said I felt much better and would go with him, so we went.

I have been selected, again, to play on Saturday but Dad hasn't. He wasn't bothered though. In hindsight, it wasn't such a good idea to take him along as he nearly had a scrap with one of our loud-mouthed players called Jonesy.

Jonesy had had a go at him for playing a poor pass and told Dad he was a useless git, so Dad pushed his chest out like a strutting cockerel, tightened his lips and tried to look intimidating. All the other players piled in to separate them. It was quite funny but I had to conceal my amusement.

The training session may not have helped Dad very much but it did me the power of good.

When we got home Mum gave me a note that had been delivered while I was out. It read:

Hi Troy

I hope you were not off school to avoid seeing me.
This is exactly the reason why we shouldn't go out with each other because we are more likely to fall out if we are boyfriend and girlfriend than if we stay as close friends.
I need your friendship. I need you. Please don't let this get between us.
All my love

Lara xxx

20 February 2003, Thursday

This morning Dad woke me up saying, 'Where is your digital camera?'

I, still feeling groggy, said that I didn't know.

'You've lent it to that Hudd lad haven't you?'

'No!' I said, wondering how the hell he could have found out.

'Oh, you didn't?' said Dad in an obviously doubting manner.

'No?' I replied, starting to think that he must have some amazing evidence to the contrary.

'So what is he talking about in this, then?' And he tossed a postcard onto my bed.

It had a picture of three topless women on one side and on the other side was written:

Dear Troy,

Just a quick note while I'm sober.
I am missing you obviously. Uncle Ray's
beer ran out Tuesday. Haven't even
rung Emma. Don't wanna come home.
The picture is nowt compared with ones
taken with your camera, fella. Superb!!!
Weather wonderful as are birds.
Hope you are well and are enjoying school without me.
See you soon (unfortunately)

Stuart P. Hudd

I looked up at Dad. He looked back at me, his lips pursed and his arms folded.

'It's a fair cop!' I said.

'Yes, you have been well and truly rumbled, so, if we ever get the camera back, the memory card containing these pictures will be confiscated, do I make myself clear?'

'Yes Dad, sorry.'

'Hmmmm!' Dad said as her turned to leave.

I called after him, 'Dad?'

'What?'

'Good luck.'

He smiled at me, 'Thanks son.'

What an idiot Spud is. I told him to keep it quiet about the camera so he writes about it on a postcard.

I texted Ed to tell him not to bother calling for me this morning, then left early so that I could meet with Lara.

She was just coming out of her house as I arrived and she waved and smiled as she shut her front door behind her. When she reached her gate I gave her a hug and said that I was sorry for being stupid and that I just needed a bit of time to get over the disappointment.

When we got to the top of Woodvale Road we were spotted by Ed, whose jaw dropped, obviously jumping to an incorrect conclusion.

'I can see what you're thinking but you are way off the mark,' said Lara.

'Oh, so you're clairvoyant now are you?'

'I don't need to be. Your face gave it away.'

'Okay then. Why are you two walking to school together?'

So I explained and Ed pretended that he didn't believe us. I realised that he was only messing around, but Lara was taken in by his teasing and went on explaining the situation over and over again until we got to the school gates at which point Ed said, 'Its all right Lara, I'm only winding you up.'

His reward was a girlie punch on the arm.

Ed said that he had received a postcard from Spud as well this morning. In his postcard Spud said that he'd shagged some girl on a beach. I said that I was surprised that he didn't write that in his postcard to Emma Hewings, as that's how stupid he his.

Just then we saw Emma crying and being comforted by some other year-twelve girls. Curious to find out why she was upset, Ed got Katie to go and investigate. Katie returned with a disgusted expression on her face.

'You won't believe this,' she said.

'WHAT?' we said in unison.

'He's only dumped her in the postcard he sent her. What a bastard! And to think I had such a crush on him.'

Ed and I had to agree with her. It was a bit out of order.

So with all that going on before I'd even entered the school building, the school day had a lot to live up to.

At lunchtime me, Ed, Katie, Meat, Kylie, Jason and Kelly went down to the icafé. Ricky Kinsella's bench was still deserted.

Vernon said that he had heard that Kinsella had been admitted to St Mary's Hospital suffering from exposure after he had passed out the other night on that bench.

The afternoon went as slowly as usual and at last I could go home and find out how Dad had got on in his attempt to get a job at Diamond Kingsland.

When I got home he hadn't arrived yet, which meant that Mum and I had to wait for an hour until he came strolling up the garden path.

We watched him glumly come in through the front door looking absolutely shattered.

Mum went up to him and hugged him. When he came into the living room I consoled him.

'It's very nice of you both, but consolation is the last thing I need right now'.

'I suppose you'll be wanting to put it all behind you,' I said.

'Yes, that's right, because in a few weeks' time I'll be commuting to Fareham.'

Mum and I erupted with cheers of joy and then Dad got a load more hugs.

Then he took me and Mum out for a meal at the Bargeman's Rest and after that to the cinema where we watched *Treasure Planet.*

21 February 2003, Friday

Back to normal this morning as far as travelling to school with Ed is concerned.

With half-term upon us, we were all trying to plan what we were going to do over the holiday.

Tom said that we must try to get out to a party or go clubbing or something as we hadn't utilised Karl's car for ages

At lunchtime Ricky Kinsella was back at his bench, a lot more sober than normal and being quite pleasant to passers-by. He even said, 'All right mate!' to a surprised Terry.

Everybody was watching the clock this afternoon until finally the bell went and we all set off for home knowing that we had a whole week away from the dreaded place.

Tom arranged for me and Ed to go round to his house this evening. We all went out in Karl's car for a burn around the island. We did a complete circuit, which took, as I timed it on my stopwatch, one hour, fifteen minutes and twenty-seven seconds. We were just about to drive back to Newport when Tom got a phone call from The Dragon, Donna, and decided to go round to her house, so we dropped him off and went back to Cowes. Karl dropped me and Ed off at the icafé where we hung around for a couple of hours before heading for home.

22 February 2003, Saturday

I spent the morning lounging around the house waiting for Southampton's away match at Everton to kick off. It was being shown live on Sky and was a half-twelve kick-off. Unfortunately I had overlooked this fact when I agreed to play for Osborne Coburg Reserves against Plessey Reserves. Our match was due to kick off at two o'clock, so I knew that I was going to miss most of the second half.

Saints were one-nil up when Dad and I left. Our game, although away, was played at a local park.

By the time our game kicked off, Saints, were still one-nil up. I scored a goal with a header to send us into half-time one-nil up. That's when I heard that Saints had lost two-one.That news put me in a bad mood.

In the second half I robbed one of Plessey's midfield players and played Pottsy through for a one-on-one with the goalkeeper. The keeper made a good attempt to save, but the ball rebounded off of Pottsy's shin into the net.

A little later I picked up the ball in midfield, beat a couple of players and did a one-two with Pottsy. When I got the ball back, I turned their oaf of a centre back and left him sat on his backside before making it three-nil. After the restart we won a corner and he was marking me. He growled into my ear, 'If you ever try vat again, nipper, I'll break your f***in' legs!'

I just made a noise like a ghost 'Woooooo!' and he went berserk. He shoved me over and kicked me a couple of times before his teammates held him back.

'Calm down Pitbull!' they were saying.

I got to my feet and looked at him as the referee tried to calm things down, and he glared back at me like a tethered Rottweiler.

'I'll f***in' kill ya!' Pitbull snarled.

'Oh, please don't,' I said in a mocking voice.

Dad came over from the touchline as Pitbull struggled once again to free himself and get to me.

'Hey, hey, come on, mate, he's only a nipper,' said Dad. 'Like beating on kids do you, mate?'

Pitbull struggled again and tried to get at Dad. Dad went up to his face and said, 'If you come anywhere near me or my family, you'll find yourself banged up quicker than you can say short fuse.'

I was impressed. I have never seen Dad act hard before.

Pitbull was, quite rightly, sent off and, to make matters worse for Plessey, I finished my hat-trick with a volley from the corner we had won before all that nonsense.

We won five-nil in the end, and as we walked back to the changing rooms one of their players warned me and Dad that we had upset the wrong man as Pitbull had already had two spells in prison for GBH.

Dad said, 'Well, if he comes near any of us either him or me will be doing time.'

We walked past the home dressing room on the way to ours and saw him sitting in there with a towel around him. He pointed at us and punched the palm of his left hand with his right fist.

'Ignore him,' Dad whispered to me. So I did.

We didn't bother showering and left as quickly as we could, especially when we were spotted by Pitbull as he climbed into his clapped-out old Ford

XR3i. Dad put his foot down and nearly crashed as he pulled out of the park driveway too quickly. We got to the Round House roundabout and he spotted that Pitbull was still trailing us. He only stopped following us when we pulled into our driveway.

We each had a quick shower before catching the results on ITV, then we had dinner.

It was after dinner that Mum asked if anyone had seen the dog. Then began the hunt. After failing to find him around the house, it was obvious that he had absconded.

Griz is not a streetwise dog and the chances of him getting run over were high, because he is daft.

We wandered around the neighbourhood, calling his name, and Mum tapped a spoon on the rim of his food bowl.

We were out for a couple of hours. It was very dark when we decided to give up, and guess who was curled up on the doorstep when we got home?

We were all mentally and physically exhausted after the day's events, so I stayed in for the rest of the evening and, with all the thoughts that we might have lost Griz forever, he got more attention than he had had for a long time.

It made us realise how much we love that dog, even if he does smell a bit.

23 February 2003, Sunday

I took Griz for a walk this morning, before we had our roast pork lunch. Then I went with Mum and Dad to Tesco, which is a thirteen-mile drive to Ryde. Mum didn't buy any frozen food so that we could go straight from there to Sandown Pier. We played crazy golf and Dad got stroppy when he finished last in our family competition.

Then we played air hockey. It was while I was thrashing Mum that Karl tapped me on the shoulder, so I went off with him and left Mum and Dad to their own devices.

I went with Karl and his mates Stevie and Nathan, as he drove, at ridiculously high speed, to Bembridge where we stopped off at their regular Sunday haunt, Bessie's Butties, which is a café bar.

We had toasted teacakes and had a great laugh making double entendres about the proprietor's unfeasible large breasts.

They call her Jugs, although not to her face. They would say things like, 'Excuse me we've run out of milk have you got any more jugs?' followed by a chorus of sniggering and, 'Do you sell baps?' and 'Can I have an udder cup of tea please.'

I don't know why we were trying to cover up our laughs because Bessie, or should I call her Jugs, was laughing just as much as we were.

'Oooh you saucy rascals,' she said. 'I feel like I'm starring in *Carry on Bessie* today! Where's Syd James?'

She even said, 'Isn't it cold today lads? I just popped outside to hang out some tea towels and you could have hung a wet duffel coat on my nipples.'

Karl got me home from Bembridge in record time, as usual. He's an amazing driver. He may drive fast but you always feel safe in his car.

He did tell me though, on the way home, that he had recently received a speeding fine. He was caught doing ninety-one miles per hour along Forest Road. He also got three points on his licence, which he wasn't happy about. He got his speeding fine notification photocopied and has had it framed. It now hangs on the wall in his bedroom.

I got in just in time to watch the second half of the West Bromwich Albion versus West Ham United match, which West Ham won two-one.

Saints are playing West Brom on Saturday, so I hope *we* can beat them as well.

Ed came round tonight and we listened to my Sugababes *Angels with Dirty Faces* CD. It is excellent. Ed showed me a picture he'd cut out from a newspaper, in which Heidi from the Sugababes had her boob nearly hanging out of her frock. It was amazing.

I wish I could see Lara wearing a similar outfit.

24 February 2003, Monday

I was woken up by Dad's angry voice this morning. He was livid because somebody had run a key down the side of his car.

I went out to take a look. There was a deep gouge from the rear light right along to the headlight on the driver's side.

Dad was so annoyed that he said that he felt physically sick. He phoned the police but they just gave him a crime number to quote to the insurance company. Then he had a moan at me because if I had had my digital camera I could have taken some pictures for reference.

Ed came round this morning and we decided to go to LA Bowl in Ryde. We got Meat, Jason Dwyer and Tom to come along. We caught the bus at the Round House and bought Rover tickets.

We had a good laugh bowling, although Jason was so rubbish that he got told off for continually bouncing his bowling ball down the alley, or whatever it's called.

Ed insisted on typing our names into the computer, so I ended up being Tory, which is probably why this bloke came up to me and started moaning on about the Labour government and Tony Blair after I had had one of my goes.

Meat was Mate, Tom was Omt and Jason was, and we couldn't work out how he'd managed it, Ksdim.

He managed to get his own name right though.

The match was won by Meat who had used his beefy stature to get several strikes.

We played on some of the games at the iCafé for an hour or so before heading for the bus station.

We all got off at Newport so that we could get a bite to eat at McDonald's.

Then we decided to go to the cinema and watch *The Lord of the Rings The Two Towers* again.

We were the only ones in there and Tom knocked his popcorn over and it went all over the floor and in our coats, which we had stuffed under our seats. He scooped up as much as he could and managed to blag a replacement carton.

After the film had finished, just after four o'clock, I phoned Dad and he agreed to meet me by the bus station and take us home.

On the way back we discussed tomorrow's plans. We have decided on pitch and putt in Sandown, so we will require another Rover ticket each.

I stayed in tonight and watched *Coronation Street*. The bloke who's been doing all those murders that everybody is getting bored about finally confessed.

It was announced on the news that Matthew Kelly had been cleared of the child abuse allegations, as I suspected he would be. He looked much older than he did the last time he appeared on television, although that might be because he had had a haircut and shaved off his beard.

We watched Tottenham Hotspur and Fulham draw one-one.

Dad let me have a can of lager while we watched, as Mum had gone to bed.

25 February 2003, Tuesday

Tom phoned me this morning to tell me that we didn't have to worry about getting the bus because he had persuaded Karl to come.

His car roared up to our drive at half past nine. I was sat in the back with Meat and Ed and felt really carsick because I was squashed and it was quite stuffy in there.

By the time we arrived at Brown's Golf Course I was struggling to retain my breakfast.

I bought a can of Diet Coke and a few burps seemed to help me feel better.

We went around the fourteen-hole course in about forty-five minutes. Ed won that game. We went around again and Ed won again, then we went into their clubhouse café and had a cup of tea and a scone.

Then Karl took us to Jungle Jim's in Shanklin - another iCafé. I was telling the lads about Jugs, so Karl took us to Bessie's Butties where we enjoyed an afternoon of double entendres and laughter, along with a couple of toasted teacakes and several cups of tea.

The day had gone quickly and all too soon it was dinner time and Karl took us all home - at breakneck speed, of course! Dad was in when I got back. He said that he had got a quote for the damage to his car - eight hundred pounds! The insurance company had been to see it as well as a bodywork expert.

Lara sent me a text message: CM 2 M9 2NITE. It took me ages to work it out. What on earth is em-nine? I thought it was a motorway.

Once deciphered, it sounded promising but I knew that there was nothing to read into it.

When I got there I was introduced to Rachel, her friend from Ventnor. She's gorgeous; short mousy brown hair, deep blue eyes with long, dark eyelashes and the figure of an eighteen-year-old. She was very friendly too and we got on very well.

She told me (when Lara had gone to make the tea) that Lara talks about me a lot and really cares about me. That made me feel wonderful.

All three of us went out for a walk along the seafront with Lara's dogs.

It was a very pleasant evening. I said, after being asked, that I would try to see them tomorrow.

26 February 2003, Wednesday

Mum wasn't feeling very well this morning. She is still suffering a lot from morning sickness. I'm afraid that I have little sympathy for her. She got herself into that situation.

I went around to Lara's house at about ten-thirty. Her Mum let me in and it was a treat to see Lara and Rachel eating toast in the kitchen in their pyjamas.

About an hour later they were dressed and made up, so I could go into Lara's bedroom and have a chat with them.

I feel really comfortable with Rachel, even though I have only just met her. They were playing a sort of truth or dare game, but without the dare.

It was enthralling to hear certain secrets about them such as when Lara nearly lost her virginity at a Ventnor beach party to this bastard called Dobbs. She was nearly too drunk to say no but managed to get away from him.

Rachel said that she had once snogged a girl, tongues and all. Lara said that it was disgusting, but I thought it was quite erotic.

I told them about Mum's pregnancy. Rachel said, 'That's wonderful.'

Lara seemed a bit off but still congratulated me. I implored them to keep it quiet. I'm sure they will; after all, they trusted me with their secrets.

Before I left, Rachel said that I could go to her birthday celebration on Friday and it's a sleepover. I can't tell the lads about this. It could be a brilliant night for me with all those girls.

This afternoon I went downtown with Ed. We stopped off at the icafé.

The local dimwit, Barry Whitticker, came up and started chatting to us inanely about all the money he'd won at the bookies with his twenty-pence-a-time bets. He was standing there, smoking a cigarette, holding it in his fingers like a biro. He also told us that Ricky Kinsella had been locked up for being in breach of his parole. Thank God for that; a bit of peace and quiet in Cowes for a while.

Vernon was moaning because someone had parked their car in his driveway before he had opened up for the day. The owner turned up and received a rally of verbal abuse as he climbed into his car and left. Vernon asked us to mind the shop while he went to get his car.

When he returned with his Jaguar, he was finding great difficulty in negotiating the small gap between the wall and the bubble gum dispenser. As he reversed in, Barry guided him. 'Come on Vee, come on.'

'Are you sure there's enough room, Barry?'

'Yeah, plenty of room Vee. Come on.' CRASH! 'Wooow!'

Vernon had reversed into his shop window. He went mad at Barry.

'You'll pay for that you dickhead!'

'You'll have to speak to my mum about that!' Barry whined.

That was a bit weird because he must be at least twenty-five years old.

Vernon handed Barry his mobile phone. 'He'yare! Call her now.'

'I can't speak to her now! She might smell the smoke on my breath!'

We just fell about laughing except Vernon.

This evening Dad and I went to football training. The lads gave me some stick for what happened on Saturday. I paid them back by giving a stunning performance on the training pitch. I impressed them so much that Silky, the first-team manager, asked me to play for them on Saturday. I declined as

Southampton are playing West Bromwich Albion that day.

Silky got me to agree to miss the next home game if Saints lose.

When we got home we watched the end of the Newcastle versus Bayer Leverkausen game before going to bed.

27 February 2003, Thursday

This morning Mum woke me up. She said that she had been to the doctor last week about her morning sickness. The doctor had prescribed some sort of homeopathic remedy but Mum was initially a bit sceptical. Now she will try anything so she sent me down to Boots to pick it up.

After picking up the tablets, or whatever they were, I went into Woolworths to look at the CDs. Unfortunately I didn't notice, until it was too late, that Pitbull was there with his two sons.

The boys, one was six or seven, the other was ten or eleven, had skinhead hairstyles with long straggly bits at the back, exactly like their father's hairstyle. The smaller of the two boys had a line of snot joining his nose with his top lip.

They started giving me loads of verbal abuse. 'You're a wanker aren't you?' the older boy said. I glanced over at Pitball, who was sniggering behind the DVD display. Then the younger boy punched me in the balls.

As I tried not to show the pain I was in, they left, laughing. A nice lady asked me if I was all right. When I left I made sure that they were out of sight and went home as fast as I could.

After lunch I went to see Lara to arrange our journey to Ventnor tomorrow night. We have decided to go by bus.

I went to Ed's later this afternoon. He said that Karl's mate Stevie was having a party tomorrow night. I said that I would be busy and I made out that I couldn't remember what I was doing.

'Your loss,' he said.

We went up to Northwood Park for a two-and-a-half-hour kick around with Karl, Stevie, Nathan, Meat, Tom and the two Jasons.

I stayed in this evening and watched Liverpool beat Auxerre with Dad as we ate our pay-day KFC Megabucket.

All this football on television lately is excellent, although Mum doesn't agree. She keeps having early nights.

28 February 2003, Friday

I woke up this morning with an abundance of zits all over my face.

Why is it that whenever I am contemplating spending time with girls my face erupts?

It was a day of waiting, which was made all the worse by the pouring rain.

I watched television until mid-afternoon when I decided to have a bath. I also shaved the bum fluff off of my face, which cut the tops off of all of my spots.

I spent the next hour with loads of bits of toilet paper stuck to my face.

I had an early dinner and went to Lara's at four thirty and we walked up to the Round House where we caught the five past five bus to Newport. Then we caught the bus to Ventnor. The journey took an hour and a half. An hour and a half with her! Bliss!

When we arrived at Rachel's I met Sam and Belinda. I felt a bit out of the girlie chit-chat that went on for the next two hours.

Rachel said that Belinda was single like me and said that we should get together. Both of us went bright red with embarrassment.

At about ten this lad called Chris turned up. He is Rachel's best friend.

'Like you are with Lara,' Rachel told me.

So he obviously wants to go out with her then.

'Chris's mum said that you can stay at their house tonight.' Rachel said. 'My mum wouldn't let you stay here, I'm afraid. Sorry!'

Shit!

1 March 2003, Saturday

So off I trudged to Chris's house where I had a night of very little sleep on his bedroom floor. I kept hitting my leg on his bass guitar and he snored very loudly.

Chris's mum cooked me a lovely fried breakfast and both Chris and I went to Rachel's house where Lara informed me that she was going to stay there for the weekend.

So I had to travel all the way back to Cowes on my own.

What a complete let-down the last twenty-four hours have been.

It was nice to have the opportunity to forget about it all as Dad and I went to the Southampton versus West Bromwich Albion match. James Beattie scored a great goal which helped us win one-nil and me avoid having to play for Osborne Coburg when Saints play Aston Villa in a couple of weeks' time.

After we got home and had eaten dinner, Ed came round to tell me about the party I should have gone to.

He wasn't very happy, as he had finished with Katie because she got so drunk that she stripped totally naked and danced around like an idiot.

I missed seeing a naked girl, yet again! I can't believe it. So that meant that both of us were hacked off with everything. He said that he wished he'd gone with me to Rachel's do.

We played CDs for a while until *The Premiership* started on ITV. Unfortunately we had to wait until midnight for the highlights of the Saints game and they only showed about thirty seconds of it.

Before he left we agreed to watch the Worthington Cup Final together tomorrow.

2 March 2003, Sunday

I had a long lie-in this morning and didn't get up until midday when Mum was serving up dinner. Nan and Grandad Brown were in the living room as I plodded wearily in. They were sat together hand in hand on the sofa. I thought that was a bit weird but it all fell into place when they announced, over lunch, that they were getting back together again.

I had a dream, during the night, that Liverpool won today's final two-nil. Both Dad and Grandad dismissed this as rubbish. 'Liverpool are terrible at the moment!' Dad said.

After lunch I went to Ed's where we watched Liverpool win, rather luckily two-nil, against Manchester United. That rounded off a bad weekend for Ed.

I quickly went home afterwards, desperate to see Dad's reaction.

He was absolutely shattered that he hadn't put a bet on it.

'Next time you have a dream like that, make sure I go to the bookies,' he grumbled.

With school tomorrow I had to spend a couple of hours this afternoon catching up on my homework.

Spud called round with my camera. Dad immediately confiscated it and told Spud off. Spud just humoured him. We went to my room where Spud said, 'Don't worry, fella, I've already copied all the pictures to disk. Here's your copy, and thanks.'

He handed me a CD and then briefed me on his holiday 'sexploits', as he called them.

He reckons that he had sex with three different girls, all of them English and older than him. 'It was the best two weeks of my life!' he remarked.

Then he came up with a brilliant idea. He said that all the lads should club together, in the summer, and go on a lads holiday. If it's that easy to get a girl on holiday, I am well up for it.

Spud stayed until we heard Dad go to bed, then we sneaked into the front room and looked at his pervy snaps on the computer. Tits everywhere! I've got to get out there somehow. At least you are guaranteed to see naked girls even if you don't get a shag.

3 March 2003, Monday

For some reason, every time the first day of term arrives, Mum has to come and wake me up, knowing full well that my alarm is set.

Dad was moaning, as he got ready to leave for work, that someone had posted a nearly empty bag of chips through our letter box last night. He had found Griz with his nose in it on enterring the hallway after getting up.

Ed and Spud called round for me this morning. Spud hasn't called in the morning for ages. He always used to drop in on Ed before calling for me, which is well out of his way considering where he lives.

At the moment Spud hasn't got a girlfriend and he was asking Ed whether he minded him having another go at Katie.

Ed looked to me as if he were trying to cover up his true feelings when he said, 'Go for it mate! It's no skin off my nose!'

So as soon as we saw Katie, Spud was over with her, chatting her up, to sideways looks from Ed.

Jason Dwyer is in Mr Vibert's class for registration, and as we queued up for Maths he said that we were going to have a life class in Art tomorrow. We all hope it's a woman. This could be my chance of seeing one naked at last.

We were all whispering about it during Maths, which resulted in several tellings-off.

At break time Spud was still hanging around Katie, and Ed was still trying to look as though he didn't care and failing to achieve it.

In Geography we were given a project which will end up being marked up as part of our GCSE exam. We have to write an essay on our region.

How tedious!

At lunchtime we went down to see Vernon, and Barry Whitticker has taken residence of Kinsella's bench.

Vernon has decided to call Barry 'Dickicker' from now on after the parking-gate scandal.

He kept calling over to Barry, 'What do you think of my new window Barry?' And, 'Has your mother come up with the cash yet?'

He knows full well that he'll get nothing out of them. After a short while Barry left, presumably to go to the bookies.

Lara came down a bit later than we did, and came over for a chat. I hadn't seen her all morning. She told me that Rachel thinks the world of me and that there is a chance that Belinda might fancy me. She told me to write Belinda a note and she'll get Rachel to pass it on when she sees her at swimming tonight.

Apparently, Belinda hasn't got a mobile phone yet.

After lunch we had a boring debate about eating disorders and the way the media try to make perfectly normal girls think they are fat. I said that I expect that even Tara Palmer-Tomkinson thinks she's fat. It's just the way women are.

So this evening my task was set to compile a note to Belinda. Unfortunately Dad and I were watching the Aston Villa versus Birmingham match, which was full of incident with Villa having two players sent off, so I was a bit distracted. After the match I went to my room to write it in peace and quiet.

Dear Belinda

I hope you are well. Having met you on Friday I noticed how nice you are. I expect Lara has told you how desperate I am for a girlfriend as she told me that you fancy me. I think she likes to play cupid. I hope you will be interested in going out with me.

I can hardly wait for your reply.

Love Troy

I put the note in an envelope addressed to Belinda, enclosing it in another envelope to Lara with a note asking her to give it to Belinda. Then I quickly skated around to Lara's and popped it through her letter box.

4 March 2003, Tuesday

It was just Ed who called round this morning. He is still in denial over Katie and claims that he doesn't care if she goes out with Spud or not. The fact that he is as miserable as sin gives the game away.

Everything was geared up for our art lesson this morning. As we waited outside the art room, I asked Mr Vibert if it was a woman that we were drawing. He said yes and all the lads became very excited, except Terry who said that we were all a bunch of toss pots.

We went in and took our places, and there was a big sheet obscuring what was obviously the model.

Mr Vibert told us that if anyone felt uncomfortable they could leave or if anyone messed around they would be asked to leave. After waffling on for a minute or so he prepared to remove the sheet. We all took a deep breath. The sheet came down and my first reaction was disappointment to see a wrinkly old woman sitting there, completely starkers. Then I thought I recognised her, but no, it couldn't be. She looked at me and winked.

A sick feeling came over me and I had to leave the room. Mr Vibert followed.

'Brown? I'm surprised to see you leave the room.'

My heart was racing and I felt a bit faint. Mr Vibert sat me down. 'It can't be that bad can it?' he said.

It was. The naked woman in the art room was my Nan.

Mr Vibert said that I could wait outside until Nan had covered up and left. That was half an hour later. I went in and everyone was looking at me. I couldn't help seeing everyone's drawings as I made my way back to my seat. Mr Vibert set everyone the task of finishing off their pictures and I went through to the storeroom where Nan had now got dressed.

'You know this is my school Nan, how could you embarrass me like that?'

'I've got nothing to be ashamed of. I didn't know it would be your art lesson, anyway.'

'But you knew there would be a chance, just from the fact that it was at my school.'

'Oh, what does it matter. It's easy money and I'm not ashamed of my body.'

Well she should have been. It was all wrinkly and yuk! I don't mean to be horrible because I love my Nan, but Grandad can't be going back to her because she looks good naked.

I went home at lunchtime to tell Mum. She said that Nan used to be a naturist when she was younger. Dad used to call her an exhibitionist and when Mum and Dad were first going out together, Mum was waiting on their sofa for Dad. She'd walked into the room naked. Mum had got a shock, but she'd only come into fetch a towel that was hanging on a radiator so that she could have a bath. She hadn't realised Mum was there as Grandad had let her in, but she didn't bat an eyelid and just said 'hello!' when she noticed her.

News soon flowed on the Cowes High grapevine and I had to put up with a hell of a lot of piss-taking for the rest of the day; how I didn't hit anyone I don't know.

When we all left I spotted Spud hobbling towards us.

'Why are you limping?' I asked.

'That bitch, Wallace, kicked me!'

I noticed Ed trying to conceal a look of satisfaction.

'Why did she do that?' I asked, stifling a laugh.

'I asked her out, and she said no. I told her that there was no need to play hard to get, as it was a waste of time. She said get lost. I said that it wasn't that difficult getting her into bed last time. She booted me in the shin. Look!'

He revealed a nasty bruise. She must have kicked him bloody hard.

It was, this afternoon, Episode Five of Maths:

'Right then. I spent the whole weekend marken ewe-er homework, didn't I, see? Par-the-tec! What have ewe got to say for ewe-er selves?'

Perplexed silence

'Get out, go on the lot of ewe go on GET OUT!!! If ewe can't be bothered to learn then I can't be bothered to teach ewe!'

Ed and I walked home and Ed was failing to hide his delight.

When Dad arrived home, Mum told him about what had happened with Nan and he said, 'It's a bit like a family initiation. You have to see your grandmother naked to join the clan.'

I said, 'That makes half of year eleven my family then!'

I had arranged to see Ed tonight after dinner, but he texted me saying: 'CANT MAKE IT 2NIGHT. CING KATIE. HOPE U DONT MIND.'

I can't say that I am surprised. He has been pining for her for the last few days. It's either that or he is desperate for a shag.

So that meant I was stuck in tonight, so I made a start on my Geography project.

5 March 2003, Wednesday

Ed told me that he and Katie were reunited last night. I told him that I was glad.

Lara met up with us on the way to school this morning and handed me a note. It was the reply I had been waiting for from Belinda.

I didn't get to read it until we got to school and I found a moment of privacy in the toilets.

Troy

When I met you the other night I didn't realise
that you were such an arrogant prat.
How can you presume that I would want to go
out with you just because I might have told
Lara that I thought you were cute?
I'm sorry but I am not interested.
Get a life.

Belinda

I flushed the letter and the envelope down the toilet. I have missed out once again. It's no big loss, though. It would've been a major hassle going to Ventnor all the time.

When I saw her at break time, Lara asked me what Belinda had written, I told her. She told me not to give up so easily.

At lunchtime we went down to see Vernon. We were chatting about that dreaded art lesson when Barry came bounding over waving a banknote.

'I won, I won. Look Vee! I won fifty quid!'

'You've been conned, mate!' said Vernon. 'That's a twenty-pound note.'

'I meant twenty,' said Barry.

Vernon snatched the note out of Barry's fingers.

'That should go towards the cost of the window, then.'

Barry looked on the verge of tears. 'Okay then Vee,' he said, and he sloped off, shoulders hunched.

'You bastard!' said Ed, as he, for a brief moment, removed his gob from Katie's.

'Serves that stupid twat right. It cost me a fortune to get that window fixed!'

'You'll get that back through your insurance, won't you?'

Vernon paused. He seemed to be trying to justify his actions in his mind.

'Th-that's not the point!' he said.

When we walked back to school, Tom lit up a cigarette.

'How long have you been smoking?' I asked.

'For a while. My girlfriend smokes so I thought I might as well do the same.'

What an idiot!

We had an assembly this afternoon where Tom was commended on his art, specifically his drawing of my Nan. The drawing has been mounted and will now be displayed, with other examples of school art, in the dining hall. What a humiliation! I'm glad that I don't have school dinners.

On the way home, Lara gave me a note. She said, 'Copy that out in your neatest handwriting and give it to me tomorrow.'

This is what she wrote:

Dear Belinda

Sorry that you misunderstood my note as
being arrogant. In fact I am far from arrogant
and have very little confidence and experience with girls.
I got my information from a third party and
things can often get confused when that happens.
I hope you can forgive me and that we can start again.

Love Troy

Dad picked up Ed and Tom on the way to football training tonight. Tom lit up in the back and Dad threatened to make him get out of the car if he didn't throw it out of the window.

Why do smokers automatically become ignorant of non-smokers? Tom never used to be like that.

Pottsy, at the football club, has started up a 'Dead Pool' where you have to pick someone famous who you think is going to die soon. Everyone chooses someone different for an entry fee of five pounds and whoever's chosen person dies first gets fifty per cent of the pot, with the club getting the rest.

I thought it was very distasteful. Dad said, 'Death is part of life, mate. You can't get away from it!'

I chose the Pope and Dad chose Kirk Douglas after initially picking James Coburn and not realising that he was already dead.

I am in the first-team squad for Saturday and Tom, Ed and Dad are in the Reserves squad. So that must mean that Silky thinks that I am better than Ed at football.

For once, when we got in, there was no football on so I did a bit more of my Geography project and wrote out the new note to Belinda.

6 March 2003, Thursday

Me and Ed met Lara on the way to school and I slipped her the note for Belinda.

When we got to school there was this awful smell around the place.

We went down to see Vernon at lunchtime and he said that he had given Barry his twenty pounds back and now Barry couldn't do enough for him. Vernon was trying to teach Barry how to say the word 'persuade' as he kept pronouncing it as 'serpuade'.

When we got back to school the stench had got worse and all the toilet doors had 'Do Not Enter' signs on them. We all had to go into the main hall where Mr Bartlett, the headmaster, said that we all had to go home for health and safety reasons. This announcement was greeted with cheers and we all left as quickly as we could.

I nipped home to change and then went down to Ed's house. We went down to the icafé until dinner time.

When we left, Pitbull, who was alighting from the Fountain Hotel, verbally abused us. He called me a namby-pamby ponce and said that I owed him twenty-seven pounds. We trotted away, hastily.

When I got home, Mum showed me this picture she'd got at her first scan which she'd had today. She was telling me where the baby's head and limbs were. I said 'Oh, yes!' but couldn't make much out, apart from what looked like its head.

Then she went and got out a similar scan picture of me, which was just as difficult to make out.

Dad was well chuffed when he looked at it (the new baby picture, not mine).

He told me that he'd driven past the school on his way home. There was a big DinoRod van there with a lot of men with hoses and the Water Board had vans there as well. It sounds like a big job. Wouldn't it be nice if we didn't have to go to school tomorrow?

I went round to Lara's house tonight but she wasn't in. She had gone to Newport to meet up with her friends from Ventnor who all go to Medina High School. She would have been able to give Belinda my new note.

Fingers crossed.

On my way back home, Spud phoned me. He was bored so I went round to his house. When I got there I noticed that his ex-girlfriend was sat in his front room talking to his mum.

When we got into his bedroom I had to ask him what was going on.

He said, 'What d'ya mean?'

'Isn't that your ex in the front room?'

'Yes, but keep it quiet. She's a neighbour and her old man is back from a cruise. He is a ships engineer.'

Infidelity is a very dangerous game that I wish I was playing (as the third party and not the victim).

We played on his Game Boy for a while, then I went home.

7 March 2003, Friday

Ed and Spud called this morning and we were all hoping for the same thing and were not disappointed when we reached the school gates to find that the teachers were there sending everybody home again.

Men were digging a trench in the driveway that leads around to where the teacher's car park is.

Jubilant, we all headed for home. Lara gave me another reply from Belinda.

Dear Troy

Thank you for your latest letter.
It's all right, I understand that you didn't mean
any harm by your first letter and I am happy
to be friends with you, although I am not interested

in going out with you. I hardly know you.
Keep writing, anyway.

Belinda

It was better than the previous one I'd got but still means I am forever single.

We all went home to change and arranged to meet at Ed's house as soon as we were ready.

I arrived first, followed by Meat, Tom, Jason Dwyer and lastly Spud. We had a couple of hours of multiplay on his football game on the X-Box.

At lunchtime we raided his kitchen for snacks. We had planned to go to the park for a kick around but it started to rain really heavily. So we had a tournament on his mini snooker table, which Ed won, of course.

Before we all left to go home for dinner, Ed let me have this superb poster of Mutya Buena, the best looking of the Sugababes. She is lovely. Ed nicked it out of one of his sister's old copies of *Smash Hits*.

I put it up on my wall as soon as I got home.

Mum asked me to tidy my room. God, what does she do all day? Women keep saying that pregnancy is a condition not an illness, so why can't she tidy the house. She doesn't work. I can never tidy up to her standard, anyway.

Karl and Tom called round this evening and unfortunately Donna was in the car, puffing away on a cigarette. This made the inside of the car very stuffy, with Tom joining in as well.

Karl drove us through Porchfield, along winding country roads, and the combination of the smoke and the motion of the car made me feel rather sick. I felt that I had to try to grin and bear it. I was trying not to look like an idiot in front of Donna. But in the end I couldn't hold on and Karl just stopped the car in time for me to yak up into the gutter.

Donna had to have a dig at me. 'Get used to it. You'll be feeling like that on Sunday afternoon, when Wolves knock you out of the Cup.'

All the windows were opened after that and they agreed not to smoke in the car.

We stopped off at Safeway's car park in Lake, where Karl let Tom have a go at driving. He offered me a go but I declined.

After that we went back to Cowes and I went to bed, still feeling unwell.

8 March 2003, Saturday

Dad and I were watching *Soccer AM* this morning when the doorbell rang. It was Pitbull and some other tough-looking bloke.

Dad dealt with it. Pitbull repeated the demand he made of me the other day.

I heard Dad arguing the toss but, in the end, he'd obviously had enough of them and I heard him shout, 'Here's thirty quid, now f*** off!' They promptly did just that.

Our first-team match was away to Plessey first team and I was made substitute. This would have been fine if it weren't for the fact that Pitbull, obviously serving his suspension, was there to watch the game.

He spent the whole match making snide comments and laughing to his mates, implying that I was gay.

To add to the misery, our team played awfully and when I went on, for the last fifteen minutes, we were three-nil down. I did manage to pull a goal back just before the final whistle, but that didn't stop that git putting his arm around me and growling into my ear, as we walked back to the changing rooms, 'You're dad moit ave everned us up financh-ally but we've still got a li'le score to se'le, aven't we?'

'If you say so,' I said.

I was glad to get showered, changed and away for home, where I watched the Arsenal versus Chelsea FA Cup quarter-final as I ate dinner with a grumpy Dad.

For his match, only twelve people turned up and Dennis, the manager, picked himself and asked Dad to run the line.

He got a load of stick from the Yarmouth players who accused him of cheating every time he put his flag up for offside. He felt like he was being used and that Dennis would only play him as a last resort. Poor old Dad!

The match on television ended up as a two-two draw.

Mum had spent the day, with her friend shopping around Southampton, and she'd bought Dad and me a Comic Relief T-shirt each. They are red with RND03 on the front.

Ed did invite me down to his house this evening but I thought I would keep Dad company. We decided to have an evening of watching *Fawlty Towers*, which ended up cheering us both up.

9 March 2003, Sunday

This morning I decided to brave Donna's irritating habits and cheer Tom on in his football match. They were short of players and asked me to play. Normally, I couldn't be bothered, but at least it meant that I didn't have to stand on the touchline with Donna.

So one of the players gave me a quick lift home to get my boots and I'd just about got into my kit and onto the pitch when the match kicked off.

I had a good match, probably because I didn't feel under pressure.

I scored our winner as well when Tom sent a ball for me down the left wing. I checked back onto my right foot and hit a crossover. The swirling wind took the ball in over the goalkeeper's outstretched hands.

Everyone told me that it was the best goal the team had scored all season. That made me feel good, so I didn't bother telling them that it was a fluke.

Even Donna said, 'Great goal, scummer!'

I had a quick shower and dashed home where Dad was waiting to leave for Southampton.

The atmosphere outside St Mary's Stadium was amazing. There were loads of Wolves fans carrying inflatable FA Cups and singing songs.

A lot of Saints fans had bought red tinsel wigs and I heard one Wolves fan say, 'You can chuck that in the bin cause you're gonna lose today!'

The atmosphere inside was electric, the best I have experienced at the stadium, and this must have helped our players to win two-nil.

We are in the semi-finals of the FA Cup. I can't describe the feelings of pride and excitement that all Saints fans are experiencing right now.

The trip back to the Red Funnel terminal was memorable with the wonderful discussions on where the semi-final would be played and who we might be playing. Everyone wants to play Watford.

I still can hardly believe it. Southampton in the semi-final. All we have to do is win this one match and it's a trip to Cardiff on May the eleventh. What an amazing early birthday present it would be for me if I could spend it watching Saints parade the cup around the streets of the city. It would be a dream come true, but it's still just a dream at the moment.

When Dad and I got home, even Mum was excited for us. She had actually watched the match on Sky and said that it was the first time she has ever enjoyed watching a football match - apart from when England beat Argentina in the World Cup last year, but she didn't enjoy that match nearly as much as this one.

Dad went out and bought a huge Chinese meal for us. He also cracked open a large bottle of Lambrini Bianco and allowed me to get a bit drunk.

10 March 2003, Monday

Ed and Spud called for me this morning and I delighted in reliving Southampton's success yesterday plus a couple of references to the goal I scored in the Sunday league match.

When we arrived at school everyone was called in for an emergency assembly.

Mr Bartlett made a speech about not throwing objects down the toilets. Then he held up a polythene bag with a manky sheet of paper in it and told us that this was the cause of the blockage on Thursday.

'It doesn't need a top detective to work out who probably threw this note down the toilet,' he announced, 'as his name is written on it.'

There was some murmuring, which was silenced by all the form teachers who were sat around the hall, minding their relative groups.

'Troy Brown!' he called to my surprise and horror, as everyone looked at me. 'See me in my office after this assembly.'

So afterwards, as instructed, I went to see the headmaster. I had to wait outside his office until he arrived and asked me to go in.

I had to stand while he said, 'Is this yours, Brown?'

He placed the polythene bag with the manky sheet of paper in it on his desk.

'This cost the school two thousand five hundred pounds. Do you recognise it?'

'No, sir,' I said, glancing at the object.

'Take a closer look.'

I could see something familiar about it but couldn't make the connection. Mr Bartlett helped me out by pointing to a word on the paper 'Troy'. Then I realised that it was the note from Belinda that I had flushed down the toilet the other day, and I felt myself going red.

'I have drafted this letter which I want you to give to your parents,' he said as he handed me an envelope.

'Do not flush anything down the toilet that isn't supposed to go down. Do you understand?'

'Yes, sir,' I replied.

'Good. Now get out of my sight!'

I made my way to the Maths lesson where I was given a good reception. Everyone was pleased that I had helped them have a long weekend.

At break time loads of people came up to me and thanked me. Terry Smith slapped me on the back, winding me.

At lunchtime I was treated like a minor celebrity with kids from lower years coming up to me and shaking my hand and thanking me. I enjoyed the attention so much that I stayed at school at lunchtime.

During this afternoon's follow-up debate about the impending war with Iraq (yawn!) Dad sent me a text message that said,'We have got Watford in the next round.'

I had forgotten to turn my phone off for the lesson so Miss Webb confiscated it.

When I got home from school I gave the letter that Mr Bartlett had given me to Mum.

She read it and took a sharp intake of breath before gasping, 'TWO-THOUSAND-FIVE-HUNDERD POUNDS?'

When Dad read it, during dinner, he went mad. 'I'm not paying that! These schools are insured aren't they?'

They wouldn't let me read it, but they told me that Mr Bartlett had asked for a contribution towards Dino Rod's bill for fixing the drains.

'I'll be seeing this Mr Bartlett, tomorrow,' he spluttered with his mouth full of lamb chop.

This evening I took a stroll round to Lara's house and, to my surprise, Spud was there. He was preparing to leave as I turned up. Lara said that there was no chance of them ever getting back together but they had decided to be friends.

I wonder if he's asked her though. He must be getting very sexually frustrated at the moment.

Lara's dad asked me if I could get him a ticket for the semi-final. I said that I doubted it. When Lara got me on my own she asked me again, but I emphasised that the tickets would probably mainly go to season-ticket holders.

'If you do get a spare one,' she said, 'please let Dad have it. For me. I'll be very grateful.'

Yeah - right!

11 March 2003, Tuesday

I was still basking in my spell of popularity at school today, although that popularity didn't extend to the teaching staff, and it hasn't led to any offers from girls yet either.

In Art, people kept teasing me by asking how my Nan was.

'She should be careful she doesn't catch a cold at her age,' Hayley Knight gibed.

'It reminded me of the eggs I had for breakfast that morning,' Jason Ince remarked.

They must have spent all week thinking up things to say to wind me up.

Mr Vibert said that there would be another life class next week for those who missed out, but with a different model, thank God. I would love it if it turned out to be one of their Nans.

At lunchtime it became apparent that Spud had managed to talk himself back into the affections of Emma Hewings. She must be a complete idiot to go out with him twice. Jason Dwyer remarked that Spud was on first-name terms with the clap clinic.

I am not sure if this is true or not, but the way he is going it could be and I hope that Emma insists on Spud using a condom.

I walked down to the icafé with Tom. He was puffing away on a cigarette, as usual. He offered me one, so I thought that I might as well see what all the fuss was about. I didn't like it. It made me cough. Tom said that you get used to it, but I can't be bothered with it. Mum and Dad don't smoke and they have led quite healthy lives.

Mum's cousin, Ian, smoked and died of a heart attack a couple of years ago at the same age that my Dad is now.

Vernon asked me if I could get him a ticket for the semi-final. I told him that it was doubtful. I hope I'm not going to keep getting pestered like this.

The afternoon was dominated by Episode Six of Maths:

'Thom-as Selby?'

'Sibley, sir?'

'Ewe've had ewer yers pinned back.'

'You're Quick.'

'Mr Quick to ewe.'

'I mean.'

'Get out.'

'Sir?'

'What do ewe want Jay-sern Dwyer?'

'That's not fair.'

'What isn't fair?'

'I own the franchise on being sent out!'

'Well don't let me disappoint ewe.'

'Aye?'

'Get out.'

When I got home from school, Dad was already there. He told me that he had sorted everything out with Mr Bartlett. He said that Mr Bartlett seemed like a very nice man and he was very complimentary about me.

The bill for DinoRod will be paid by the insurance.

He also said that he was told today that he is starting in Fareham on Monday.

It was on the news that the motorbike rider, Barry Sheen, had died. Just to think that he survived some horrific crashes only to be killed by cancer. I bet he would have preferred to have gone out in a race.

This evening me, Ed, Katie, Lara, Meat, Jason Dwyer and Spud went round to Tom's house (Donna was already there, of course) to play Consequences. It was so funny.

The funniest one read as follows:

Ed wrote:	Spud
	Went out with
Meat wrote:	Troy's Nan
	They met at
Tom wrote:	B&Q
	He said:
Katie wrote:	How big are your boobs?
	She said:
Lara wrote:	That's quite enough of that thank you
	Consequence:
Troy wrote:	They spilt up and he wrote a book called
	VD for Beginners

Spud thought that it was really funny. He asked who had written the last line and when I put my hand up he came over and shook it.

Still laughing he chortled, 'VD for Beginners. Nice one, fella!'

I managed to keep out of Donna's way as she became rather friendly with Lara and Katie. I guess she couldn't really have a go at Saints now we are in the semis. The only thing she said to me was, 'Come on Watford!' as we all went our separate ways at the end of the evening.

12 March 2003, Wednesday

Ed's sixteenth birthday began with a phone call from him asking me to call round at his house on the way to school. So I gulped down my breakfast and headed round there.

He has got a new computer, which is slightly more powerful than mine, surprise surprise. He also said that he is getting the new Game Boy Advance SP when it comes out later this month.

His computer has this software on it that is a recording studio, so we have decided to form a band. I am going to play drums and Ed is going to play keyboard, as he used to take lessons until last year. Ed's dad has a drum kit in their spare bedroom and he said that we could use it.

When we got to school, Ed was greeted with a big kiss and hug from Katie. She told him he'd get his present tonight.

Meat can play guitar so he's in the band.

Now we need a bass player and a singer. I instantly thought of Chris in Ventnor, so at break time I asked Lara to get his telephone number for me from Rachel.

Everyone involved is very excited about the band and we did very little good work at school as we were all trying to write lyrics in our rough books.

Lara came up with Chris's phone number at lunchtime and I gave him a call. He was really pleased that I'd thought of him and said that whenever we had out first practice he would come over to Cowes on his moped.

Brilliant! It's all coming together nicely.

So we all got told off for daydreaming this afternoon.

We have arranged our first practice for Friday evening at Ed's house, as he has most of the equipment we need.

This evening Dad took quite a lot of persuading to go to football training, but eventually he did.

Unfortunately he fell out with Dennis after he asked Dad if he'd like to run the line for the Reserves on a regular basis. Dad finished the argument saying, 'You can stick your f***ing Coburg up your arse!'

He waited in the car for me, Tom and Ed to finish, and as we travelled home he said that he was happy to give us a lift to and from training but he didn't want anything more to do with the club.

I am still in the first team on Saturday.

13 March 2003, Thursday

This morning Spud asked Ed and me if he could join the band in some capacity, so we said that we would give him an audition as a singer. He said he couldn't come on Friday because he was seeing Emma Hewings that night.

At break time Ed seemed to disappear. I couldn't find him anywhere. Then he just turned up at our woodwork lesson saying that he had had a long chat with Katie and they have decided to become just friends and not girlfriend and boyfriend any more. They didn't want to ever split up on bad terms.

A letter was given out saying that, for Comic Relief, we could go to school looking silly, as long as we paid one pound for the privilege. That should be a laugh.

Jason Dwyer is coming dressed as himself.

Ed came round this evening to watch the Celtic versus Liverpool UEFA Cup match. It was all played in good spirit until a Liverpool player spat at some Celtic fans.

14 March 2003, Friday

I went to school today wearing my Red Nose Day T-shirt, my Big Hair Nose and red hair. My mum had bought some red hair-dye spray especially for the day.

Most people had had the same sort of idea.

Ed brought a harmonica to school, which he is hoping to be able to play in the band. Unfortunately he needs a lot of practice.

The 'looking funny' theme spread throughout the teaching staff. Even Mr Bartlett wore a red wig. Lessons continued as normal, but were not taken very seriously.

Terry nearly had a fight with a fourth-year boy who laughed at him. The boy thought that Terry's realistic-looking red nose was all part of the fun, when it was in fact the result of a scrap he had had last night.

We went down to see Vernon at lunchtime and he too had entered into the spirit of things. He said that he would be donating all the profits from the icafé today to Comic Relief.

Barry wore his nose upside down and Vernon asked him if he'd like to borrow his nose-hair clippers.

When I saw Dad this afternoon, he was quite emotional after having worked his last day at MP Graphics.

This evening, me, Tom, Meat and Chris met at Ed's house for our first ever practice. We didn't play much music, though. We just discussed our name while watching *Comic Relief* on television.

We ended up agreeing on the name 'The Henry Ross Organisation Band' or THROB for short. It was named after Lenny Henry and Jonathan Ross who presented parts of the *Comic Relief* programme. The rest came from Ed's dad who is a Beatles fan and thought that it sounded a bit like the name of one of the Beatles old LPs.

15 March 2003, Saturday

Tom phoned me at around lunchtime. Silky had phoned him and asked him to come along with the first team, so he was after a lift.

On the way to Wroxall, he told me that he had had a chat with Jason Ince this morning. Jason's older brother is in the Navy and he was called away this morning. Jason thinks that it means that we will be at war within the next forty-eight hours.

I am trying not to think about what might happen to all of us if they bomb

Portsmouth or Southampton. One nuclear bomb on either of those cities and we are all dead.

I won't blow my own trumpet about my performance in our four-nil win, but if it hadn't been for me we would have drawn nil-nil.

On the radio, on the way home, they announced that Dame Thora Hird had died. That means that Ed has won the Dead Pool. Typical of him!

We also listened to the end of the Fulham versus Southampton game. Tom was taking the piss because Portsmouth were winning one-nil and we were losing two-one. I was feeling very glad that Karl wasn't with us to gloat. Tom soon shut up, though, when Michael Svennson scored an injury-time equaliser. Dad and I went mad. Dad nearly over-steered the car into a hedge.

When I saw Ed this evening and told him that he had won the Dead Pool he was overjoyed, but his mum overheard and asked us to explain the rules of the Dead Pool to her. She got on her high horse about morals and things and Ed was forced to agree to give his winnings to Comic Relief.

At last, he doesn't end up smelling of roses.

While he sulked we messed around with the drums and keyboard and we think that we have the beginnings of our first song.

He told me that he and Katie have decided to be close friends because they now know that they can't have a romantic relationship but they still need to see each other.

16 March 2003, Sunday

I had a long lie-in this morning and Mum got me up at eleven-thirty when Nan and Grandad arrived for lunch.

They were all lovey-dovey; it was so sickening. When I was eventually given the chance to leave, I quickly went down to Ed's house. We finished writing the song. I wrote the words:

> Seen you walking down the street,
> The kinda girl I wanna meet,
> Sexy body, pretty face,
> The best of the human race.
>
> CHORUS
> The question's always easier to find than the answer,
> The question's always easier to find than the answer.

I stand in front of the mirror,
Going through my lines,
Thinking 'bout next week,
Imagining you'll be mine.

CHORUS
The question's always easier to find than the answer,
The question's always easier to find than the answer.

You make my heart flutter,
When I think of you,
I love to say your name,
Yes I do.

CHORUS
The question's always easier to find than the answer,
The question's always easier to find than the answer.

Will you be my girlfriend?
Please say yes,
I'll let you take your time,
It's hard I guess.

If you um and ahh,
The answer's negative,
I wish that I was not,
So sensitive.

CHORUS
The question's always easier to find than the answer,
The question's always easier to find than the answer.

Don't shy away like all the rest,
I hope the answer will be yes.

CHORUS
The question's always easier to find than the answer,
The question's always easier to find than the answer,

The question's always easier to find than the answer,
The question's always easier to find than the answer.
I hope the answer will be yes,
I hope the answer will be yes,
I hope the answer will be yes,
I hope the answer will be yes.

When Meat arrived, after his football match, we played the song to him. He loved it and joined in learning his part on guitar.

We practised it for the rest of the afternoon, made a demo CD and I phoned Chris but he couldn't make it. He said he'd come over tomorrow night.

Meat and I left together and, as we walked home, Meat said that Pitbull had been playing for their opponents this morning. He'd given Meat a message for me - I have got to watch my back.

'That could be difficult!' I quipped. 'Your back is one of those things in life that you know is there but you hardly ever get to see it yourself.'

'A bit like the contents of a girl's knickers,' Meat retorted.

I had to stay in this evening and do my homework. Boring.

17 March 2003, Monday

By the time I got up this morning, Dad had already left. He had to catch the six-fifty Red Jet so that he could get in nice and early on his first day.

Mum gave him a good luck card from us. She said that Dad was choking back the tears when she gave it to him.

Why is it that women like to imagine that men are as sentimental as them?

Mum and I watched, on *GMTV*, the depressing posturing that Bush and Blair are doing in preparation for this ridiculous war.

Dad's and my semi-final application forms arrived in the post.

The weather was lovely as me and Ed walked to school. We enthusiastically discussed this evening's get-together of THROB.

At lunchtime, Spud and Tom came round to my house to listen to the demo of our song, which I have called 'I hope the Answer will be Yes.'

They both thought that it was excellent.

This evening I had dinner with Mum, as Dad was still travelling home from work. He still hadn't arrived when I left to go round to Ed's.

Chris was already there. We played him the song and he said that it was rubbish. He said that we should start by learning existing songs, so, once we got over the disappointment, we started practising the Oasis song

'Wonderwall'. I had to sing but it wasn't very good.

We finished at ten and I went home where I found Dad asleep in front of the television.

18 March 2003, Tuesday

Another nice day! It was a shame to be stuck inside classrooms all day.

At least we could go down to town for lunch. For a change we sat on the sea wall at the pontoon and fed the swans.

This afternoon I attended an astonishing Maths lesson, which turned out to be the Final Episode of Maths (with Quickey in it):

'Right then class. I am retiren, see? So this is my last day and I would like to say that, in my thirty-five years as a teacher, ewe are the worst class I have ever had the misfortune to teach.'

'Nothing like going out on a high then, eh, sir?' (Jason gets out of his chair and walks towards the door)

'Where are ewe go-en Jay-sern Dwyer?'

'Just saving you the bother of sending me out, sir.' (Quick follows him out of the door)

(You can hear the muffled shouting from outside)

'GEETT IN!' (Jason takes his seat)

'Now can I make myself quite clear. *I* send people out of this classroom, 'right?'

'I was just bowing to the inevitable, sir.'

'Jason Dywer, shut ewer mouth!'

'It's a waste of time me being here.'

'SHUT UP!'

'Wait for it!'

(Quick bared his teeth and filled his lungs for one last, inevitable catch-phrase)

'GEEET OUT!'

It was a great relief, but he must be ill to leave before the end of the school year.

This evening I stayed in to see Dad and to watch the Manchester United versus Deportivo game. It was rubbish. United lost two-nil.

Dad said that he didn't mind travelling to Fareham to work but he feels more tired when he gets home.

He is thinking of buying an old runabout to use over there.

19 March 2003, Wednesday

Today was dominated by the imminent war. School was just as insignificant as usual. Lunch was spent with Vernon and Barry, who was proudly displaying his two pounds and thirty-seven pence winnings.

Dad arrived home from work at six-fifteen and had already had a takeaway, so we immediately left for football training. He dropped me, Ed and Tom off and said that he would come back later to pick us up.

When we got home the news programmes were predicting that war would begin overnight. They also said that eighteen or so Iraqi soldiers tried to surrender. Well, that's not very many out of several thousand.

20 March 2003, Thursday

It has started! The Americans began bombing Baghdad overnight. All the breakfast news programmes were taken over by it - a good reason to avoid watching television.

We had an assembly at school in which Mr Bartlett asked us to pray for our servicemen and servicewomen who are out there. Of course we all did just that. I thought of Jason Ince's brother who is already on his way out there.

At lunchtime Ed and I went down to see Vernon, but all he wanted to go on about was the war. When we went back to school for the afternoon I got the idea for another song. I wrote it in my rough book during my History lesson.

Surroundings change us,
I have no doubt,
But not too much,
Inside and out,
You can't see happiness in a willow,
Whose branches, to the ground, hang so low.

The air you cannot breathe
Comes at the end of a word,
But news spreads so fast,
Now everyone's heard
That you can't find love in the barrel of a gun

That is pointed at your head as if in fun.

Sometimes the saddest things are said by the happiest people,
Sometimes the funniest jokes are told by the loneliest people.
We might know, then we might not,
But they can't solve all the worlds' problems in an agony column,

Perhaps it's a bad dream and one day I'll wake up,
With an apple in my hand in the Garden of Eden.
But then that's just a dream,
And I'm only young.

When Dad arrived home, as me and Mum were watching the Hallmark Channel, which seemed to be the only channel without war coverage, he told us about his trip to work this morning.

He said that the seven-twenty Red Jet was full and the last three people were trying to get on. The steward announced that there were two seats left so they were taken up by two of the three people waiting, so you would have thought that they would have stuck to the rules and set sail without the unlucky passenger. But not, apparently, when that passenger was Ellen MacArthur. She managed to find a non-existent seat on the bridge before they set sail, five minutes late.

Dad moaned, as he missed his connection and got into work late.

'She's got her own bloody boat,' he grumbled. 'Why couldn't she have sailed across herself?'

I went round to Ed's to see if he'd like to help write the music to my song but he was out, so I watched the Liverpool versus Celtic game with Dad. The first half was on BBC2 and the second half was on BBC1. Why? Because of extended bloody war coverage, that's why!

21 March 2003, Friday

When Ed called this morning I told him that I'd called at his house last night. He said that he was round at Lara's house. I felt a huge surge of jealousy come over me as he said it. He had been invited round there when he bumped into Lara and Rachel as they strolled up Egypt Hill past his house. It was the first time he had met Rachel and they took an immediate shine to each other.

The fact that it was her he was interested in and not Lara made me feel a little less jealous, but I still wished that I could have been there.

It was nice to get the last school day of the week out of the way, but my plans of an evening of song writing were scuppered when Ed told me that he was going round to Lara's as Rachel was staying for the weekend.

I tried to invite myself round but he asked me to stay away because he wanted to ask Rachel out and he couldn't do that with me around.

This evening's television schedule was ruined by war coverage again and all the soap operas were shuffled around.

They even had some cross-party politicians doing broadcasts asking us all to support our servicemen and servicewomen in the Gulf.

We may not support the government for going to war, but we are hardly not going to wish our own soldiers well, are we? What kind of people do those idiot politicians think we are?

22 March 2003, Saturday

I was awakened by the phone ringing at nine this morning. It was Dennis, Osborne Coburg's reserve-team manager, who was desperately short of players for their match today. Dad told him that we were not going to be used at the club's convenience.

The recent weather has turned rather summery, so me and Dad washed the car in the morning sun.

Ed came round as we were rinsing off and he told me that he was now seeing Rachel. He has arranged a date with her for tonight. So I'm left to another Saturday night in front of the television.

Dad and I embarked on the twelve-thirty Red Jet and caught the courtesy bus straight up to the ground.

Apart from us there where just these two blokes, a woman and a little girl sat together at the back. If the buses aren't used, they might stop the service and that would be a shame.

There were a lot of people selling gimmicky FA Cup semi-final wigs. Dad bought me one. I actually wanted a commemorative semi-final baseball cap, but he didn't get me one of those despite the several blatant hints I dropped as we browsed the club megastore.

We played Aston Villa and were awful, going two-nil down, but we eventually came back to draw two-two after a last-minute equaliser by Kevin Davies.

I got my programme signed, before the game, by Matthew Le Tissier, an absolute legend of the club. He gave up playing at the end of last season.

It was a good game despite our poor performance. I only hope that we make up for it in the semi-final.

So, as I suspected would happen, after our steak and chips I stayed in and watched television with Mum and Dad.

23 March 2003, Sunday

More good weather encouraged Mum and Dad to persuade me to go out with them for the day.

We set off at nine-thirty to shop at Tesco and returned home to pack all the shopping away before heading straight back out again, this time to shop around Newport. It was so warm that I was able to stroll around without my jacket on.

At two we set off to Sandown, where we went to a pub that we have never been to before The Caulk Heads. It was recommended to Mum by a friend. I ordered a delicious half a chicken and chips and Dad got a huge roast lamb dinner that put Mum's large portions to shame.

We left there at four and got home at about four-thirty, in time to watch the rest of the Arsenal versus Everton game.

I went round to Ed's this evening. He wasn't seeing Rachel as she had gone back to Ventnor.

We spent the evening trying to work out the music to the song I wrote on Thursday.

When I got home, I used the inspiration I had got from the recent nice weather to write this song.

The smell of freshly mowed grass,
An evening spent on the patio,
A day spent on the golf course,
Making love on a secluded beach.

CHORUS
And it's good to love,
When the sun is shining.
Give a smile to everyone,
And you can laugh too.

A town full of beautiful girls,
Cut-off jeans and tight T-shirts,

Vanilla ice cream with specks of sand in,
You can't hide the sunburn on your nose.

REPEAT CHORUS

Hanging washing on the line,
The TV stays off in the evening,
Cricket and tennis and electric fans,
And summer holidays.

REPEAT CHORUS

The occasional shower doesn't matter,
You can't please everyone.
But when the flowers are out,
And so are the bodies, summertime's here.

REPEAT CHORUS

24 March 2003, Monday

God, can school get any more boring? I sit in lessons trying to find the subject matter interesting but it is so hard. I wish July would hurry up and arrive.

I know that qualifications are important, but why can't they make school a place that you look forward to going to. The only thing I like about it is seeing my mates and girls.

Lunchtimes are getting a bit boring as well.

At least Ed told me that he wasn't seeing Rachel until the weekend so we could do some practising.

So this evening THROB, including Chris, united at Ed's. Chris didn't like the new songs we had written, surprise surprise, so we ended up learning one he has composed, called 'Out o' Town.'

In my opinion that song is rubbish, but the others reckon it is good so we have to play it.

I left at nine and got home in time for the second half of the Bolton versus Spurs game, which I watched with Dad.

Dad and I chatted about the fact that James Beattie has not been chosen for the England squad, despite being the top English goal scorer in the league.

Dad tried to get on the phone-in show, *You're On Sky Sports* but there were several others complaining about the same thing, even one Pompey fan!

25 March 2003, Tuesday

This morning I got a letter through the post from some solicitor saying that I might have to be called up as a witness at the trial of that murderer. I hope I'm not. What if he gets off and comes after me?

When Ed and I walked to school we had a chat about last night's practice.

He admitted that he really thinks that Chris's song is crap too and when we met up with Meat we asked him and he agreed.

At break time we had a meeting and decided that we should kick Chris out of the band. But then we had the problem of who would deliver the news to him.

We decided to choose by holding our breath and the first person to give up had to do the deed. Meat lost.

The next task was to try to replace him. Tom said that he would have a go. He used to take guitar lessons at middle school. The only problem is that he hasn't got a bass.

This evening we all skived off football training and met at Ed's to see if we could find Tom a cheap bass on eBay. We did. For thirty-five pounds, plus eleven-pounds-fifty postage. It comes with a carry case and looks quite good in the picture. We all chipped in twelve pounds and Ed paid by Nochex. So hopefully it should be here by the end of the week.

Meat phoned Chris and gave him the bad news and he didn't seem too bothered. 'I was thinking of leaving actually. Your band is shit anyway.'

26 March 2003, Wednesday

Ed and I met Lara on the way to school this morning. She asked me why I hadn't been round recently. I explained about THROB and she asked if she could come and watch us practise. Ed and I had to explain that we hadn't properly learnt any songs yet. She took the piss out of us.

'Not much of a group, if you don't know any songs.'

This made me and Ed feel that we had to get down to some serious practising tonight. Unfortunately it had to be without Tom who was seeing Donna this evening.

At lunchtime we trudged on down to the icafé. When we got there we found Vernon chatting to this normal-looking bloke that we didn't recognise. The bloke was nice and friendly towards us and he looked a bit like Ricky Kinsella, so I asked him if he was any relation to Kinsella.

To everybody else's astonishment, and mine, the man *was* Ricky Kinsella.

He had sobered up and smartened himself up and was quite the gentleman. We couldn't get over it. Even Terry was gobsmacked and Kinsella started chatting to him and apologised for the ruck they had had a few weeks ago.

Then he went over and sat on his bench and had a chat with Barry Whitticker.

No one believed us when we got back to school.

This evening me, Ed and Meat practised until ten o'clock. We would have gone on longer but Ed's mum sent us packing.

27 March 2003, Thursday

A few people had gone downtown last night to see Kinsella for themselves and weren't disappointed, finding him in the icafé joking with Vernon and drinking Sunny-D.

So at lunchtime the same crowd as yesterday trooped down to the icafé.

Things were going quite pleasantly until Barry asked Terry, 'Excuse me, but are you a homo?'

We all took a step away, expecting Terry to unleash a violent attack on Barry. But all he did was say, 'Where did you get that idea from?'

'Mr Kinsella told me.'

All heads turned to him. Terry asked Kinsella, 'So where did *you* get the idea from?'

'*He* told me,' he replied. I looked around to see where he was pointing and found everyone looking at me. 'No I didn't!' I said. 'It was Spud!'

'Oh, yes, that's right,' said Kinsella. 'Sorry.'

Terry asked me to go for a little walk with him. I expected to receive a pasting as he frogmarched me to the pontoon.

'Before you hit me,' I said, 'You've got to know that I never said anything.'

'I'm not going to hit anyone,' He responded.

'Why not?'

'Why should I? It's true. I *am* gay.'

I felt my jaw drop and my cheeks going red. Terry went on.

'I will only hit anyone who has a problem with that. Do you have a problem, Troy?'

'No not at all. I-I'm just surprised. Very surprised. Are you sure?'

Terry ignored that question. 'So you can tell all that lot and if they can't cope with it tell them I'll deal with them in my usual way.'

I had to ask, 'Does this mean that Jason is too?'

'That's not for me to say,' he said.

I took that as a yes.

Terry left and I went back to the icafé, totally stunned. When I told them, they didn't believe me - except for Kinsella and Whitticker.

With all that on my mind, I could not concentrate at all this afternoon.

This evening we practised again. Tom came along but his bass hadn't been delivered yet, so he just filled in by singing badly.

28 March 2003, Friday

As we approached school this morning, we all wondered if Terry would have to face any uncomfortable questions but neither he nor Jason Ince were there.

When we went down to the icafé at lunchtime, Ricky Kinsella came up to me and apologised for dropping me in it yesterday.

He's like a completely different person now. He's really nice. I don't really know what to make of it. Spud came down with us and could hardly believe the transformation. He also got an earful from Kinsella for stirring it about Terry being gay.

Actually, when Spud was told about Terry he said, flippantly, 'What are you telling me for? It was me who told you in the first place!'

Vernon was showing us his new car. He's got this gorgeous silver Audi TT. I wish Dad had bought one instead of that embarrassing Ka.

This evening I was left on my own as Ed had gone to visit Rachel, Tom was seeing Donna and Meat was seeing Kylie.

So I assumed that I would be spending the evening in with Mum and Dad. But to my joy, I got a phone call from Lara, who was lonely as well, and I spent a wonderful evening with her.

She complained to me about not having a boyfriend. I said that I could help her with that problem but she just laughed and said, 'Oh, you're so sweet. You always know what to say to make me feel good.'

I wish she'd say something to make me feel good. Like 'Make love to me Troy now!'

I stayed there until gone midnight and the time just flew by. When I got in, Dad was snoring, very loudly, slumped in his chair. Mum had obviously got fed up with the noise and gone to bed.

29 March 2003, Saturday

After breakfast this morning, Dad handed me thirty pounds and told me to go out and buy Mum something for Mother's Day and for their wedding anniversary, which is on Tuesday. So I went downtown, but the lack of decent shops in Cowes meant that I had to take the bus to Newport and shop there.

I arrived back home at lunchtime, with a box of Dairybox, a bunch of flowers, and a card for their anniversary and for Mother's Day, which I'd bought at Sainsbury's.

I turned out for Osborne Coburg this afternoon. I scored, but we lost two-one.

Tom also played but Silky took him off after just thirty minutes as he was so out of breath. I think that smoking isn't agreeing with him. He didn't hang around to see the rest of the game and left with Donna. I phoned him on the way home and he said that he won't play for Coburg again.

I arrived home just in time to see the Liechtenstein versus England match kick off. We ate our steak and chips as we watched England win two-nil. They were wearing their new kit for the first time. I'll have to buy that when it's in the shops.

This evening I also got the call-up for the Sunday league game tomorrow morning.

30 March 2003, Sunday

It was a bit of a drag having to get up early to play football.

Mum loved all her Mother's Day goodies.

I left for Northwood Recreation Ground at nine-fifteen, ready to help put the nets up, but when I got there the players were all ready in their kit and the nets were up. I realised, all too quickly, that we had forgotten to put the clocks forward last night.

The team started with ten men while I changed. This must have annoyed Tom, who was substitute. He stood with Donna, arms folded, watching the game with a face like thunder. Donna smiled at me as she puffed away on her cancer stick. I saw her offer him one but he didn't take it. In fact, soon afterwards he was shouting at her. At half-time I noticed that she was no longer there. He said that he had dumped her. He had just got fed up with her.

This was great news and it made up for the fact that we were one-nil down. I was taken off with ten minutes left. I was feeling tired anyway.

I persuaded Tom to come around to Ed's this evening, for a practice - a sure way to cheer him up.

This afternoon I went out with Mum and Dad for a meal at the Eight Bells. I had a lamb roast. It was delicious.

In this evening's THROB band practice we decided that we should advertise for a singer. So we designed a poster for the school noticeboard for an open audition, to be held at Ed's next Sunday afternoon.

I walked home with Tom. He blamed Donna for his drop in football form, as it was her who got him into smoking. He smoked a cigarette as we walked and said that it was his last one.

Good for him! It is nice to think that I won't have to see that stupid cow again.

31 March 2003, Monday

I can't bloody believe it. I saw Tom this morning and he told me that after he'd parted company with me last night he went round to see Lara and had somehow managed to get back with her. What's the matter with her? Surely she can't be as desperate as I am for love?

We pinned the poster up at break time. It seemed to attract quite a lot of interest.

It was sickening at lunchtime, seeing those two snogging non-stop at the icafé. Ricky Kinsella wasn't down there. Apparently, according to Barry, he was attending an interview with Red Funnel. I can't imagine him ever having had a job. I wonder what he put on his CV?

Special skills: Downing two bottles of Scotch in five minutes.
Employment history: Walking Pascall Atkey's dog a few times.
Education: Discarded copies of the previous day's *Sun*.

He arrived back from his interview just before we had to leave for school. I asked him what work he had done in the past and was amazed when he told us that he used to be a teacher.

When we got back to school I told Spud. He said, 'Are you sure he didn't say that he used to be a taster for Teachers Whiskey?'

How can someone who is clever enough to be a teacher let himself go like that? It is such a waste.

When I got home I told Mum about Kinsella and she said that she knew he used to teach because he once taught her when she was at Cowes High. She said that he got the sack for coming to school drunk, after his much younger lover dumped him. He has been down and out, for most of the time, ever since.

1 April 2003, Tuesday

Today is Mum and Dad's sixteenth wedding anniversary.

I got a letter from Portsmouth Football Club this morning. It read as follows:

> *Dear Mr Brown*
>
> *I came to watch you play for Osborne Coburg against Yarmouth the other week and was quite impressed with your abilities.*
> *I am pleased to be able to offer you a week's trial at our football club.*
> *Please report for training, at the above address, at 9 a.m. on Monday 14th April.*
> *If you have a problem with this arrangement please contact me on the number above.*
> *The club will refund your travelling expenses, so please keep all receipts.*
>
> *Yours faithfully*
>
> *Ken Scully (Scout)*

So I was pretty excited as I went to school with Ed. But my balloon was burst when he realised that it was April Fools Day. I wonder which bastard did it. I wish I knew so that I can get them back.

Surely a better wind-up would have been a letter from Saints. It would have been difficult going to Pompey and trying to play with passion for them. But, for a chance of professional football, I would have given it a go.

It rained today and, as it has been sunny for the last couple of weeks, I suppose it was bound to rain on the first day of April.

The rain kept us at school during all the breaks, so that was a drag.

This evening I went to Ed's. Meat and Tom were there. I was surprised that Tom could tear himself away from Lara. We practised our songs. We are getting quite good at them now.

When I got home I had the house to myself as Dad had taken Mum out for the evening.

2 April 2003, Wednesday

I had to get up and make my own breakfast this morning, as Mum and Dad were still in bed. Dad took the day off.

Our FA Cup semi-final tickets arrived in the post. Thank goodness for that! I was getting worried that we might miss out because of a mistake by the club or something.

At school still, nobody owned up to sending me that letter, probably because it's got around that I am annoyed about it.

Quite a lot of people asked me about the singing audition this weekend, so we are going to have to have a quick turnover.

Tom and Lara were in a mood with each other at lunchtime. Lara caught him smoking when he'd told her that he'd given up. Tom, stubbornly, told her that it's up to him when he gives up.

I told him to get some Nicorette.

At lunchtime we went to see Vernon. Kinsella was full of the joys of spring because he'd got the job at Red Funnel. Maybe his life can finally get back on track now.

When we got back to school we received news that Terry had been in a major fight. A homophobic sixth-former said something to him that he didn't like and he apparently went berserk. Both Terry and the sixth-form boy were sent home.

This evening all the lads skived off football training again so that we could watch England beat Turkey two-nil.

Dad bought me the new England home shirt. He got himself one too. It was nice to have it for a few minutes before Ed got one.

3 April 2003, Thursday

Lara and Tom have split up again. Lara announced the news when Ed and I met her on the way to school. They will remain friends but Tom won't, or can't, give up smoking and Lara can't put up with it.

We also found out that Terry had escaped suspension for his fight when Mr Bartlett heard of the provocation involved. So he faces a week of detention.

Meat said that his parents would be out for most of tomorrow evening and, with Kylie doing so much swatting lately, we are having a get-together there. At last I get to do something on a Friday night.

Despite Kinsella having a job now, he had his lunch break with us at the icafé. Tom asked him to go to the pontoon shop and get him some cigarettes as he didn't have his ID card with him.

I stayed in this evening. Dad had phoned to say that he had to work back and would be late home. I decided to have a long bath, and when I came out and went into my room I was shocked to receive a punch in the face.

I hit the ground, not knowing what was going on. After a few moments I realised that Spud was there ranting something at me. I didn't take in most of what he said because I was so shocked and I was in a bit of pain.

He had been waiting for me in my room and had been poking around. He started reading my diary and read the part where I told Lara about him and Katie.

'Well you shouldn't look in people's private things,' I said.

'Well a private conversation between you and me didn't mean anything to you did it?'

I couldn't really answer that one.

Anyway, he told me that our friendship was over and that he never wanted to see me again. Then he left.

I picked up my diary and checked that none of the pages had been ripped out before putting it away in my drawer. Then I checked my face in the mirror. I had a red mark on my cheek. At least I wouldn't get a black eye. I then went out into the hallway where I saw Mum slapping Spud around the face. She must have heard the commotion. He left and Mum came up to me and asked me if I was all right. She was clearly upset.

'What did he say to you?' I asked her.

'It's not what he said to me, it's what I said to him. That's all he's got to worry about.'

'Why? Did you threaten him with an assault charge?'

'No, I just told him a few home truths.'

I told her not to let any of my friends into my room ever again without my knowing.

She said that she wouldn't, apologised and started crying. So I hugged her. That's when I felt her quite substantial bump for the first time.

'Have you felt it move yet?' I asked.

'That's the first time you have asked any questions about the baby. I thought that you didn't care about it.'

'Of course I care!' I lied.

Shortly after all that Dad arrived, but we didn't mention any of recent events to him.

4 April 2003, Friday

The mark on my face didn't develop into anything overnight and I got a pleasant surprise this morning when Lara rang the doorbell. She asked me if I was all right.

Spud had called at her house immediately after leaving me and told her everything, but Lara said that she told him a few home truths as well and that made me feel so much better. Then Ed arrived and we both told him the full story on the way in to school.

As we entered the school gates, Spud was there.

'Wanker!' he sneered.

I didn't have to retort as Ed jumped in, 'I think we all know who the wanker is around here and it's certainly not Troy.'

'What is he then?' said Spud. 'He's definitely not loyal or trustworthy.'

'He knows the difference between wrong and right,' said Lara, to my delight, 'unlike you.'

Spud grunted and walked away. I thanked my two friends from the bottom of my heart. This is one of the most wonderful moments of friendship I have ever experienced and, if I have lost Spud as a mate, well I can live with it. I always found him quite irritating anyway.

This evening me, Lara, Ed, Rachel, Tom, Katie, Kelly and Jason Dwyer all went round to Meat's house where he was with Kylie who decided that she couldn't miss the event.

I spoke to Meat while he made everyone a drink, and he was annoyed because they could have had the house to themselves for the evening. They haven't done it yet (sex) and it was a perfect opportunity.

We played this game where you spin a bottle and have to kiss whoever it points to. I went first and it pointed to Lara and I gave her a peck on the lips. That was nice but it could have been better because when Ed spun it and it pointed to her he got a full-on kiss, tongues and all.

Everyone did with everyone else, except when it was boy on boy, which is all I managed to get for the rest of the evening.

5 April 2003, Saturday

Me, Mum and Dad all trooped over to Southampton on the nine o'clock Red Jet so that Mum and Dad could do some pre-match shopping. I let them get on with it and went to all of my usual shops.

I then went into BHS and had a cup of tea and read the paper. Just before leaving I went to the toilet, and when I came out of the cubicle and started washing my hands I heard an unfriendly voice.

'Well, fancy meeting you here, poofter boy!' It was Pitbull. 'If I'd known you were a scummer I would have given you a kicking a while back.'

With all the warm weather we have been having recently, he was taking the opportunity to wear a T-shirt. He lifted up his sleeve to reveal a Portsmouth badge tattoo.

He grabbed my ear and growled in it, 'I hope you lose today and I look forward to seeing you next season.'

I gathered from that that he was threatening me with violence at the Saints v. Pompey fixture next season.

He then left the toilet after giving me a clip around the back of my head.

I resisted the temptation of being cheeky to him because I thought that I wouldn't be able to go to the game if I ended up in Casualty.

I went to the ground at around twelve-thirty and hung around the players car park so that I could get my programme signed by some of the players.

I went in the club after that to watch the second half of the Manchester United versus Liverpool match which United won four-nil. Dad joined me during the match.

With one eye on next week's semi-final, I expected us to lose today against relegation-threatened West Ham United, but instead we threw away a one-nil lead and drew one-all.

I saw Pitbull again on the ferry on the way back. He just gave me a few hard- nut stares that time.

When I got home, Mum had bought me a load of cheap clothes from Primark. I can't wear them when my mates are around. They would rip the piss out of me.

6 April 2003, Sunday

9.15 a.m. I had a horrible dream last night and I am writing it down straight away, otherwise I know I will forget it.

I was standing by the side of a road waiting to cross when I saw Pitbull glaring at me from the opposite curb.

I heard a speeding car approaching, then felt my legs being punched and kicked. Pitbull's horrible kids were attacking me.

I blindly pushed one of them out of the way and he went sprawling into the road. Pitbull ran into the road to try to save him but the speeding car hit the boy. Then I woke up, sweating.

11.30 p.m. I was right to write that dream down because I had forgotten about it until just now when I read it again. Anyway, back to today's events.

THROB assembled at Ed's just after lunch so we could set up the audition. We requisitioned Zoe's room so that the applicants could sing into the karaoke machine. Speakers were attached so that we could hear in Ed's bedroom. Then they could sing without the embarrassment of having to see our reactions. That, as it transpired, was a good idea.

Six people turned up, plus Zoe who insisted on having a go as payment for us using her room. She has the voice of an angel but she is too young and a girl. The others were all tone deaf, so we ended the session with two problems. One we still had no singer, and two our sides hurt so much from laughing.

Meat laughed so much that he scratched the back of his head on a picture hook as he slid down the wall, collapsing in a contorted heap of hysterics. It was all because Jason Dwyer got the lyrics to Robbie Williams' 'Eternity' totally wrong and kept on shouting 'Bollocks!' whenever he missed a note.

So it was a great afternoon of comedy, even if it wasn't supposed to be. Fortunately we recorded the event and were able to have more laughs as we made copy after copy of Jason's performance.

When I got home, I played it to Mum and Dad and they fell about laughing as well. Dad asked for a copy to take to work.

I went to Lara's to play it to her whole family, but her mum got offended by the swearing on the recording.

7 April 2003, Monday

On the way to school, Ed suggested that, as I was the only one who seemed to be able to hold a note (when I am not concentrating on playing the drums), I should give up the drums and become the lead singer. He thinks that it will be easier to find a drummer. When we saw Meat he said that we should give it a try.

Sad news went around the school this morning that Katie's Nan has died. She was Katie's only living relative on the island and now she is on her own. What is going to happen to her? Surely, at sixteen, she is too old to go into care and she can't support herself. It looks as though she is going to have to leave the island and move in with her relatives in Ipswich. This is an awful situation to be in when you are so close to your GCSEs.

Lara, Kylie and Kelly all went to see her at lunchtime and were very sad when they returned. I think that they had been crying as they all had red eyes.

Poor Katie, she hasn't had a lot of luck in her life. I thought I could go and see her and offer her some support, but people might think that I am trying to take advantage of her while she is down. However, really I do care for her, as a friend.

At lunchtime me, Meat and Ed discussed the idea of going to see Katie this evening and decided that we had to, whether we liked it or not. We had to show her that we were thinking of her.

When we arrived we found Spud there. He obviously pretended that there was no problem between us for Katie's benefit, which surprised me because he's usually such a selfish git. He left soon after we arrived, giving Katie a sympathetic hug and a kiss on the cheek.

'Look after her, fellas!' he said as he left.

I saw him out and he said, 'We'll put on a front, for Katie, yeah?'

I nodded.

Katie would try and sound cheerful one minute and burst into tears the next. Ed spent most of the evening holding her.

It wasn't much fun being there. It was so difficult finding the right words to say. I found it so hard that I kept quiet for most of the time.

The time crept on to eleven o'clock and the prospect of her being left alone in that house was nearing. Ed couldn't leave her and stayed. Meat and I went home, although I phoned to let Ed's parents know what he was doing. The battery on his mobile had run out during the evening.

8 April 2003, Tuesday

There was a thing on the news this morning that scares me much more than the war in Iraq. There is a killer bug going around the world.

Death is a thing that young people see very little of in this country. That could soon change. We may all be feeling like Katie in a few months' time.

I wasn't surprised to be leaving my house alone this morning. I bumped into Lara along the road and told her about Ed having to stay at Katie's last night.

'Did he now?' she asked, with a suspicious tone to her voice.

'There's nothing in it,' I insisted. 'Oh, don't tell Rachel. I don't want to lose another mate because of my big mouth.'

'Well if Rachel knows about it, he's been honest hasn't he?'

'I doubt she does. Ed's mobile battery ran out while we were round there.'

'That was convenient.'

After putting up an advert for a new drummer for THROB, I had to contact

Ed to let him know what had happened. I expected to have to wait a while because I thought he was going to bunk off school, but he turned up at breaktime.

I told him about Lara and he said that it was all right because, about ten minutes after we'd left, Katie's auntie and uncle from Ipswich turned up and Ed went home.

I quickly went to tell Lara but she had already texted Rachel.

Ed said, 'I don't care. Katie's a mate in trouble. If Rachel can't accept that, then she is too high maintenance for me.'

So I wasn't surprised when Ed came round this evening to show me the text he had got from Rachel: 'U R DUMPED U BASTARD.'

Ed didn't stay long. He went off to see Katie.

I stayed in to watch Manchester United get beaten by Real Madrid.

9 April 2003, Wednesday

Ed came round, as usual, this morning. He told me that Katie has left to stay with her aunt and uncle. They are going to have the funeral there as well. I hope that she hasn't gone for good, but I rather feel that she probably has.

Instead of going down to the icafé at lunchtime, we had a kick around at Northwood Park. Jason nearly got run over when he chased the ball into the road. We recognised the speeding car as Karl's. He pulled over and joined in. He decided to come to football training tonight and offered to give us all a lift, which I knew would please Dad.

So, that evening, off we sped to football training. Silky made a few snide comments about our lack of attendance recently but still put me in the first team for Saturday. We were looking forward to having a burn around in Karl's car, but the idiot left his lights on. Why he had his lights on in broad daylight is a mystery to me, but I expect it had something to do with posing.

I had to phone Dad, who wasn't too happy about having to come out and fetch us. He also helped to jump-start Karl's car.

If the news reports are to be believed, it looks as though Saddam Hussein has lost his grip of power over Iraq. Let's hope that is the case and that our soldiers can come home soon.

10 April 2003, Thursday

It was snowing this morning as we walked to school. Snow in April! I have never experienced that before. It didn't settle, though, and as the day went on the sun came out and, despite the chilly breeze, it was more like a spring day.

The nice weather gave us an excuse to have another kick around at the park. Terry joined in and during the session Pitbull drew up in a car and shouted, 'Hey, you know he's a nancy boy don't you lads. Keep yer arses away from him!' He laughed out loud and sped off. He was driving a taxi.

Terry was standing there like an agitated bull, ready to chase after him.

'Don't worry, mate. It was me he was referring to,' I said.

'Why? You're not gay!'

'He's just got it in for me. Ever since I got him sent off once.'

'If I see him again'

'Just leave it, Te. He's not worth it.'

Terry soon calmed down and we continued with our game.

I had a chat with Dad tonight, and told him that I really don't want to go back to school next year. I asked him to put in a good word for me at Diamond Kingsland. He said that he would do his best. He also told me to try as hard as I can with my exams. So I stayed in and did three hours of revision.

11 April 2003, Friday

The last day of term is always the slowest of days. It was still chilly but we warmed ourselves up by playing park football at lunchtime.

With two weeks to kill, a party has got to be organised along with auditions for our, so far, unanswered advert for a drummer.

This evening Dad arrived from work at six-fifteen. He came home with two tickets for tomorrow's Portsmouth versus Sheffield Wednesday match. Portsmouth are top of Division One and Sheffield Wednesday are bottom. If Pompey win, they will have guaranteed their promotion to the Premiership, so why Dad wants to go to that game beats me. He told me that the tickets were for the away supporters' stand.

I have already agreed to play for Coburg on Saturday but Dad is pestering me to tell them I can't play.

After dinner we went out to buy the DVD of *Harry Potter and the Chamber of Secrets*. We watched it as a family this evening.

12 April 2003, Saturday

After constant badgering and nagging from Dad, I finally gave in and agreed to go with him to Fratton Park.

I phoned Silky and told him that I couldn't play. He went mad.

'You are the most unreliable player I have ever worked with!' he moaned. 'You are wasting your talent watching football when you should be playing. Don't bother coming to training this week, I've had enough of you.'

Well, if that's his attitude he can get lost. I have to pay two pounds every time I play for them, so it shouldn't be a problem if I don't want to play.

We took the train to Fratton and wore plain clothes. I have to say that Fratton Park is the grottiest football ground I have ever been to. There is graffiti everywhere and it's like your next door neighbour's dodgy conservatory that he has made out of corrugated plastic.

The fans are noisy enough but they would be just as noisy in a nice ground.

As it happens, Dad and I enjoyed our day as Sheffield Wednesday fans. Pompey went one-nil up after a mistake by Wednesday's captain, but with fifteen minutes left Wednesday equalised and we went berserk. Even better, though, was the winner, which came from a dodgy free kick by a Portsmouth defender, which was charged down by the Wednesday striker who went on to score, to the delight of the Wednesday fans. It was the last kick of the game.

Dad and I had to pretend to be disappointed as several Pompey fans told us that it would be all right when they won their game on Tuesday night.

I hope this minor pleasure is a prelude to immense pleasure tomorrow afternoon.

I didn't go out tonight so that I could have an early night in preparation for tomorrow.

13 April 2003, Sunday

An early start, for a Sunday. We were up at seven. We drove round to East Cowes via Newport, as Dad couldn't be bothered to catch the floating bridge. We parked the car and caught the Red Funnel car ferry.

There were quite a few Saints fans on the eight-thirty sailing. We had our breakfast on the ferry - a full English.

We walked up to St Mary's Stadium and were amazed by the sight of a hundred or so coaches parked end to end around the stadium. Our coach was coach three, which was difficult to find as they weren't parked in numerical order.

The coaches set off at ten. The journey went quite smoothly until we approached Birmingham and things got congested. We came down this road which was full of half-drunk Saints fans waving and cheering at us. We could see that Villa Park was quite close, but the police directed us away from the ground.

We ended up parked a mile away and had to memorise the route as we hiked back in the direction that we had just come from.

It was astonishing to see all the Saints fans, who seemed to have taken over that area of Birmingham. Any Watford fans that were seen were teased.

One couple in Watford shirts walked past a pub and the Saints fans sang, 'Does she take it up the arse?' They seemed to take it in a good-humoured way.

When we reached the ground we started trying to find the Trinity Road Stand, where our seats were situated. We also wanted to buy a programme but only found them in a kiosk with a huge queue emanating from it. We joined the queue, but a Saints steward told us that they were also on sale inside the ground, so we went in.

Our seats were in the top tier and it made me a bit dizzy at first as it was so high up. It was a brilliant view. Right on the halfway line. We sat there for an hour and a half, watching, on the big screen, the end of the other semi-final where Arsenal beat Sheffield United one-nil.

Then we watched the stands gradually fill with fans and soaked up the growing atmosphere.

You always feel that something will go wrong even if, on paper, yours is the better team. So it was a surprise when Brett Ormerod put us in the lead just before half-time.

Our second goal was greeted with hysteria as we all started to believe that we were in the final. A bloke in front of me popped to the toilet just before our first goal and he did the same thing just before James Beattie forced the Watford defender into conceding an own goal.

The only goal he actually saw was the goal that meant we had a tense last five minutes. Watford's Marcus Gayle headed in from a corner. But it didn't matter in the end and we hugged each other at the final whistle. Dad was very emotional; he had tears in his eyes.

We stayed inside for a few minutes to see the players celebrating and then made a joyous journey through hordes of celebrating Saints fans, back to our coach. Dad bought a couple of T-shirts, which had 'FA Cup Final, Cardiff 2003 Southampton' printed on it. Someone had taken an expensive gamble that we would win.

It took about an hour for the police to begin escorting us to the M6. On the way back, everyone on the coach was silently happy about being in the final and the fact that we had qualified for the UEFA Cup, everyone apart from one bloke who couldn't understand why we weren't singing. He took a phone call and spoke deliberately loud saying, 'I'm on a crap coach here, mate. You would have thought that someone had died, not that we have reached our first Cup Final in twenty-seven years. They're all a bunch of wankers!'

The bloke in front took exception to being described in that way and a fight nearly ensued. Fortunately it all simmered down and we had a quiet three-hour journey back to Southampton. We waved at passing cars whose passengers waved back at us in celebration.

We had to wait at the ferry terminal for one hour before catching the eleven- forty ferry back to East Cowes.

We arrived home just after one in the morning, tired but proud and happy to be Saints fans.

14 April 2003, Monday

Dad had taken the day off work so Mum let us lie in until lunchtime. She had recorded coverage of the semi-final on Sky so we watched it while eating lunch. A cooked meal was welcome after a day of eating sandwiches and crisps yesterday.

Both Dad and I wore our T-shirts for the day. After lunch Mum got a phone-call from Grandad Stenning. After a conversation with Dad it transpired that we had been invited to stay with them in the days leading up to the FA Cup final.

Penarth is only a few miles from Cardiff. The good thing about that is that I will have a few days off school; the bad thing is that I don't know anyone up there so I will probably spend most of the time revising.

I went to Ed's to tell him all about the day. He said that everyone except Arsenal fans, Portsmouth fans and Rodney Marsh would be supporting us in the final, which made me feel good.

We took our skateboards out and went down to see Vernon at the icafé. He told me that we had no chance in the final, then Ricky Kinsella butted in. 'Rubbish! Saints for the Cup. Come on you Super Saints!' I ended up having a really good chat with him while Ed played on a fruit machine.

We were talking about good and evil in relation to George W. Bush's reasons for attacking Iraq. Bush thinks that Saddam Hussein is evil (and I happen to agree with that) but Kinsella said evil is a matter of opinion as some Iraqis and a lot of Muslims believe that Bush is evil.

That means that nobody really knows who is and who isn't evil. No one except God.

We talked about why the Harry Potter books are so successful - the simple fight between good and evil. In books, good always wins out in the end. I said that not everyone faces evil in life and he disagreed saying, 'Everyone has to face an evil in their life. Mine is alcohol. I may never win that battle.'

'I hope you do,' I said.

'So do I,' he said. 'What is your evil, son?'

'I don't know. Myself I suppose.'

He laughed. 'We are all our own worst enemies. My father in Ireland once told me - he was a priest you see - evil cannot be destroyed, only defeated. The trouble with that is that something that has been defeated but not destroyed lives to fight another day.'

I tried to ask him about teaching and his mood changed.

'It's time to change the subject, boy,' he said.

Then he made the excuse that he had to get back to work, and he left.

I watched the news during dinner. The Severe Acute Respiratory Syndrome (SARS) virus has started killing healthy young adults in Hong Kong. I am petrified. It sounds exactly like the Spanish Influenza bug from the First World War.

It is scary enough worrying about dying myself, but to top that you would have to watch, helpless, while friends and relatives died.

Karl Sibley slipped me an invitation to his eighteenth birthday party. It is tomorrow night at the Temptation Club in Newport. It should be a laugh.

15 April 2003, Tuesday

This morning me, Ed, Meat and Tom got together for a THROB practise. It all went well. We let Zoe play the drums. She's good. It's a shame she's not suitable for the band.

We practised until mid-afternoon. We now know five songs.

After dinner I got ready to go out and went round to Tom's house to have a few drinks before we all caught the bus to Newport.

We were all quite tipsy by the time we got into the club, which is supposed only to let in eighteens and overs. Karl had a word with the doorman and we were allowed in.

To my shock, one of the bouncers was Pitbull. He just gave me a few tough looks. I guess he didn't want to risk his job or image by picking on a fifteen-year-old. Having said that, he knew how young I was and would have been well within his rights to kick me out.

So, once we were in, the drinks flowed. There were hordes of gorgeous women in there, including Lara, but none was interested in any of us lot.

We still had a great time, though. I was the most drunk I have ever been by the time we left, at two in the morning.

Pitbull threatened me in my ear, but I was so drunk that I couldn't make out what he said.

We decided to walk back to Cowes. We had a great laugh singing songs and messing around. I didn't get into bed until four in the morning.

16 April 2003, Wednesday

I felt so ill this morning. I was sick when I got up but just felt awful for the rest of the day. The mere thought of alcohol turned my stomach. I don't think I'll ever touch another drop. I was drinking all sorts of different drinks. I know they say that you shouldn't mix your drinks but it's a bit difficult when they are being bought for you and Karl had two hundred pounds given to him to spend on drinks.

Mum was moaning, saying that we shouldn't have even got into the club in the first place, but she had to admit that she got up to the same sort of thing when she was my age.

I got up at one o'clock but didn't feel like eating anything. Mum gave me lots of orange squash to drink.

Ed phoned me this afternoon. He was feeling the same, as was Tom, and everybody else. It was a brilliant night though.

I realised why Pitbull was leaving me alone for most of last night. Pompey have finally won promotion to the Premiership. He must have been thinking about that all evening.

Dad came home at six and had another moan about the same sort of thing Mum was moaning about. He said that he could report the club and they would lose their licence, but Mum reminded him of when he used to go to the old Zanies Club when he was fifteen and he shut up. They met there.

We had dinner together, then I had to decide whether to go to football training or to stay home and watch the Arsenal versus Manchester United game. I stayed in. From what Silky said, the last time I spoke to him, I wouldn't be welcome anyway.

17 April 2003, Thursday

The weather today was like it usually is in August glorious! I went round to Ed's and we called Tom and Meat and went down to the Green at Gurnard to sunbathe and play volleyball.

Lara, Kelly, Kylie and Rachel met us down there. Oh what a treat it was to see them in their bikinis. When they played against us in a game of volleyball, I started playing badly as I couldn't keep my eyes off them, especially Lara who is perfect. God has been striving for millions of years to create the perfect woman and has finally got it right with her.

In fact, Lara came up with a brilliant idea. 'Why don't we have a beach barbecue?'

So we set about arranging it. Meat knows this secluded place along the coast past Gurnard near Thorness. All we need to do is get people to bring their own drinks, sleeping bags and food.

Meat and Tom will go there during the afternoon to gather wood and make the fire ready for the event tomorrow night.

We texted the people that we wanted to invite. Ed has got a tent that sleeps eight. It's going to be excellent and I can hardly wait.

This evening I decided to set out ten romantic targets that I want to try to achieve before I am twenty-one:

1. Kiss a girl/woman (on the lips) (non-platonic).
2. Kiss a girl/woman (tongues).
3. Get a girlfriend.
4. See a girl/woman naked (no older than Kylie Minogue).
5. Touch a girl's/woman's breasts.
6. Touch a girl's/woman's genitals.
7. Have sex with a girl/woman.
8. Have regular sex with a girl/woman.
9. Have sex with a variety of girls/women.
10. Get married.

18 April 2003, Good Friday

I went round to Lara's this morning. She was lounging around in a vest top and she wasn't wearing a bra. I know this because when she bent down I could see her nipple though the arm of her top. Oh joy! She's got small ones, nipples, I mean. Her boobs are about a large handful. Exquisite! Thank God for this early summer weather. It doesn't count as seeing a woman naked, but it's the first time I've ever had a bit of luck in seeing any parts of a girl. It has made my year and it was Lara as well. Magical!

We walked up to Place Road Stores to stock up on supplies. We met Karl in there and piled it all in his car. Then we went to Gurnard Marsh and parked up before carrying the stuff to the barbecue site. It took twenty minutes to get there. Meat and Tom had done a fine job in collecting loads, of wood and the fire was ready to start.

Karl and Lara walked back to Karl's car to bring back the second load of supplies while I helped gather yet more wood. They came back just over half an hour later with Kylie and Kelly. Ed arrived soon afterwards and we all helped set up his tent in a nearby field.

Rachel and Chris brought a tent with them as well, which the girls claimed.

By the time all the tents were up, it was time to set the fire going. Then Jason Dwyer, Jason Ince and Terry turned up with loads of food, drink and a large music system.

There was a lot of cider and we all got drunk quite quickly. We cooked sausages on the fire by running them through with a stick. We didn't have to worry about getting food poisoning because they were all burnt to charcoal. We were all so drunk that we didn't care.

A few other people from our year turned up and some of Karl's mates including some nice-looking girls. Tom got off with one of them. Laura I think her name was.

Rachel got off with one of Karl's mates. Another one of his mates tried it on with Lara but she wasn't interested.

This girl, Claire, was in an unconscious state by the fire. She had been sick and was barely responsive. Meat and Tom were snogging their relative girls. They badgered me into kissing this paralytic girl. She kissed me back and we stayed together for an hour or so. Eventually she said that she'd better go home so I walked her the mile and a half to the Round House where she went on without me. She seemed keen to get away.

I think that when she'd sobered up a bit she'd realised that she didn't want to be kissing me. Anyway, I made my way back to the barbecue.

By that time, there was only Lara, Kylie, Katie and Rachel there, out of the girls. Ed, Meat, Karl, Tom, Jason Dwyer and Karl's mate Stevie were also there. The party was over and everyone was tired and drunk, so we made our way to the tents.

The girls plus Karl, lucky git, stayed in the smaller tent and the rest of us squeezed into Ed's tent.

We'd all been asleep for a while when Karl came into our tent. He'd been kicked out for snoring and it wasn't long before he started keeping us awake.

Tom had a go at him and they had an argument, which resulted in Tom storming out of the tent and sleeping in the field.

He returned a while later, shivering. He lay across our legs and I got cramp. It hurt so much because I couldn't straighten my leg out.

What a brilliant night though.

I don't count the kiss with Claire because she didn't know what she was doing, but it would have been level two.

19 April 2003, Saturday

I expected to feel rough this morning after the amount I drank last night, but, maybe because I stuck to cider, I didn't feel too bad, just a bit tired.

We were all hungry and had not made any provisions for breakfast.

We packed the tents away and cleared up the rubbish from the beach. We even put seawater on the remains of the fire, to be as responsible as possible, although this was because the girls had insisted.

By the time I got home I was ravenous. I had a bath while Mum cooked me a couple of bacon sandwiches.

With all the fun we have been having, I nearly forgot that I was going to the Southampton versus Leeds United game today.

Dad and I went over late. We caught the two o'clock Red Jet and went straight into the stadium. The game was really good. We haven't played as well as that since the four-nil victory against Tottenham. We won three-two but we were three-nil up until the last ten minutes when our stand-in goalkeeper, Paul Jones, felt a bit sorry for Leeds and let them have two goals.

We went straight back home and enjoyed our steak and chips.

On the news they reported that a busload of students had arrived back in the country after a trip to Hong Kong. They are being held in quarantine in case they have SARS - which is fine, but they are being kept on the Isle of Wight!

Why couldn't they be kept on an unpopulated island? Why risk people here? I am so angry and frightened.

There are lots of islands north of Scotland, where hardly anyone resides. There are over one hundred thousand residents on this island.

They tried to say that it wasn't in the league of the Spanish Influenza virus of 1918 because that virus killed fifty million people. But this virus has already killed a few thousand. Who knows how many people will be dead in two years' time, when this epidemic has run as long as the Spanish Influenza bug did?

Dad told me that he had the same fears when he was my age. The AIDS virus had just reared its ugly head and he can remember some of his friends fearing that everyone would be dead in a matter of months.

But exchanging body fluids is the only way to pass on the HIV virus. SARS is a mutation of the common cold which is airborne and bloody easy to catch.

I phoned Ed but he said that he was tired. I felt knackered as well so I crashed out on the settee.

I woke up just as the highlights of our game were being shown on *The Premiership*.

20 April 2003, Easter Sunday

Mum and Dad had a lie-in this morning and I got up (as I have done for as long as I can remember) to get my Easter Egg.

When I arrived in the living room all I found was some chewed-up cardboard packaging, tin foil, puke and a collapsed Griz. The git had destroyed my Easter Egg. It was a Milky Bar one as well!

I confined the dog to the yard and woke Mum up so that she could clear up the mess.

Nan and Grandad Brown arrived for lunch with an Easter Egg and we went out to Pizza Hut. After our meal we went to the adjoining cinema to watch Rowan Atkinson in *Johnny English*. It was so funny.

When we got home, Mum and Dad gave me a replacement egg. Griz had continued to be sick on the newspaper that had been laid for that purpose.

I went around to Ed's for the evening and he thought that Griz eating my Easter Egg was hilarious.

21 April 2003, Monday

Griz was still being sick today. If he continues like this we'll have to take him to the vet.

It appears, according to news reports, that China has been lying about the extent of the SARS problem in their country. Apparently it is much much worse than they have previously admitted.

It has just dawned on me that this could be the beginning of the end of the world that Nostradamus predicted.

For the latter part of the morning, THROB got together for a band rehearsal. Zoe filled in, again, on drums and we finished at three and went up to Northwood Recreation Ground for a kick around with Karl, Stevie, Terry and the Jasons.

Tom spotted a black and white rabbit disappearing into a hedge, so, assuming it had escaped, we went looking for it.

We all took a section of both sides of the hedge and foraged around. I heard Ed shout, 'There it is.' From right opposite Meat, who was next to me, the rabbit suddenly emerged and headbutted Meat on the nose, before hopping away and being caught by Terry.

Those of us who had seen it were in hysterics, so that was Terry, Karl, Jason Dwyer and me. Every time I relive the image of that rabbit butting Meat I can't help chuckling to myself. I only wish we could have videoed it. We would have easily won two hundred and fifty pounds from *You've Been Framed.*

When I got home for my dinner, Dad told me that Saints had lost three-two at Birmingham, after being two-one up.

After dinner, Mum persuaded me to mow the lawn. That was a drag.

Me, Ed, Tom, Karl and Jason went round to Meat's to watch the report on how Charles Ingram tried to con his way to a million pounds on *Who Wants to be a Millionaire?*

We all think he deserves a bit of money, just for the sheer gall of it, especially if they are going to make a movie about it.

It was announced on the late news that S-Club are splitting up. We all, except Kylie, cheered. The bad news is that S-Club Juniors are to continue as S-Club 8.

22 April 2003, Tuesday

Someone has died in Wales after coming back from the Far East. They are examining him to see if he died from SARS. I'm praying that he didn't. This is a massive threat to humanity.

How many of my friends and family will I see die? Will I die? Knowing my luck I will. If it is a mutated cold virus, perhaps you will be able to catch it twice? Then no one will be safe from it.

All this worry is playing havoc with my complexion. I spent nearly an hour this morning in the bathroom, taking the tops off whiteheads with a razor blade. Then I dipped my face into a sink full of diluted Dettol.

I went around to see Lara this morning. She was messing around on her computer. She said I could play on it for a while, whilst she had a shower. She was preparing to travel over to see Rachel.

I did a search, hoping to find something interesting. I typed in the word 'secret'. The result was a folder called Spud's Secret Girlfriend. In the folder was an image. I opened it. It was a picture of Spud with my mother in what appeared to be Arctic Road.

Why has Lara got this picture in a folder named Spud's Secret Girlfriend? And what was my mum doing with Spud?

I couldn't ask Lara, otherwise she would have known that I had been poking around her computer.

When she was ready she left for Ventnor and I went home with lots of questions and scenarios bouncing around in my brain.

Surely the married woman wasn't Mum? God, what if it was? It can't be, she loves Dad. What would Dad do if he found out? My God! What if the baby isn't his?

There must be an innocent explanation. I know Spud has complemented my Mum on her looks, but she's well old enough to be his mother. It's ridiculous. What am I thinking of? It can't be that. She must have just been at the wrong place at the wrong time and Lara must have jumped to the wrong conclusion.

I tried to put these stupid ideas out of my head for the rest of the day. But in the end I had to confide in someone, so I went to see Ed.

I asked him,'Ed, why do you think Lara has got a folder named Spud's Secret Girlfriend on her computer with a picture of Spud with my mother in it?'

Ed's eyes opened wide and his jaw dropped open. He jabbered and stuttered for a few moments, then composed himself before saying, 'I don't know! God, I bet you're a bit confused. I would be.'

Then he said, 'I'm sure there's an innocent explanation for it.'

Which is exactly what I think.

'Maybe I should ask Lara?' I suggested.

'No, don't do that,' he said, 'Just forget about it, mate. There's obviously nothing in it. You would have noticed something, wouldn't you?'

He's right. If they had been seeing each other, I would have noticed something. This made me feel a lot better.

I stayed around there until after the Barcelona versus Juventus match had finished. We watched it on ITV2.

When I got home, Dad was still up but Mum had gone to bed, which got me thinking. I haven't seen them cuddling on the settee for ages.

23 April 2003, Wednesday

As I lay in bed this morning, I devised a cunning plan to allow me to find out what the image on Lara's computer was all about.

She'd recently upgraded her computer to Windows XP so I went around there to show her the in-built screensaver that displays random images from her My Pictures folder. It was that folder that contains the mystery file.

Just as I'd planned, the image appeared, fairly quickly because she has very few digital photographs on her hard drive.

'What is that picture all about?' I asked her.

'Oh, that was when you lent us your camera to try to catch Spud with his mystery woman. Unfortunately, the only woman we saw him with was your mum.'

'And what was he doing with my mum?'

'Isn't she good mates with Spud's mum? They left the house at the same time. That's when we snapped this picture.'

Lara is right, of course. Mum and Spud's mum are friends. Spud's mum was a hairdresser and used to do Mum's hair. So, as I suspected, it is all innocent so I needn't interrogate Mum over the matter.

Lara said that the screensaver would be good if she had some more pictures on her computer. So I went home and got my camera. We took lots of snaps of her and her mum and dogs and brothers and downloaded them to her hard drive.

After medication, Griz is showing signs of recovery from his, near fatal, chocolate binge.

Our FA Cup final ticket application forms arrived this morning. I filled mine out while I ate lunch, although I had to leave the credit card details for Dad to fill in when he came home from work.

He will drop them in to the ticket office tomorrow.

This evening we watched a fantastic football match where Manchester United beat Real Madrid four-three but still went out of the Champions League. Ronaldo was awesome!

24 April 2003, Thursday

Dennis from Osborne Coburg phoned me this morning to see if I was still interested in playing fror them. I said that I wasn't.

The disturbing thing was that he asked how I got on with my trial at Portsmouth. He said that he had heard that Pottsy had got taken on but he hadn't heard anything about how I got on.

My God! I think that letter I got on April the first was genuine. If anyone finds out that I ignored the chance of a trial at a, now, Premiership club, I will be a laughing stock.

I am so disappointed. Why did they have to send it to me on April Fool's Day? I'm a better player than Pottsy, so I could have been taken on as well.

This is bloody typical of my luck!

So my day was ruined before I'd even got started. I decided to stay in and watch the *Back to the Future* trilogy DVD box set that I got for Christmas but hadn't watched until today.

25 April 2003, Friday

I instigated a conversation with Mum this morning and asked her if she'd seen anything of Spud's mum since me and Spud had had our disagreement.

She said that she had had a chat with her at the Health Centre last week, where Spud's mum works now. Spud's mum said that she was sorry about his behaviour and that Mum was well within her rights to slap him around the face.

I asked her when was the last time she had been round to her house for a cup of tea.

'Why all the questions?' she asked.

'I don't want to be responsible for the break-up of such a long friendship,' I said.

'Don't worry, we are still very much friends and I was at her house just a few weeks ago.'

'Was Spud there?'

'I think so, why?'

'We never did find out who his secret, married girlfriend was.'

'Where is this leading?'

'That day me and Dad went to the Liverpool game, Lara and Tom tried to take a secret picture of Spud and this mysterious secret woman but the only picture they got was one of him with you.'

'Oh, so I'm this secret woman am I?' Mum said in a clearly irritated voice.

'Don't be silly. I was trying to find out if you saw him with any older women that day.'

'Oh! I see. No I didn't. We just walked into town together.'

'Did he meet anybody there?'

'I can't remember.'

'I guess we'll never know.'

'Does it really matter?'

'No, I suppose not.'

That finally settled it in my mind that Mum wasn't this woman. I finally realised what a ridiculous notion it was and I feel a bit stupid even thinking such a thing.

The rain today prevented Meat, Ed and I from indulging in any outdoor activities, so we stayed in and watched every episode of *Fawlty Towers* on DVD. Comic perfection! And it's always so much funnier when you watch it in a group.

Dad brought us back a Chinese takeaway this evening. It was lovely. I had chicken fried rice with Hong Kong style sweet and sour chicken.

We watched the news as we ate, and they still insist on putting the SARS epidemic behind 'the ending the Iraq war' stories. The Iraq war won't kill us. This virus will.

26 April 2003, Saturday

Dad went with some of his mates to the away match at Charlton. I was quite glad that I wasn't going, as the manager, Gordon Strachan, said that he will not risk injuring players for the FA Cup final. So I felt that we were bound to lose. We did, two-one.

Dad's car was caked in dirt from the roadworks outside St Mary's Hospital so I washed it. It was quite nice with the hot sun beaming down on me. When the car dried, however, it looked as though I hadn't even touched it. So I washed it again and the same thing happened. What a waste of time!

Ed came around as I was finishing and persuaded me to go to the beach with him. By lunchtime it was really hot. So we went down and picked a deserted spot beyond Gurnard Sailing Club. After an hour or so, Lara and Rachel turned up in bikinis. What a bonus! I'm sure I could see the outline of Lara's pubes through her bikini bottoms. It was so tantalising. It was around then that Ed and I decided to take a dip to cool down. The water was painfully cold. We didn't want to look like wimps so we bore it for as long as we could. When we came out the girls seemed to know that we were cold because Rachel said, 'That was brave of you! You wouldn't catch us going in when the water is that cold.'

It was also around that time that the sun went in and the temperature dropped.

I was glad to get into a nice hot bath.

I met up with Lara, Rachel, Kylie, Kelly, Jason, Meat, Stevie, Tom and Karl outside the Woodvale Hotel. We had pooled all our resources and Karl had bought three bottles of Vodka, which we consumed over the next two hours as we first walked then staggered up and down the seafront. We also went into the town because we all developed a joint craving for chips. We ate them on the way back to Gurnard and they tasted especially nice.

It was a brilliant night of drunkenness and laughs. When I got home, Dad noticed the condition I was in and made me down a pint of water before sending me to bed.

27 April 2003, Sunday

Today was the most uneventful day of the year, so far.

After a trip to Tesco with Mum and Dad, I spent the rest of the day watching football on television with Dad: Manchester City versus West Ham United followed by Tottenham Hotspur versus Manchester United and finally the most difficult match to sit through, Porstmouth versus Rotherham United. We had to watch Pompey get presented with the First Division trophy. We can only hope that Southampton can eclipse that achievement by winning the FA Cup.

The last normal term begins tomorrow. Exams and freedom will follow that term.

28 April 2003, Monday

The old routine! Ed arrived, as usual, at eight-thirty and we plodded our weary way to school. When we got there I thought I was seeing things when I spotted Katie chatting to Lara, Kelly and Kylie by the bike sheds.

We quickly went over to see what was going on. She seemed back to her old happy self and gave us both a big hug.

'I'm sorry you split up with your girlfriend because of me,' she said to Ed.

'That was her fault not yours, mate,' Ed replied. He received another hug.

Katie went on to tell us that she'd been left her grandmother's house so she had moved back into it with her nineteen-year-old cousin from Norfolk. Her cousin, Hannah, is a nurse and she has arranged a transfer to St Mary's Hospital so that she can help Katie get through her exams and get used to being a homeowner.

Her Nan also left her some money which is in a Trust. She will get a monthly allowance as well as the money that Hannah brings in so she should be able to get by quite nicely.

I am so glad she was able to come back.

Our conversation was ended when Spud turned up and was obviously overjoyed to see her. We left as Katie went through her story again, for his benefit.

At lunchtime it was raining so we stayed in the common room and chatted. The obvious thoughts were for a 'welcome home' party for Katie, to be held, naturally, at her house. She said that she'd have to clear it with Hannah but it should be OK.

This evening Me, Ed, Meat, Kelly, Kylie, Jason and Lara all went around to Katie's where we had to suffer the company of Spud. We steered clear of each other.

We didn't get to see Hannah. She was working nights. We watched *I'm a Celebrity Get Me Out of Here* until midnight.

29 April 2003, Tuesday

Today, in Art, Mr Vibert sprung a life class on us, as there had been a long delay in finding a model after my Nan's embarrassing appearance. Today's model was a bloke. He was bald and in his fifties and I was sure I had seen him somewhere before.

After the lesson I saw the man in the corridor and I knew I'd recognised him from somewhere, especially now he was dressed. He said, 'All right, Troy!' as he passed me on his way out.

'All right,' I said, still straining my brain to remember who he was.

'It's amazing what one will do to scrape some money together after you're made redundant. How's your dad getting on now, any good?'

Then it dawned on me. It was Dad's old boss, Derek.

'Oh yes, thanks. Yes, he's doing fine.'

'Good, I'm glad. He's a good lad is Kevin. See you then.'

'Cheers,' I said as I waved him off.

Isn't that sad?

At lunchtime me, Ed and Terry went down to see Vernon, as we hadn't seen him for over two weeks. He wasn't there and he, rather unwisely, had left Dickicker minding the shop. So we decided to sit and eat lunch in the Red Funnel terminal building. They have got a hot drinks machine there.

Terry went to the loo and that idiot, Pitbull, came through the automatic doors. I hoped that he wouldn't spot me but he did.

'Hallo Poofter Boy,' he sneered.

Terry came out of the toilet.

'OI!' he called. 'Who are you calling "Poofter Boy"?'

'What's it to you? You 'is boyfriend are ya?'

Terry advanced towards Pitbull.

'Come on then,' said Pitbull in a typically hardnut fashion.

'Yeah? Come on then!' replied Terry.

'Yeah?' said Pitbull.

'Yeah!' said Terry.

Then it all stopped when this little old lady came into the terminal room. Pitbull broke away.

'Hello Mrs Jennings,' he said to her, in a charming voice.

'Hello Pete,' she replied, handing him her bags.

'The cab's just out'ere, love,' he said, beckoning her to follow him.

He is a taxi driver! And his real name is Pete! We took the opportunity to head back to school.

After school I went home with Ed to have a quick listen to his Pink CD. When I got home I found Mum and Spud in our front room. Spud had his hand on Mum's belly.

'What the hell is going on?'

They looked quite innocent.

'The baby moved,' Spud said. 'I could feel it!'

'What's it to you?'

'Just interested,' he said. 'I've come because I think it's time to bury the hatchet.'

'Why don't you just punch me again?' I retorted.

'I'm really sorry we fell out.'

I grunted. He continued. 'Look, I was wrong to look in your diary and you were wrong to tell Lara. We're even. Okay?'

He stretched his hand out to me. Weak as I am,I shook it.

He made small talk for the hour or so we spent chatting in my room before Dad arrived home from work.

Why have I got such a nagging doubt about him and Mum? I wish something would arise to quell my suspicions.

There was a THROB practice this evening and we decided to record the songs we had learnt and split up.

So we spent the evening recording the six songs and left Ed to create the CDs.

30 April 2003, Wednesday

Our FA Cup final tickets arrived this morning. We will be in line with the edge of one of the penalty areas. I can hardly wait. What a day that is going to be, win or lose.

This lunchtime Ed, Terry and I went back to the pontoon to see if Pitbull was there. He was, sat in his cab reading something. We waited for him to get out and disappear so that Terry could post a copy of *Gay News*, which he'd just nicked from the Newsagent, through his sunroof. Then we waited for him to return. When he did he found the magazine and got out of his car to scour the area for the culprit. The expression on his face was fantastic. It was a mixture of surprise, rage and embarrassment.

We expected him to deposit it in the nearest available bin, but he appeared to get back in his cab and read it. Then the Red Jet arrived and he got a customer.

We are planning more pranks over the next few days and it serves him right.

This evening I went round to Ed's to help him make covers for the THROB CDs.

When I got home, Dad was distraught. He had been to the MP Graphics reunion where he had been told that Stan had been killed in a horrific road accident. He had been racing through Porchfield at night when a fox had run out in front of him. He swerved straight into a tree. He didn't even manage to miss the fox, so he died for nothing.

I am a bit upset as well. I really got on well with Stan when I had my week at MP Graphics. He's the first young person I've ever known that has died.

1 May 2003, Thursday

I spent a lot of time today thinking about Stan and the stuff we got up to when I was on work experience. It is difficult to picture him dead in my mind, when all I can remember about him is a young man with loads of energy and full of life. I got told off for daydreaming a couple of times.

Ed brought the THROB CDs in for all the band members and Jason Dwyer, Jason Ince and Terry all want copies. I don't know if they want them to take the piss out of us or not but Ed said he would burn off a few copies this evening.

At lunchtime, me, Terry and Ed went down to the pontoon for Revenge Part Two. This time Terry tied a bottle of Coke to the back of Pitbull's car while he was in the toilet. We had to wait a few minutes before he drove away and it was so funny. He didn't even notice as he drove with the bottle dragging behind. We ran around the block to watch him drive on around the corner and up the hill. We saw the bottle split and Coke spraying everywhere as he continued to drive on, oblivious.

Dad was still a bit melancholy this evening - understandable, because he had worked with Stan for over a year.

2 May 2003, Friday

I had lots of hot flushes at school today. The sweat under my arms was showing through my shirt so I had to wear my jumper to hide the problem and this only made the sweating worse.

During break time Terry somehow managed to photocopy his arse. At lunchtime he stuck the picture to the rear window of Pitbull's car. Pitbull did check his car before departing this time, but he didn't check his windows.

We told Tom about it, as he was the first person we saw when we got back to school.

The subject got changed, at some point, to nicknames. The funny thing was that he told us that his ex-girlfriend's nickname was Snowy.

'Why?' we all asked.

'Because her name is Donna Bull,' said Tom.

'Yes?'

'Well, people think it sounds like Abominable, if you say it quickly,' said Tom. 'The Abominable Donna Bull.'

That tickled me. I couldn't stop laughing about it for the rest of the day. I have got a sore throat now because I have been laughing so much. It's funny how some things just make you laugh, even if they aren't really that funny.

I felt rather tired this evening, so I declined Meat and Ed's offer of a DVD and popcorn night at Ed's house.

3 May 2003, Saturday

This morning the sore throat had got worse and it had spread to my chest. I also had a pounding headache. I took some cold and flu tablets and went over to Southampton with Dad. We got a table in the social club but there was a chain-smoker on the next table and my chest got heavier and heavier as the afternoon progressed.

By kick-off time I had the shivers and Dad said that my lips were turning blue. I thought about missing the match and walking back to the ferry terminal, but my breathing was so shallow that I thought I might as well stay at the match and get the free bus back at the end of the game.

It was Southampton's last home league game of the season and we drew nil-nil with Bolton Wanderers. It was probably just as well that we didn't score, because my lungs couldn't have taken any cheering.

I hardly touched my dinner and I went to bed very early.

4 May 2003, Sunday

I didn't sleep much last night. Every breath hurt and my head was throbbing. I couldn't take any Nurofen because Mum said that I couldn't take more than the stated dose per day.

I lay in bed all day. I didn't feel like doing anything else. I did get a bit of sleep though, after Mum gave me a dose of cold and flu tablets with the toast that I forced down.

I was able to watch Arsenal lose the championship to Manchester United when they lost three-two at home to Leeds. I also watched live *I'm a Celebrity Get Me Out of Here*.

5 May 2003, Monday

I was even worse today. I coughed up some blood this afternoon. Mum said that if I'm no better tomorrow, I will be seeing the doctor. At least I won't have to go to school.

I did get up for a couple of hours in the evening to watch the soaps with Mum and Dad.

6 May 2003, Tuesday

Dad took the day off so that he could go to Stan's funeral.

I still felt rough when I woke up but I was, at least, able to shift some phlegm that had been sitting on my chest for the last three days. So I was spared the doctor.

As the day went on I felt better and better. It now just feels like a bad cold.

7 May 2003, Wednesday

I was well enough to go back to school today and Mum told me that because of my days off sick we wouldn't be going up to Penarth until next Thursday. The original plan was Monday.

I had to put up with the usual, 'Did you have a good skive?' jibes. Terry and Ed had put a hold on the Pitbull campaign for the last few days, so at lunchtime we headed on down to the pontoon to resume proceedings.

Ed had printed out a photograph of his one-fingered salute and Terry stuck it to Pitbull's passenger-side wing mirror.

We went back to school where Tom and Meat were eager to hear the story of what had just happened.

After that, Tom amused us all with the impressions of the noises that The Abominable Donna Bull used to make in bed.

I wish I had some amusing sexual anecdotes to tell my mates about. The nearest thing I have to one of those is when my Nan caught me masturbating when I was sleeping there last year. I couldn't tell them about that. It was the most awful experience of my life. My Nan made things worse by asking me, the following morning, if I would like a box of tissues in my room.

Lara has taken to wearing a short skirt to school now, with all this summer weather. I think it should be banned because I can't concentrate on the exams with all this beauty in such abundance in one person.

This evening I made the mistake of listening to Southampton getting stuffed six-one at Arsenal. We have got no chance in the final. I am so pissed off about it.

8 May 2003, Thursday

Terry nearly got caught this lunchtime when Pitbull pretended to go to the toilet and only hid around the corner while Terry tried to stick a big sticker on the back of his cab that read, 'Yes I am as ugly as I look'.

He chased after him but was nowhere near fast or fit enough as Terry found refuge in the icafé. The good thing about that was that while they were chasing each other, Ed was able to stick the sticker properly on Pitbull's cab.

When we met back up with Terry, Kinsella was in there having his lunch break. He offered me two hundred quid for my cup final ticket. I turned him down and Vernon said, 'I'm not surprised he turned that offer down. I read in the paper that a Saints fan paid ten thousand pounds for a ticket'. Mine only cost Dad eighty. But I wouldn't sell it for any money, even if we do have to sit through Saints getting beaten.

We got to see Hannah this afternoon. She met Katie at the school gates, dressed in her nurse's uniform. Wow! She is absolutely stunning. Spud was with us and he was going mad with sexual frustration. He walked with them, as his house is in the same road. I wouldn't be surprised if he has shagged her by tomorrow morning.

9 May 2003, Friday

A beautiful sunny day began with the usual call from Ed. School was a bit boring today because we had to put a stop to our lunchtime pranks for safety reasons - Terry's safety to be precise.

All the lads enjoyed the fact that all the girls were wearing less clothing, and lunchtime was spent sunbathing in the school field. Well, actually, the girls sunbathed we ogled.

When I got home, Mum was out and there was a note in the hallway, which read:

Troy

There is a new carpet in the front room, so take off your shoes.
Feed the dog and let him out. I'll be in at 5.30.
Love you

Mum

So I took off my shoes, let the dog out and fed him. I then went into the front room to admire the new carpet, which is a cream colour.

Griz trotted in, seconds later, having downed his dinner in one and then it happened. He scooted around the carpet on his backside leaving a brown trail behind him. I was horrified and rushed into the kitchen to see what cleaning stuff I could find. I got some kitchen towel and some Fairy Liquid and started scrubbing. The kitchen towel just disintegrated leaving a right mess which I was still trying to sort out when Mum and Dad arrived home.

They went mad. Mum even kicked the dog who then received a grounding to the kitchen. Half an hour later, Dad had cleared up the mess, with the help of next door's Vax and the instructions of Mum.

We had to put up with Griz's whining all night though.

10 May 2003, Saturday

This morning I helped Dad dismantle the old shed. We didn't have the facilities to take the scrap wood to the dump, so we piled it in our driveway and Dad painted the words 'Free Wood' on a plank. Then we went to the hospital where Mum had her scan. You really can see it's a baby. They found out the sex as well. It's a girl. Mum always wanted a girl. If I had been a girl, Mum wanted to call me Helen, after Helen of Troy. So you'll understand where they got the idea for my name.

After that we went into Newport so that they could shop around Mothercare for baby girl's things. Yawn!

Eventually we went home where we found the pile of wood still outside our house minus the sign. Someone had just taken the sign so Dad had to paint a new one that read 'All This Wood Free (except this sign)'.

This afternoon Dad and I watched the play-off semi-final first leg between Wolverhampton Wanderers and Reading. Unfortunately Wolves won. We want Reading to get into the Premiership.

This evening Ed, Meat and I met up with Jason Dwyer, Kelly, Kylie and Spud at Katie's house where we watched *Die Another Day* on DVD.

Spud was flirting, unsuccessfully for a change, with Hannah. It was rather pathetic to watch.

11 May 2003, Sunday

We all crashed out in Katie's living room - all the lads that is. The girls all slept in Katie's and Hannah's bedrooms.

Hannah and Katie cooked everyone breakfast. It was delicious: bacon, sausages, eggs, tomatoes, mushrooms and hash browns. It well made up for the poor sleeping arrangements.

Back at home, I had lunch with my grandparents, who seem to have packed in their lovey-dovey behaviour, thank God! In fact the atmosphere seemed to be a bit tense until Mum showed them her latest scan picture.

This afternoon Dad and I watched the Chelsea versus Liverpool match. We couldn't bring ourselves to listen to Saints getting stuffed by Manchester City in their last ever match at Maine Road. To our amazement, though, Saints actually won one-nil and finished eighth in the league.

Sky Sports News kept on going on about West Ham United's relegation and we had to wait until midnight to see any highlights of the Saints match.

12 May 2003, Monday

Apparently the war in Iraq has been over for a while. The first I knew about it was when I heard a report on the news that ended with the words 'since the war'.

I had a chat with Spud at lunchtime. I teased him about his lack of a girlfriend and the conversation ended up on the subject of his following in his father's footsteps. Spud's Dad spent his youth sowing his wild oats and eventually settled down, happily, with his mother. Spud intends to do exactly the same thing.

Unlike Spud, though, his dad was actually quite nice looking, apparently. According to Spud, he used to look like Shane Ritchie who plays Alfie Moon in *Eastenders*. Spud looks more like Tyrone from *Coronation Street*.

He reckons that Hannah will give in to his charms, eventually. I hope not. It would knock him down a peg or two to be turned down for once in his life.

When I got home, Mum gave me a letter that says I have to attend the trial of Trevor Marsh as a witness for the prosecution. It was what I was dreading. The trial has been set for September at Winchester Crown Court.

I spent the evening revising. I might as well make an effort with these exams, as they are the only ones I will be doing. I watched Phil Tufnell win *I'm a Celebrity Get Me Out of Here*. He's done really well. He only gave up cricket in the last month to become a celebrity.

13 May 2003, Tuesday

I told Ed about the letter I got yesterday and he said that he was surprised that he hadn't got called up to give evidence, as he had been there when Marsh tried to abduct me. I hadn't thought of it but he is right. If it hadn't been for Ed, I could be dead.

There I go again, demonstrating my poetic abilities.

All this court business put me in a bad mood for the day and I declined Ed and Terry's invitation to go down and wind up Pitbull at lunchtime.

It was just as well, as only Ed returned from the mission. Terry had been arrested after Pitbull caught him sticking a fake, printed-out and cut-out numberplate reading 'UID 10T' on his cab. Pitbull pinned Terry down until the police arrived. He was unaware that Ed was watching from the Newsagent's window.

In my depressed state of mind I moaned to Dad this evening, saying that going to the Cup Final was pointless, as it is obvious that we are going to lose.

He said, 'Moments like this are rare. Forget about whether we win or lose. Just try to savour the day and the attention the club will receive from the media. Remember hundreds of clubs entered the FA Cup but only Saints and Arsenal made it to the final. That's a hell of an achievement. It would be nice to win but I know, too, that we will probably lose. I'm going to enjoy the day, though. It's twenty-seven years since we were last in the final, and in twenty-seven years from now I might be dead!'

It is still going to be depressing having to put up with everyone telling me that it was obvious that we weren't going to beat Arsenal.

I wish we could win it. That would be fantastic, but I know we are going to lose. How can I enjoy the day, knowing that?

Ed and I went to see Terry this evening. He has got a bruise on his cheek where Pitbull pressed his face against the road while he waited for the Old Bill to arrive.

Terry is still out for revenge and refused to tell us what he is planning.

'It's something I'm going to have to do by myself,' he said.

Ed was worried that Terry would be annoyed with him for keeping out of the way when he was in trouble, but Terry didn't blame him.

'There's no point both of us getting nicked,' Terry said.

14 May 2003, Wednesday

I'm not happy! All my alleged friends are planning a beach barbecue for this weekend. Why bloody plan it when I am away? I'm really pissed off but I pretended that I didn't mind, as I didn't want to be accused of being a party pooper.

Terry took a sicky today, so Ed and I went to see Vernon. While we were hanging around outside we saw Pitbull drive past and he gave us an evil smile and made a rude gesture with his finger.

This evening Dad brought home a bag of goodies from the Saints Megastore: yellow and blue rosettes, scarves, flags and yellow Southampton shirts with the words 'FA CUP FINAL 17th MAY 2003 MILLENNIUM

STADIUM' ironed on in between the badge and the shirt logo. Talk about getting into the spirit of things. He even bought a yellow and blue wig for Griz to wear. He didn't look happy as he was set up for a photograph sporting the wig on his little head.

Southampton will be wearing yellow and blue in the match as they lost the toss to wear their first-choice kit. Arsenal's first-choice kit is red.

Well, my school week is over, thank God! Mum, Dad and I spent the evening packing a few items for the weekend, and then Dad and I watched Real Madrid get knocked out of the Champions League by Juventus.

15 May 2003, Thursday

Nan and Grandad Brown arrived at about seven-thirty this morning, ready to mind the house and the dog for the weekend. We caught the eight-thirty ferry and had a full English breakfast during the voyage to Southampton.

The journey to Penarth took three hours once we had driven off the ferry. We were greeted with the usual handshakes and bear hugs from Grandad Stenning and slobbery kisses from Nan Stenning. Yuk!

Having said that, Mum escaped a bear hug because of her now obvious condition.

Once we had unpacked and consumed the cheese and pickle sandwiches they had made for us, we were taken on a walk to see the sights of Penarth. This consisted of the sea, or should I say Severn river front, the park and the town where Mum and Nan spent ages shopping.

In the afternoon we were taken to a local pub for dinner. I have to say that I find the local accent very irritating. They all say 'he-yer' instead of here and 'Caaadiff' instead of Cardiff.

This evening they all went out to the Rugby Club, and I elected to stay in and watch the First Division play-off semi-final between Sheffield United and Nottingham Forest. After Sheffield United won, I went for a poke around the house.

In a box at the bottom of a wardrobe in my grandparents bedroom, I found a red diary, which had 'Alison Stenning Diary 1986' written in it in various coloured felt-tip ink.

Just as I was about to flick though the pages they all arrived back from the club and I had to bury the book back in the box and make out I'd been in the bathroom.

1986 is the year I was conceived. I can't wait to read about it, but how will I get a chance now?

16 May 2003, Friday

Nan brought me breakfast in bed this morning. It was lovely - boiled eggs with toasted soldiers.

Nan and Grandad offered to take us all into Cardiff to go shopping. I tried to get out of it so that I could pilfer that box of Mum's diary, but they all made it impossible for me to refuse.

So we went in and had lunch at Yates' before walking around the city. We went to the Millennium Stadium, which was all dressed up in FA Cup banners ready for tomorrow. We saw several Southampton and Arsenal supporters in and about the shops, wearing club colours and replica shirts. I didn't bother wearing my yellow Saints shirt because I am saving it for tomorrow.

We went back to Nan and Grandad's for dinner. I hoped they would all go out again for the evening, but no such luck.

I couldn't even sneak into the bedroom during the evening because Nan and Mum spent most of it in there.

I spent the evening watching television with Dad and Grandad before going to bed at ten-thirty.

17 May 2003, Saturday

At last, the big day had arrived - the FA Cup Final. More breakfast in bed was followed by a couple of hours watching Sky TV.

Dad and I got dressed up in our yellow gear and Mum painted our faces in yellow and blue halves. Then the effect was finished off with yellow and blue curly wigs before Grandad transported us into Cardiff.

It was eleven o'clock and the place was full of football supporters of both clubs, all soaking in the atmosphere and alcohol.

We bought our match programmes, which shocked Dad when he saw the price was eight pounds fifty. We had to buy seven copies in total for ourselves and for people who had asked Dad to get them one. Dad asked the man in the kiosk if they had any bags but he didn't. He gave Dad a box to keep them in though, and Grandad took them home with him so that we didn't have to carry them around all day.

It started raining quite heavily and we went to a fish and chip shop to shelter and eat lunch. Then we braved the elements again and went to buy some official merchandise from the FA stall, but the Southampton one had sold out.

Fed up with the rain, we went into the stadium when the turnstiles opened at one o'clock.

A lot of other Saints fans must have had the same idea because the Saints end of the ground was nearly full by two o'clock. The Arsenal fans must have all decided to stay on in the local pubs.

There was merchandise on sale inside, which made up for them selling out outside. I bought an official Cup Final pin badge.

We sat in our seats, which were right in front of an executive box that was full of Saints fans enjoying a meal. The view of all our supporters wearing yellow and blue, and waving flags, was breathtaking. The Arsenal end didn't fill up until about fifteen minutes before kick-off.

When the teams came out of the tunnel, our end of the ground was awash with yellow and blue flags, balloons and confetti whereas the Arsenal end was just full of applauding Arsenal fans.

I won't go on about the match. We lost one-nil but it didn't matter. It was an amazing experience and we all left the stadium full of pride for what our team had achieved this season.

On the way back to the rendezvous point, where we had arranged to meet Grandad, a lot of Arsenal fans commented on the magnificent way that all the Southampton supporters had conducted themselves. We stayed back to see the cup presented and, apparently, that doesn't usually happen.

When we met Grandad he said, 'Commiserations!,' but we were happy because we will have at least one UEFA Cup match to watch next season, and we had played well enough to avoid ridicule.

When we got back to the house, Nan had a lovely meal of spaghetti bolognese ready for us. It was delicious. We spent the evening watching the match again but from the viewpoint of the BBC's coverage, which Grandad had videoed for us this afternoon. The six hours of coverage took us up to midnight and, with getting caught up in all the excitement of the day, I missed the opportunity to get the diary out of the box. We leave tomorrow morning, so how the hell am I going to get it?

18 May 2003, Sunday

I could get used to this breakfast in bed routine but this was the last morning of such luxuries. We had a lie-in until ten after staying up late last night.

The car got packed and everybody got ready to go. I made sure I had my backpack with me just in case the opportunity would arise and it did as Nan and Grandad came out of the house to wave us off.

'I've forgotten my diary!' I lied.

‘I’ll get it for you,’ said Nan.

‘No, no, I know exactly where it is.’

I ran into the house and, fortunately, wasn’t followed by anyone. I went, as quickly as I could, into Nan and Grandad’s bedroom, snatched Mum’s diary from the box in the wardrobe and stashed it in my backpack before, triumphantly, rejoining Mum and Dad in the car. Doing this also meant that I avoided a bear hug and a slobbery kiss.

The three-hour car journey, followed by the one-hour ferry trip seemed to take weeks because I was desperate to read the diary.

When we arrived back on the island, I had to wait even longer as Dad insisted that we went to the Eight Bells for dinner.

Finally, at just after six, we arrived home and unpacked. I hid both diaries in a safe place in my room, which I had to do now after Spud read mine that time. Then all I had to do was wait for my parents to go to bed.

I went to see Ed this evening. The beach barbecue was cancelled due to bad weather, which I was very pleased about. We might have it this weekend.

Terry got suspended for a week after news of his shenanigans with Pitbull reached Mr Bartlett. The lucky git! That means he gets two weeks off including half-term.

Ed also told me that an open audition had been advertised in the paper for a TV programme called *Rock Stars The Bands*. He thinks that we should reunite THROB and go for it. I agreed. I might get on TV!

I went home after half ten but Mum and Dad were still up, watching TV. I went to my room but I didn’t want to risk Mum walking in on me while I was reading her diary. She has often crept in without me noticing. I couldn’t risk it. I had to be sure that they were asleep.

19 May 2003, Monday

I fell asleep, waiting, last night. I’m afraid that I had to skive off school today, so I pretended to leave for school and took my backpack along to our beach barbecue site, where I was guaranteed not to be caught skiving and wouldn’t be disturbed.

Finally I was able to read it. I began by reading the month in which I was conceived. I counted nine months back from June 1987 and read from September 1986. Her writing wasn’t as detailed as mine is, as she only had a few lines to write in. I was shocked by what I read. Specifically:

3 September 1986, Wednesday
Today is my due date but no signs. Pauline, the midwife, visited me and told me to rest. She said that it would be all over soon.

4 September 1986, Thursday
Still nothing. I just want to get this thing out of me. Kevin came to see me tonight. He's a diamond. I don't know what I would have done without him.

5 September 1986, Friday
Mum and Dad left me in the house alone this morning. Wicksey must have been keeping an eye on the house because he called just after they left. He said he still wants me after I've given up the baby. I'm not sure I want him after everything that's happened.

6 September 1986, Saturday
It started when I had a shower. My waters broke. I'm in St Mary's now in agony. Why is it taking so long? Mum is with me, thank God! Kevin is here as well. He is keeping Dad company in the waiting room, bless him!

7 September 1986, Sunday
At last it is over. The baby was born at 9.30. A boy. I didn't want to see him and they have taken him away. They asked me what I'd like to call him so I said Peter. It was the doctor's name. Now I can get my life back. I am very sore down below. I have got stitches where they cut me to get him out. Kevin stayed with me all day.

8 September 1986, Monday
Wicksey visited me but Dad caught him and told him if he ever catches him near me again that he will make his life hell. I'm going home tomorrow.

* * *

30 September 1986, Tuesday
I am so in love with Kevin. What other man would have stood by a girl in my position. Cathy offered to take me out tomorrow night. I can't

wait.

1 October 1986, Wednesday
I went to Newport to shop with Mum for a new frock for tonight. Cathy picked me up and we went to Zanies. It was quiet but I had a great time dancing until Wicksey turned up. I was drunk and ended up kissing with him. He offered to take me home. Cathy tried to persuade me not to but I assured her it would be OK. I don't know how but we ended up doing it in the back of his car. I feel so ashamed of myself.

2 October 1986, Thursday
I am frightened that history is going to repeat itself. I haven't started taking the pill yet and he didn't use anything.

I spent most of the day in my room crying. Kevin called and cheered me up. How could I do this to him?

He bought me the 'Rain or Shine' single by Five Star, in an attempt to cheer me up.

3 October 1986, Friday
I couldn't stand the guilt any more so I told Kevin everything. To my amazement he immediately forgave me. He understands how messed up I am at the moment. We made the most beautiful love I have ever had. It was so much better than last time. I know now, he's the one.

4 October 1986, Saturday
I spent the whole day with my beloved Kevin, cuddling and making love. Bliss. He took me out this evening. Tonino's Italian Restaurant. So romantic!

5 October 1986, Sunday
Mum and Dad were out this morning when I was woken up by Wicksey. He pleaded with me to go away with him. We argued and didn't notice Mum and Dad arrive home. Dad went mad and Wicksey ran off like a scared animal.

* * *

21 October 1986, Tuesday

It was a miserable day today. It poured, all day. I still haven't had a period since the baby was born. The doctor said that it is perfectly normal as he prescribed me another course of pile cream. I heard that Wicksey has been sacked. I hope that is an end to it all.

Kevin came around and posted a request for me on the Ocean Sound radio station.

22 October 1986, Wednesday

Complete joy!!! Kevin asked my Dad if he could marry me. Dad gave him a big hug and said,'Welcome to the family.' Only thing now is that he hasn't asked me yet!

* * *

25 October 1986,Saturday

Went on a long walk with Kevin. We stopped at the chalets in Gurnard where he went down on one knee and proposed. I didn't waste any time in saying 'Yes' I am so happy, excited and in love.

* * *

16 December 1986, Tuesday

My 18th birthday. I went out to the Sloop for lunch with Mum, Dad and Kevin, who took the day off work to be with me. This evening was my party at Brook House in Binstead. All my friends were there and Kevin surprised me by announcing the date of our wedding: Ist April. Wicksey turned up at one point, drunk, but Dad and Uncle Gordon physically removed him. I felt a bit sorry for him, but only a bit. I'm so glad that I can put all that nightmare behind me now and look to a happy future with Kevin and our baby. Yes, I found out today that I am pregnant again. This time I'm absolutely delighted. I'm sure Kevin will be when I tell him.

17 December 1986, Wednesday

I told Kevin about the baby and he cried. I was worried for a while until I realised he was crying from happiness. I will have an ultrasound on 23rd January to find out how far gone I am. They can't make an estimation because I never had a period after I gave birth. There is just a nagging worry that the baby might be Wicksey's.

I can't believe I didn't look to see if there were any more diaries in the box. So from that, the man I have called Dad all my life might not be my natural father.

If you count forty weeks back from my birthday you find the day that Mum slept with Wicksey. I've got to do some careful detective work now. If I am wrong about my suspicions and Mum and Dad find out, they will be ever so hurt. I have to find out for sure. But it isn't looking too good.

Who is this Wicksey bloke? Obviously a man with the surname Wicks.

On top of all that, I have got a brother out there somewhere and soon I'm going to have a sister. From an only child, I am now one of three. Where is my brother? What if he wants to make contact with Mum? He is less than a year older than me, so it won't be long before he knocks on the door. How will Mum take it? Why haven't they told me about all this?

I have got so many questions that I can't ask.

I returned home at the time I would normally do, so as not to raise any suspicions.

Mum could tell that there was something wrong with me. I just told her that I had a headache, which wasn't far off the truth.

I spent the evening in my room, mulling over things in my head.

20 May 2003, Tuesday

I wrote my sick note last night before turning in and managed to get mum to sign it after telling her it was a note to say that she was giving me permission to be excused from games. Mum was half-asleep after returning to bed when I had eaten my breakfast, so it was very easy.

Then it was off to school, as normal. I told everyone who asked that I needed a day off to get over the disappointment of Saints losing the Cup Final. Some people believed me, some didn't.

The day went by in a bit of a haze. I didn't bother joining the rest of them as they all went down the town for lunch. I just milled around the school, thinking of scenarios of the way the story might continue. I also thought about hitch-hiking to Wales to get my hands on the next diary.

I saw Lara and she said that she would be at home this evening so I got myself invited around there. I bolted down my dinner and headed for her house as soon as I could.

I got her to swear on her mother's life not to tell a living soul, including Rachel before telling her the full story.

She said that it shouldn't make any difference who my natural father is because my dad (Kevin) is the one that brought me up and has given me love all these years.

'Maybe he doesn't know that he's not my dad?' I said.

'You don't know that either,' she replied. 'He loves you, and nothing will change that and that is all that matters. *I should know.*'

'What do you mean, I should know'?

'I'm adopted and so are my brothers.'

I felt a bit guilty and awkward.

'Yes, well of course you are right,' I said. 'But I really want to know one way or the other.'

'Give yourself some time to calm down and get your thoughts together. In time you might realise that things are best left as they are.'

That was good advice and I think I will follow it as best I can.

She also told me that there is someone else, in our year, that I know very well who is adopted, but she wouldn't tell me who it was because she had promised to keep it to herself.

21 May 2003, Wednesday

Lara spent more time than usual with me today and did a good job at diverting my thoughts by going on about the barbecue this weekend.

Ed reminded me about the reunion of THROB and I agreed to go round to his for a practice session. Tom and Meat also agreed to come, and Spud was roped in to audition for the vacant drummer position.

The session went well and Spud was passable on the drums. He should be all right with a bit more practice.

When I got home I was really disappointed to find out that Lara had called for me and I had missed her.

She might be the person to keep me together at the moment. I have been avoiding my parents as much as possible at the moment, for obvious reasons.

22 May 2003, Thursday

Lara called for me this morning and we waited for Ed before walking to school together. Ed is really excited about the prospect of getting on the *Rock Stars The Bands* programme. It's all he went on about. I find it difficult to find the same enthusiasm.

Terry visited school at lunch time. He has managed to get Pitbull charged with assault. Good for him! He has still got grazes and bruises on his face.

Terry persuaded me to join him, Jason Ince and Ed downtown at lunchtime.

We went to the icafé to antagonise Pitbull from a distance. We waved at him and poked our tongues out. All he could do was give us the toughest and most intimidating stares that he could muster. He also went a very funny shade of pink. I recognised it from my time at MP Graphics. It was magenta.

At home this evening I passed small talk with Mum and Dad over dinner. Dad told me that the lads and I have been invited to play in Osborne Coburg's twentieth anniversary match on Saturday afternoon.

That will be a good opportunity to burn off some nervous tension.

We had another practice at Ed's house tonight. I wish I had gone to Lara's.

23 May 2003, Friday

The welcome last day of the last normal term passed very slowly. We had an assembly in which all the teachers wished us luck in the forth-coming exams, which begin immediately after the holiday.

This evening me, Ed, Spud, Meat, Tom, Lara, Kylie, Kelly and Karl all went round to Katie's house to watch the launch night of *Big Brother*.

When the first housemate went in the house I was amazed. She looked so like Lara that they could have passed as sisters. Her name was Anouska. I joked to Lara, 'That isn't your long lost sister is it?'

She gave me the dirtiest look I have ever seen her give. I immediately shut up.

Later on, when she had got me on my own, she asked me if what I had said was a dig at her being adopted. It took some persuading on my part to convince her that it wasn't.

That was close. With that misunderstanding she could have easily said something about my problems and I am regretting telling her.

They did the nominations tonight as a surprise and, to my dismay, the stunning Anouska, who Spud said has got the best tits he has ever seen, was one of the housemates nominated for eviction.

I will be gutted if she gets voted out. It will only be jealous women who will vote for her.

24 May 2003, Saturday

A nice sunny day meant that the beach barbecue arrangements could go ahead. We spent the morning taking stuff out to the site - tents, sleeping bags and cool boxes.

We made it to Cowes High School field for the match at the same time as everyone else - two o'clock.

I was on the current Coburg team and we were playing against Coburg Old Boys.

First of all there was a penalty competition. I buried my first round kick with style but hit the second kick so hard against the bar that it had to be retrieved from the halfway line.

We played in a kit similar to Aston Villa's from the nineteen-eighties. To my amazement the Old Boys went in four-nil up at half-time. I couldn't understand it. Most of them were bald, fat and grey haired, yet every time they attacked they seemed to score.

We got a goal back early in the second half but they immediately scored again. Then this fat, bald bloke, who everyone had been taking the piss out of because he had spent so much time on the pitch without hardly getting a touch, nodded in from a perfect cross from the left. That just made it clear that it wasn't our day. So, despite playing by far the best football and creating most of the game's chances, we lost seven-two. Just like Saints!

As the game drew to a close it began to rain and we thought that the barbecue would have to be cancelled.

When I got home, Dad announced that Bournemouth had won their play-off final against Lincoln. I had forgotten all about the play-offs. I'd really wanted to see that game.

I had a quick bath then joined a small crowd outside Place Road Stores where Karl was buying the booze. So far the weather was behaving itself.

It behaved itself long enough for us to consume all the cider available before the heavens opened and we rushed to take shelter in the tents.

25 May 2003, Sunday

It rained for most of the night and made a terrible noise as every drop thundered against the tent. It did stop in the morning and we all got dirty as we packed the tents away and carried the camping stuff back along the coastline path.

I got cleaned up in time for lunch with Mum, Dad and Nan and Grandad who hardly spoke to each other. After that I went to Ed's to watch the Cardiff versus Queens Park Rangers play-off which was won by the former one-nil.

I left after that and, instead of going home, I went to see Lara.

I told her about the worries I had had on Friday night, when I thought that she might have told someone if she'd got upset enough with me. She said that even if she could save my life by telling someone she wouldn't because she never breaks a promise under any circumstances.

I told her that she could tell someone if it would save my life. No secret is that important!

I explained that I thought that Anouska from *Big Brother* was one of the most beautiful women I had ever seen and that I thought that she looked like her without brown skin and she understood what I had been getting at.

She thanked me but said that Anouska was much prettier than her.

I really enjoyed spending this evening with Lara. It was just like the evenings I spent with her a couple of months ago.

26 May 2003, Monday

I watched *Big Brother Live* on E4 this morning and Anouska's hair has reverted to Afro. It was straight when she entered the house. It makes her look less like Lara but she is still gorgeous. I couldn't keep my eyes off her breasts while she was doing a rowing task.

It was lovely and sunny today. THROB had a practice at Ed's before we all watched the First Division play-off final, which was won comfortably by Wolverhampton Wanderers three-nil. I wanted Sheffield United to win.

After the match I was forced to do some revision by Dad after he had a go at me for being irresponsible.

He should know all about responsibility after possibly bringing up someone else's son.

27 May 2003, Tuesday

This morning Mum made me revise until lunchtime before she let me go out. Then I met up with Ed, Spud, Tom, Jason Dwyer and Meat for a kick around at the park.

We are going to have another beach barbecue on Saturday night, to make up for the bad weather we had last weekend. At least that is something to look forward to. When we'd finished, Spud walked home with me. He wanted to have a chat. He told me that he is back with the mystery woman that he was seeing a few months ago.

I was surprised that he was prepared to tell me, after the time he found out that I'm not very good at keeping secrets.

I have decided to read *Hary Potter and the Goblet of Fire* to catch up before the new book comes out. So I spent the evening reading.

28 May 2003, Wednesday

This revision grounding is getting tedious. Every morning of my last holiday is being wasted. I might as well be at school. It's much easier there. You don't have to do any work.

The sun was out today and we took advantage of it by going down to the Green to stare at Lara, Kelly, Kylie, Rachel and Katie in their bikinis. We also played football.

It is so frustrating only being able to look at these examples of beauty when I see Meat and Jason cuddling up to Kylie and Kelly respectively. I did notice Tom gazing at Lara longingly. Well he had his chance!

It was THROB band practice this evening and I have to say that I am finding it very difficult being enthusiastic about these sessions. I wish I could leave but I feel as though I will be letting the lads down.

29 May 2003, Thursday

I tried to get out of revision this morning by lying in, but Mum was on the ball and made me do three hours. I didn't get out until two o'clock. I went around trying to find everyone, but nobody was in and all mobiles were switched off.

It turns out that they had all gone to the cinema to watch *Kangaroo Jack.* I am so pissed off with Mum for allowing me to miss it.

I did meet up with the THROB lads for yet another boring practice this evening, but today was a totally wasted day.

30 May 2003, Friday

I had a row with Mum this morning, when she tried to get me to do another three hours of revision. I ended up storming out of the house without breakfast.

It is just as well that I stormed out. I could have got wound up enough to accuse her of all the things that are festering in my mind at the moment. I am hoping that all these thoughts will start going away soon and I can get back to normal.

I went to Ed's and he made me some toast and Marmite. It's funny how it always tastes much nicer at someone else's house.

We went to the barbecue site to make preparations for tomorrow night. Karl, Meat and Tom met us there and we gathered loads of wood for the fire.

The sun was hot so we spent the afternoon there swimming and sunbathing. It was a great laugh.

I managed to avoid going home as we had fish and chips from Chip Ahoy down Victoria Road.

This evening we all piled round Katie's house again to watch the first eviction show of this year's *Big Brother*.

I was gutted when Devina McCall announced Anouska's name. It must have been all the women of the country voting, jealous of her incredible beauty.

The dreaded moment, when I had to face Mum, came when I arrived home. To my surprise, she put her arms around me and apologised.

'I'm sorry, sweetheart. It's m' hormones I know you've been working very hard on your schoolwork. Don't worry, I won't hassle you any more unless your results are bad.'

I felt quite guilty after that.

31 May 2003, Saturday

After breakfast this morning I did a couple of hours of revision without any prompting. Then I attended a practice at Ed's.

Afterwards, we took some acoustic equipment out to the barbecue site where we met Tom and Karl. We put the tents up, then Karl left to get the booze, leaving THROB to rehearse the acoustic set we had decided to do for the evening.

I was very nervous about singing in front of people, but we all felt that it was time to see if we could do it. It was also the first time that I have felt enthusiastic about the band for a while.

Soon people started arriving and the barbecue got under way.

There was a lot more alcohol available than usual. We performed our six songs before getting too drunk and got a big ovation. I got a real buzz out of it and hoped that it would lead to a groupie or something but nothing happened.

The wind picked up as the evening went on and, once all the drink was drunk, we went to find the tents but couldn't find the big one anywhere.

We couldn't all fit in the small one so a few of us, including me, volunteered to go home. We left Ed, Lara, Kylie, Jason, Katie, Rachel and Meat at the site and staggered along the moonlit path, formulating theories on what had become of the tent.

The winning scenario was that the farmer who owns the field had removed it to punish us for using his field without permission. The reason he didn't remove the smaller tent must have been because he thought that we might catch him.

1 June 2003, Sunday

I left the house early this morning so that I could meet up with everyone at camp. When I got there, I found the place deserted but I did find the missing tent, which was straddling a hedgerow right over the other side of the field.

I removed it and packed everything away before struggling with it on my way back along the path. When I reached Gurnard Marsh I phoned Dad, who came and picked me up.

I was pouring with sweat after that, so I had a bath then went to Ed's to find out what had happened.

He told me that he had got off with Lara. My heart sank.

He then said that he went for a walk with Lara and Rachel and they needed a wee and did it in front of him. He saw their 'genitals' as he called them. My heart sank still further.

Then he got very passionate with Lara, so much so that she said that she wanted to have sex with him but couldn't because she was on her period.

They found that they couldn't all fit in the remaining tent so they packed it up and went home.

I am devastated! Lara told me that when she loses her virginity she wants it to be special and that she thinks that you should be going out with someone for six weeks before considering sex. Yet she obviously considered it with Ed after six minutes. How could she? I'm so angry with her.

It was on my mind all day as I attended lunch with Mum, Dad, Nan and Grandad.

Nan and Grandad have patched up their differences. They have decided to sleep in their own houses as the problem was that Nan can't put up with Grandad's night-time habits of snoring and farting.

Mum explained my bad mood away by saying it was because I was nervous about my exams.

With Ed's comments on my mind all day, I had to phone Lara to hear her side of the story.

I was disappointed to hear that Ed was telling the truth, but Lara said that she was very drunk. She said that she wouldn't be going out with Ed. It was a one-off.

Then I put my foot in it and said, 'You could have got pregnant from that one-off!'

She yelled, 'I don't think it's any of your business what I do in my sex life. Why don't you get your own and f*** off!' Then she hung up.

I went to bed and, for the first time since I was thirteen, I cried.

2 June 2003, Monday

Mum turfed me out of bed this morning. I didn't feel like going in but Ed called round and I went to school with him. I didn't say much and he guessed that it was because of him and Lara.

'Look, mate,' he said, 'we were both pissed out of our heads. I'm sorry if it upsets you but there is nothing else I can do about it!'

'Its all right. I don't blame you. I blame her. I thought the world of her but now I know that she is a hypocrite and a bit of a tart!'

We didn't do much at school. All we did was collect our exam timetables and go home again.

I confined myself to my room and spent the rest of the day on my own.

I laid out some exercise books so that whenever Mum came in with a cup of tea it would look like I was revising.

Spud texted me to remind me about *Big Brother's Little Brother* on E4, probably because Anouska is on it this week, but I didn't even feel like watching her. It would have reminded me of Lara.

3 June 2003, Tuesday

I went into school with Ed. We took our English paper-one exam in the main hall with Mr Castle and Mrs Bowen presiding.

It took two-and-a-half hours. Afterwards we saw Lara in a corridor. Ed said, 'Hi-yer!' I just ignored her but I felt that she ignored me first, anyway. This upset me and I declined Ed's offer to go round to his house for a session on his X-Box.

I confined myself to my room again until the England versus Serbia and Montenegro match came on the television. I watched it with Dad and he didn't notice how down I was, being more interested in the football. He was moaning because James Beattie didn't get on until five minutes from the end. At least there were two Southampton players on the pitch for five minutes.

4 June 2003, Wednesday

This morning was our Biology paper-one exam. I don't think I did very well but hopefully I can redeem myself when I do paper two.

Mum went shopping in Southampton today, so I had the house to myself after the exam.

I just lounged in the front room watching *Big Brother Live* until Mum returned. Then I went back to my room for some simulated revising.

Mum had bought me some fruit and nut chocolate: 'A reward for working so hard,' she said.

5 June 2003, Thursday

I felt a bit better today and I went to Newport with Mum to do some shopping. Once we'd arrived there, Mum got some cash from the cashpoint. I watched her type in her PIN number. It was her year of birth, backwards.

We had a buffet lunch at Pizza Hut.

It was nice not having any exams. At least there would be no risk of bumping into Lara. I did, however, bump into Donna Bull outside McDonald's. She was on her lunch break. She was actually quite pleasant. She still smokes though. They all were, her and her friends. She's had her hair cut. She really looked quite nice.

We went around HMV and Mum bought the R Kelly CD single 'Ignition Remix'.

It was nice of her not to ask me any invasive questions. I wish I could pluck up the courage to ask her the questions that are banging around in my brain at the moment.

I worked on my computer this evening, ready for my Computer studies exam tomorrow afternoon.

6 June 2003, Friday

This morning was an incredibly boring Geography exam. Three long hours. Then Ed, Spud and I went down to see Vernon and have lunch.

We were down there earlier than usual and Kinsella was there, having his lunch break. I had my first laugh in nearly a week when Kinsella quizzed Spud about when, as he put it, 'Some little git plopped an ice cream on my head.'

It was hilarious seeing Spud squirm and stutter, as he tried to explain that it was Terry and not him. Eventually Kinsella let Spud know that he was only pulling his leg.

'It's all right, both myself and Peter, the taxi driver, have marked young Terence's card.'

We returned to school for the Computer Studies exam. It was a doddle.

I was invited round to Katie's this evening but I declined, in case Lara was there. At eight o'clock I got a text from Ed: LARAS NOT HERE CUM ROUND. So I did and we watched another *Big Brother* eviction show. Ed,

Tom and Spud were there with Hannah. She looked so sexy in her nurse's uniform.

I think that I am starting to realise that there are plenty of beautiful girls in the world. Unfortunately, none of them is interested in me.

7 June 2003, Saturday

I had a lie-in this morning. I got up at midday and had a brunch of a bacon and sausage baguette from Tiffins. Obviously I had to skateboard downtown to get it. I sat in Tiffins, feeling a bit stupid, on my own. I had just finished my cup of tea when I spotted Karl, Tom and Stevie going into Woolworths. I quickly caught up with them.

They asked me what I was up to and I told them I was bored and, thankfully, they asked me if I'd like to hang around with them for the day.

We set off, at very high speed, for Bembridge and Bessie's Butties where Jugs hasn't changed a bit. To my surprise she remembered me. We spent a couple of very pleasant hours there enjoying smutty humour.

Jugs has a collection of funny postcards, which she showed us. I thought that she seemed like one of the characters in them.

When we left we headed back towards Newport, over the Downs. Karl sped around a blind corner and was suddenly confronted by an idiot on a horse there. He had to swerve onto a grass verge to avoid hitting the horse and another car coming in the opposite direction. Fortunately we were at a picnic area. If it had been just another hundred yards up the road, we would have gone over a cliff.

The woman on the horse had the cheek to give Karl a right mouthful before she continued on her way.

After checking to see if the car was all right, we continued on our way. We overtook the woman. He gave her a wide birth but revved up the engine and tooted the horn as he went past. The horse didn't seem to be bothered but the woman was shaking her fist. Stupid cow!

Karl dropped me and Tom off at Ed's house where Meat and Spud were also waiting. It was time for another THROB get-together and we discussed the song we would perform at the audition.

Spud said that we should perform a cover version and he brought along his dad's Hollies CD and played us a track called 'He Ain't Heavy, He's My Brother'. It's quite good, so we spent the evening trying to learn it.

Ed's Dad brought in a Chinese that we'd all chipped in for and we ate it during a break. I was starving by that time.

We finished at ten-thirty because Zoe was on her way to bed.

8 June 2003, Sunday

I got a sarcastic greeting from Dad when I got up for lunch. 'Oh, you still live here, do you?' he said.

I humoured him.

Nan and Grandad came around for Sunday lunch, as usual, and I had to answer questions about my exams.

We had another band practice this afternoon and then we went to Northwood Park to play tennis.

Spud and I played Ed and Tom with Meat umpiring. Ed and Tom won six-three, six-two. There's a surprise. That's the last time I let Spud talk me into playing on his side.

I spent the evening in my room listening to my Pink CD. Then I watched *Big Brother* and went to bed.

9 June 2003, Monday

No exams today so I watched a bit of daytime TV on my own. Mum went out in the morning. I soon got bored and went out myself.

I went down to see Vernon. He told me that he had seen Spud walking through the town with an older, pregnant, woman.

I asked him which way they went and he told me. It had only been a few minutes earlier, so I set off to try to find them.

After looking in every shop, I eventually found Spud sat in Shooter's Hill Café.

'What are you up to?' I asked. He looked very uncomfortable, especially when this woman returned from a visit to the toilet.

It was the woman I had seen him with all those months ago, when I was sat in Tiffins with poor Stan.

'This is Christine,' Spud said.

I said 'Hello' and shook her hand.

I can understand why Vernon thought she was pregnant. She has got a big arse and she isn't slim. She looks like she is in her late twenties.

I didn't stay long, I could see that Spud was finding my being there very uncomfortable.

I went on my way and met Mum as she was coming out of Bailey's. I resisted the temptation to tell her about it. I don't think she would have been interested anyway.

Then I realised that this meant that the slight doubt about whether there was something going on between her and Spud had now been laid to rest.

In fact it has helped to restore a bit of faith that I had lost in her, although I need to find out about this baby she had before she had me. As soon as the exams are over I am going to have to find out. I wonder if I can get my hands on a birth certificate from Somerset House? Even if I do, it might not say who the father is. All I know is that the man's surname is Wicks.

Tonight Spud came round for a chat, not surprisingly. He told me that Christine had kicked her husband out and that he was sometimes living with her and her daughter. She lives in the same road as him, Arctic Road. That's convenient. It all seems to happen down that road. Katie lives in Arctic Road as well.

When he left he said, 'Cheers, fella. It's nice to be able to get it off my chest at last. It's been so hard keeping it to myself.'

10 June 2003, Tuesday

I had another lie-in this morning because our English paper-two exam wasn't until this afternoon.

I saw Lara on my way to the exam, which, again, was held in the main hall. She blanked me so I returned the compliment.

I think I have failed English. I couldn't get into it, especially when I was asked to write a poem. I just wrote the lyrics to the song I wrote a while back: 'Surroundings change us'

This evening I stayed in and watched TV with Mum and Dad.

11 June 2003, Wednesday

No exams today and I, very sadly, spent most of the day watching *Big Brother Live* on E4, something I told myself that I wouldn't do after last year when I ended up staying up until two o'clock in the morning most nights.

Dad arrived late, after he had given blood. He told us that he had seen Kinsella at the donation. He was giving blood as well.

I am surprised they accept his blood. Maybe they can give it to alcoholics that end up in Casualty.

So we had a late tea then watched England just about manage to beat Slovakia two-one. On digital TV you can switch the commentary off and just have the crowd noise, so Dad and I did our own commentary. I wish I could have recorded it, it was really good.

12 June 2003, Thursday

This morning I attended our History exam, which was held in our History classroom. Mr Vibert looked after us. I think I did all right with the paper.

This afternoon I went round to Tom's house. As we sat in his sitting room, sipping tea, it struck me that he bore absolutely no resemblance to either of his parents. He would have confided in Lara and I very much think that he is the other person in our year that is adopted.

Well, I'm ashamed to say that I watched *Big Brother Live* for the afternoon until Karl arrived home from work. He told us that Stevie is borrowing his dad's launch for Saturday night and that they are going along the River Medina to have a free look at the Isle of Wight Festival of Music. I have booked myself a place. It should be a laugh.

We had a band practice this evening, which went well. Spud brought around a brilliant song called 'The Caravan of Love' by a band called The Housemartins. He reckons that Fat Boy Slim had something to do with the song, so it would be a cool song to cover. The only trouble is that the song is sung a cappella on the record, so we had to create a musical background for it and speed it up a bit. It sounds punky.

13 June 2003, Friday

Today I had to attend the exam for my worst subject, Maths. I have failed.

We had another band practice this afternoon and 'Caravan of Love' is coming together superbly. With the weather finally turning summery, we went to the park for a kick around.

This evening I went round to Katie's to watch the *Big Brother* eviction show but Lara was there. I didn't bother speaking to her and she didn't bother speaking to me. I left as soon as the show finished and walked home on my own.

14 June 2003, Saturday

Tom phoned me this morning and invited me to go out to Compton Bay with him, Karl and Ed. The weather was perfect for the beach. We got there at eleven and got a lovely spot.

We had a great laugh. At one stage we buried Ed in the sand and made a huge sand penis for him and Karl found some dead grass that he made into pubic hair. Then Tom set fire to the grass. The expression of panic on Ed's face was hilarious.

We ogled some lovely girls but no one was topless. Early in the afternoon Spud turned up with Meat, Jason Dwyer, Kelly, Kylie and Katie. They had come by bus and it had taken them two hours to get there.

I was drooling at the girls in their bikinis.

We had a game of cricket and everyone fell about laughing when me and Ed got confused about who was supposed to be bowling and ran straight into each other, ending up in a heap on the sand.

We played volleyball against the girls. Apparently Katie popped out of her top just as I was taking a shot and I missed it.

Things were going really well until around three o'clock, when Lara and Rachel turned up. Rachel is obviously in the same mood as Lara with me because she hardly managed a glance let alone say anything to me.

I went for a walk on my own, to get an ice lolly. Ed came to find me and told me that Lara and Rachel were sunbathing topless. Normally I would have been quite excited by this but I couldn't be bothered.

It did cross my mind, though, that I should have brought my digital camera with me.

We left soon after so that we could get ready for the evening boat trip.

Me, Meat and Ed met Karl, Tom, Spud and Stevie in East Cowes. The launch *The Nellie Maud* was berthed at the Power Station, where Stevie's dad works.

The good thing was that there was plenty of cider on the boat and we were all pissed by the time we reached the concert site.

We could hear the music all the way along the three-mile river journey. Paul Weller was on stage when we got there, although we couldn't see him because the stage was facing away from the river. It was really good and there were lots of similar little boats on the water doing the same thing.

It finished at around ten o'clock, so we sailed back to Cowes and most of us ended up puking up over the side of the boat.

Stevie dropped us off near the floating bridge at around midnight. An excellent lads' night out.

15 June 2003, Sunday

With yet more scorching weather what else could we do but go to the beach again. This time Karl took us (me, Tom, Ed and Stevie) to Ryde beach. We got there at just after ten a.m. Even, at that time, the sand was hot to step on.

The tide was out, so it was a long walk if you wanted a dip, and after missing out on a swim yesterday, we all went in to the tepid water. It was lovely.

After midday, though, the tide turned and the water became colder, which was strange because the temperature on the beach was stifling.

We had a game of beach football, which was quite difficult because the sand on Ryde beach is much finer and more powdery than Compton Bay sand. We had to stop when these two young girls started complaining because we were covering them in sand.

We stayed there until five and then Karl white-knuckle rode us back to Cowes.

Nan and Grandad were still there when I arrived home. In my absence they had all decided to have their roast dinner at teatime. They had spent the day out and had had a light lunch at the Caulk Heads in Sandown.

I was delighted to be having a nice big meal. I was famished.

This evening we had another band practice at Ed's.

16 June 2003, Monday

It was good to have no exams today because the weather was really hot and sunny again. This morning Ed and I played tennis at Northwood Park. He won six-four, six-seven, seven-six. So he beat me on a tiebreak. I get so frustrated when I play against him. He always gets the lucky breaks; plenty of net cords for example.

After that we played putting. He beat me on the last hole. After that I decided to challenge him to a round of real golf.

We had a quick lunch at my house and I dug my clubs out of the shed and relieved them from hibernation.

Cowes Golf Club is a nine-hole golf course and you have to go around twice to do a full round. Ed hired his clubs but still had ridiculous luck. I was three shots ahead at the halfway point but I sliced my tee shot at the eleventh out of bounds, then my second at the fourteenth ended up in the drink. We ended up level after the eighteenth hole and I was going to settle for a draw but he insisted that we had a play-off, which he won when he hit his tee shot at the second to within four inches of the hole and won with a birdie.

We finished at teatime and I was absolutely shattered so I stayed in and watched TV.

17 June 2003, Tuesday

None of THROB had exams today so we all assembled at Ed's for a band practice. Spud got in a sulk when we decided to dump his two song choices for the Beatles' 'Things We Said Today'. Ed's dad is the one who suggested that we did a Beatles cover as they are popular with all generations.

By lunchtime we thought that staying inside in this weather was a bit stupid. We went to Gurnard to mess around at the beach. I didn't have to worry about bumping into Lara as she was at school. So I was able to relax and have a really good laugh with the lads.

I had my camera, so we took the opportunity to have our first ever band photo shoot. I took them all on the self-timer.

Up to this evening I didn't know what was happening on my birthday. But Mum and Dad told me that they are treating me to a meal at the Eight Bells. So bang goes any chance of a piss-up. I suppose it is just typical of my luck that my sixteenth birthday would fall during the exams.

I spent this evening in my room listening to my Blur *Think Tank* CD and then my Sugababes CD. Then I watched *Big Brother* and went to bed.

18 June 2003, Wednesday

I walked down to town with Mum this morning and we parted company at the icafé where I stopped off to chat to Vernon. We were chatting for a while when Christine walked past. She waved and smiled at me. I waved back and Vernon said, 'Who's that?'

I said, 'You should know. That's the woman you saw with Spud last week!'

'No it isn't,' he said. 'I told you the woman he was with was pregnant.' Then he stopped himself as he spotted something through the window. 'It was her in fact.'

'It can't have been,' I said.

'Why not?'

'That's my mum!'

'Oh dear, oh dear, oh dear,' said Vernon. 'Who's got a little jacket spud in the oven then?' he chortled.

I didn't think it was funny. 'SHUT UP you twat!' And I stormed out of the icafé with Vernon's voice calling after me, 'Hey! I was only joking.' He stepped out of the icafé to call, 'Troy! Come on. Don't be stupid!'

I didn't follow Mum. I went off down the seafront to try to calm myself down. Vernon had spelt out my own suspicions but what has Christine got to do with all of this?

Then my mind started to clear. Obviously Spud had just been strolling down the road with Mum on his way to meet Christine. He had told me all about her, unless he was lying and was using her as a decoy. But why would she do that for him?

I went back into the town in the hope that I could find her and ask her what was really going on between her and Spud. But I didn't find her. Maybe I'll have to go round her house to ask her personally.

I went round to Spud's but he was out. I could have knocked on every door in Arctic Road but I didn't.

Eventually I gave up and went home to a very cheerful Mum. So at least Spud wasn't seeing her, unless the reason she was so cheerful was that he had been there all the time I had been out.

She was even lovey-dovey to Dad when he came home from work. Dad kissed her and then kissed the bump saying, 'Hello Junior!' Then he cheerfully called to me, 'Do you want one as well, Troy?'

'No thanks,' I groaned.

'Suit yourself!' he replied.

I did phone Spud tonight to see if I could go around and see him but he said, 'Sorry, fella, I'm seeing my woman know what I mean?'

Mum went out tonight, as well. She was going out for a drink with Angela. Or so she said.

With all this going on I only found out about David Beckham's move to Real Madrid on the ten o'clock news.

19 June 2003, Thursday

I met Spud at our Biology paper-two exam this morning. He had a glint in his eye.

'Did you see Christine last night, then?' I asked as we were preparing to go into hall for the exam.

'Yes I did,' Spud replied in a matter-of-fact sort of way.

I felt much better after that and that was good, otherwise I could never have got through the paper.

This evening me, Spud, Terry, Tom, Ed, Meat and the Jasons all met up with Karl, Stevie and Nathan for a game of cricket at Northwood Recreation Ground.

We all had our own go at batting, with the person with the most runs winning. Ed won, yet again.

There were actually some good programmes on television tonight so I stayed in. There was an interview with J. K. Rowling, author of all the Harry Potter books. Dad really fancies her.

'There's nothing more attractive than a beautiful woman with brains and money,' he said. 'And she's my age as well, you know?'

'Maybe you should write a book then, Dad?' I teased.

'You know, that's a bloody good idea!' he said, in a voice full of revelation.

20 June 2003, Friday

This morning Mum invited me to go shopping with her in Southampton. We caught the nine o'clock Red Jet and caught the free bus to West Quay where we spent three hours looking in John Lewis, Waitrose and Marks & Spencer.

She picked up lots of cheap baby clothes. I was getting rather bored as it approached lunchtime and I was regretting going with her. I could have gone to Ed's house.

We had lunch at KFC and then went out of West Quay and into the High Street. Unfortunately Mum made a beeline for Mothercare. That was it for me. I went off to Virgin and HMV for an hour before meeting back up with Mum and helping her lug a heavy bag full of shopping back to the ferry terminal.

All was well until we arrived back in Cowes. Ricky Kinsella had been one of the hands that tied up the Red Jet as we docked, and he was standing by the entrance to the passenger gangway as we disembarked.

'Hello Ali!' he said to Mum. 'You're not this lad's mum are you?' He was referring to me. 'I had no idea.'

'Yes, he's mine,' said Mum.

'And you haven't been at the pies have you?'

Mum chuckled, 'No I haven't.'

'Congratulations. When's it due?' asked Kinsella.

'The twenty-fifth of September,' Mum answered, trying to ease herself back into the tide of people walking down the gangway.

'Oh that's wonderful. You're looking so well,' smarmed Kinsella.

'Thank you and so are you,' said Mum as someone let her into the procession. Pregnancy is a ticket for politeness.

'Nice to see you!' Kinsella called. 'Bye!'

'You too, Wicksey. Bye!'

A feeling of suppressed panic came over me as Mum led me to a taxi. As we were driven home I asked Mum, 'What did you call Kinsella as we left him?'

'Wicksey. Why?'

'Why Wicksey? I don't understand.'

'It was a pet name I had for him. We used to be good friends before you were born.'

'Oh,' I said as answers to questions were starting to form in my mind.

Of course, he used to be a teacher and lost his job after a relationship with a student. That student was Mum. He must think that I'm his son. Maybe I am!

When we got home I retired to my room to try to get my head around everything.

If I could wish for anything in the world I would wish that he were not my father.

Dad came home from work, but I asked if I could have my dinner in my bedroom. When I had finished I carried my tray to the kitchen and heard a conversation between Mum and Dad.

'We should tell him after his birthday,' Dad said. 'If he takes it badly it might ruin his big day.'

'Okay.' said Mum, 'but I'm dreading it. What if he ends up hating me?'

'He's got to be told. It's time.'

Just then my knife slipped off my tray and crashed to the floor, startling Griz who barked.

'Okay there, love?' Mum called.

'Yes, sorry,' I called back.

I went back to my room and lay on my bed. I couldn't get to sleep. I couldn't stop the scenarios churning around in my brain even though I wanted to.

I hope I can get off to sleep tonight.

21 June 2003, Saturday

I did get off to sleep eventually because Dad woke me up with a gift. He had gone out at midnight to buy me *Harry Potter and the Order of the Phoenix.*

I thanked him groggily. It was eleven-fifteen and he told me that he and Mum were going to go to Tesco.

'Coming?' he asked.

I shook my head and made out that I was going to go back to sleep. I heard them leave and then put into practice the plan that I had formulated while trying to get to sleep. It was time for me to leave.

I packed my backpack with a few essentials: three pairs of socks, three pairs of underpants, deodorant, a spare pair of jeans, a T-shirt, a Saints shirt, my new Harry Potter book, my toothbrush and toothpaste, Game Boy, camera, Mum's diary, this diary and some snacky food from the kitchen.

When I reached the hallway I noticed that Mum had left her purse in the kitchen. I opened it up and removed her debit card, then went down to town and drew three hundred pounds from the cashpoint machine. When I had folded the money into my wallet I spotted Christine walking up the High Street, so I decided to follow her. I followed her all the way to her house.

I stood outside her gate trying to pluck up the courage to knock on her door.

'Troy!' a familiar voice called. It was Karl. 'What are you up to? Want a lift anywhere?'

'No thanks' I said as Karl reached me.

'What are you up to anyway?' I asked.

'I've just been to see Katie about renting a room off her,' Karl replied. 'Anyway, I'll see yer la'er mate. I had to park the car right down the other end of the road.'

I said goodbye and decided not to confront Christine for the moment. I headed for Katie's. I was going to ask her about the room.

I had just arrived at her house when a little boy shouted at me, 'OI! WANKER!' It was a little boy with a skinhead haircut except for a long bit hanging ridiculously over his collar. He had a line of snot joining his nose with his top lip. It was Pitbull's youngest son.

I was just about to ignore him when the other little lout turned up. I heard the roar of an engine down the road, then spotted Pitbull across the road looking at me menacingly.

The younger boy spotted him. 'DAD!' he yelled.

The roar of the car engine became louder and I got a terrible feeling of déjà vu. The boy suddenly made a run for the other side of the road just as the car was upon us.

Pitbull screamed, 'NOOOO!'

I made a grab for the only part of the boy I could reach - his straggly bit of hair. He squealed in agony as the car roared past. Pitbull was desperately trying to get across but another car prevented him from crossing, as the boy lay grizzling on the pavement holding the back of his head.

I made a run for it and he called after me, 'OI! COME BACK 'ERE!'

I ran straight down to the Red Jet and hardly noticed Ricky Kinsella who was crashed out on his bench with an empty bottle of whisky lying next to him.

I timed it well and was the last person on just as they were about to set sail.

As the Red Jet pulled away from its berth, an amazing sensation of freedom washed over me.

When I arrived in Southampton I went to a hairdressers that I'd always seen on my way to football matches, in St Mary's Street. I had a grade one and I didn't recognise myself when the bloke finished. It took him five minutes and I had to pay him fifteen pounds. He must be raking it in.

After that I headed for Southampton Central Station and bought a one-way ticket to Penarth.

After the train departed, I got out my new Harry Potter book and began reading. A few stations down the line the inspector arrived to check my ticket.

''Arry Po'er?' He nosied. 'Is that a good one of 'is?'

'So far so good,' I replied.

'Yeah,' he continued. 'I used to like his mum's books when I was a lad. *Pe'er Rabbit, Mrs.Tiggy Win'le, Tale of the Flopsy Bunnies* wonderful!'

He was interrupted by his mobile phone as I stared at him disbelievingly. When he'd finished his conversation he chortled, 'Old Farmer McGreggor, he used to make me laugh! Sadistic bastard!'

'So you haven't read 'Harry Potter and the Philistine's Phone', then?' I asked sarcastically.

'No, no, I 'aven't read any of 'is books, mate!'

It was that that made me realise that I had left my phone at home. It doesn't matter, though, because I don't need it.

Thankfully, after that, he moved on.

I arrived at Cardiff Central Station at around four o'clock. I then caught the next available train to Penarth and got off at Dingle Road Station, which is the closest to my grandparents' house.

By this time I was famished. I had to keep an eye out for my grandparents as I got myself a fish cake and chips.

There is a bed and breakfast place right opposite my grandparents' house. I asked them if they had a room available that faced the road. They did and I gave the landlady, Mrs Long, thirty pounds for the night.

The room is just a bedroom with a television a bed and a chair in it. There was also a tallboy in which I put my backpack.

I took up surveillance at the window, but nobody alighted from the house before I started to feel really tired.

What a day!

22 June 2003, Sunday

My sixteenth birthday. Mrs Long brought my breakfast to my room at seven-thirty. Once I was washed and dressed I took up my vantage point, but by mid-morning I was getting very bored. I was also missing the fact that I had no presents, so I decided to go into Cardiff and buy myself some.

I paid Mrs Long for a second night and carefully made my way to the railway station.

Once in Cardiff I went to the cashpoint machine and drew out another three hundred pounds. I had a good time browsing all the shops.

I had lunch in Burger King, which is right next to the Millennium Stadium. It looked different from the last time I saw it.

I bought myself a portable DVD player and both Harry Potter DVDs. I had dinner at KFC, then headed back to Mrs Long's house. I got there at six-fifteen.

Once again I took up a position at the window, but the lights stayed on and nobody left. I gave up at around nine o'clock and watched the first Harry Potter DVD in bed.

This was not the way I had expected to spend my sixteenth birthday. I do feel a bit lonely at the moment, but I must do what I have to do. It's gone too far now.

23 June 2003, Monday

Another delicious fry-up greeted me first thing this morning, and after I had freshened up I sat at the window and at last saw Nan and Grandad leave their house together. They looked rather flustered and Grandad heaved two large suitcases into the boot. So obviously they are going away for a few days.

I watched them drive off and gathered my belongings together. I thanked Mrs Long and headed around the block.

If Mrs Long had seen me walk straight across the road I think she would have found it a bit odd.

I reached my hand into the letter box and retrieved the emergency key that dangles on a length of string inside and I let myself in.

It was fantastic to have the whole house to myself. Once inside, I wasted no time and ran upstairs to Nan and Grandad's bedroom. I pulled out the box I had been longing to get hold of all these weeks but there were no diaries in there. I couldn't believe it, so I searched the house. I even got the stepladder and had a look in the loft but there was nothing there.

The only thing I found, right at the bottom of the box I'd originally dug out, was a letter which read as follows:

12 August 1987

My dearest Ali
I had to write to you one last time. I am going away and I want to persuade you to leave Kevin and live with me.
I have never stopped loving you and, as you know, I have given up everything for you.
Please think carefully about the life you want for the children and yourself. You know we were good together. Please, please, PLEASE give it a try. I know I can make you and the boys happy.
Yes I mean both of the boys. I'm sure that it's not too late to get Peter back. Then you, the boys and me can live happily together as a true family.
We both know that you married him on the rebound. I know he is a nice man but he is not me. I am the father of your children. That must mean something to you.
I am here until Friday. You know where to find me.

Forever

Richard Kinsella
Your Wicksey

So I didn't need the diary after all. It's all written there in blue biro. I folded the letter into Mum's diary and then had a long bath.

Now I know the truth I feel surprisingly calm. I thought that if I heard the worst that I would go mad, but I suppose that I have had plenty of time to get used to it.

I still love Kevin, even if he isn't my natural father, and I certainly don't want anything to do with Kinsella, or should I now say, Dad.

The only thing now is the question, whatever happened to my long lost brother, Peter? I'm not in a hurry to find that out either.

I spent the day lounging around the house watching television. *Big Brother* has done a housemate exchange with *Big Brother Africa* so that was interesting to watch as the African housemate entered the UK house.

I also used Nan's washing machine to wash my filthy clothes. I could get used to this independence.

I ordered an Indian takeaway delivery tonight - absolutely delicious. I have run out of money.

24 June 2003, Tuesday

I went into Penarth town to draw out another three hundred pounds. I hope this money will last me a bit longer than the other money I have drawn out.

I couldn't go back home now, even if I wanted to, after nicking all that money from my Mum and Stepdad. I have really dug a hole for myself.

I spent the day watching Wimbledon on television. I raided Nan's freezer to make my lunch and ordered a pizza delivery for my dinner.

I am starting to miss Ed and the lads. I wish they could be here with me.

The only bad thing about this experience is being on my own. I hate it.

25 June 2003, Wednesday

I got a shock this morning. The doorbell rang and I peeped through the curtains and saw Mrs Long there with a policeman. I held my breath and, thank God, they left. That made me realise that I had outstayed my welcome in the house.

Mrs Long must have seen me pop out yesterday to get my money.

I spent the day trying to remove all trace of my having been here and I packed all my things together and carefully sneaked out late in the afternoon.

It was probably a good time to go because Nan and Grandad are bound to return soon.

I headed for Cardiff again and booked myself into the Hilton Hotel for the night.

One hundred pounds got me an en-suite room with a TV and PlayStation. I had a lovely roast lamb meal for supper. A have never enjoyed a meal like that as much before.

I played on the PlayStation for a couple of hours before turning in.

26 June 2003, Thursday

A wonderful buffet full English breakfast greeted me this morning in the hotel restaurant. You could just keep going up and getting more.

I just loved it there so much, I had to spend just one more night there so I went to the bank and drew out another three hundred pounds. Then I walked around all the shops and ate lunch in McDonald's.

I had chicken korma for dinner at the hotel, then I settled into my room to watch the Confederations Cup semi-final match between France and Turkey. The French and Turkish players were all crying during the national anthems. I wondered why.

Then they reported that Marc-Vivien Foe collapsed and died in the other semi-final, playing for Cameroon against Colombia. He played for Manchester City last season and Harry Redknapp was trying to sign him for Portsmouth.

God, he was only twenty-eight. They showed some footage of him collapsing. He just collapsed in the Centre Circle with nobody anywhere near him.

His whole family were at the match, including his young baby. That made me think of my family, and for the first time since I have been away, I really miss them.

What have I got myself into?

27 June 2003, Friday

After another wonderful breakfast I checked out of the hotel and went to the bank to draw out another wad.

When I got there, there was a man at the machine who was in a strop. He was thumping the machine with the palm of his hand.

'Sorry mate!' he said. 'I put my card in and it doesn't ask me for a PIN number. It just spits my card back out.'

'Oh!' I said.

'I tell you what mate,' he suggested, 'You put your card in and see if it'll except yours.'

So I did as he asked, expecting to get the same result as him, but the transaction went through perfectly. I folded the money into my wallet and headed off to the market.

I eased through a bustling passageway, squeezing by shoppers, and I was quite relieved to get out of the crush.

I thought that I'd better buy myself some new batteries for my DVD player, but when I reached for my wallet it had gone.

I panicked and retraced my steps, hoping to find it lying on the pavement somewhere, but it was no use. Now I only had eleven pounds and sixty-two pence of lose change that I had in my pocket. I knew that I was going to have to sleep rough from now on.

Totally and utterly devastated, I went back to the market where I invested in a sleeping bag. That cost me six pounds and ninety-nine pence.

I phoned the bank from a phone box and pretended to be my dad. They asked me two very simple security questions.

'Can you tell me your mother's maiden name?'

'Hall,' I replied.

'Your date of birth?'

'Ninth of February nineteen sixty-six.'

I successfully cancelled the card.

It was just as well that I had had a huge breakfast. I lasted out until the early evening before I got hungry. I had a Happy Meal for my evening meal, then I went off to try to find somewhere safe to sleep.

I went to Bute Park where I found a vacant bench. There was a huge black man who seemed to be watching me from another bench. I felt very uneasy, so I settled down with my backpack on.

28 June 2003, Saturday

I had very little sleep last night. When I awoke, the black man was still asleep on his bench.

It was five-thirty; far too early, but the cool morning air and sunshine helped to prevent me from getting back to sleep.

I went to the drive-thru McDonald's and had two Bacon and Egg McMuffins and a cup of tea. I kept the paper cup so that I could get water from the park toilets. I packed it in my backpack.

I spent the last of my money on three Snickers bars to keep me going whenever I got hungry. I ate two of them straight away.

I managed to get the same park bench as last night. The black man nodded at me and he gave me a friendly smile.

He didn't attack me last night, so I felt a bit more relaxed tonight.

29 June 2003, Sunday

I was awakened by huge rumbles of thunder. The black man came rushing over to me. It was still dark.

'Come on,' he beckoned in a distinctive African accent. 'Follow me. You don't want to be getting that sleeping bag wet, now.'

I did as he asked and he led me to the toilets where there was a shelter. We got there just before the deluge started. A couple more down-and-outs arrived to share the small space with us.

He introduced himself to me.

'My name is Robert, but I am known as Kwami,' he said.

I introduced myself and we spent the morning talking about how we ended up where we are now.

Kwami is originally from Ghana. He married an English woman but it all broke down. There was some trouble with her family and he had to run away. He told me he was twenty-eight years old. I told him that I was sixteen and he said that my parents would be frantic with worry.

'I doubt it,' I told him. 'One of them is a drunk who has had nothing to do with me all my life and the other is a pathological liar.'

He's actually a really nice man. I spent the day with him.

He earns money at Cardiff's railway stations, busking with his ukulele.

He bought me my lunch and my dinner, which was really good of him, even if it was just a McChicken Sandwich for lunch and a Burger King burger for dinner.

We spent the evening singing songs with his ukulele and he said that we could do duets tomorrow, so that I could earn my own keep.

30 June 2003, Monday

I was having a nice sleep until the rain came in and we had to seek shelter at the toilets once again.

Kwami and I began our busking stint at eight-thirty, outside Cardiff Central. We must have been good because the takings were up. When we broke for lunch I decided to sell my DVD player. Kwami took me to a second-hand goods merchant who offered me eighty pounds for it; ninety including the two Harry Potter disks. I had no choice but to take his pitiful offer.

I felt a bit low after that, but Kwami soon had me cheered up after another busking session, this time at Queen Street Station.

I treated us to dinner this evening. We pigged out on a seven ninety-nine bucket from KFC.

Tonight I told him that he was the first coloured bloke that I have even known.

'Coloured?' he said. 'Have you not noticed, Troy, that I am a black man? Coloured - Hugh! Do I have a rainbow emanating from my arse?'

'I'm sorry,' I said. 'I didn't mean to be racist.'

'Unfortunately, young Troy, racism is a human characteristic. We all have it within ourselves to be bigoted because of the way we are. It is how we control that instinct that decides whether we are racist or not. But we are really all racists.'

'I'm sorry,' I said.

'Don't be silly, Troy. The only way we could stop racism is by having all cloned men and all cloned women, but even then the cloned men would find something about the cloned women to abuse. It's totally wrong, but it is an incurable part of being a human being.'

'Yes,' I said.

'You are a white boy. The fact that I have noticed that technically makes me a racist, but you are my friend so I hope that will help you to forgive me for being a bigot. Having said that, you were not being racist, just curious.'

1 July 2003, Tuesday

It rained again in the early hours of the morning. I took the opportunity to finish my Harry Potter book. Later in the morning I sold it to the second-hand shop for three pounds.

We had another enjoyable day busking. I suppose that I can say that this is my first job. I can also say that I have officially left school.

I feel very lucky to have met Kwami. If it hadn't been for him, I don't know what would have happened to me. I feel like I've known him for ages, but I only met him on Saturday.

Somebody had thrown a copy of the *Western Mail* in one of the park bins. There was an article in it on a new housemate that has entered the *Big Brother* house because she is a local woman. Weirdly enough, she is from Penarth. I do miss being able to watch *Big Brother* but I am quite happy here with Kwami and I'm not gay or owt.

We went to a launderette this evening, where we washed our dirty clothes and ate a portion of chips.

2 July 2003, Wednesday

Isn't it typical that as soon as I have to start sleeping outside, we never get a night without rain!

We began busking at eight-thirty. During several breaks, Kwami told me about his website designer brother, who lives in London. He obviously misses him a great deal. He hasn't been in touch with him for over three years.

I told him that he could have my last forty-pounds but he said that he wouldn't dream of travelling there without me! I was quite moved by that.

We must have been performing well because some toff dropped a fifty-pound note into Kwami's ukulele case. Kwami called after him. He thought that he'd made a mistake but he just called back, 'Keep it! I've had a lucky day and I want to share it.'

We couldn't believe our luck. We packed up for the day and counted our takings, ninety-three pounds and thirty-two pence.

'Well, I think this has happened for a reason,' I told Kwami. 'It must be God's way of telling you to go and visit your brother.'

Kwami reiterated that he wanted me to go with him. I agreed and we booked tickets for tomorrow. We only had enough for a one-way ticket, thirty-two pounds each.

We still had enough left to enjoy a Chinese takeaway, just a portion of chicken fried rice each.

This evening we went to the swimming baths for a swim. It also meant that we could have a shower. We both stank.

I swam in my Saints shorts. After that we had twenty pounds left between us.

We spent another damp evening talking about, or I should say Kwami was talking about, what he and his brother used to get up to as boys in Ghana.

3 July 2003, Thursday

We were both awake early, albeit wearily. We knew that we would get some sleep on the train. Our train was due to leave at nine a.m. The three hours we had to wait seemed like an eternity, but it eventually passed and we were comfortably on the train where we had a breakfast of two rounds of toast and a cup of tea each.

After finishing that, it wasn't long before the monotonous rocking motion of the train sent both of us off to sleep.

In no time at all, it seemed (although it was two hours later), we arrived at Paddington Station. Then we caught the tube to New Cross and at one-fifteen we were standing outside a house preparing to knock on a door.

'I hope he still lives here, after all this' said Kwami.

With obvious trepidation, he took a deep breath and knocked on the door.

The fact that a black man answered the door wasn't for me a guarantee of it being his brother, as New Cross was full of people of various ethnic origins. The man, however, looked completely shocked to see who was standing at his door.

'Kwami? KWAMI!' And he flung his arms around him and kissed him very firmly on the cheek. Kwami hugged and kissed him back with equal enthusiasm.

Several minutes of keen reacquaintance followed before I was finally introduced and we were invited inside.

Kwami's brother, Koo, was very hospitable and immediately offered us refuge and full use of his house.

Better was to follow after he had gone out to fetch his daughter home from school.

In walked the absolutely stunning Ellie.

I got to know Ellie while Kwami and Koo prepared dinner. She has just turned fifteen and we seem to have clicked.

As the two reunited brothers were totally enthralled in each other's company and in catching up on the last three years, Ellie and I chatted and played music in her room.

They went out to the pub. We stayed in and watched Tim Henman get knocked out at Wimbledon again and *Big Brother.*

It was lovely to be able to sit down and watch TV again. After *Big Brother* had finished, Ellie went to bed.

I was left on my own in the living room. The pissed brothers staggered in at eleven-thirty. Kwami got the spare bedroom and I got the sofa. Kwami offered me the bed but I insisted on having the sofa, and it was wonderful to know that I was going to have a night of undisturbed sleep.

4 July 2003, Friday

I never thought that I would ever say that I enjoyed a boring day. It was nice to see Ellie first thing in her pyjamas. She went to school, though, and I spent the day listening to Koo and Kwami talking about old times.

I watched the Wimbledon matches when the rain let up.

This afternoon Koo showed me his website and business. He operates from home and I have to say it is very impressive.

He seemed impressed with my knowledge on the subject.

He sells African idols online. Apparently they have been bewitched by a witch doctor to relieve stress, or so he says. He showed me one of them. He had a huge stash of them in a cupboard. 'Produce of Tunisia' was stamped on all the boxes. I suppose, at least, they do come from Africa.

It was a welcome break from boredom when Ellie arrived home. We had a dinner of Spaghetti Bolognese, then Koo and Kwami went out to the pub.

Ellie and I talked about previous loves. It turns out that we both have none.

'Have you ever kissed a girl?' she asked.

'No I haven't,' I shyly admitted, having forgotten about the girl at the barbecue.

'I haven't kissed anyone yet either,' She confessed.

'Oh!' I said.

There was an uncomfortable pause and then she said words that were music to my ears. 'You can kiss me if you like.'

My knees and elbows suddenly began shaking as we leant to kiss each other. Her tongue shot straight into my mouth. It danced around like a pea in a whistle. It was absolutely wonderful.

We enjoyed it so much that we carried on kissing and cuddling, and as the evening went on I even stopped trembling.

We had to stop abruptly when we heard the door open and the brothers arrived home. Ellie went to bed and I had the most awful ache in my balls and my groin. It felt like someone had kicked me in the crotch a hundred times.

But I didn't care. I have achieved the first two of my romantic targets in one night.

5 July 2003, Saturday

There were some delightful looks and smiles from Ellie over the breakfast table this morning. Koo disappeared into his office to work for the morning and Kwami, Ellie and I played Monopoly.

It was quite frustrating not being able to touch her. Kwami won the game.

Koo emerged from his office at two o'clock and it didn't take much persuasion for Kwami to be tempted out to the pub.

As soon as the door slammed shut, Ellie's mouth and mine were cupped. She led me to her bed. My heart was racing with hope and excitement. In fact I got so excited that I made a bit of a mess of my pants.

I tried to put my hand down her knickers but she stopped my wandering hand.

I was moving too fast. Idiot!

I made an excuse saying that I could smell my own BO, so that I could take a shower and change my soiled underwear. Then the brothers returned with an Indian takeaway.

This evening we settled down to watch *Big Brother* but it wasn't on because there was a bomb scare at the studio. The brothers went out again and Ellie said that she was tired and that she was going to bed.

I was disappointed but tried to pretend that I wasn't. So I sat and watched TV until the brothers returned home, pissed. They both went straight to bed so I settled myself down on the settee.

She's obviously gone off me already.

6 July 2003, Sunday

I was awakened at around twelve-thirty a.m. Ellie was tapping me on the shoulder. 'I can't sleep. Can I have a cuddle?'

I was overjoyed as she climbed next to me on the settee. We kissed for a while but that was all.

I don't know how much later it was, but suddenly the light was on and Koo was raging, 'WHAT ARE YOU DOING WITH MY DAUGHTER YOU

SCUM?'

We both jumped up and pleaded our innocence, which was true. He didn't want to believe us.

He started running towards me and yelled, 'I'LL KILL YOU!' Ellie squealed, 'NO, DADDY!' and jumped out of the way. He was just about to grab me when Kwami appeared from nowhere and rugby-tackled him.

They wrestled on the living room floor for a few seconds before Kwami managed to pin his brother down, snarling and spitting insults in my direction. I could hear Ellie crying in the hallway.

'Get out, Troy,' Kwami called. 'Get your stuff and run away as far as you can. I can't hold him forever.'

'But I haven't done anything!' I pleaded.

'GO NOW!'

So I quickly grabbed my things and left. I'll never forget the look on Ellie's face as we exchanged glances before I shut the door behind me.

I was now alone in London at three o'clock in the morning, penniless. This is the first time that I wished none of this had happened and that I could go home.

I missed Ed and Griz, and the lads. What was I doing here?

I headed for the main road and started thumbing for a lift. Eventually a lorry driver stopped and picked me up.

I told him that I was heading for South Wales but he said that he was heading off up north, so he took me to the North Circular road and told me where to walk so that I could hitch to the M4.

A few drivers stopped but it was a while before I found someone that was heading for the M4. I did get lucky, though, because a lorry driver carrying second-hand office equipment picked me up and he was heading for Swansea. His name was Bob and he was kind enough to buy me a fillet burger and a Coke when we stopped off at a service station.

He dropped me off at a service station near Cardiff. It was ten a.m. and I was shattered. I soon got a lift into Cardiff city centre from a man driving a Ford KA almost identical to my stepfather's.

Even though I was desperately hungry, tiredness took over and I snoozed on my park bench for the rest of the morning and the first part of the afternoon. In the second part of the afternoon I sold my Gameboy Advance and my camera and got fifty pounds. I was finally able to get some food. I bought a large fish and chips but I couldn't eat it all for some reason. Then I tried my luck at an off-licence and bought myself a bottle of whisky.

I went to my park bench and started drinking the whisky. It was revolting but it made me feel so much better.

7 July 2003, Monday

I woke up with a thumping headache and the smell of alcohol and puke issuing from a puddle by my bench. The whisky bottle was lying empty close by. It suddenly dawned on me. There I was collapsed on a bench with an empty bottle of whisky lying beside me - like father like son! This was the final bit of evidence that I am Ricky Kinsella's son. Troy Kinsella!

It was after lunchtime before I started feeling a bit better. I went to the swimming pool to have an expensive shower but I needed it. I had a swim as well. Then I went to Burger King to while away the afternoon.

I retired to my bench. I so miss home but I can't go back after everything. I wish something would happen that would make me feel like it was worth not killing myself.

8 July 2003, Tuesday

Things just get worse and worse for me. Some bastard stole my money while I was sleeping. I am now officially destitute.

I sold my watch for a pitiful fiver and my Saints shirt for the same amount, and the bloke in the shop only bought it because it had got Matt Le Tissier's autograph on the back. I expect he'll sell it on eBay for forty.

So I had a McDonald's breakfast for two pounds and ninety-seven pence, including a cup of tea; lunch at Burger King, three pounds fourty-seven; and dinner at KFC, three pounds fourty-nine. I have got seven pence left.

Well I should sleep safe tonight as I now have nothing left worth stealing.

9 July 2003, Wednesday

It was stiflingly hot today. I had to swallow my pride and headed for the railway station ready to do some old-fashioned begging. I tore out a blank page from the back of my diary and wrote 'HOMELESS, PENNILESS, PLEASE HELP' on it.

I didn't know what time it was until I arrived there - eight twenty-seven.

My baseball cap was laid out in the hope of collecting cash. For half an hour I had received nothing. Then I put my last seven pence in the cap and gradually pennies started to drop into it.

By ten-thirty it had become quiet and I counted my hoard - three pounds seventy-one. So I bought two McChicken Sandwiches, some fries and a small Diet Coke. Then I headed back and set up in the same spot.

I don't know how long I had been sat there but somebody reached down and lifted me up by my T-shirt. He dragged me over to a corner snarling, 'I'm going to make you pay for what you did to my daughter.'

It was Koo. He had caught up with me. I just waited for the first painful blow. I heard the thud of fist against face but felt nothing.

'Come on ven!' called a familiar voice. The sun was in my eyes and I couldn't see who it was. I turned away from the light and caught a glimpse of Koo sprawled on the ground.

I picked up my bag and cap and I was literally frog-marched away from the scene.

''ello yeah I've farned 'im.'

That voice was very familiar. I looked back to see who my rescuer was. 'SHIT!' It was Pitbull. He had caught up with me as well. He was on the phone, so it was easy to shake him off. I ran as fast as I could.

'NO, TROY! IT'S ALL RIGHT COME BACK 'ERE!' He yelled after me. I rounded a bend and was caught by somebody else.

'LET ME GO, PLEASE!' I begged. 'THERE'S A MAN AFTER ME.'

The man put his arms around me. 'It's all right son,' he said.

'Dad?'

Pitbull soon arrived, panting and perspiring profusely.

'Oh fank gord fer vat!' He puffed.

'Come on, mate,' said Dad. 'Let's go home'.

I wasn't in a position to refuse.

We were soon all sat in the car; Dad and Pitbull in the front and me in the back.

As we pulled out of the car park, Pitbull craned his neck to say, 'What you did savin' my boy after all what we dun to yer! I'll never forget vat.' He reached his hand through the gap between the two front seats to shake my hand.

I shook his hand and he gave me a smile, which was so unlike him. He looked kind. 'I'm sorry,' he said. He looked like he was going to cry and he sniffed and wiped his eyes as he turned to face the front. 'Vat's ze problem wiv vis wever. Bloody pollen!'

'Yeah!' said Dad. He raised his voice as he spoke to me. 'It'll be all right soon, son.'

It was a long, silent drive back to Southampton. I pretended to be asleep to prevent any inane conversation.

On the ferry Dad, bought me shepherd's pie and chips. It was delicious. Pitbull apologised again when Dad popped to the loo.

He told me that if I ever needed anything in future, I was just to call him.

As we got into the car and prepared to drive off the ferry and into East Cowes, I started get the worst butterflies in my stomach I had ever had.

The floating bridge was in, for a change, and Pitbull said his goodbyes and walked home. In no time at all we were parked up in our driveway.

I had hardly got out of the car before Mum had thrown her arms around me. She spouted some highly emotional stuff that I couldn't decipher, slapped me around the face saying, 'How could you do this to me?' Then she tearfully hugged me again. She hugged me so hard it felt like Grandad, then I realised that it was Grandad hugging me as well.

Dad prised them off me and allowed me to go into the house and let me take a wonderful long bath.

I stayed in there for an hour: then had a shave and got dressed.

When I walked into the front room they were all gathered around the dinner table. Mum, Dad, and Nan and Grandad Stenning. Even Griz was looking at me in an expectant way. It was wonderful to see him. I gave him a huge cuddle and he reciprocated with lots of licks and tail wags. Then I sat down to face the music.

There was a short silence, then Dad spoke. 'Now I want you to be completely honest. What on earth happened to make you put us through the last few weeks? I don't believe that Pete had as much to do with it as he thinks he did. Was it your exams, girls, drugs?'

'NO!'

'Well what then?' said Mum, her eyes red and wet.

I then explained about the diary I found in Nan and Grandad's wardrobe and about my suspicions that Mum had been seeing Spud and all the other things that had made me act in such an impulsive way.

'What diary?' Mum asked. I fetched the diary and showed all of them the evidence.

'This is silly, Troy,' Mum said. 'This is your Dad.' She grabbed Dad's forearm. 'It's obvious!'

'Not when you read this!' I said, passing her the letter from Kinsella.

She took time to read it and pushed it to the middle of the table. 'This is bollocks!' she exclaimed, 'The man was delusional! You were four weeks premature for f***'s sake! Sorry Mum! It is biologically impossible for anybody other than your father to be your father. Want proof? Right! Wait here!' She got up and left the room.

Dad was flicking through Mum's diary. Grandad Stenning was whisper-grumbling to Nan about Kinsella.

Mum returned with another diary and slammed it down in front of me opened at:

Friday January 23rd 1987
Joy! Relief! Ultrasound revealed my due date to be July 20th. My baby is Kevin's. At last I can really look forward to this baby.

Then she turned the pages to:

Sunday June 21st 1987
I've had a show! I think. I'm panicking now. It's four weeks to go. Too soon.

Monday June 22nd 1987
I went into full-blown labour just after midnight and Kev rushed me in. I was frantic with worry. I really thought that I was losing the baby. The midwives were wonderful but I was too far gone and gave birth at 4.27 a.m. A beautiful boy, who is, thank God, the spitting image of his dad. 4 lb 9 oz. He's in an incubator but they say he's doing fine. It's early but not too early.

I felt very stupid for a moment, then I remembered my illegitimate brother. 'What about Peter?'

'You'll meet him tomorrow,' Dad said. 'He's coming around for tea.'

I felt confused, and stupid. Seventy-five per cent of my reasons for leaving had just been quashed. Desperately tired, I just wanted to ask Dad one question. 'How did you find me?'

'Bank statement!' he said with a curl of his lip. 'But we'll talk about that later.'

Oh my God! All that money! What have I done?

Being tucked up in my own bed at last gave me a similar feeling to when I was tucked up in bed at the Hilton Hotel a couple of weeks ago.

Despite everything, it's great to be home.

I wonder how far this Peter will have to travel to get here. I hope he doesn't stay the night.

10 July 2003, Thursday

A glorious night's sleep was halted when Mum came in with a cup of tea. She sat on my bed.

'Why didn't you talk to us? Are we that frightening that you can't approach us and ask us face to face?'

'I'm really sorry, Mum.'

'Well, at least you're back now and things can start getting back to normal.' She winced and placed her hand on her sizeable bump.

'Was that a kick?' I asked. Mum nodded and placed my hand on her belly. The baby kicked my hand, surprisingly strongly.

'Looks like another footballer in the family is on the way,' Mum said softly.

I looked at my clock radio. It was nearly midday! I heard the doorbell ring and Dad poked his head around the door. I noticed that his knuckles were all red and bruised. 'Somebody for you, Troy,' he said.

I put on my dressing gown and headed for the front door. It was Pitbull and his younger son, still with what must be a permanent line of snot on his upper lip.

''Allo, mate,' said Pitbull. 'Liam's got summing'e wants ta say t' ya.' He gave his son a nudge.

'Fank you uncle Twoy,' Liam squeaked. Then he put his arms around my waist and hugged me. He left a patch of snot on my dressing gown as he went back to his father.

'We got you a present,' said Pitbull. He handed me a brown paper bag and I took out the contents. It was a brand new wallet with five pounds in it. I looked up at him and was almost hypnotised by the look of kindness in his eyes.

'Thanks,' I said in a way that didn't reflect my gratitude.

'A late birfday present,' he said.

Pitbull insisted on taking a photograph of me with Liam. They then left and I went to the kitchen to put my dressing gown into the washing machine.

Nan was in there, hand-washing Grandad's trousers.

'Washing machine broken down has it?' I asked.

Nan told me that she was trying to get bloodstains out using Vanish Oxy. He and Dad had trouble changing a wheel last night.

After I had got dressed, Mum and Dad gave me my birthday presents. It was a bit weird because I had forgotten all about it.

A brand new Saints shirt was the first thing I opened. Then I opened 'Donkey Kong Country' for the Gameboy Advance that I used to have.

I got a card with fifty pounds inside from Nan and Grandad Brown and one with sixty from the Stennings.

It was all a bit put on, but I appreciated it. Then Mum said, 'there is something else we need to tell you.'

I braced myself but it didn't help the blow, 'Your grandfather had a heart attack a couple of weeks ago. He's getting better, though. He's in St Mary's. That's why he hasn't been to see you.'

I hadn't even thought of Grandad through all this. Was it worrying about me that set off the attack?

I went to the hospital with Dad, who now had a bandage wrapped around his hand.

Grandad was full of spirits and was delighted to see me. He was on form with his wittiness, and the only way you would have known that he was unwell was because there were loads of tubes coming out of him. I hope that me coming home will help him to get better.

Ed, Tom and Meat came to see me this afternoon. It was wonderful to see them. I never realised how much I had missed them. We had a great laugh catching up, but my departure meant that THROB missed out on the audition for *Rock Stars The Bands*. The group have now officially split up.

Jason and Kelly have split up. Spud is going back out with Lara and the amazing thing is I don't care.

They all left when Dad let me know that Nan and Grandad Stenning were leaving. So, after a quick bear hug and slobbery kiss, they were off.

Just before tea, Spud turned up. I was surprised that he was allowed in as I was nervously awaiting the arrival of Peter. There was an uncomfortable ten minutes or so while he asked me what I had been up to and I gave him the shortest answers possible. Then Mum started serving tea.

'Aren't we waiting for Peter to arrive?' I asked.

'He's here!' Mum said.

'Where?' I asked.

'You're sat next to him,' Mum replied.

'Ha ha ha, very funny. This is Spud, Mum! aka S-t-u-a-r-t. Not P-e-t-e-r.'

'Stuart is the name his adoptive parents gave him. Peter is the name I gave him. Stuart Peter Hudd.'

I felt the blood draining from my face. I was suddenly struck dumb.

'I've been trying to give you hints for ages,' Spud said.

I felt rage building up inside me. 'How long have you known?'

'Since Christmas. I dropped a big hint in the postcard I sent you from Turkey.'

'What big hint?'

'I can't remember it word for word but it was something about the beer running out at Uncle Ron's and missing you. If you take the first letter of every word it spelt 'I am your brother.''

'Couldn't you have just TOLD ME?'

'I couldn't! I promised Mum.'

'Who? My mum, your mum or OUR MUM!'

I was suddenly screaming with rage. 'F***ING HELL!' I kicked the pouffe across the room and stormed out of the house.

Dad started to follow me. 'Where are you going?'

'Don't worry!' I called. 'I'm just going for a long walk. I'm not leaving the island.'

It was a long walk as well. Two hours up and down the coastal road between Gurnard and Cowes. It ended when I decided to walk through the town. I saw a poster with my face on it in the window of the icafé. I went over to take a closer look. The word 'missing' was above my face and someone had stuck a 'Found' sticker at the bottom.

'Ah, the traveller returns!' said Vernon through the window.

He then apologised because he thought that it was his fault that I'd run off.

I spent the next half an hour explaining the whole story to him. It made me feel a hell of a lot better to get it all off my chest.

'It's just as well Kinsella isn't your dad,' he said when I'd finished spinning my yarn.

'Why do you say that?' I asked.

'Because someone put him in hospital last night. Beat the shit out of him. He's on life support and everything.'

My God! Dad had bruised knuckles and Grandad had blood on his trousers. Either of them had a good motive.

I then headed home. When I got there, Spud had left and Mum and Dad were sat on the sofa looking very worried.

'It's all right!' I said. 'I've calmed down now. Just give me some time. Please.'

'Okay, son!' Dad said.

'Oh!' I remembered. 'Sorry I swore!'

11 July 2003, Friday

This bloke from the *County Press* came around this morning to interview me about my running away. I gave him as little real information as possible. He took my picture with Mum and Dad.

Spud came around after lunch, with Lara (for emotional support I suppose). Lara hugged me and apologised for being horrible to me. She was yet another person who felt responsible for my actions. I wonder how many more people think it is their fault?

Spud went on about all the subtle clues he tried to give me, even ringing the coded letters on his postcard from Turkey.

Apparently, the songs he was trying to get THROB to play were another clue. 'Caravan of Love' has the line 'He's my brother' in it and the song 'He Ain't Heavy, He's My Brother', speaks for itself.

A lot calmer than last night, I just said, 'Either tell me straight or don't tell me at all.'

Then he said that he hoped that we could soon start being brothers. I told him, as kindly as I could bearing in mind that I plainly don't want him as my brother, that it would take some time for me to get used to the idea.

'I was sorry to hear about Kinsella,' I said to change the subject.

'What about him?'

'Oh, sorry, I thought you'd know. He's in hospital on life support. Someone beat him up the other night.'

'Ah well, serves him right the drunken bastard,' Spud said. 'Somebody was bound to retaliate to his insults one day.'

I thought that was a strange reaction. Maybe he doesn't know that Kinsella's his dad, I thought to myself.

The conversation moved on to my adventure, now that Lara had got over her awkwardness. When the subject was worn out I asked Spud, 'Did Mum say anything about who your dad was?' His face dropped. 'Oh, sorry. You don't mind me asking do you?'

'No, of course not. She said that she doesn't know because she was paralytic at a party and someone took advantage.'

This is excellent. I have some ammunition against Spud.

When they had left, I casually told Mum that Spud didn't know who his father was.

'I know,' she said.

'Well, under the circumstances, don't you think it would be a good idea to tell him?'

'Have you already forgotten your reaction when you thought he was your father?'

Touché!

'Don't tell him, Troy.'

'Okay' I said. She then gave me a hug and I enjoyed doing an evil smile over her shoulder, a là Janine Butcher from *Eastenders* .

Now I have got to think of some coded way to let him know the truth.

Big Brother was good tonight. That Lisa from Penarth was evicted, but the previously evicted Jon was voted back in.

12 July 2003, Saturday

Mum and Dad reaffirmed their invitation to take me to Blackpool with them in a couple of weeks time. I agreed once they had made it quite clear that Spud would not be joining us.

A scorching hot day. I went down to Gurnard with Ed, Tom, Meat, Jason and, unfortunately, Spud. We met some of the girls down there - Lara, Kylie and Katie.

We sunbathed quietly. A grumpy Terry joined us with a stunning black eye. Nobody asked until we got a moment alone together. He told me that his dad found out that he was gay the other day and went ballistic. Poor sod.

He also told me that he was joining the army. I said, 'I'm surprised you aren't joining the Navy' before I realised that it might upset him, but to my relief he started laughing.

'Nice one mate,' he chortled, 'At least I've got one loyal friend around here.'

For one worrying moment I thought he was going to hug me, but we just gave each other a knuckle-to-knuckle greeting.

When I went in for my dinner, Mum told me that we would be getting two foreign exchange students on Monday, for a week. She had spent the day preparing the spare bedroom, which is next to mine.

Fingers crossed it will be two girls. Foreign girls are less inhibited about sex, or so I have heard.

This evening the first episode of *Rock Stars The Bands* was on. That git, Chris's was on with his band playing my song 'I Hope the Answer Will Be Yes'. He had changed some of the lyrics, but it was still my song. Bastard! They got through to the next round as well.

13 July 2003, Sunday

Nan came round for lunch today. Grandad will be allowed to go home tomorrow, if the doctors give the go ahead. He will need a heart bypass operation but there is a bit of a waiting list.

Dad said he would pay for private treatment but doubts he has enough money left. That made me feel terrible, as it was me who squandered thousands on my jaunt to Wales. If it prevents Grandad from getting the treatment he needs, I will regret my actions for the rest of my life.

After lunch a policeman came round to ask us if we had seen anything of Ricky Kinsella's attack or whether we knew if he had any enemies. Some lies were told.

Another caller this afternoon was Karl Sibley. He looked as though he'd been trying to pluck up the courage to come and see me, and when he told me that it was him that nearly ran over Pitbull's son, Liam, I understood why. He thought that he was partly to blame for my departure.

I assured him that it had nothing to do with him and we went out for a drive.

We went to Bessie's Butties. Jugs was there but was obviously not wearing a bra because her tits were hanging so low that she looked like she had an exaggerated beer gut.

She was happy to admit that she found that her bra had been chafing her in the extreme heat of the day. It was thirty-one degrees today.

When I got home, Mum was sunbathing in the back garden. She looked horrendous with her massive, moving bulge. Yuk!

This evening I attended a lecture by Mr Kevin Brown entitled, 'You'd better get yourself a job soon, otherwise you are going back to school in September'.

He's right, unfortunately.

14 July 2003, Monday

Dad took the day off work and dragged me to Newport and the Job Centre.

There were plenty of summer jobs available but it was a bit pointless applying for any of them when we are going away soon. However, I humoured Dad and put my name down on some sort of register. Later, in the afternoon, we drove over the floating bridge to Red Funnel's car ferry terminal in East Cowes. There we awaited the arrival of the latest group of foreign students. The two girls that joined us are fourteen and Austrian. One is a bit of a loudmouth. She is what *The Sun* would describe as a freckly, roly-poly, ginger, curly-haired girl called Greta. The other girl, Monica,is a slim, dark-haired girl with no redeeming features bar a hairy mole on her top lip. They both seem quite nice and can speak very good English. We took them home and allowed them to settle into the spare room while Mum cooked dinner. After dinner they went out to meet up with some of their friends. Ed phoned me to say that one of the girls staying with them was gorgeous. So I went around there to investigate. He wasn't wrong. Eva is about five feet tall with ample breasts, a minute waist and she is beautifully broad across the beam. Ed was already in an advanced state of smarminess, which obviously gets lost in translation because most British girls would have told him to get lost ages ago. However, it was working a treat on Eva who giggled at every word Ed said. I left him to it, feeling a bit jealous, as I was left with my pair of munters. I didn't see Monica and Greta again this evening as they sneaked straight into their room when they got in.

15 July 2003, Tuesday

Mum told me today that we are getting an au pair when we get back from Blackpool. One of our former foreign exchange students, a Swedish girl called Annicka, has always kept in touch since she stayed with us in 1999.

She even came for a visit two years ago, when she brought her brother with her. But that visit went a bit stale for me when Annicka caught me rummaging through her knickers. When I realised she was watching me I was busy sniffing a crusty pair. I was sniffing them extra hard because, despite the crustiness, all they smelt of was fabric conditioner.

It took me a long while to get over the embarrassment.

Now the eighteen-year-old Annicka will be returning and, I suspect, keeping her knickers out of my reach.

When Greta and Monica came home after their group meeting I played badminton in the front garden with them. I managed to make Ed's smarminess look like charm. It seems to be working. Lots of giggling.

This evening was spent chatting and messing around in their room. I really enjoyed it.

Although I don't fancy either of them, I still imagined what it would be like to have sex with them.

Mind you, I seem to do that with any unrelated female I meet these days. Am I a pervert?

16 July 2003, Wednesday

It's funny how a crop of wiry hair growing out of a mole can be hideous and similar hair growing out of a vulva can be exquisite. Monica's mole was difficult to keep your eyes off, as droplets of milk kept on getting caught in the hair as she ate her cornflakes this morning.

I got a phone call from the Job Centre. A DIY shop in Cowes is looking for a shop junior, so I went down there for an on-the-spot interview.

The shop manager is called Colin. He is a softly spoken man and seemed very nice. After showing me around the shop he asked me a few questions, which I answered, then he asked me when I could start. I told him that my parents had booked a holiday at the end of July. He said that he could see no problem with that. It would be taken out of my holiday entitlement.

So I start on Monday. I can hardly believe it. I've got a job. I can leave school. The only problem is working Saturdays, but I'm hoping to negotiate that once I've got my foot in the door.

Mum was really pleased. I was hugged, of course. Ed was chuffed as well. He told me that he thinks he will probably go back to school and take his 'A' levels.

Spud paid Mum a visit this afternoon. I was in such a good mood that I didn't mind. He told me that he was thinking of going to the Tech College to learn to be a builder. The Austrian girls arrived while Spud was still here and he told me that he reckons Monica has got her eye on me. I don't know where he got that idea from.

The funny thing is that this evening I was tidying my room when there was a knock on the door. It was Greta.

'Monica has asked me to tell you zat she theenks you are handsome,' she announced.

'Oh!' I said, totally stunned.

'Do you er like her?'

'Well, yes. Of course I like her.'

'Good!' And, before I could say another word, Greta turned on her heals and left, shutting the door behind her.

A minute or so later there was another knock on the door. I expected to see Greta as I said, 'Come in.'

Monica stood there, smiling shyly.

'Hello,' I said.

'Hello. Do you like me?' Monica asked.

'Of course I do,' I said, again.

She then advanced on me. 'I like you too.' And before I knew it her arms were around my neck and her tongue was in my mouth.

It was nice, but I had to turn the light off to take my mind off her face. We fell on the bed and kissed and cuddled passionately for ages. Eventually I plucked up the courage to put my hand up her top. To my pleasure and relief she didn't resist as I cupped her left breast in my hand. I felt her nipple but I didn't know what I was supposed to do with it and she certainly wasn't going to tell me.

Our encounter ended when we heard footsteps along the hallway and Monica hid behind my bedroom door - wisely, as it happens, because Mum poked her head around the door to check on me.

Monica gave me a final passionate kiss, which wasn't so pleasant with the light on, then she went back to her room.

I went to bed, feeling rather full of myself. I have achieved level five, but still need to achieve levels three and four to even things out. Especially level three.

17 July 2003, Thursday

As I was settling down to sleep last night and reminiscing about my clinch with Monica, I realised that I couldn't feel the hairs on her mole while I was kissing her, and when I saw her first thing this morning it appeared that she had trimmed them.

She beamed at me over breakfast, which was sweet. I might as well go along with this attention because she leaves on Sunday. They left after breakfast and went to school to meet up with their chums.

I went to Ed's and told him all about it.

'She's not too bad,' he said, 'What's the matter with you? She's fourteen though, isn't she?'

'Yes.'

'Hmmmm. Bit dodgy,' Ed pouted.

'Well Spud the Stud always used to say 'If the roof's thatched move in,''I retorted.

'Yeah, and he also said, 'If it bleeds shag it!' Which pissed me off because he said that the week my then eleven-year-old sister started her periods. She's still only a kid two years later.'

'Yes, but they think differently on the continent, don't they?' I argued.

'I suppose so.'

I don't know why I was arguing the point. I don't think it is very likely that sex is on the cards. He might be a bit shitty because he has failed in his attempts to get off with sexy Eva.

This evening we had another session of passionate smooching. This time I tried to put my hand down her knickers, but the same thing happened that had happened in London. She grabbed my hand to stop me. She did move it up to her breast though.

Things came to an end when I told her I was tired, when really I couldn't stand the pain in my testicles any more.

18 July 2003, Friday

I have made page two of the *Isle of Wight County Press* There is a picture of me with Liam and the heading 'Hero Runaway Returns'.

Cowes boy Troi Brown, 16, who ran away last month after saving little Liam Bull, 6, from certain death, has returned, enabling Liam to thank his hero.

Liam's father, Peter 36, of Arctic Road, Cowes, said, 'Troi is the whole family's hero. He doesn't know what he's done for us saving Liam from that speeding car.'

When asked about Mr Brown's disappearance Mr Bull added, 'We had a problem with each other which got out of hand, mostly my fault. I bullied him, I suppose, and I'm very, very sorry that he felt so bad that he had to run away. That's why I went up with his father to help find him.'

Mr Bull went on to say that Mr Brown should receive an award for his actions.

They could have spelt my name right!

Reading the paper this morning, it is reported that Southampton's star player, Wayne Bridge, has put in a transfer request. He wants to move to Chelsea as they now have a millionnaire new chairman who has made one hundred and twenty million pounds available for players. His wages are likely to be trebled. I wish some super-rich Russian would take over our club. It really annoys me that we can't compete with the wages clubs like that can pay. I expect James Beattie will be the next to go.

Also, Portsmouth play their first league game at midday on August the sixteenth, so if they win they will top the Premiership for three hours. They will be able to brag that they have been top of the Premiership - something Saints have never achieved. They may also finish the first weekend above us as we are playing away from home and are likely to lose.

I went to school today for the last time. It was strange putting on my school uniform again. We all went in to spend a morning saying goodbye to one another. We had a party in our form room - nothing too mad, just cake (made by Miss Steele) and red spray dye for our hair.

We had an assembly before lunch and Mr Bartlett said goodbye to all of those that were leaving and wished us all luck.

Apparently we are the best year he can remember in his time as headmaster. I'm sure he said that last year.

There were tears when we were told that we could all go. Lots of hugs from the girls. That was nice. I went home.

When Monica and Greta came home from school, Monica said that I could play for the Austrian team in a football tournament at Cowes High tomorrow. All the various nationalities represented in the foreign exchange company called EF will have teams. That should be a laugh.

I watched *Big Brother* in my room tonight with Monica and Greta. Monica pretended to get jealous when she asked me if I thought evictee, Nush, was pretty. I was, of course, totally honest and said, 'She is beautiful.'

'Do you seenk I'm bootyfool?' she asked, bottom lip protruding and looking up at me through fluttering eyelashes.

I stupidly hesitated and she got up, gave me a formal kiss on the cheek and left my room saying, 'I'm tired, goodnight.'

19 July 2003, Saturday

I wearily got up for breakfast at nine (much earlier than usual, for a Saturday). Monica was giving me the silent treatment, but as soon as Mum cleared away the breakfast things she had her arms around me saying, 'I'm very sorry. Do you forgeeve me?'

I gave her a peck on the lips, by way of showing forgiveness, even though there was nothing to forgive. I noticed her mole stubble when we kissed. When we sat down to watch the Saturday morning television programmes, I noticed Dad showing some bloke the car. Then the bloke drove off in it. Dad has sold the car to raise money for Grandad's operation. I feel terrible.

I went down to the pontoon to see Terry off with Ed, Meat, Katie and the Jasons. He is off to start his Army training. Jason Ince was struggling to keep it together. It was difficult watching Terry say goodbye to his mum and his brother and seeing the strange lack of affection from his father. It was also strange to see the usually hardnut Terry almost in tears as he waved from the window of brand new Red Jet Four as it sped away from the terminal.

Spud turned up late and missed the whole thing. He was dressed very smartly.

'Sorry I'm late. I was at an interview,' he announced.

He had alighted from the Red Funnel office.

'What job are you going for?' Katie asked.

'Kinsella still hasn't come out of his coma, so they are temporarily filling his position - hopefully with me - and if he snuffs it I might get the job for good!'

I bit my lip so hard that I nearly drew blood.

This afternoon I thought that I was going to be playing football for the Austrian EF team, but the Austrian boys took exception to me so I ended up hanging around the changing rooms with Monica. I kissed her a lot, but it was more for her benefit than for mine.

When we got home, Dad was cleaning his new car - an L reg Seat Ibiza. It cost him four hundred pounds with a year's MOT and Tax. He could see that I was looking guilty. He told me not to worry as the operation would cost more money than I squandered in Wales.

They say that to enjoy pleasure you have to suffer pain, and my pleasure of spending two nights in the Hilton Hotel will be paid back with the pain of being crammed into the back of a Seat Ibiza on a three-hundred-mile car journey next week.

After watching Chris's band 'Panache' go through on *Rock Stars The Bands* this evening, I enjoyed my last night of kissing and cuddling with Monica, who cried when we said goodnight. I said that I would write to her.

20 July 2003, Sunday

I had to walk down to the ferry terminal in East Cowes this morning because there wasn't enough room in the car for me with Mum, Dad, Greta and Monica.

Monica and I exchanged a more formal kiss than we were used to as we said our goodbyes, and then they left with the rest of their group.

After that, I got a place in the car and we went to see Grandad. Nan is living with him at the moment to look after him.

He got quite emotional when Dad told him that he was going to pay for him to go private for his operation. They hugged, and Mum and Nan also had sore looking eyes.

We couldn't take them out, so Mum and Nan cooked a lovely roast chicken dinner for us all. Grandad's portion had more vegetables and less gravy than the rest of us.

We spent most of the afternoon there, watching the climax of the Open Golf Championship on television.

Grandad even found some time for a bit of banter with me. I said, 'When you're better I'll have to arrange a thrashing for you on our golf course.'

He barked (mock sharply), 'WHAT?'

I said, 'Eh?'

He growled, 'Whaduya mean?'

I said, 'Whaduya mean? Whaduya mean?'

He said, 'Whaduya mean? Whaduya mean? Whaduya mean?' And so on.

This evening I compiled a CD of my favourite songs for the trip up to Blackpool. I copied Blur's 'Crazy Beat' twenty times. I completely love that song.

I am going to fall asleep listening to it as I am having an early night ready for work tomorrow.

21 July 2003, Monday

Mum woke me up this morning with a cup of tea and a plate of toast. Nice service!

I put on my best shirt and trousers, watched *GMTV*, then set off for the town.

Cowes DIY is right opposite the marina, which is quite busy at the moment in the wake of the recent Admirals Cup and the forthcoming Cowes Week Regatta, which we will miss because of our holiday.

I arrived early and had to wait for Colin to arrive and open up.

'What are you dressed like that for? You'll get those ruined,' he said as I followed him through the door. 'Go home and change into something that you don't mind getting dirty.'

So an hour later (changed into jeans and a T-shirt) I arrived at the shop again to belatedly start my first day's work.

I was first introduced to Bill who claimed to be a Scouser but the only accent I could detect was a local one. He was tall and gaunt with a seventies-style mop of mousy hair, and side-burns.

Then I was taken to the back of the shop to meet Jean, a short, giggly woman with short, jet black hair. Colin left me with Jean, who spent the morning showing me how to weigh out portions of pet foods and bag them up.

It was also my job to make the tea when Bill requested it and sweep the shop when it was quiet.

I hoped that I might get a chance to serve customers at the till but it didn't happen.

At lunchtime I went to see Vernon. He told me he'd just seen Spud who spent his lunch break in a similar way.

Kinsella still hasn't regained consciousness. This was a state he was used to in his heyday. Vernon said that he'd heard that Kinsella's brother had been visiting him in hospital. He is a doctor in Cork, Ireland. So at least *he* didn't make a mess of his career.

This afternoon I had to cut sheets of plywood with a handsaw. It was very hard work. I ended up with a blister on my thumb. When five-thirty eventually arrived I was really knackered.

I watched *Sky Sports News* during dinner and saw that Wayne Bridge had joined Chelsea. He didn't look right with a blue shirt. Southampton have signed Chelsea's Graeme Le Saux as a replacement.

22 July 2003, Tuesday

I had a chat with Bill this morning. It was Colin's day off. I won't be having a day off during the week because I won't be working on Saturday.

Bill told me that he was a single man in his forties and he doesn't like children. He calls them trainee human beings. I still didn't get to have a go on the till and Bill hinted that I probably wouldn't get a chance in the near future. My job was general dogsbody, or as he calls it, shop floor technician.

We had a delivery before lunch, which I had to lug into the shop and then check against a list before either opening up and stocking on the shop shelves or stowing away in our storeroom.

The twenty-five-kilo bags of cement were the hardest to carry. Bill said that he couldn't help with those because of his dodgy back.

Vernon and I spent lunchtime ogling the women that walked past the icafé.

Jean worked a half-day today, so I looked after the pick-and-pack end of the shop.

This evening I went round to Ed's house and we played on his X-Box for a while until about nine forty-five when I went home to watch *Big Brother*.

I can't make my mind up who I want to win. There are four people to chose from Cameron, from the Orkneys, he says that he believes that the Bible is true and that he disagrees with gay people having the same rights as straight ones because the Bible says that man should not lie with man.

The Bible has been translated several times in the past two thousand years, but who knows what is the right way of interpreting it? If it were that easy, then there wouldn't be so many branches of Christianity.

Saying man should not lie with man implies that it is wrong to be a homosexual, yet it doesn't say that man should not lie with child and we all know that to be totally wrong.

I think that a lot of the Bible's true meanings have been lost in countless translations. It basically preaches that man should be good, kind and love everybody, which is the thing that everyone should take notice of. If a gay man or woman loves someone of the same sex, that is a wonderful thing. How can it be wrong? I must admit, though, the thought of kissing a bloke makes my stomach turn.

Continuing on the subject of *Big Brother*, there is Steph, a dinky Brummie woman who spends the whole time in the house gasping and yapping in a high-pitched voice. When the beautiful Nush left on Friday, Steph was relieved as she couldn't bear the fact that the men in the house fancied Nush and not her.

Hot-headed Irishman, Ray, has been entertaining, but he flies off the handle at the drop of a hat and has spent most of his time in the house breaking the rules. It is blatantly obvious that all he is interested in is the seventy-grand prize money.

Finally, Scott seems a great bloke but he is a Scouser and I said from the beginning that I didn't want him to win.

Ah the shallowness of being a *Big Brother* fan.

23 July 2003, Wednesday

Today wasn't much fun and it wasn't much like shop work as I spent the whole day clearing rubbish from the backyard. The only time I saw the interior of the shop was when I arrived, during my lunch break and when I finished.

I don't really want to spend my working life watching the clock and wishing for the end of the day.

I asked my dad tonight how much it would cost for Grandad's heart bypass. His answer made me feel a bit better because my spend-up is a drop in the ocean by comparison. It will cost nearly fifty grand. Grandad is paying most of it himself from his savings and the money he got from Great Nan's estate in January.

Spud came round this evening to see Mum. I put up with him and even stayed in the room as we exchanged tales of our first few days at work.

He seems to be having a better time than me. After he had finished chatting with Mum, we went into my room for a chat.

I asked him how he was getting on with Lara.

'Oh great. I think she's the one,' he said.

'You said that about Christine,' I remarked.

'That was just a smokescreen. To keep you guessing.'

'So you didn't shag her then?'

'Nowhere near it. She's a bit old for me, mate. And she's a mate of my mum's. We're good friends.'

I was so close to asking Christine all about their relationship just before I ran away.

Such a lot of deception. No wonder I was confused.

24 July 2003, Thursday

Today was a bit of a mixed bag at work. It was Bill's day off and at least I didn't have to do such menial tasks.

I cut up wood, sorted out seeds, weighed out bags of rabbit food, posted letters at the post office and did the banking.

Lunch was spent at the icafé. Spud was there this time. Vernon must have told him that I had my lunch break between twelve-thirty and one. He made small talk about my forthcoming holiday. I humoured him.

This evening I went round to Ed's house. Tom and Meat were there. Tom told me that he had got a summer job working at Bessie's Butties.

'How the hell do you get out to Bembridge?' I asked.

'The bus leaves from the pontoon,' Tom explained.

'That must cost a fortune.'

'Nah! Bessie pays for it.'

The others and I exchanged looks but said nothing.

Meat said that he was going to go back to school in September, which is good because Ed will have some company.

25 July 2003, Friday

My last day before my holiday was a slow one. I filled in for Jean. Ed popped in for a visit while I was filling bags of Irish moss peat. He hung around so that I could spend lunch with him. It meant that I didn't have to meet up with Spud. I didn't tell him that though. He would have wanted to meet up with him. We went to Tiffins.

I was amazed when I opened my wage packet. Four hundred and thirteen pounds and ten pence!

'Don't get too excited, Troy,' Colin said when he saw my jaw drop. 'This is your holiday pay as well. So, in fact, it is three weeks wages.'

'Thanks,' I said.

'You've done well this week. Keep it up and enjoy your holiday.'

The shops were closed, so I couldn't treat myself to anything and, when I got home, Mum told me that I would now have to pay my 'keep', as she called it.

'How much will that be.' I asked, apprehensively?

'Your dad and I have decided on fifty pounds a week.'

I disappointedly handed over a hundred and fifty pounds.

I spent the evening packing and watching boring Cameron win *Big Brother*. I had eventually voted for Scott.

26 July 2003, Saturday

I was turfed out of bed at four-thirty so that we could catch the five-thirty car ferry from East Cowes.

The roads were clear and, despite several piss stops (Mum's constricted bladder), we arrived in Blackpool at eleven-forty. Dad drove straight into the town so that Mum could book tickets for Andrew Lloyd-Webber's *Cats* show, then we headed along the speed camera-guarded coastal road through Cleveleys to Fleetwood where we checked in at the Cala Gran holiday camp.

Our caravan was supposed to be top graded, but it absolutely stank of BO, cigarettes and sick. We opened up all the windows as it was hot and stuffy. Mum sprayed everything with Febreeze.

Everything was unpacked and we had a KFC dinner before settling in for the evening.

27 July 2003, Sunday

Today we went to Blackpool Zoo. Mum spent a lot of the day in the zoo's various toilets. I found it a bit boring, but the red pandas and the lemurs were cute.

It was a relief when we headed into Blackpool town and found the

Buccaneer's Bar where we enjoyed a delicious roast turkey carvery. Dad was well pleased as it was quite reasonably priced.

We headed back to Cala Gran and enjoyed the facilities at the complex. I beat Dad at bowling. Mum and Dad had several very competitive games of air hockey, which Dad eventually won, probably due to Mum's condition as I completely thrashed him when I played him.

Mum went off to play bingo while me and Dad had lots of games of pool, then we went back to the caravan and bed.

28 July 2003, Monday

It was raining as we got up this morning, so we decided to go to Blackpool Tower for the day.

Mum had a bit of a funny turn in the lift on the way up and got fussed over by the smelly lift attendant. When we reached the top, Dad and I helped her to a seat and she soon started feeling better. She said the smell of the lift attendant and vertigo had had a funny effect on her.

It had stopped raining and the view from the tower was genuinely breath-taking.

We left the tower for an hour so that we could enjoy a buffet lunch at Pizza Hut. On our way there, a woman stopped me and said, 'Will you buy a charm?'

I said, 'No thank you.' And as we walked on Mum said, 'She'll curse you now.'

'Why?'

'I'll think you will find that she is a pagan witch.'

I was paranoid for the rest of the day.

After lunch we went to the Tower Circus which was really good.

We spent another evening in and in a way I wished that Spud had been invited then I could have had someone to agree or disagree with about the standard of girls here.

There are quite a few pretty ones with all the right equipment but they all act quite young, so I haven't got a clue how old they are and none of them is giving me a second glance.

29 July 2003, Tuesday

Rain-went to the Sea Life Centre-boring-went to Waxworks Museum - boring - had fish and chips for dinner-boring-went to the complex again and watched some crappy thing called the Bradley Bear Show. The young kids loved it but I thought it was boring so I went back to the caravan to watch TV nothing on went to bed bored.

Dad is treating me to something tomorrow should be interesting.

30 July 2003, Wednesday

The day began with a boring shopping trip to Blackpool. While I was sat in Pizza Hut, staring out of the window at the passing women, I devised a grading table:

1. Would not shag under any circumstances.
2. Could shag if I was paid to.
3. Would shag for free.
4. I think she is quite sexy but don't think that all my mates would agree.
5 I think she is sexy and I think my mates would agree.
6. I think she is sexy and I know that my mates would agree.
7. Really nice looking.
8. Absolutely gorgeous.
9. Top totty.
10. Perfect.

Backdated marking: Lara (9), Monica (3), Ellie (5), Hannah (8), Katie (4), Amy Nuttal from *Emmerdale* (10).

I found out what Dad's treat was this evening. He took me to watch a pre-season friendly at Bloomfield Road. Blackpool lost two-one to Blackburn Rovers.

31 July 2003, Thursday

We watched the weather forecast this morning and were told that rain was due. So we decided to go to the cinema.

We watched the new cartoon version of *Sinbad*, despite me hearing a review saying that there was no computer-aided animation in the film. That proved to be utter rubbish because most of the film was made up of it. It was really good.

The fact that one of the voices in the film was provided by Catherine Zeta Jones is quite topical at the moment because John Leslie's ordeal against sex charges is now over. Dad said, when Mum was out of earshot, 'If it were me,

I would have got through the pain of the last year, happy in the memory that I had once shagged Catherine Zeta Jones when she was at her best.'

We had bangers and mash for dinner at the pub across from the cinema.

It turned out that the weather had been glorious all day. Bastard weathermen!

1 August 2003, Friday

Our original plan to go to the Camelot theme park was scuppered when rain was forecast on the television.

We went to Safeway to buy some ingredients for spaghetti bolognese, which Mum and Dad cooked up for our main meal of the day.

Once again, the sun came out and the day was wasted. I went swimming and ogled at the amazing young adolescent breasts on view at the pool. They had the bodies of women but the faces and actions of little girls. It was difficult to tell how old they were but I guess they could have been as young as twelve, which made me feel like a major pervert.

Why aren't people's brains ready for sexual attraction before their bodies? These young girls look great in bikinis but they are only children. It just isn't right. Why can't girls have some reliable visible indication of their age? Like a mole that vanishes the moment they reach the age of sixteen (preferably a hairy one).

I left the pool pissed off with myself for stooping so low and because of the fact that there were no similar sexy-looking girls of an acceptable age.

2 August 2003, Saturday

Boredom with a capital, emboldened, italicised 'B'. I had to sit through *Cats* for two-and-a-half hours, including a moment when one of the cast suddenly appeared next to Mum through a fire exit. Mum loved it but I was totally embarrassed.

It was so annoying because elsewhere in the Blackpool Winter Gardens was the World Matchplay Darts Championship Final, which I would have loved to watch, and in nearby Lytham St Anne's the Women's Open Golf Championship was being played.

3 August 2003, Sunday

We spent the day at the park before going to the Chuckle Brothers show at the Grand Theatre.

I expected it to be rubbish but it was quite good.

4 August 2003, Monday

I wrote out a few postcards this morning before we departed for Camelot. I thought that I would take the opportunity to get my own back on Spud and incorporate a cryptic clue similar to the one he sent me when he was in

Turkey.

Dear Spud

I was a bit bored so I decided to write you a poem.

Kindness is never sold.
Even life laughs at
Idiots sat yawning on utterly
Rotten dawns and days.

Troy

Dad and I went on the new ride at Camelot, the Whirlwind. It is a fast moving, steep roller coaster where the car you ride in turns as you travel, petrified, around the track.

It was quite a good park, albeit a lot smaller than Thorpe Park. We enjoyed our day in the hot sun though.

5 August 2003, Tuesday

I sent my postcards this morning. I saw a ten-out-of-ten girl in Bispham Sainsbury's and made a fool of myself when I walked into a display while I was ogling her with my tongue hanging out. She was slightly oriental and completely perfect.

This evening we went to another show at the Grand Theatre. This time some unknown comedians called Billy Pearce and The Grumbleweeds were the stars of a very entertaining and funny show.

I did remember a couple of the gags from the Chuckle Brothers show the other night that were used in this show, though.

6 August 2003, Wednesday

This morning the weather forecasters were warning us that today was supposed to be the hottest day on record, but all we got was mist and murk.

We spent the whole day at the Pleasure Beach. Me and Dad went on the Big One, the new Spin Doctor ride, the ride that shoots you up in the air at high speed, and the Avalanche, amongst others. It was the best day I have had on this holiday.

Mum had to sit out all the rides because of her bump, so we went to a show called Eclipse to split up the day.

7 August 2003, Thursday

Mum got a phone call this morning and when she had finished it she turned to me and said, 'Oh, Troy what have you done?'

'What's the matter?' I asked.

'You promised me that you wouldn't tell Stuart about Wicksey,' she said.

'I didn't,' I half lied.

'He deciphered your pathetic coded postcard.'

Rumbled, I went on the defensive. 'Well he deserves to know!'

'Maybe, but it's going to be very hard for him now.'

'Why?'

'Ricky Kinsella died last night.'

I felt the blood filling and then emptying from my face and felt an unseen force pull me into a seated position.

Mum turned to Dad, 'Kev, I'm sorry, but I have to go to him.'

Dad scowled at me, then said, 'Come on you can help me pack.'

I was completely in the doghouse for the rest of the very long day. It was so hot in the car. We had even more piss stops on the way home than we did on the way up. We got home at seven p.m. Mum got Dad to take her to Spud's, leaving me alone with my guilty thoughts.

Why is it that when I try to get the revenge I deserve all I get is my comeuppance?

8 August 2003, Friday

Spud came round today. I expected to get a torrent of verbal abuse from him but all he said was, 'Did Alison tell you not to tell me about Kinsella?'

I nodded.

'Thought so. Thanks anyway. I'm glad you told me, but I wish he hadn't snuffed it before I could have spoken to him, knowing what I know now.'

He looked a bit emotional and I felt a bit sorry for him. Or was it a bit guilty? I don't know. Anyway, I persuaded him to have a round of golf with me in the roasting sunshine. I won.

As we talked, on the round, he told me that when he went to the hospital Ricky Kinsella's younger brother was there. The brother asked Spud who he was and when Spud told him that he was Ricky's son, he snarled, 'How dare you? My brother has no children. You're just a grave-digging bastard.' Then he told Spud to leave in a very impolite fashion.

Why would he think Spud was grave-digging when Ricky was little more than a tramp?

When we'd finished, he had a salad lunch with us before leaving to see Lara.

I had another round of golf in the afternoon, this time with Dad. He popped over to Southampton this morning to get us tickets for tomorrow's final pre-season friendly against Parma. I won our game as well.

At dinner this evening I remarked that Spud seemed all right with the whole situation.

'So we needn't have come home early after all,' Dad moaned.

'I'm sorry!' Mum replied with a quivering bottom lip.

That would have been a good time for Dad to end the gripe, but no. Obviously caged-up frustration got the better of him and he started ranting and Mum let go with floods of tears. I left them to it.

I went to see Ed who was knackered after a day at work. He told me that there was going to be a beach barbecue tomorrow night.

We went down to a good vantage point along Baring Road to watch the finale of Cowes Week - the fireworks.

9 August 2003, Saturday

It was so hot today. There was nowhere to hide from it. I had a lukewarm bath before breakfast and went to Southampton with Dad later in the morning.

We went to West Quay where most of the women I noticed were graded between six and nine. Southampton is definitely the city with the highest consentration of beautiful women in Britain.

We window-shopped for a while before heading for St Mary's Stadium. The air conditioning in the club megastore was delightful, but the heat outside felt even worse when we left with a bag containing new shorts and a match programme.

At least we were in the shade in the Kingsland Stand as Saints won one-nil. When we got on the bus we had to suffer the awful sight of that fat bloke off ITV's *The Premiership* with his shirt off. His name is Steve Bull.

After we arrived home, I scoffed down my dinner quickly and headed for the barbecue as fast as I could.

All the usual crowd were there, including Spud and Lara. Everyone was already drunk and I grabbed a bottle of cider that Ed had saved for me and drank it very quickly in order to catch up. Then I politely consumed some charcoal sausages that Jason Ince had impaled on a stick and incinerated on the fire, which, because of the heat of the day, was totally unnecessary.

A few people went to cool off in the sea, all in swimming costumes, but I kept my eyes open in case the drink might unearth some exhibitionist behaviour, but as usual I saw nothing.

A few people retired to the tent, but it was so warm that me, Ed, Katie, Meat, Hannah and Tom all slept on the beach next to the dying fire.

10 August 2003, Sunday

When I got home, sand in all my extremities, I had a quick bath before our roast lunch which Nan and Grandad attended. Dad had driven out to pick them up as Grandad still can't drive yet.

He is having his operation privately but he has to lose a stone in weight before he can be admitted, so Mum served him up with a salad, which he scowled at before consuming it like a pig at a trough.

I went to see Ed when Dad took Nan and Grandad back home. He told me that Spud and Lara were seen shagging in a sand dune last night.

I felt a pang of jealousy. I thought that I had got over all that. I also felt a little disappointed that the perfect Lara was no longer pure and untouched. But my reaction was mild compared with the way I would have reacted if it had happened a few months ago.

I had a fairly early night to prepare for the dreaded return to work tomorrow.

11 August 2003, Monday

I was welcomed back to work with a morning of bagging up portions of rabbit and bird food with Jean.

Spud popped in this morning to ask if I could meet him for lunch. When I did meet him he just wanted to talk to me about the fact that he had decided to go to Kinsella's funeral tomorrow. He feels very nervous. He has never been to one before and he asked me if I would mind if he asked my mum to go with him.

I did mind, but something made me say, 'It's up to Mum, not me. Ask her.'

'I didn't want to do anything to upset you any more than you already are,' he added.

I was surprised he had noticed my disapproval. I thought that I had done a good job of hiding it.

'No, go on and ask her,' I insisted.

I said that partly hoping that she would say no but, the more I thought about it during the rest of the day, the more I knew that she would go with him.

When I got home from work I was reacquainted with Annicka.

'Hello Troy,' she said in her Scandinavian drawl. She came over and kissed me on the cheek. She looks just as fine as she did the last time I saw her.

At dinner she was the centre of attention. Her English is superb now. I can remember how poor it was when she first arrived; so much so that I was able to call her all sorts of rude names without her knowing what I was saying.

Spud came round as Mum was packing away the dinner things. Dad took over and Spud was introduced to Annicka.

'This is my older son Stuart,' Mum said as they greeted each other.

I could hardly believe my ears and I'm sure I saw a look of discomfort on Spud's face as she said it.

'I'll explain that later,' she added.

After Spud had left, Mum came over to me and said, 'Troy. I thought I'd better let you know that Stuart has asked me to go with him to his father's funeral. I hope you and your dad will understand.'

'So you're going then?' I asked, already knowing the answer.

'Yes I am.'

Life is shitting on me all the bloody time. I didn't want Spud as a brother and I don't really want this new baby sister I am about to get. I have absolutely no control over the things that are happening to me.

If she wants Spud so much, maybe he should move in and I should move out.

Suddenly, life on the streets of Cardiff is beginning to look attractive again.

12 August 2003, Tuesday

This morning I ate my breakfast on the chair opposite Annicka, who was wearing a very loose dressing gown. You could see right up her legs and I was waiting for the moment when she would reveal whether she was wearing any knickers or not but, as usual, I didn't ever find out.

It was Colin's day off at work so it was quite a relaxed day. The town is still quite busy even though Cowes Week is over.

When I got home, Annicka had cooked dinner. It was an Indian dish. It was very nice but the portions were a bit ungenerous. Mum said that the funeral was a bit hard for Spud.

'His brother had a go at Stuart, calling him a lying b ..' she said.

'Better than being called a lying wasp!' I quipped.

Mum ignored the spontaneous wit. 'The priest told me that he is a doctor. I'm not sure I like his bedside manner. When I tried to explain that Stuart was telling the truth he looked me up and down and said, 'The both of you are wasting your time if you think you are going to get anything out of this. I am his only next of kin.' Poor Stuart. He didn't know what to say or do. I took him home. He was quite upset. He didn't deserve that. I know the man is grieving but that was very harsh.'

After a rather long pregnant pause, where no one knew what to say next, she continued. 'It's not as if he had anything to leave behind, otherwise why was he living as a down-and-out in Cowes?'

Of course the one thing that I had forgotten about was the fact that since the man died it had become a murder and *South Today* had a small article on the matter, appealing for witnesses. They showed some grainy CCTV footage of a man who was entering the pontoon at the time of the attack. He did look rather familiar but I couldn't quite put my finger on who it was.

I stayed in this evening and watched my first live match of the new season - the Carling Cup match between Macclesfield Town and Sheffield United.

13 August 2003, Wednesday

It was supposed to be my day off today, but I went into work to plead with Colin so that I could have home-match Saturdays off. My bargaining point was that I would always work my day off and all Saturdays when Southampton were playing away, apart from specially arranged exceptions, for no extra money.

Colin said, 'I don't know. You haven't been here long have you?'

'No, I know, but Dad has already bought a season ticket for me.'

Colin shook his head and rubbed his chin with his thumb and forefinger. I tried another bargaining point. 'You can lower my wages as well if you like.'

Colin's eyebrows, which are very bushy, shot up, creating a very wrinkly forehead.

'Okay then. On a trial period! You will work every day and finish on home-match days at one forty-five. That should give you enough time to catch the two p.m. Red Jet.'

My face shone with gratitude. It meant the end of the pre-match drinks in the Dell Supporters Club Bar, but otherwise what a resounding result.

So I worked today, as hard as I could, and I hope that Colin was impressed because I was shattered when I left at half five.

Chelsea were playing the first leg of their Champions League qualifier this evening and the BBC were showing the match live. With Chelsea trying to buy the championship, I hoped that they would fall flat on their faces but they didn't. They won the away leg and are more or less through.

Mum warned me to knock before I entered the bathroom because Annicka refuses to lock the door when she has a bath.

So maybe I can, accidentally on purpose, walk in on her and finally get to see a naked woman.

It wasn't tonight though, as when I went to have my bath I could smell the fact that Annicka had just vacated the bathroom. I found some pubic hair in the plughole, but I soon realised that they could well have been Dad's so I quickly flushed them down the toilet.

14 August 2003, Thursday

I was watching *GMTV* this morning and they were making a fuss over the fact that A-Level students receive their results today. When I watched the news this evening, they were saying that the exams are too easy, that's why so many people are passing. Well what is the point in staying on and doing your A levels if you are not going to pass them? Why can't the students get the credit they deserve for the hard work they have put in? I am dreading the arrival of my GCSE results!

It was a long day at work today. While I was there I got a text message from Ed saying: 'SAINTS HAVE JUST SIGNED KEVIN PHILLIPS'. I was desperate to find out if this was true. Surely my Southampton couldn't have made such a top signing? But they had. I so wish I was going to the Leicester game on Saturday.

Dad was overjoyed when he came home. 'What a signing!' he beamed. 'This is nearly as good as when we signed Kevin Keegan!'

I had a quick dinner and afterwards I joined Ed, Meat, Tom, Karl, Stevie and the Jasons for a crap game of cricket at Northwood Park.

I haven't mentioned this for a while, but I am still desperate for a girlfriend.

15 August 2003, Friday

I became a bit paranoid this morning when they were reporting on the news that three thousand people have died in France because of a government cover- up. I immediately thought of SARS, but it turned out to be because of the unusually high temperatures of the recent heatwave. They hit forty-five degrees Celsius at one stage. The French government has announced a state of emergency, but the hot spell seems to be nearly over so it unfortunately seems to be too little too late.

Surely, if you get too hot, can't you lie in a cool bath or something and drink lots of water to keep your body temperature down?

Also there has been a huge power cut that has blacked out most of north-east USA and Canada. How the hell can that happen? When we have had power cuts it is usually just our side of the street that loses power.

They don't think that they are going to be able to restore the power for days. This is the USA we are talking about. The world's most technologically advanced country. If you wrote it in a novel it would be too far-fetched.

They, of course, paranoid as they are, thought that terrorism was involved. But it probably happened while George W. Bush was having one of his electro-therapy sessions at the asylum.

Dad took my Saints shirt with him to work this morning so that he could pop to St Mary's Stadium and get 'Phillips 7' printed on the back of it.

I enjoyed gloating today at Bill who is an Everton fan. 'Not such a small club now, are we?' I said.

'Maybe not, but you'll never be as big as The Toffeemen,' he pathetically retorted.

Colin wasn't in today, so Bill gave me my wages this morning and I treated myself to a Tiffins' bacon baguette for lunch.

It was a good day at work today. It didn't drag as much as usual.

It actually rained tonight. Annicka went out. She looked very sexy in the hot pants and bikini top she was wearing.

Dad presented me with my shirt, but some idiot in the shop put 'Philips' on the back. They missed off an L. Dad hadn't realised until I pointed it out to him and when I did he wasn't very happy.

16 August 2003, Saturday

I asked Colin this morning if I could have the radio on for this afternoon's match. He said, 'Don't take the piss. If our customers wanted to listen to football while they shopped, they would be carrying their own radios.'

Pitbull swanned in this afternoon with a huge grin on his face.

'I've got some good news, young Troy,' he beamed.

'I hope it's news that I will feel good reason to smile about as well,' I said.

'Now I don't know about vat,' said Pitbull. 'Free fings. One. I've got ve manager's job at Cowes Park Rangers, Sunday league team. Two. Pompey won veir first Premiership game two-one. And free. Safamton are ge'in stuffed at harf toim by Leicester.'

My heart sank. 'What's the score?' I asked.

'Two-nil. And they're lucky it ain't more, apparently.'

I prepared myself for some teasing but Pitbull just asked me, 'What are you doin' on Sundee mornin'?'

I told him that I usually have a lie-in but he persuaded me to turn out for his new team.

The games were long over by the time I got home and I was very pissed off.

'What's the matter with you?' Dad asked.

'Well Pompey won and we got stuffed,' I answered.

'What are you on about? We drew two all and Kevin Phillips scored a wonder goal!'

This news immediately lifted my mood.

I was preparing to go out and see Ed when the doorbell sounded and it was Lara in tears.

'What's the matter?' I asked as I led her to my room.

'Stuart's finished with me!' Lara sobbed. 'Says he's fallen in love with someone else.'

'Oh!' was all I could say in reply.

'Who is she?' Lara asked.

'I don't know,' I said, quite honestly.

'You must do. He is your brother.'

'Only in his and my mother's minds, not mine.' I said, trying not to sound bitter.

Lara just looked at me through teary eyes. She seemed to look a bit disgusted but I expect that was just me misreading the expression on her face, since she was so upset.

I made her a cup of tea then walked her home.

So what I feared would happen did happen. She gave her virginity away to somebody who wasn't worthy of receiving it.

When I arrived at Ed's, he was playing badminton in his back garden with his sister, Zoe. God she is developing fast. She was playing in hot pants and a bikini top and I was struggling to keep my eyes off her rather large, bouncing breasts as she moved athletically around the garden chasing the shuttlecock that Ed was hitting wherever he wanted, with great ease.

I took over and was beaten as well. We played on until it got dark then went inside to watch the first *The Premiership* of the new season. I left at eleven forty-five when they had shown Southampton's bit.

17 August 2003, Sunday

I got up at nine and ate a high-energy breakfast, which consisted of cornflakes and a Mars bar, then headed off up to the park ready to help put up the nets.

Pitbull had forgotten to tell me that he had also roped in Ed, Tom, Karl, Stevie, Nathan, Meat, Jason Dwyer, Jason Ince and, worst luck, bloody Spud!

'Who have you dumped Lara for?' I asked him. 'She came around last night in tears.'

'Annie,' he whispered. 'Shhhhh! Not 'ere. I'll tell you about it later, fella!'

Fair enough, I thought, and we proceeded to get everything ready for the match.

We played Southern Vectis and our kit is like Inter Milan's - black and blue stripes. It is brand new and looked really good. In contrast, Southern Vectis had green and white stripes.

Pitbull, rather aptly, barked instructions from the touchline, but he didn't have much to moan about as we won five-nil. I was a bit unfit and I had to come off after about fifteen minutes of the second half. That wasn't before I had helped Ed complete a hat-trick. It was four-nil then, and Spud replaced me and scored himself when big Nathan pulled the ball back from the byline to Spud, who scooped the ball into the roof of the net.

When the game had finished, we took the nets down and Nathan went over to his girlfriend.

'Hasn't she got googly eyes?' Tom remarked.

'I was going to say that,' I said.

Karl chuckled, 'You'll see why soon.'

'What do you mean?' we all asked at once.

We didn't have to wait long as when we got in the showers we saw that Nathan had got the biggest dick I have ever seen. It looked like a toddler's leg dangling down there. No wonder her eyes bulge out like that.

This afternoon I went to the annual Garlic Festival in Newchurch with Mum, Dad and Annicka. It was packed! Most of the island must have been there. There was a lot of top totty there. But I can't remember seeing any garlic, funnily enough.

We met up with Spud and his parents, and then I discovered who Annie was as Annicka and Spud immediately greeted each other with an embarrassingly tonguey snog.

Spud's parents were friendly enough but looked uncomfortable and soon made their excuses and left to look around the various show tents.

I must admit that if it hadn't been for the abundant crumpet, I would have been bored.

We went to the Bargeman's Rest for dinner and then home where I stayed in.

18 August 2003, Monday

I went to see Vernon at lunchtime. We were talking about our win yesterday and Vernon said that Pitbull had approached him to sign but Vernon had refused. He hadn't realised that me and my mates were playing for the team and he was now showing distinct interest in joining, so I spent the lunch break trying to get him to sign. His skill and experience would be a huge asset to the team. He is an Island League Division One standard player and we are in Division Three. By the end of the lunch break he had agreed to come along with his boots on Sunday morning.

I spent the afternoon at work making sure that all the perishables were on the shelves in the correct date order and disposing of any out-of-date products.

Whenever I cut up sheets of board I have a terrible time trying to keep the saw going in a straight line. Surely it would pay Colin to buy a jigsaw.

This evening I had a round of golf with Ed. I was winning by four shots after the first circuit, but I started to think about the possibility of beating him and my game went to pot. After I sliced my tee shot into the grounds of Cowes High School at the final hole, I got in a mood and slung my driver away, narrowly missing an elderly golfer who was heading back to the clubhouse.

'Bloody yobs!' he moaned.

'Sorry, it slipped out of my hand,' I lied.

'Then I suggest you get a new glove,' he said.

'This hand!' I said, waving my gloveless right hand at him.

The man just raised an eyebrow and continued on his way to the clubhouse.

19 August 2003, Tuesday

I got groggily out of bed this morning and headed for the bathroom only to bump into Spud.

'What the bloody hell are you doing here?'

He just winked, grinned, walked into Annicka's room and shut the door behind him.

I went to see Mum in the kitchen.

'Do you realise that Spud has stayed the night in Annicka's room?' I asked her.

'Yes, I just found out. Don't worry, I'm going to have a little chat to those two.'

After a long day at work I came home and asked Mum how the little chat went.

'It's all right. They assure me that they are taking the relevant precautions,' she said.

'That's not the point. I have to pay rent to live here. Spud seems to be staying for free.'

'It's not rent, it's keep and he only stayed as Annicka's guest, and mine for that matter. Anyway, what does it matter? He is family, and can you please refer to him as Stuart when talking to me. I hate the name Spud!'

He came around this evening and disappeared into Annicka's room. I expect to see him again tomorrow morning.

Later in the evening Mum said that it was nice for Annicka to find a friend of her age group to associate with.

'It must be difficult for her living in a strange country with no friends at her age.'

Her choice, I thought.

20 August 2003, Wednesday

As I had suspected, I had to endure Spud's irritatingly cheery demeanour at breakfast this morning.

'I could get used to this,' he said, smiling a knowing smile in the direction of Annicka.

'So could I,' Annicka drawled.

They snogged.

'Some sort of rent, then, is perhaps in order,' I said in an attempted teasing way. Annicka giggled and Spud gave me a bit of a dirty look after seeming to check that Mum was out of earshot.

At work today I had to help this bloke, Rob, paint the back of the shop.

We had to climb onto the roof and I hate heights so I didn't have a very good day. I was so relieved to be able to put my feet back on terra firma.

I stayed in this evening to watch England beat Croatia three-one. James

Beattie only played the last fifteen minutes, but he did set up a superb goal for Frank Lampard although he got little credit for it. Then he flicked the ball on for Kieron Dyer to score but it was incorrectly ruled offside.

Beattie has got three caps now for England but has only played just over sixty minutes in total. Oh well, England's ignorance is Southampton's gain.

21 August 2003, Thursday

Today gave a new meaning to the phrase D-Day. I got my GCSE results and Colin allowed me some free time to go to school and get them.

Here they are:

History D
Biology D
Mathematics D
English Language D
Geography D
Geology D

The only exceptions were:

Art and design A
Computer Studies A*

So I passed them all just!
Ed texted me his:

History B
Physics B
Mathematics A
English Language A
Geography B
Geology C
Art and design B
Social Studies A

Jammy bastard! Typical of him to do better than me! Tom texted me his:

History C

Biology C
Mathematics C
English Language C
Chemistry D
Physics D
Art and Design D
Computer Studies B

I wonder if that clay penis he made once had any reflection on his Art grade?

I didn't see Spud until surprise, surprise I got home from work. Mum told me to wait until Dad got home before I revealed my results, but Spud bounded in and announced his, with Annicka hanging off his spare arm:

History A
Biology A
Mathematics A*
English Language A*
Physics A
Chemistry A
Art and Design A*
Social Studies A*
Being a flash tosser A**
Annoying the hell out of me A***
Shagging anything that looks like its legs are slightly open A****
Gitness A*****
Being someone I like having as a brother G

(I made up the last five.)

Mum hugged him and said in a corny way, 'You've obviously got your father's brains. Let's hope you haven't inherited any of his weaknesses.'

I felt, later, that they were trying not to make me feel inadequate when I announced mine later and Dad treated us all to a Chinese to celebrate.

I have been upstaged again but it is my own fault. All I had to do was pay more attention at school, and if I'd known the way things would turn out, I probably would have.

22 August 2003, Friday

Today was a crap day at work. Everything went slowly. The only break was lunch when I saw Jason Ince mincing through the High Street looking like he had turned up to the wrong Notting Hill Carnival.

'Hello, what the hell are you wearing?' I asked him. He was wearing a ridiculously colourful shirt and a pink baseball cap. Then I noticed his black eye and fat lip. 'You're not wearing that stuff to detract from your battered face, are you?'

He wasn't in a good mood. 'Trevor Smith's fists did this to me when he saw me having a laugh outside the Pier View. He came over, called me a son-stealing evil poofter, then punched me in the stomach and the face before your friend Vernon arrived to pull him off me. He spat at me while I was cowering on the ground and then he left.'

Jason had a bit of a tear in his eye and I felt really sorry for him.

'So are you wearing these clothes in protest?'

He didn't answer me. He just made his excuses and went on his way. All this reminded me about the CCTV video that was shown on *South Today*, the man that was seen at the scene of Kinsella's attack, it was Trevor Smith. I knew I recognised him but with all that is going on I just forgot.

I spent the afternoon trying to decide whether to tell the police or not. I thought of the battered faces of Terry and now Jason and knew that Trevor was a menace, but I had to do it discreetly so I wrote a letter and posted it in at the Police Station before heading home.

Spud was already there when I arrived home. He was being entertained by Annicka in her room. I asked Mum about the fact that he had stayed every night since those had two got together and Mum told me that he had paid her some money to help towards his keep. So that has just given him the green light to become a permanent resident.

It isn't that bad at the moment because I hardly see anything of him. He's always in Annicka's room.

This evening I went out with Karl, Ed, Tom and Meat. We met Stevie, Nathan and his googly-eyed girlfriend at Medina Leisure Centre for a swim.

Nathan drives an old mini and Karl drives a souped-up RS Turbo. From that evidence, blokes do drive powerful cars to make up for insufficiencies in the trouser department.

In the pool we marvelled at this gorgeous girl with an absolutely perfect figure. It took us a while to realise who she was and then she called over. 'Hello Tom, hello Troy.'

It was the Abominable Donna Bull who can no way be described as abominable now.

Both Tom and I greeted her with our mouths open.

'God, she's blossomed a bit since you went out with her,' I said to Tom.

'She looks just the same to me. Must be something wrong with your eyes, mate.'

After the swim we went up to the bar where Karl managed to get us all a pint of lager. It was very naughty of their barman not to check our ages, but a very nice pint of lager.

23 August 2003, Saturday

It was awful watching the clock slowly tick its way towards one forty-five when I could leave and catch the ferry to Southampton for our first home game of the season.

Birmingham City were the visitors and in the first half we should have had the points sewn up, but in the second half it just went from bad to worse and in the end we were lucky to come away with a goalless draw.

I have never ever seen Southampton win their first home game of the season. It was rubbish and it put me in a bad mood for the rest of the day.

I went around to Ed's tonight. We watched *Rock Stars The Bands* and Chris's band get voted off the show on the final round before the finals. Good. So the day ended on a good note.

24 August 2003, Sunday

Today we played against Cowes Social, a very physical team, so physical, in fact, that Pitbull himself played and he'd phoned early this morning and persuaded my Dad to run the line. Spud came along as well, and I enjoyed it when he looked pissed off at the stick he was getting about the love bites on his neck and chest and the scratches on his back.

Pitbull's decision to play turned out to be not such a good idea, as he was sent off after he headbutted their centre back, who had started getting shirty with me when I left him on his backside, after some silky skills that set up Paul Squires to put us one-nil up. That was a strange thing. It was just like the moment me and Pitbull first met, but the difference was that the bloke apologised to me after the game.

The fact that they won three-one might have helped him come to his senses.

Today's team comprised Bob Murphy in goal; Tom Sibley, Peter Bull,

Nathan Edge and Stuart Hudd in defence; Karl Sibley, Edward Case, Vernon Chandler and Nathan Salter in midfield, and Troy Brown and Paul Squires up front. Stevie Perry and Jason Dwyer were subs.

After the match I went home for lunch. Nan and Grandad were there and Spud and Annicka also joined us but looked quite uncomfortable with not being able to touch each other. I'm sure they relieved themselves the moment they were excused from the table.

Spud said that he was going back to school to do his A levels. He admitted that he was surprised to get such good grades and thought that he had better put them to good use.

Grandad said that he thinks that he might be able to get his operation on the NHS. He has already lost a stone in weight.

Mum went to bed and Dad and I washed up. Mum is huge now and is finding life very uncomfortable. She is drinking lots of pineapple juice because somebody told her that it helps to bring on labour.

On *Meridian News* tonight they said that the police have arrested somebody in connection with the murder of Ricky Kinsella after an anonymous tip-off. They didn't name the man but I bet it's Trevor Smith.

During the afternoon, Dad recorded the two televised matches and we managed to avoid finding out the scores and watched them both this evening. I fell asleep, though, halfway through the second match.

25 August 2003, Monday

Bank Holiday. I had a wonderful lie-in this morning. More so for the fact that Spud had to work and wasn't in the house.

He would have to have been out of the house anyway because Annicka is in full-time au pairing now. Mum is spending more and more time resting her huge bulk.

It was Annicka who made me my breakfast and she seems to have got into the routine of giving us what we like instead of continental breakfasts.

I ate my breakfast in the living room opposite Mum, who was lounging in her pyjamas with her bump sticking out. Whenever the baby moved she unwrapped her hideous mound to show the freakish shapes moving around and protruding from it. It reminded me of *Alien* but she and Dad think it's wonderful.

After I had finished my brekkie I decided to pay Lara a visit for old time's sake.

She looked particularly beautiful which made me think that maybe Spud hadn't ruined her by shagging her.

We had a lovely chat until we got onto the subject of my inability to get a girlfriend. She told me that I am an old fuddy-duddy.

She said, 'You moan about things like an old man does.'

I asked, 'What do you mean?'

'It's difficult to think of an example.' She thought for a while. 'I remember when Tom started smoking. You were always going on and on about how much you hate smokers.'

'Well I do!'

'I know, but Tom's young. He's just experiencing things for himself.'

'I don't have to experience things to know that they're bad for me.'

'There you go again. You also went funny when I got off with Ed at that barbie. If I'd had sex with him my Dad would have taken the news better.'

'That was because I was jealous and you would have been engaging in underage sex.'

'I rest my case!'

I left after a couple of hours and couldn't stop thinking about what she'd said as I walked to Ed's house.

Ed and I went down to town and I bought a ten-pack of Marlborough and a packet of Swan Vestas. Ed asked me what I was doing and I told him, 'Trying to get in touch with my youthful side.'

We hung around the icafé for a while, then we both went to our respective homes.

Annicka was cooking dinner. Dad was mowing the lawn. Mum was chatting with Spud.

After our dinner, which was mushroom omelette and sweetcorn, I went to my room and lit a cigarette. I then smoked it as best as I could as I coughed and gagged profusely. After about ten minutes of finishing the thing, I began to feel quite nauseous.

I tried to fight the feeling, as I can't stand vomiting, but it beat me and I chucked up in the toilet and didn't feel much better afterwards. After about an hour the feeling passed and I flushed the other nine cancer sticks down the toilet. I was now very hungry so I went down to Chip Ahoy in Victoria Road on my skateboard and bought a Sausage Special.

I am definitely never going to be a smoker and I have gone right off omelettes.

26 August 2003, Tuesday

Back to work, worse luck. We had a massive delivery of heavy bags of Irish moss peat, gravel and cement which I had to single-handedly carry to the storeroom behind Colin's office.

At lunchtime I saw Jason Ince again. He has reverted back to his hardnut image and re-emphasised it by having his head shaved.

'All right Troy!' he said, in a much more cheerful voice than last time.

'Hey! Jase!' I replied.

'Got a letter from Te. He's lovin' it.'

'Good.'

'Did you 'ear about his dad?'

'Sort of.'

'Yeah. He done over Kinsella. I 'ope they throw the book at him, the mad, homophobic bastard.'

'Yeah!' I agreed.

He went on to say that he was thinking of going into the forces himself. I went back to the original subject.

'How does he feel about his dad?'

'Pleased, I expect, he 'ates him.'

'He didn't say, then?'

'No. He wrote the letter before 'is dad's arrest.'

Well that confirmed in my mind that Trevor Smith killed Ricky Kinsella. Then, during the afternoon, Trevor Smith walked into the shop and bought a box of quarter-inch masonry nails. Bill served him.

''Ello mate. How's it going?' he said.

'Not good. I'm out on police bail.'

'Oh, sorry. I didn't know.'

'Yeah right. It's been on the telly an' everything.'

'Sorry mate, I don't take much notice of what's on the News.'

Smith looked a bit disappointed as he paid for his goods and left.

'Shit!' Bill said. 'I wonder what he's been up to?'

'Murder,' I responded.

Bill looked like he was about to part company with a large turd. I had to laugh to myself as I went off to cut up some sheets of plasterboard.

This evening I stayed in and listened to the football on the radio. Saints drew nil-nil at Leeds but Portsmouth went to the top of the Premiership after thrashing Bolton four-nil.

Southampton are playing Manchester United on Sunday, by which time

Portsmouth will be seven points above us after they have beaten lowly Wolverhampton Wanderers. I will then have to put up with Pitbull gloating. This is a terrible start to the season.

27 August 2003, Wednesday

Colin took the day off today so it was a nice, relaxing day.

This evening, Ed and I went to Northwood Park and played putting. He won, as usual.

When I got home there was an Irish bloke sat in our living room.

'This is Doctor Kinsella,' Mum said. 'Wi-Richard Kinsella's brother.'

She went on to tell me that the good doctor had managed to wangle a night in our house because he wants to get to know Spud.

He now knows, apparently, that Spud is truly his nephew after his brother left instructions with his will about how to find his son. It said to look for Alison Stenning.

Spud, though, was on a night shift tonight, so their meeting will have to wait until tomorrow. Meanwhile Dad moved the cot out of the nursery to give the doctor room.

So this evening I had to sit through tedious stories about his life in Ireland. It was interesting to note that he made no reference to his relationship with his brother over the years.

I was eventually able to retire to my room, which I had to share with Griz who refused to stop barking at the doctor whenever he saw him.

I set about predicting how many points Saints would get this season. It wasn't a very good total. Forty-one means we will probably get relegated.

The doctor retired to his room shortly after I did. Annicka was out for the evening, so I took the opportunity to sneak into her room and listen in on the suspicious doctor through the crack in the partition doors.

I could here him mumbling to himself.

'You can do it you know you can. Just focus your mind. Focus.'

I heard him igniting a lighter. Dad wouldn't be happy if he knew he was smoking.

As I was eavesdropping, Annicka returned and switched on the light. Obviously this was an awkward situation for me.

'I erm sorry.'

'My pantie drawer is over there, Troy,' she drawled.

'Yes, and mine is in my room, Annie. So if you don't mind, I'll just go and rifle through them now.'

I didn't return to my room. I went into the living room to ask why this obviously shifty character was being allowed to stay in our house.

'He's Stuart's family,' Mum said.

'Well then perhaps he should be staying at Stuart's family's house where there is a spare room since Stuart has been staying here,' I retorted. Then I exaggeratedly stormed off.

I crept back down the hallway to listen at his door. I heard mumbling again.

'You can do it you know you can. You've done it before. Just focus your mind. Focus.'

What was he babbling on about? I decided to go out into the back garden to see if I could see anything through the gap in his curtains. With his light on I knew that he wouldn't notice me.

Mars was at its closest point to the Earth for sixty thousand years and I could see it twinkling, bright red, in the sky as I sneaked around to the back of our bungalow.

There was a tiny opening in his curtains. I peered through. I could see him holding a spoon with some golden syrup in it. He was heating it up from underneath with a bare lighter flame. I could see his lips were moving. He was obviously still muttering to himself.

I have an awfully uneasy feeling about that man.

28 August 2003, Thursday

I had a restless night's sleep. When I got up and went to get my breakfast, I walked in on a conversation between Mum and the doctor.

'I'm ever so sorry. He has stayed here every night for the last couple of weeks and he chooses tonight not to. If only he'd had his phone switched on.'

'Don't you worry now, Alison,' the doctor said in his smarmy Irish accent. 'Oim sure we'll meet up very sewn.'

Then he noticed me. 'Helleow dare yoong Troy. Did ja sleep well?'

'Yes, thank you,' I lied.

I went to work feeling very uneasy. I took my bike with me so that I could ride home at lunchtime.

When I got home I noticed that the curtains were drawn and, when I tried to get in, my key wouldn't operate the lock.

The place seemed deserted. What was going on? I felt very uneasy again, as if somebody was watching me. I walked deliberately down the garden path and away from the house. Then I rode to the entrance to the golf club and made my way to the back of our house via the golf course. I received several complaints from aged golfers but ignored them.

My bedroom has a sliding patio door for a window. I carefully tried to open it, with success. I crept in. The house was quiet. Griz was curled up on my bed. He was very pleased to see me and jumped off the bed and headed for the open patio door. I let him go, as he obviously needed a pee.

Then I carefully opened my bedroom door and crept down the hallway to the nursery. The door was open and the doctor's things were strewn everywhere the lighter, the spoon, a used syringe and some official-looking papers.

I took a look. There was a letter from a solicitor that said that the estate of Mr Richard Kinsella goes to his son Peter, first-born son of Miss Alison Stenning, who was given up for adoption at birth.

What estate? The man was a tramp.

I also found some Internet printouts that all seemed to relate to a similar subject: how to kill someone without trace.

I then became very worried and scared. My heart started racing and my lips started tingling.

'Hello dare, Troy.'

I jumped and turned around.

'Oi was hopen you wouldn't get involved in moi little venture, so oi was.' He was now leaning over me.

'You seemed such a noice lad too. 'Tis sooch a shame, so it is.'

'What are you doing?' I asked, trying to sound unaffected by the situation. I blindly started scrolling through the menus on my mobile phone. I was trying to remember how to find the voice recorder. I hoped I'd got it right as the doctor continued.

'Well that half-broother of yours has inherited what is roitly moin. I tort dat polishing off moi broother whoil he was so vulnerable in dat hospital, would mean dat all dat was his would become moin. It should be moin. Oi have lived dare all dease years. Not dat alcoholic waster. Den, just as oim abewt to foind ewt it's all roitfully moin oi discover dat he has a son and dat dat son of his doesn't even know he's got an inheritance in Oireland.'

'But your brother was a tramp!' I said.

'He initially chose to live dat way so as he could stay near to your ma, leaving me tew build a good loif at home. A loif oi worked too fookin hord for to give away to some stranger. Oim sorry you got involved.'

He had some cloth tightly wrapped around both of his hands and stretched out as though he was going to strangle me.

I have never been so scared. Just then, there was a startling noise. It was Griz barking. It distracted the evil doctor just long enough for me to kick him as hard as I could, in the crotch. He screamed in pain and dropped to his knees. I kicked him again as hard as I could, this time in the head. He flopped to the ground. I did it again. Griz was barking like mad, and then I thought of Mum and the drawn curtains.

I removed the cloth from the doctor's hands and tied his hands tightly behind his back. Then I got my old school tie and tied his ankles and feet together. I phoned the police as I ran down the hallway to the front room where I found Spud unconscious in the living room with the gas fire on full. I thought that he was dead and I started shouting and crying. I opened the patio doors and turned the fire off. Then I tried to wake him up.

He was a bit groggy. The bastard had made him drink a bottle of Scotch. I called an ambulance.

The ambulance came and the paramedic said that Spud should be all right after a few pints of water.

The police took the evil doctor away and told me I had done well. Then they cordoned off the nursery and asked us to leave the house while they conducted their investigations.

Dad came home from work and was a picture of panic. Then Mum and Annicka arrived. They had been shopping together in Newport. They showered Spud with concerned affection.

Spud and I gave statements while we waited for the investigating officers to finish their work in the house.

Mum, Dad and I had to go to Grandad's house to stay the night.

Spud went home and took Annicka with him.

Dad and Grandad chatted about the day's events for as long as our eyes could stay open.

I still can't really believe what happened today. It was like it was happening to someone else or I was doing things instinctively. Whatever caused me to do what I did, I am so glad my family is all right.

Just before bed I remembered my phone and checked it to see if the recording was on there. I carefully saved it.

The only unfortunate thing about all this is that that thug, Trevor Smith, will probably be let off now. But if he hadn't beaten Kinsella up he would still be alive.

29 August 2003, Friday

Dad phoned both his boss and mine to explain the situation and why we couldn't go to work today, which was a relief as I wasn't really up to working and I didn't want to get the sack.

The police called round during the morning and told us that we could go home. They took my phone, so now I am without a phone again.

We picked up Annicka and Spud on the way. There were a lot of hugs when we got in the house, apart from Spud and me who just shook hands.

Griz, the real hero in all this, got some fuss as well.

Mum and Annicka did some feverish cleaning for a few hours while me, Spud and Dad watched television.

Southampton have been drawn against Steaua Bucharest in the UEFA Cup. So that will be a quick exit, then.

At dinner time Dad went out to get a KFC, leaving Spud and me alone together.

Spud broke the awkward silence. 'I know you aren't happy having me as a brother, but I want you to know that when I found out that you were my brother, I was so proud. I still am.'

I just listened, trying not to get emotional. He continued. 'We are still good mates, though, aren't we?'

I got up, walked over to him and gave him the truest, most affectionate hug I could muster. 'Too right we are.'

We hugged for what seemed like ages. It was good. It was right.

Dad returned with the food, which was eaten heartily. As we finished, a policeman called round to tell us that the flue to the gas fire had been deliberately blocked. The doctor was trying to asphyxiate Spud.

He also admitted administering something called Ricin into Ricky Kinsella's drip in the hospital, which slowly poisoned him over a week or so.

Trevor Smith is still being charged with GBH.

What a couple of days! I kept Griz with me in my room tonight. He is so precious. He saved us all and he doesn't even know it.

30 August 2003, Saturday

Lying in bed last night I couldn't get to sleep. I was thinking about what would have happened if Mum had been in the house and the doctor had decided to overdose everyone with heroin, but it's obvious that an addict like him wouldn't want to waste any on people he could kill in a clean way.

It upsets me that he was in our house and could have killed my family, not to mention Annicka. It would have been awful for her parents, being so far away.

Mum told me this morning that Annicka was on the phone to her parents for ages last night. Apparently they were pleading with her to come home. She went to bed crying. She was on her own as Spud stayed at his house.

I could hear her crying as I lay awake in my bed. I thought, seriously, about going in and seeing her, maybe cuddling her. Then I imagined one thing leading to another. I thought that with her in her current frame of mind that it would be a good opportunity to take advantage of the situation and finally offload this burden of virginity that is hanging around my loins like an overdose of Viagra.

Dad took another day off and I went to work. Colin, Jean and Bill all interrogated me about what had happened, so I had to relive the whole thing again.

At lunchtime Colin insisted on taking all of us to the Fountain for a snack. He called me a hero and said that I deserved it. I felt rather unworthy but it was very nice of him and I ate my Welsh rarebit with gratitude.

Spud came in the afternoon and asked me how Annicka was. I told him that she wasn't good and he said that he was finding it difficult coping with her, now she is in an emotional state. I told him that I heard her crying herself to sleep last night, and that he should stay with her tonight. I could hardly believe what I was saying. I was asking Spud to stay the night and not feeling like I was contradicting my feelings about him.

He went away, but when I got home Mum told me that he was with Annicka in her room.

He re-emerged midway through the evening, while me and Ed were surfing the Internet, trying to find a way of getting rid of a virus called Master Blaster that was playing havoc with my Internet connection.

I activated the worm-killing software and did a search for virus file by typing in BLAST. It didn't find the virus file, as it had been successfully eradicated, but it did find a file called blasting.doc.

I opened the file, which was a Microsoft Word document with the heading 'Blasting Spaceships by Kevin Brown'.

Dad is writing a story. Me, Ed and Spud read excerpts and laughed at bits that weren't supposed to be funny.

I had to write some of it down:

His mighty hands caressed her perfect, firm, lily-white orbs. Her nipples stood proud and erect, like beckoning fingers drawing his mouth towards them. He gave into their desire and his mouth engulfed them. He massaged her whole breast with his lips and tongue.
'You can bite them if you like,' she sighed.
He obeyed and she gasped and writhed in ecstasy. Her hand reached for his throbbing shaft and desire sent waves of pleasure pulsating through his body.
She rolled him over and moved her head down to the epicentre of his libido. She consumed it in her mouth and throat.
He felt the tingling and then electrifying pangs of his sexuality tightening in his loins as she sucked on his bloated bell end. It tightened and tightened until its tension threshold was breached and the physical manifestation of his desire surged again and again into her mouth.
He never imagined it could ever feel like that.

We read it over and over again. It was hilarious. Especially the "bell end" bit. Dad could have a real talent as a comedy writer.

Of course it was a bit gross as well.

Spud said, 'God, he's done over a hundred pages. I hope he's backed it up.'

I said, 'Brilliant idea!' and rummaged around for a floppy disk which I used to copy the file to.

Then I deleted the original.

'What the bloody hell are you doing?' Spud said.

'It's just a laugh. I just want to see if he notices and, if he does, the expression of relief on his face when I hand him this disk.'

'That's bang out of order, Troy. He'll go mad. Put it back on there. Come on. That's stupid.'

'Oh, shut up. It's safe on this disk,' I said, waving the floppy disk in Spud's face.

Spud just shook his head, disapprovingly. Boring git!

I put the disk in my bedside cabinet.

31 August 2003, Sunday

This morning we played away at Bembridge, and Pitbull kept himself out of the team. Dad was delighted to find himself named among the substitutes. Vernon brought his brother, Jonathan, along for a game and Pitbull put him straight into the starting line-up.

We won the game one-nil. Jonathan passed me the ball while I was standing in the centre circle. I turned and started running towards the Bembridge goal. I was looking for one of my teammates to pass to but nobody was offering. Also no Bembridge player seemed to want to make a tackle, so I dropped my shoulder a couple of times, rounded the goalkeeper and slotted the ball home. It was an easy goal to score when nobody is prepared to challenge you, but my teammates and Pitbull were going well over the top with praise.

'That was the best goal I have ever seen,' said Paul Squires.

As we prepared to leave, Pitbull came up to me. He put his arm around me and said, 'Son, you're a class player, you really are. You could play in the Premiership if ya put your mind to it.'

It was strange to hear him speak in coherent English.

Dad was happy as well as he had been given twenty minutes of the match, after he came on for Meat, who'd twisted his ankle.

Today's line-up was: Bob Murphy in goal, Tom Sibley, Jonathan Chandler, Nathan Edge and Stuart Hudd in defence; Karl Sibley, Edward Case, Vernon Chandler and Nathan Salter in midfield; and Troy Brown and Paul Squires up front. Stevie Perry, Jason Dwyer and Kevin Brown were subs.

Dad drove back to Cowes quite hastily. We got back home at one o'clock and walked very briskly down to the Red Funnel terminal to catch the one-thirty. At the other side we caught a taxi which dropped us at St Mary's Stadium at two o'clock-kick-off time.

There was a slight delay to the start because it was a pay-per-view game, so we just about saw the kick-off as we moved along the row to our seats.

We were playing the champions, Manchester United, and we had a wicked game. James Beattie scored a well-deserved winner with just three minutes left, sending all of us, and probably most of the country, into ecstasy.

We headed back to the ferry and got home in time to watch the whole of the second half of the Manchester City versus Arsenal game. Arsenal won and went top of the Premiership.

Annicka has gone home to Sweden. Her dad travelled all the way from Malmo to take her home. Now Mum has no au pair and is on the verge of giving birth. She didn't seem too worried, though.

'My mum will come and help, if I need her,' she said.

More slobbery kisses on the way then. Hopefully she'll stop giving them to me and will concentrate on the baby. Maybe I should buy the baby some breathing apparatus, just in case.

Actually, I think that it's about time Spud received some of them. She owes her recently found grandson a lifetime of them. I won't bother getting him anything to help him breathe, though. I expect he'll wangle his way out of it anyway.

This evening Dad and I watched the recording we had made of today's game and it was just as sweet second time around.

1 September 2003, Monday

Spud came in to see me at lunchtime. He has finished working for Red Funnel now. He was quite upset actually. He said that his mum is now taking Prozac and he feels that it is his fault for spending so much time with my mum. His mum naturally feels rejected. There wasn't much I could say to dispel his feelings on the matter, as he was probably right.

He also said that he had received a letter from a solicitor in Ireland regarding the estate of Ricky Kinsella. He has got to go and have a meeting there, all paid for by the estate.

He is going on Friday night and has asked me to join him as he travels there with his mum and dad. I felt a bit honoured and accepted. It will be an adventure. I am really looking forward to it. Colin even let me have Saturday off, without even batting an eyelid.

We fly back on Saturday evening, in time for Spud's birthday on Sunday.

Spud was at our house when I got home from work. Mum was quite pleased that I had agreed to go with him.

I did say, after Spud had left, that I expected that Kinsella's estate would consist of a couple of crates of whisky, which wasn't well received.

Karl took me, Ed, Tom, Meat and Jason Dwyer to Medina Leisure Centre for swimming.

I jokingly said that he should drive us to Loftus Road when Saints play Fulham away on Boxing Day.

'The way you drive, we could leave Southampton at three o'clock and arrive at the ground half an hour before we left.'

He didn't quite understand what I was getting at. He just said, 'Yeah! That would be wicked! Go for it. Let me know when you want the money for the tickets.'

'Mate, the game is on Boxing Day.'

'So what? It'll be wicked. A few of us can fit in my car. We'll have a great day out.'

The others weren't quite so enthusiastic about the idea, but I went along with it. Maybe he'll forget about it over the next two months. I'd rather travel up with the Saints Travel Club. At least they know where the ground is. I doubt Karl does.

2 September 2003, Tuesday

I found out today, from the Oracle of all Cowes' gossip, that Trevor Smith had been banged up for six months for GBH. It's just as well Jason Ince didn't report the assault he received from him. Vernon heard the news from a mate of his that works at County Hall.

Doctor Kinsella has been remanded in custody without the possibility of bail. The magistrates sent him to some prison hospital as he is suffering severe withdrawal from heroin. They also think he might be a nutter. So that's two pieces of scum off the streets in one go.

After thinking about the agreement Colin and I made regarding football, it made me think that the Fulham away game might be the only away game I will be able to go to this season, as the shop will be closed on Boxing Day. I think that I will go to it after all.

Maybe if we follow the Travel Club coaches we will be able to find the ground all right.

I went to the park this evening to play cricket with the lads. I had the great pleasure of bowling Ed out for a golden duck. He, of course, blamed the bad light.

I told Karl that I was up for the trip to Loftus Road. He told me to sort the tickets out the next time I go over, and he didn't believe me when I told him that the tickets probably won't go on sale until a couple of weeks before the game.

3 September 2003, Wednesday

The day at work faded into the part of my brain that files insignificant memories, as this evening, after dinner, Dad decided to work on the computer and had a major paddy about his disappearing file.

He was stomping around panicking and I calmly asked him to leave it with me for a while as I had a disk with a programme on it that could retrieve recently deleted files.

'I didn't' delete it!' he crowed.

'It's easy to accidentally delete files. Also, if the file is saved on a part of the hard disk that has a bad sector on it, it could have been lost that way.'

I knew that all that computer jargon would go right over his head. I went to my room and retrieved the disk.

I calmly inserted the disk into its slot and double-clicked on its icon, which then displayed the disk's contents.

Then I was the one panicking. The disk was empty. I searched for hidden files. Nothing! What the hell had happened?

I couldn't have not copied the file to the floppy. I'm sure I saw it displayed in the disk's window before I ejected it. Or was it? What have I done? I tried everything to try and retrieve the original file that I'd deleted, but failed.

I felt like I was announcing a death when I told him. A death that I had caused. I felt like a murderer.

He was nearly in tears. 'Three months of work gone,' he sobbed and he went to his bedroom.

I felt destroyed. Spud told me not to do it. Why didn't I listen? How can I live with the guilt?

4th September 2003, Thursday

I lay awake for most of the night, trying to think of a way of salvaging my situation. No doubt Dad had a similar night of insomnia that probably involved silent snivelling. His red eyes this morning matched mine. He decided to take a sickie and Mum was quite pleased. I was little use at work with my preoccupation with guilt.

At lunchtime Ed, Meat, Lara, Katie and Spud visited me in their school uniforms. Everyone, except Lara, had black sixth-form ties. Lara is in year eleven and therefore wore the usual red tie with diagonal silver stripes.

Spud reminded me about our trip tomorrow, so when I got home I packed an overnight bag before dinner was served.

Dad was still miserable. I went to Ed's house to play footie in his back garden with his ever increasingly beautiful sister and him.

5th September 2003, Friday

Dad gave me one hundred pounds in cash this morning, to keep me going on the trip.

The day dragged today but finally, at five o'clock, Spud turned up to go with me to catch the five-thirty Red Jet. Colin let me go early.

We had a taxi booked to take us to Stanstead Airport where we caught a flight to Cork with Ryanair.

On the trip I obviously told Spud about my predicament with Dad and, to my great relief, the bugger had taken a copy of Dad's file and deleted the one on my disk, to teach me a lesson. I could have had a right go at him but I am just so relieved that I can repair the situation when I get home. I need to create a story to explain why the file has reappeared, though.

As soon as the plane crossed the Irish coast, we entered a wall of cloud and the resulting rain was constant.

A taxi had been arranged to pick us up from Cork Airport and take us to our accommodation, which was a pub called The Leaping Leprechaun. The bad thing was that we had a room with a double bed in it. His parents had their own room. I was hoping that he would share with them. The good thing, though, was that the TV had Sky.

After freshening up we went out with his parents. It was nearly ten o'clock by then. We ate at a Chinese restaurant and then it was time for bed. We lay in bed flicking through channels. The weirdo illusionist, David Blaine, is staying in a perspex box suspended over the Thames for six weeks with no food, only water.

Before he went in, he said that he was worried that he might lose his mind in the latter days of the attempt. How can you lose something that you never really had in the first place?

6th September 2003, Saturday

We got up at seven after a very uncomfortable night in which I was forever removing Spud's arm from me. I complained about it to him, but he just told me that I was talking rubbish.

We all had a full English breakfast and had a walk around Cork's shopping centre before our meeting with Mr Cootes, which was scheduled for nine in the morning.

I expected to be meeting an Irishman, but Mr Cootes spoke in a broad cockney accent.

He personally took us out to see Kinsella's house. It is huge. It is a three-story detached building set back from the road in what I guessed to be the outskirts of Cork.

Inside it was full of all the doctor's crap and it smelt very stale.

After the tour, he took us to a street where every other house seemed to be a pub. There he set about his business, which basically was asking Spud what he wanted to do with the house now that it was his.

'Mine?' Spud said, with eyes like saucers and mouth agog.

'Yes, Mr Hudd. This house is rightfully yours as part of your father's estate.

Cootes then went on to explain that the doctor had taken full advantage of his brother's exile and milked the family's estate, which now only consisted of the house.

Spud said, eventually, when he was able to gain control of his mouth, 'Sell it. It's no use to me. I don't want to live in Ireland.'

We went back to Cootes' office where Spud signed a few papers and that was it.

Spud asked, 'How much do you think it will go for?'

'It's difficult to say. I will phone you when the estate agents have come up with their valuation.'

Mr Cootes shook hands with each of us in turn before we left. We had lunch at McDonald's where Spud started talking about the fact that he was guaranteed at least fifty grand from the sale. His dad was trying, in vain, to keep Spud's feet on the ground.

I felt rather envious.

We spent a couple of hours looking around the shops and then headed for the airport. We landed in Stanstead at four-thirty and were back on the island at seven. I had missed all of England's two-one victory over Macedonia but fortunately I was able to watch Wales lose against Italy.

I was knackered and I went to bed straight after the game.

7th September 2003, Sunday

We had a home game against Plessey this morning. Spud turned up, to my surprise, considering the fact that it was his seventeenth birthday today. He had disastrous news as well. His dad had used the disk with my dad's file on it to send a picture to a website that sells African stress idols yesterday.

'Why couldn't he e-mail the bloody picture?' I asked.

'The website didn't list an e-mail address and had instructions to send the picture on disk.'

Something flickered in my mind. 'African stress idols? Will your dad know the name of the website?'

'I expect so.'

So after the game, which we won two-one with two assists by me for Vernon and Ed, who got the winner, I went to Spud's house.

The website is Koo's. What a ridiculous coincidence! He posted it last night, so I have to go all the way to London in time to intercept the postman. Spud insisted on coming with me and paying for the trip! He is beginning to grow on me.

I will have to pull a sickie on Monday.

We then went to my house where Mum had prepared a special birthday lunch for Spud, who looked both surprised and overwhelmed by the effort that had been put in. Nan and Grandad Brown were there and enthusiastically joined in the chorus of 'Happy Birthday to You'.

I told Mum and Dad that I would be spending the night at Spud's as he was having a little get-together for his birthday. This was a lie.

After dinner there was a knock at the front door. It was Annicka. She had returned and this seemed to make Spud's day as, after Annicka explained her return, he spent the rest of the evening in her room.

He came out at nine and we went to the ferry terminal. I took my backpack and we caught the twenty-two fifty-one train to Waterloo.

8th September 2003, Monday

So there we were at Waterloo Station at midnight. I still had eighty pounds left from our trip to Ireland, so I used some of it to get a taxi to New Cross. We arrived there at twelve forty-five in the morning.

There were some girls hanging around a street corner and Spud tried to get me to shag one of them.

'Come on. I'll pay. You keep going on about wanting to offload your cherry and they are there, happy to take it from you.'

'Yes, I desperately want to end my virginity. I am the most unwilling virgin in the world, but I want to know the person that I shag, see them around from time to time and be able to look at them with a glint in my eye.'

'What difference does that make? It's just sentimental crap.'

'It's how I feel. Anyway, you must be able to remember who you lost yours to?'

'Yes, of course, Katie Wallace, but at the time I would have settled for a hooker.'

'And I would have settled for Katie, as I know her.'

We soon found Koo's house and started our long wait for the postman who could have arrived at any time over the next twelve hours.

There was a seat near the house, so we sat there and talked about inane things to pass the time, like trying to remember the order of eviction of every *Big Brother* contestant from series one to four, a quiz about anything we could think of and charades.

The hours passed slowly but eventually the lightness grew and various milk floats and early-morning joggers started appearing.

At about seven forty-five I saw Koo coming out of his front door. I hid my face as he walked straight past us.

'That was close. I hope he's out for the day.' I said to Spud.

Finally the postman appeared. We went to Koo's front door, ready to intercept him. Spud became impatient and went over to him while he was just a couple of doors away. I could here them bickering.

'I sent something by mistake. I don't want it to go through the letter box.'

'I'm sorry, son, but you will have to take that up with the person whose name is on the front of the envelope, unless you want me to call the police.'

I didn't hear the rest of it because I was grabbed from behind and hauled through the front door.

'Got ya you f***in' rapist bastard.' It was Koo's voice.

He pushed me to the floor and tied my hands behind my back with his belt. Then he dragged me by my feet into his sitting room, heaved me into a seated position and then he must have punched me, because the next thing I knew was that I was regaining consciousness.

'The police are on their way,' he said. He was pointlessly brandishing a baseball bat.

'What are you doing?' I asked, and as I moved my lips to speak I realised that my lip was sore and swollen.

'ELLIE!' he called.

Ellie came into the room, her eyes full of tears and her belly swelled. Koo pointed at his daughter's belly.

'There is the evidence that will see you put away. You know what they do to rapists and child molesters in prison don't you?'

'But they will need DNA evidence that I have had sex with her.'

'What do you think that is? A cushion?' He pulled up Ellie's T-shirt to reveal a bare bulging, belly.

'Koo, I am a virgin. It is impossible for me to be the father.'

'Bullshit! You lying bastard, shit, rapist c***! Ellie told me you did it. You calling her a liar?'

'Yes!' I said, looking at her with the most contempt filled look I could muster.

Koo brandished the baseball bat and swung it above his head, obviously ready to batter me, but Ellie stood in his way and screamed, 'NOOO, daddy! He's telling the truth. It wasn't him who got me pregnant.'

This did stop Koo swinging his bat, but he wasn't immediately convinced.

'I told you it was Troy because I thought that we would never see him again. I wanted to protect the real father.'

'Who is the real father, then?' Koo asked.

'I can't tell you that.'

'Why not?'

'Look at the way you are acting. I can't put the baby's dad through that.'

'Why not? He raped you didn't he?'

'No, he didn't. I love him.'

At this, Koo dropped the bat and sat back into an armchair. Then he put his head in his hands. At that moment Spud appeared at the door. Koo stood up again.

'Who are you and what are you doing in my house?'

I intervened. 'This is my brother, Stuart. Stuart, this is Ellie and her hospitable father, Koo. If you would like to tie your hands behind your back and whack yourself in the mouth, you can join in the thrilling experience I am having right now.'

Koo's lips were pouted in bewilderment. 'Oh I erm. I'm sorry here, let me help you.'

Then the police turned up and Koo explained to the suspicious looking officers that there had been a little misunderstanding.

He untied me and sent Ellie to get something to treat my lip. He then gave us some breakfast. We had a short chat, and I found out that Kwami had stayed in Cardiff after they had chased me there. They are not having anything to do with each other.

Then we were sent away so that Koo and Ellie could sort a few things out. We had the package with us with an Isle of Wight postmark, so our mission was accomplished.

We took the tube to Waterloo Station and were back in Southampton just after midday. We went to West Quay for lunch and admired the abundance of crumpet that adorned its huge concourse.

Spud took the opportunity, as we consumed our portions of Popcorn Chicken and Fries, to say, 'Do realise that you called me your brother?'

'Well you are aren't you?'

'Yes. Yes I am,' He said with a smile of pride on his face that I couldn't quite comprehend.

'That's the best birthday present I have ever had,' he added, tears welling in his eyes.

'Okay, easy, ya wuss, no big deal!'

Then we went home and I went straight onto the computer to replace the missing file only to find, to my horror and infinite disappointment, that all that was on the disk was a picture of Mr Quick, my former maths teacher.

I just can't believe it, but at least I had been inadvertently cleared of a sexual offence that I hadn't committed.

I had a really early night tonight as I started to doze off during *Emmerdale*.

9th September 2003, Tuesday

I woke up at five and couldn't get back to sleep, so I got up and watched breakfast television for a while.

At work I was lumbered with all the menial jobs: unloading the delivery lorry, sawing sheets of board and sweeping the shop floor, punishment for having yesterday off.

'What was wrong with you, then?' Bill asked, in a 'knowing I was skiving' voice.

'Puking, most of the time.'

'Is that how you got that fat lip of yours?'

'What?'

'Did you whack in on the rim of the toilet?'

'Er, yes.'

He didn't believe it but didn't take it any further.

At lunchtime Spud bounded into the shop in his school uniform, followed by the rest of his sixth-form gang and Lara.

He plonked a box on the counter, which I was minding while Bill was in the loo.

'Take a look in there,' he instructed.

I did as he said and found an African stress idol and a floppy disk. My floppy disk!

'I've checked it. It's on there and I have backed it up on my computer, just in case.'

'Nice one!'

'Yes, I didn't realise that he returned the disks with the idols.'

'No.'

'So we needn't have gone yesterday.'

Bill was eavesdropping.

'NO, BUT IT'S ALWAYS BETTER TO GO TO THE DOCTOR WITH SOMEONE, JUST IN CASE YOU COLLAPSE ON THE WAY.'

'What? Why are you shouting?'

Ed nudged Spud and the penny dropped.

'You're right. I didn't mind, anyway. I'm glad you're all right now.'

They all headed for the door.

'YOU MIGHT HAVE GOT ILL AFTER YOU CAUGHT YOUR LIP ON THE RING PULL OF YOUR FIFTEENTH CAN OF LAGER AT MY BIRTHDAY PARTY ON SUNDAY NIGHT,' Spud called as they left.

Bastard!

Bill scowled at me.

This evening I reinstalled the file on the computer but I didn't tell Dad. I'm hoping that he will find it and think he overlooked it before.

Ed came around this evening and curiously invited me round to Lara's house. My initial suspicions were confirmed when they absurdly announced to me that they were going out with each other.

'I know you've got a soft spot for Lara, so we thought that we had better tread carefully.'

'I am very fond of Lara,' I said, 'but I stopped flogging that dead horse a long time ago.'

Lara looked insulted.

'No offence,' I added.

10 September 2003, Wednesday

The build-up to tonight's match between England and Leichtenstein dominated today. The morning papers reported that James Beattie would be starting the match with Michael Owen and Wayne Rooney up front in a line-up that was designed to score goals.

I had to put up with the usual speculation about whether Beattie was good enough to play for England and people saying that he will have to move to a bigger club to really prove himself.

Surely being the Premiership's top English striker for *tiny little* Southampton should double his credibility. A player whose goals kept a team up single-handedly, or even footedly, surely must be exceptional.

I hoped all day that he would shine in the match but, although he hit the bar and worked hard, the credits went to England's actual goal scorers in the match, Rooney and Owen.

I watched the match at home with Dad and went to bed a bit deflated. If he has to leave to further his career, it means that the big-money club will always corner the market, which can only be bad for the game.

Since Chelsea were taken over by a multi-billionaire there are rumoured to be a horde of similar Eastern European rich boys gagging to buy Premiership football clubs.

What happens when football goes out of fashion or they get bored with it and want to waste their money on something else? It can't be good for football.

I hope that none of them has ever heard of Southampton. I hope also that our chairman, Rupert Lowe, loves the club enough not to accept a big personal pay day at the expense of the club's future security.

11 September 2003, Thursday

The papers were all slagging off James Beattie, which is bad for his England prospects but good for Southampton because he will probably score on Saturday.

Today is the second anniversary of the destruction of the World Trade Centre in New York. I don't think that anybody will forget where they were when they first heard the news.

I was at school and Mr Bartlett called us all into a special assembly. He told us that we would witness, on the television news, images that would stay with us for ever; that they would fascinate us and horrify us, but that we would find it difficult to avoid watching them over and over again because we would find it hard to believe that what we have seen isn't a special effect from a Hollywood blockbuster.

He also said, 'Remember, when you watch those planes hit the towers, that you are watching hundreds of people dying in a single instant.'

How right he was and how wrong the hijackers were. How wrong George Bush is for not trying the course of understanding the religious beliefs of other nations. How wrong Osama Bin Laden is for the same thing. They should lock both of them up in the same lunatic asylum and throw away the key.

I tried to work on autopilot today. I find it so boring but I don't want to feel that way. I long for the end of the day. I really want to enjoy being at work. Maybe if I tune my mind to it I can try to enjoy it but the day is so monotonous.

It's the same chores, the same surroundings, the same customers and no day off. I know that's my fault. If there was a nice-looking young girl there, I would love going in but then I would just get frustrated because no nice-looking girl is going to be interested in me. Come to think of it, no girl is going to be interested in me.

Spud was around our house tonight, shagging Annicka, I expect.

Dad found that his file was back on the computer but wasn't overexcited. I asked him why. He said, 'I soon realised that I had taken the precaution of backing all my stuff up onto CD a couple of days before that night. I had forgotten, in all the panic, that I only had to rewrite a couple of paragraphs. Sorry if I went a bit mad, but you do lose a bit of short-term memory when you get older.'

I'm not going to say that I don't believe it, because this sort of thing always happens to me.

12 September 2003, Friday

My positive attitude didn't work and I had an awful day today. It was wonderful when five-thirty finally arrived.

At home, Dad told me that he had bought a ticket for next week's Spurs match, which is away.

Mum said, 'What if I have had the baby?'

'I'll play it by ear, love. Obviously I won't go if you have had or look like you are going to have it.'

Bastard! I wish I could go, but my agreement at work prevents me.

I helped Mum wash up and noticed that I am now considerably taller than her. I got Dad to measure my height. I am now five foot ten. I have grown five inches in the last nine months! It is no wonder some of my shirts are becoming tight. Added to this is the fact that I have recently noticed hairs growing out of my chest.

This evening, Karl and Tom came round. Karl has got a new car. It's wicked. It's a red Renault Five Turbo with an excellent aerofoil attached to the roof. It rocks! I thought that his previous car was fast but it was nothing compared to this.

We had a great evening tearing around the island after we had picked up Ed and Lara.

13 September 2003, Saturday

With the prospect of an afternoon of football, the working day was all right.

With Southampton playing bottom side Wolverhampton Wanderers, we expected a win but you can't guarantee anything as a Saints fan. However, the team, for once, did what was expected of them and won two-nil. This was even with the referee having a terrible game. He gave us a penalty for nothing when our striker, Kevin Phillips, tripped over his own feet with nobody anywhere near him. Then he booked our defender, Graeme Le Saux, because a Wolves player ran into him.

Before the game, Dad was moaning because the Saints Travel Club had sold out of tickets to Spurs, so he's going to have to take the train.

When we got home for dinner, Mum presented me with a copy of David Beckham's autobiography *My Side*, which Dad immediately borrowed to read on the way to work.

This evening me, Karl, Tom, Spud, Annicka, Ed, Lara, Meat, Kylie, Katie and Hannah got some booze and got totally wrecked on the beach, just past Gurnard Sailing Club. We got a small fire going and turned it into a little beach barbecue when people started bringing food. Someone even brought a CD player and we had The Darkness, Linkin Park, Starsailor, and Blur keeping things lively.

Gradually people started gatecrashing the party. I went for a walk with Jason Dwyer, to see his new motorbike, and we walked past Hayley Knight and Stevie. When we returned, Stevie was on top of Hayley. I couldn't see much in the dark, but Jason said that Stevie was shagging her.

I said, 'No he wasn't' and Jason Ince interceded by saying, 'Yes he was. I prodded something with a stick that turned out to be his willy. It had definitely been somewhere unmentionable.'

'Why did you prod it?' I asked.

'I thought they were horsing around with a sausage, so I thought I'd put an end to the shenanigans by skewering the sausage with a stick. When I tried, he yelped in pain and I apologised and left.'

'Dirty stopout,' Jason Dwyer said.

'Lucky git,' I said.

When we decided to call it a day we were all staggering noisily home and people were stopping to puke over garden walls and into flowerbeds. We were not a good advert for our generation.

14 September 2003, Sunday

During the night I succumbed to the uncontrollable desire to throw up and woke up feeling terrible. Why is the result of such a good night always a terrible hangover? It's not fair.

I was useless in our away game against Seaclose this morning. Fortunately Vernon was on fine form and turned in a performance worthy of his former professionalism and his hat-trick helped us win three-two. Dad played for the last half an hour, after coming on to replace me. He played really well and it was his defence-splitting pass that set up our winning goal. I felt really good for him.

I hardly touched my roast dinner. Nan and Grandad were around as usual and I had to put up with teasing from them. At least Spud wasn't there to join in. He, fortunately for him, suffered his ill effects at home.

I gradually felt better during the afternoon, while watching the two live football matches on offer, and by dinner time I was ravenous. Our salad dinner did not satisfy my craving, so I went down to the Chinese takeaway with Ed and Lara, who came along to keep me company. We went to the icafé to see Vernon but soon regretted it, as we had to relive his goals again.

When I got home, I then had to relive Dad's assist over an over again but I didn't really mind. It was good to see him having a good opinion of himself for a change.

I had to sit through Mum's soaps. If anyone is aware of the current *Coronation Street* storyline in which an unconscious Roy is supposed to have got Tracey pregnant, how could he have done it?

Well, it brings a whole new meaning to the phrase, 'Came a Cropper'. (Roy's surname is Cropper.)

After the soaps finished, Mum waddled off to bed and Dad and I watched the film *Ali* on the movie channel. It was brilliant.

15 September 2003, Monday

The weather at the moment is more like July than September, which makes being stuck indoors even more frustrating.

Spud came to see me at lunchtime with his cronies, who all happen to be beloved friends of mine.

He has been summoned back to Cork this weekend. Apparently he has to sign some very important papers. He is obviously intrigued and excited. Also, he told me that he is taking Annicka with him this time.

He was worried that I might be annoyed about this, but the only thing that worries me is that I am going to be here on my own with a mother who is ready to pop. For once I will be happy to be at work, just to be out of her way, just in case anything drastic happens.

At home this evening I voiced my concerns to Dad while watching the game between Leicester and Leeds on Sky. He assured me that he would not leave if it looked like Mum might be on the verge of dropping.

'She could be fine in the morning and suddenly go into labour and give birth,' I said.

'It takes a bit longer than that, mate! She was in labour for eighteen hours when she had you.'

'Yes, but I was her first.'

'Second.'

'Oh, yes!'

How could I have forgotten?

16 September 2003, Tuesday

There was this woman who came into the shop today. She had the sexiest ankles I have ever seen. They were shapely and slender, so much so that they could have been sculptured. I had never thought the ankle to be a part of a woman that could be described as sexy before and I relayed this thought to Bill.

'You've got the beginnings of a fetish there, mate,' he remarked.

'What do you mean, fetish?'

'I've got some porn DVDs at home in which men finish by shooting their loads over women's ankles.'

What the hell is he on about? I was only remarking about a girl's ankles and now I'm a pervert? He's the one who sits at home watching porn on DVD and probably straining his wrist as a result!

I wonder if he'll lend me any?

Tonight I stayed in to watch Sky's coverage of the Champions League. You can watch all eight games at once. It's superb.

17 September 2003, Wednesday

Same old grind at work today, but it was all right. I was quite busy, so the day went quite quickly.

When I got home, Mum was having a lie down, a pastime she seems to be doing a lot these days.

Annicka cooked dinner for us. We had lasagne and chips, which Mum ate in bed.

After dinner I went to the Northwood Recreation Ground to play cricket with the lads. I bowled an innocuous ball to Ed and it hit a conker, which was lying, unseen, on our makeshift wicket, and hit him on the side of the head.

I felt really bad. He's got a hell of a bump on his head. When I went into bat he bowled a deliberate bouncer at me. I blindly swung the bat at it, in self-defence more than anything else, and caught it on the meat of the bat. It headed straight for Ed, who, in the failing light, tried to catch it. He mistimed his grab at the ball and it hit him on the top of the head. It was another bump for his collection.

'You vicious git!' he moaned.

'Sorry!' I said.

He seemed a bit off with me after that as we went down the town to play at the icafé.

When I got home, Spud was sitting in our living room watching TV with Mum, Dad and Annicka. He is staying the night. I'd wondered how long he would stay away. Well, it wasn't very long.

Arsenal got thumped three-nil in the Champions League. Ha, ha.

18 September 2003, Thursday

I have accumulated two days' holiday since I have been working and I intend to take them as soon as possible.

It was yet another day of bagging up birdseed, dog food and rabbit food. Why can't I have a go on the till? It's so unfair.

I was thinking, today, that if Mum goes into labour tomorrow, Dad won't be able to go to the Spurs game and he might give his ticket to me. I will use one of my days off if that happens.

At home this evening I tried to make Mum jump by popping a crisp bag behind her. I hoped that might start her off, but she has had a few shocks recently so I might have known it would have no other effect on her, other than to make her bollock me.

She said that it had woken the baby up inside her and she was now being kicked black and blue, under her ribs.

Yeah right!

19 September 2003, Friday

I was hoping to receive a phone call today saying that Mum was on her way to hospital, but I didn't.

Spud and Annicka came in to see me on their way to the ferry as they were travelling to Ireland.

When I got home this evening there was no change in Mum. She had no pains, other than under her ribs, and she is still spending most of the day in bed, so how is she going to go into labour? She did stay up, though, after I got in from work, and she cooked the dinner.

'So it's all right for me to go tomorrow?' Dad asked her.

'Of course it is. If it wasn't, I'd let you know. I know my body, Kev.'

Dad beamed.

Bollocks!

I went to see Ed to see if he was in a better mood. He was with Lara and was quite happy. He explained his attitude of yesterday by saying he was feeling frustrated because Lara was on her period.

'No I wasn't!' she said as she elbowed him in the ribs.

We spent the evening watching the DVD of *Lord of the Rings The Two Towers*. I was awakened as the end titles rolled up the screen.

20 September 2003, Saturday

Mum cooked us a delicious full English breakfast this morning and was full of the joys of spring, which alleviated Dad's anxiousness over the possibility of her suddenly going into labour.

He left to catch the eight-thirty ferry.

I left Mum, who had decided to clean the house to her standards.

'These Scandinavians must live in dust-filled houses judging by Annicka's cleaning.' She commented.

The day dragged, as it usually does on a Saturday when Saints are playing and I can't listen to the match on the radio.

Our match today had added interest as Tottenham's manager, Glenn Hoddle, who walked out on Saints two-and-a-half years ago to manage them, an act that has turned Tottenham into arch-rivals only exceeded by Pompey, was expected to get the sack if they lost.

To be there at the match that sees Hoddle's desertion finally get its expected result would have been superb. Dad kept me informed during the match with text messages. At five past three I received this message: 'ONE-NIL BEATTIE HEADER FROM OAKLEY CORNER.'

Then at three forty five, 'TWO-NIL BEATTIE FREE KICK.'

We won three-one. I wish I could have gone.

When I arrived at home I found Mum holding her belly and panting.

'Oh Troy, thank God you are here. It's started. I'm in labour.'

'Oh my God! I'll call and ambulance.'

'Too late. It's coming now,' she gasped. (My nightmare had come true.) 'Quickly, go to the bathroom and get somc towels.'

I did as she asked and when I returned she was still holding her belly but this time she was in stitches of laughter.

'I'm sorry love,' she chortled. 'I couldn't resist it the expression of horror on your face!'

I wasn't amused. She had to go and sit down.

'I've been planning ow! that all day. I wish I'd oooh! filmed it now. I could have sent it in to *You've Been Framed*. Ha, ha, ha, OOOWWW!'

She winced in pain and held her belly with both hands. In a few moments the pain passed.

'Oh dear! That was a big one.'

A few moments later 'OOOOWWWW! GOD! SHIT! IT'S STARTING!'

'You won't get me again,' I responded, suspecting a repeat performance.

'No, this really is it!' she said, with an expression on her face that let me know that she really was serious.

'I'll phone an ambulance, then,' I said.

'Don't panic. It'll be hours yet. We'll wait until Dad comes home and he can take us in. I'll make us a cup of tea.'

She got up and went to the kitchen where I heard her call out, 'Oh no!'

I quickly went to see if she was all right. She was standing in a puddle of water with red specks in it.

'My waters have gone!' he said. 'Go and get me one of those towels, love. I'm going to have to change. You can make the tea.'

'Perhaps an ambulance will be a better idea?'

'Look! Stop panicking. I know my own body. Dad'll be home in a couple of hours.'

I heard her moaning loudly from the bathroom where she stayed for half an hour or so. I called to her through the door to make sure she was all right and she said that she was having a bath.

I waited for another half an hour during which I heard lots of moaning and groaning. Eventually Mum emerged, in her dressing gown, looking very much the worse for wear.

'What time is it?' she asked, panting and moaning as she did so.

'Half past seven,' I said.

'Have you tried ringing your father again?'

'Yes, but his phone is still turned off.'

'I'll be complaining to the Southampton Travel Club about their stupid rule about having to switch off your mobile phones on their coaches. I'll be having words with your father about being such a stickler for rules under these circumstances. Oh, here comes another one! OOOHHHH!' She staggered to her bed and sat down, then rolled awkwardly onto her back.

'I'll wait here until your father gets home,' she said.

At eight o'clock I tried to phone Dad again. This time I got through. He was still on the coach, travelling along the A33. He also told me not to panic and to tell Mum that he would be home just after nine.

I told Mum this and her reaction was weird. She got out of bed and ran another bath.

'You've just had a bath,' I said.

'WELL, I'M HAVING ANOTHER ONE, OKAY?' she bellowed, just before howling in pain again. She slammed and locked the bathroom door.

The clock ticked on. I paced the hallway hoping to hear the rattle of Dad's key in the front door lock.

Eight-thirty arrived and there was a huge scream from the bathroom.

'TROY! HELP!'

I ran to the bathroom door. 'What's the matter?'

'I can feel the head!' Mum said. 'IT'S COMING!'

'Dad'll be here soon,' I yelled.

'I CAN'T WAIT THAT LONG! THE BABY'S COMING NOW! OOOOWWWW! AAAAAAGGHH!'

'I'll call an ambulance!'

'IT'S TOO LATE FOR AN AMBULANCE! I NEED YOUR HELP, NOW! GET IN HERE AND HELP ME!'

'But the door's locked! You'll have to let me in!'

'I CAN'T F***ING STAND UP WITH A BABY'S HEAD STICKING OUT OF MY CROTCH, YOU IDIOT! KICK THE DOOR IN!'

I leaned my back up against the wall opposite the bathroom door and kicked hard against the handle of the door. It swung open with ease, splinters of wood shooting in all directions.

The sight of my mother stark naked, lying in a bath with her legs spread-eagled and the top of a baby's head sticking out of her vagina was not an image of feminine naked beauty I had ever wished to see.

Mum told me to support the baby's head and pull gently as she tried to push it out. I had to touch my mother's vagina to do this. I felt as though I was going to be sick.

I didn't want my first memory of touching a woman's vagina to be the one woman whose vagina I never ever wanted to see or touch, along with every other female relative of mine, except my aunt, Cathy.

Mum felt the urge to push and she did with all her might. Her face turned purple with the strain. The baby's head moved until its neck was held by Mum's vagina. Its squashed-up little face looked like it was grimacing.

'I think the head is out!' I said.

Mum looked down and gasped. She looked like she was about to cry. Then the urge to push came again and I heard myself encouraging her. 'Come on! One big push!' I said.

Mum's face went purple again and she strained and then started panting and out came the baby. I caught her and handed her to Mum. The bloody and naked little cherub cried straight away and went bright pink as she screamed.

'Hello!' Mum said to the baby. 'Hello! You're out now!'

The baby cried. I wrapped her in a towel and covered up Mum's bits with another towel. Then Dad arrived.

He took one look at the scene and fainted. I called an ambulance and we were all taken to St Mary's Hospital.

Mum and the baby were checked over by doctors and Mum was kept in overnight. Me and Dad went home to a very quiet house.

Before we went to bed, Dad poured out a glass of whisky for both of us and made a toast. 'To my kids,' he said as he downed his in one.

'To us,' I replied, as I downed mine in one and nearly gagged. It tasted disgusting.

21 September 2003, Sunday

All the shenanigans of last night caused me to miss *The Premiership* and our goals against Tottenham.

I had to phone Pitbull and tell him that we wouldn't be able to play this morning. He wasn't happy but accepted our reasons with his congratulations.

Dad spent the morning phoning people with the good news. He kept having to say, 'We haven't decided on a name yet,' and 'Yes, Troy helped deliver her. Yes, our Troy. It's true!'

At the earliest possible time, we made our way to the hospital to see Mum and the baby.

Now she was all wrapped up in her baby things, I could look at her properly. Mum made me hold her. I never thought that this would happen to me, but I had this overwhelming and sudden feeling of love; a feeling I don't understand and find difficult putting down in words, but never-the-less I love that little girl, my sister.

'What do you think of her?' Mum asked.

'She's beautiful!' I said, turning away to conceal my building emotions.

'She looks exactly like you did when you were born,' Dad said.

I blushed, but it was all right as I was showing the baby the view from the window.

'I couldn't have given birth to her without your help, Troy! You were fantastic!'

'You didn't give me much choice, if I remember!'

'You were great. We haven't got a name for her yet. Have you got any ideas?'

I looked at the baby's sleeping face and her perfect, tiny little fingers.

'She's like a little angel isn't she?'

'Yes,' Mum and Dad said together.

'Angel,' I whispered to the baby. 'Little Angel-ina. How about Angelina, like Angelina Jolie?'

'Perfect! That's a beautiful name.'

Mum beckoned for me to give Angelina back to her.

'Hello Angelina. I'm your Mummy. This is your silly old Daddy.' Dad waved back in the way people usually wave at babies. 'And this is your big brother, Troy.'

I felt a wonderful warm sensation of pride surge through my veins.

During the day, several visitors came and went: Nan and Grandad Brown; then Spud and Annicka arrived. Spud couldn't believe that I had helped bring Angelina into the world but he agreed that the name fitted.

'I've got some news,' he said, 'but we'll wait until everyone is home and settled.'

We tried to persuade him to give up his secret but he wouldn't budge, and when Nan and Grandad Stenning turned up and he got a dirty look from Grandad, he and Annicka left.

I thought that I had managed to escape the slobbery kisses and bear hugs, but once Mum recapped the story I was covered in drool and bruises.

Soon it was time for all visitors to leave and we headed for home. Nan and Grandad Stenning have booked into the Fountain Hotel and Dad went out for a booze-up with his mates leaving me at home alone.

It was nine p.m. and I decided that it was time for me to have my own little celebration. I got a half-pint glass from the kitchen and made up a cocktail of brandy, gin, whisky, port, pernod and sherry. I downed it in one and was absolutely pissed out of my head in seconds.

I nearly forgot to say. Glenn Hoddle got the sack from Tottenham. What a brilliant weekend! I'm pissed.

22 September 2003, Monday

I have never had such a bad hangover in my life. I puked so much that I felt as though my stomach was going to come out of my mouth.

I drank a pint of water and stopped being sick, but still felt very fragile as I went to work.

I was quite proud of myself for going in. I could easily have taken a day off sick, but I thought that if I went in and owned up that my fragile state was due to alcohol abuse, then when I really needed to take a sickie it would be swallowed by Colin and Bill a lot easier.

What I actually got at work today was a torrent of stick. I didn't tell them about my involvement in Angelina's birth, just the fact that she had arrived.

They understood why I had got drunk, though.

I gradually felt better as the day went on.

When I got home from work, Mum and Angelina were home. Nan and Grandad Stenning and Spud were there as well. Spud was cuddling her and looking totally uncomfortable as he made oochie-coochie noises to her. I noticed the scowl on Grandad's face, but if Spud had seen it he seemed to ignore it.

Griz was a bit wary. He kept sniffing her. Dad said that he weed himself when they arrived home from the hospital.

Annicka made our dinner, which was bangers and mash with onion gravy. Her English cooking is certainly improving.

After dinner, Spud told us his news. They have got a buyer for his house in Cork. A multimillionaire has offered him a sum of money for his house.

We all gasped when he quoted the figure: 'Seven hundred and fifty thousand pounds.'

Spud said that he saw no point in continuing at school now. Mum argued with him about it, but he said, 'What's the point. I can live off twenty-five thousand pounds a year for the next thirty years. That's without taking the interest into account, although I am going to spend two hundred and fifty grand of it when I get it.'

That set Mum off again, but Spud was adamant. He can still live on twenty-five thousand a year for the next twenty years, not including interest.

Grandad put an end to the discussion when he said, very grumpily, 'It's his money. Let him do what he wants with it.'

On the News tonight they reported that ex-world boxing champion, Frank Bruno, has been admitted to a mental hospital. Poor old Frank! My Dad's met him and said that he's a lovely man.

We had to turn the television up to hear the news as Angelina chose this time to have a screaming session.

Ed and Lara came round this evening to see the baby, although I think that it was more for Lara's benefit than for Ed. Lara had a cuddle but Ed politely declined when Lara offered Angelina to him.

He did predictably say, 'She's lovely. At least she hasn't got her brother's ugly mug.'

Ed told me that Cowes Park Rangers lost three-nil on Sunday. They were so short of players that Pitbull had to play under my dad's name as he was suspended, and he got sent off again for a professional foul.

This was confirmed when Pitbull called this evening to warn Dad that he would be receiving a fine from the Hampshire FA very soon. Pitbull handed over the fine to Dad in cash and asked him if he wouldn't mind pretending to them that it was him.

Dad didn't have much choice but to agree.

23 September 2003, Tuesday

Little or no sleep was achieved last night thanks to Angelina's screaming.

Two important letters arrived through the letter box this morning: Dad's fine from the Hampshire FA and a letter from the courts reminding me that I had to give evidence next week. It filled me with dread. I took the letter to work to show Colin, as I will have to take the day off and don't want to waste a day's holiday.

I wonder if I will have to do the same thing at some stage concerning the mad Doctor Kinsella who is still institutionalised. God, he might be chatting to Frank Bruno right now!

Talking of Bruno, the papers have been very unkind to him. I like him but they are just taking the piss out of him. I don't think it's right. It's not his fault he is ill.

I could hear Angelina's screaming on the corner from Battery Road as I approached our house. It wasn't the most welcoming of noises.

Mum, Dad and Annicka all looked very weary. Dad decided to get a KFC for dinner and I kept him company on the trip for some peace and quiet.

Griz is still behaving strangely. When Angelina cries he howls, and when she sleeps he sits and stares at her.

Dad registered the birth today and showed me the birth certificate Angelina Ethel Brown. They have done it again! They gave her the middle name Ethel after Dad's grandmother who died a year ago, and I was lumbered with Abel as a middle name after my late great-grandad, a name I must delete by deed poll at the earliest available opportunity.

Spud came round this evening, fresh from his first ever driving lesson. I didn't see much of him. He confined himself and Annicka to her bedroom.

I was considering going out this evening, but I was so tired after last night that I decided to veg out in front of the TV and watch Cardiff play West Ham in the Carling Cup. It was a good game actually, as West Ham came from two-nil down to win three-two.

24 September 2003, Wednesday

3.17 a.m. Note to self: Buy some earplugs.

4.09 a.m. It finally went quiet half an hour ago but I couldn't get off to sleep.

5.33 a.m.Note to self: Look into rented accommodation.

7.02 a.m. Just got off and it is time to get up. I have a new name for the baby: Thunderlungs.

Nan and Grandad Stenning came in to see me at work on their way home and duly embarrassed me with their overexaggerated and physical goodbyes, and they invited themselves on a tour of the shop when we were at our busiest. I didn't get bollocked for it though.

I can remember vividly the first Southampton match that my Dad took me to. I was six years old, in October 1993. It was in the days of Ian Branfoot, a very nice man according to Dad, who met him at an Isle of Wight Saints function once, but a terrible manager for Saints.

His crime? He dropped our best player from the team. Matthew Le Tissier's goals had kept Saints in the top flight of English football for several seasons. Anyway, there we were, languishing in or near the relegation zone, as per usual, with our only hope of survival sat on the bench.

In the evening game that Dad took me to, we were playing Newcastle United. Dad had managed to get us tickets because sales were down due to poor recent results and the fact that the match was being shown live on Sky. Branfoot decided that night to play Le Tissier, probably to prove that he would have no positive effect on the team. The opposite happened. He scored two of the most memorable goals in Premiership history and we won two-one. I was hooked on Saints from that point on.

In subsequent years and with some different managers, we flirted with relegation and Matty saved us.

Dad had been on the waiting list for a season ticket for a couple of years and in 1997 he got them and we began going regularly from then on. Still we flirted with relegation, but since we moved from our old decrepit but quaint stadium, The Dell, to the plush and grand St Mary's Stadium, our team has gone from strength to strength.

A cup final last season meant qualification for the UEFA Cup tonight, and me and Dad headed there for our venture into European club football against Romanian giants Steaua Bucharest.

Saints brought out a new special European shirt for the occasion to which I remarked, 'What's the point of bringing out a new shirt for just one game?'

‘Money.’ Dad replied.

‘Rip off!’ I said.

We saw this enormous bloke dressed in the only clothes that he could buy that would fit him. Isn’t it ironic that a man who has obviously had no exercise in years can only wear a tracksuit?

I missed the start of the second half because I had ordered a cup of hot chocolate, sat back in my seat, then taken a sip only to find that I had spent one pound twenty on a cup of steaming hot water. I had to go and complain and was given a cup of hot chocolate, but by then I had missed five minutes of the second half and annoyed the spectators along our row, who had to stand up to let me in.

I told the bloke next to me that I had ordered a cup of hot chocolate and been given a cup of hot water and he said, ‘I’m surprised you can tell the difference.’

Steaua went one-nil up in the first half. In the event of a draw, away goals count as double, so even though we equalised in the second half and probably deserved to win it, the game finished one-one and I can’t see us getting a win in Romania, so we are out after just one game.

Dad and I arrived home at eleven-fifteen and found Mum lying on the settee fast asleep with Angelina also asleep in her arms. Dad gently removed Angelina, placed her in her Moses basket and carried her to their bedroom. He returned with a duvet, which he gently placed over Mum, then we both went to bed.

25 September 2003, Thursday

Mum woke up this morning panicking. She awakened to find Angelina missing and Dad got told off for scaring her. The ensuing argument woke Angelina, who transformed into her alter ego, Thunderlungs.

I left them bickering and went to work.

Spud came to see me at lunchtime and suggested that we must try to get to London to indulge in the country’s latest craze Blaine-bating.

All you have to do is get on a train to Tower Bridge and throw an egg at the perspex box that David Blaine is suspended in over the River Thames. The trick is doing it without getting beaten up by his security guards.

I can’t do it this weekend because of football, but I told him that I would keep it in mind for next weekend.

It was all nice and peaceful when I arrived home, and I had a cuddle with Angelina while I watched *Meridian Tonight*. It is quite soothing to hold a sleeping baby.

I ended up staying in as Ed was seeing Lara and Meat was doing his own thing. Spud was, of course, seeing Annicka.

26 September 2003, Friday

Very little sleep last night due to Thunderlungs. I'm getting a bit fed up but I did get some earplugs from Boots this lunchtime, so I hope that will cure the problem.

The weather is turning colder. I had to wear a T-shirt in bed for the first time in months. I also had to wear my jacket on the way to work.

You can tell how boring things are at work because I have hardly ever got anything to write about it.

This evening Ed, Lara, Meat, Jason Dwyer, Tom, Kylie and I went to Katie's house to play Twister.

Jason suggested that we play Strip Twister and my heart leapt with hope, but the girls weren't up for it. We had a good laugh.

27 September 2003, Saturday

Thunderlungs started up last night so I put my earplugs in, which led to me oversleeping this morning. I had to leave for work in a hurry and consumed my toast along the road.

The bright sunshine that blazed through the shop window was a misleading guide to the temperature outside, which definitely has an autumnal feel to it.

Dad called into the shop when it was time to leave to watch the football.

The match itself was terrible, if you are a Saints fan. I know that no team can play well in every game, but you always live in hope that your team can. Today Middlesbrough played like we normally do and worked hard to win the ball in every position. We were deservedly one-nil down after only fifteen minutes and I knew at that point that we would not recover.

Kevin Phillips got sent off in injury time for kicking the arse of a Middlesbrough defender who had sneakily stamped on his foot.

Pompey's defeat by Birmingham helped to stop the day becoming a complete disaster and means that we remain above them in the league.

I have over a month to wait now before I go to any more games as all our games for October are away from home. What a drag!

This evening I went round to Ed's house where we watched this disgusting porno film in which girls were having sex with animals. All the lads found it very funny, but I had to shut my eyes because I would have embarrassed myself by being physically sick. How can people really get turned on by such perverted filth and how can the women involved bring themselves to do it?

Nothing on Earth would make me do anything like that.

Me, Meat and Jason spent the night in Tom and Karl's front room. His parents have gone away for a dirty weekend in Newquay.

28 September 2003, Sunday

A good, albeit uncomfortable night's sleep which has increased my desire to seek rented accommodation.

We had a home game in the Isle of Wight Sunday League Cup. A full-strength side faced Cowes Social, which meant Dad had to run the line.

We won four-nil and I scored a brace. Vernon nipped in front of me and headed in from Ed's corner when I was just about to head it in myself for a hat-trick, the bastard.

Pitbull was ecstatic. We found out the name of Nathan's googly-eyed girlfriend today. She's called Helen. I think I will continue to call her Nathan's googly-eyed girlfriend, unless I need to catch her attention.

Spud made me laugh when he said, 'I bet her gynaecologist needs to use potholing safety gear when examining her.'

It was lunch as usual at home with my parents and the doting grandparents. Both Mum and Annicka cooked the spread, which was one of the best we have ever had.

Then the men all sat down to watch a brilliant pay-per-view match in which Charlton Athletic beat Liverpool three-two.

Grandad's got a date through for his op. He is going in on Monday week. He is petrified.

Talking of petrification, my long awaited court appearance is tomorrow. I can't wait for it all to be over.

Mum tried to show me how to change Angelina's nappy. It wasn't pleasant. I breathed through my mouth.

So it was another evening in. I get the feeling that my group of friends is disbanding. I am seeing so much less of them nowadays.

29 September 2003, Monday

A day off work would normally be a thing to look forward to, but today I had to make the trip to Winchester Crown Court for the trial of murder suspect and definite pervert, Trevor Marsh.

Dad is still on paternity leave, which was convenient, so he came with me. We arrived at the court building bang on time. I was so nervous that I had to go to the toilet several times.

I had my David Beckham autobiography with me and I looked at lots of the words without taking any of them in. I was surprised to see Ed there. He was sitting with his Mum along the corridor. We exchanged waves but weren't allowed to speak to each other.

Most of the day was spent waiting. The morning ended and we had to go for lunch.

At one time I thought that they would never call me in but finally, at eight minutes past three, I was summoned in.

I had to take the stand with every eye in the court on me, including Trevor Marsh, whose stare sent a chill down my spine.

Then I had to take the oath and this barrister started asking me questions. He just asked me to tell the court what had happened when I met Trevor Marsh before the Millwall game. Then he said, 'No further questions, my lord.'

I was preparing myself for a horrific cross-examination, but the judge asked the other barrister if he would like to question me and he declined.

I left the courtroom on a high. It was over. Months of worrying and it was so easy.

When Dad and I arrived back in Southampton we went to the Saints Megastore in West Quay. Dad bought Angelina a Saints Babygro. Then we went home.

This evening I went round to Ed's house to see what had happened to him and he told me that he went through exactly the same thing. He had watched the local news but there was no mention of our contribution.

I stayed there for a while and played X-Box games as Lara was spending the evening at Rachel's house.

I actually watched *Eastenders* tonight, as it was the big, long-awaited return of Dirty Den. The annoying thing was that we had to wait until the end of the episode to see it. Then it was DUFF DUFF DUFF duffduffduffduff-duffduff et cetera.

30 September 2003, Tuesday

I can't believe it. I have been asked to give evidence at Doctor Kinsella's trial now. A letter arrived this morning.

Shit!

In fact Spud has as well. March the first is the dreaded date.

So it was back to work today and it was as uneventful as ever. Dad came in to see me as I finished today. He wanted some company during his blood donation this afternoon.

Spud went with him for his first ever donation. I am still too young as you have to be seventeen.

Dad has got a silver donor card and I noticed that it said 'Blood Group AB' at the bottom left corner.

'That's the same as me,' I said.

'I guess that proves you're my son then,' Dad said.

'Not if Mum is also AB,' I teased

'Your mother is O.'

'Oh!'

Then Spud returned from his interview with the anaemia nurse with a plaster on his finger.

'Did you find out your blood group?' I asked him.

'No!' he said. 'I already know it.'

'What are you then?'

'AB, why?'

'AB-Y? I didn't know there was a Y blood group!'

'NO AB, WHY? Double you hayche why!'

'Hey! That's the same as us!' I said. 'Welcome to the club.'

'What's the big deal? We *are* related.'

'I know, but I suppose it just makes us even more blood brothers if we have the same blood group.'

They both looked at me as if I was talking bollocks which I, of course, was.

I blagged a cup of tea and a biscuit with them before we all went home for dinner.

1 October 2003, Wednesday

I have booked this Saturday off work. I know I could have booked a day in which we are playing football, but I need a long weekend.

Karl came bounding into the shop this afternoon and he thrust an invite to Stevie's eighteenth birthday party at Colonel Bogey's tomorrow night into my hand.

A minibus will pick us all up from the Round House.

What a bonus! I haven't had a good night out for ages.

He also reiterated his desire to go to the Fulham away game. I told him to remind me about that a month before the game, otherwise we would miss out on tickets.

It was another night in watching the Champions League, although I watched it on my own as Dad was busy browsing the Internet.

I expected to see Spud tonight but he didn't turn up, so I phoned him about Saturday. He's up for it.

The jury delivered their verdict in the Trevor Marsh trial; not guilty of murder! I can't believe it. He's been put away, though, for two years for abduction and attempted abduction and for having obscene images of children on his computer.

They must be the most incompetent jury of all time.

2 October 2003, Thursday

After another long day at work and a delicious dinner of shepherd's pie, I met up with Tom, Karl, Meat, Lara, Katie, Kelly, Stevie, Nathan, Helen, Kylie, Hannah, Spud, Annicka, the Jasons, and a handful of people that I don't know and we were taken by minibus to Sandown.

As soon as we got inside the club, the drinks were flowing and we danced and drank all evening.

I noticed this very plain-looking girl hanging around me on the dance floor. She made a point of trying to speak to me.

She must have been drunk because she said, 'I REALLY FANCY YOU!' over the din.

I didn't bounce the comment but I thought that I might as well take advantage of the situation. When the music stopped and we left the dance floor I grabbed her and snogged her. Later, with the lights on, I could see that she was actually quite ugly but I shut my eyes and performed some tongue wrestling with her. I could hear my friends egging us on.

We had to leave the nightclub and, as we waited for the minibus to come and take us home, I continued snogging with the girl whose name was Mandy.

The coach came and she slipped me a piece of paper with her mobile number on it. I took it with little intention of following it up.

3 October 2003, Friday

I didn't feel too bad this morning, just a little tired. I had a great time last night.

Spud and the rest of the sixth-form posse visited me at lunchtime to give me some stick.

'Hey Troy, what did it say on the door handle of Bogey's as we went in?' Tom asked.

I had to think for a bit. 'Pull?'

'That's right. It wasn't supposed to mean pull a bird.'

'Ha, ha, very funny.'

The girls asked me when I was going to see her again. I told them that I didn't know.

During the afternoon I couldn't help thinking that this girl was obviously keen on me, so maybe this could be my big chance to finally get a shag.

I eventually convinced myself to do something that I hadn't originally planned to do. I phoned Mandy and arranged to meet her.

After dinner I got Dad to take me to her house, which is in Ryde.

Mandy goes to Ryde High School. She is in the sixth form. She is seventeen years old and has terrible eczema. She has this awful flaky skin all over her face. She has dry lips and buck teeth. She looked even worse than she did on Thursday night, now I was sober and the light was on.

We spent three hours cuddling and snogging on the settee in her front room. Her family were occupying their dining room, which is where they usually spend the evening. My groin ached so badly that I could hardly walk when I left.

Dad asked me what was wrong. I said that I was just a bit stiff. He said, 'I bet you are!'

Target number three has been achieved, and I am officially going out with Mandy. At last I have a girlfriend. I just wish I fancied her.

4 October 2003, Saturday

After a very bad night with Thunderlungs in which even the earplugs didn't work, a nap on the train to Waterloo was welcome.

Me and Spud headed for Tower Bridge, but the whole day was one big let-down when we were searched and relieved of our eggs by security guards before spending half an hour staring at this shape in a perspex box.

So we went home. I listened to Saints lose to Newcastle on my radio, but the pain was relieved by the news that Pompey had also lost at home to Charlton.

When I got home, Mum got me to change Angelina's nappy while she finished preparing dinner. This was all right because it wasn't a pooey nappy.

Then she showed me how to administer some medicine called Infacol. It is supposed to help cure something called colic, which is the reason for Angelina's constant grizzling.

I am getting a bit suspicious that I may be being groomed for babysitting.

5 October 2003, Sunday

This morning we had an away game against Rookley. With all of our players fully fit we ran riot, winning nine-nil.

I won us a penalty in the last minute and, after having already scored a hat-trick, I persuaded Dad to step up and take it. He nervously stepped up but I don't know who was the proudest when his toe poked it in off the crossbar, him or me.

At lunchtime Mum and Dad announced that they would be spending next week in Penarth with Nan and Grandad. They asked me if I would like to come but I declined. I have to work, anyway.

'No parties!' Dad said.

I wouldn't dare trust certain people to behave themselves in my house.

I went to see Mandy for the rest of the day. We kissed and cuddled for most of the time, in her bedroom. My whole groin was throbbing even worse than last time. Dad arrived to take me home at nine.

Before leaving, I invited her around to stay the night next weekend. She jumped at the chance.

'Aren't you going to ask your parents?' I asked.

'Oh, they won't mind,' She said.

I will have to buy some condoms.

6 October 2003, Monday

At lunchtime today, I went to the Co-op to try to buy some condoms, but they kept them behind the tobacco counter and I couldn't just ask for them. Everywhere, except Boots, had the same arrangement, but I couldn't buy them from Boots as I'd discovered that Hayley Knight had started working there.

While I was at home this afternoon, eating my dinner, I found out that Grandad was desperately disappointed because his operation had been cancelled at the last minute.

I thought that the condom problem was solved this evening, when Tom came in to say that we were all going to the pub tonight with Karl. I thought that I could get some from the machine in the toilets.

So when we were at the Union Inn I went to the loo several times, but I was never alone long enough to buy some.

Everyone thought that I had some sort of illness, but I just said that I had drunk a lot during the day. I was drinking blackcurrant and lemonade in the pub. They asked us all for ID, so there was no chance of any under age-drinking, unfortunately.

During a game of darts I noticed that the pub had got quite empty, so I went to the loo only to find that the bloody condom machine was empty.

Shit!

7 October 2003, Tuesday

I worked today on autopilot. That way the day didn't seem to drag so much.

This evening Spud was around, seeing Annicka. He told us that the sale of the house had gone through. He said that all he needed to do now was provide a blood sample to prove that he is Kinsella's son and he will be rich. The lucky sod!

'When will you receive your money?' Mum asked.

'In a week or so.' Spud said. 'Then Annicka might be booking a holiday, if that's all right, Alison?'

'I should think so.'

'We'll discuss it first,' Dad interrupted. He glared at Mum.

'Okay!' Mum glared back at him, more effectively.

Dad went very quiet after that. So Mum tried to lighten the proceedings by taking the piss out of me. She started to recite my old early childhood quotes.

Once she was about to brush my teeth for me when I refused to let her, demanding to brush my own teeth.

When Mum asked why, I said, 'I've got an oyster in my mouth,' which actually meant I had an ulcer.

I was watching an aeroplane leave a trail in the sky and asked my Mum what the long cloud coming out of the plane was called. Mum replied, 'A plane did it.' From then on I called them plane didits.

One Easter I recited the story of Jesus's death to my grandparents. 'Jesus died on the cross. Then he was buried in a cave and he came back to laugh.'

I used to call a car park a par cark.

I used to call a blouse a blawers.

I used to call a hospital a hostiple.

At Christmas I always used to have trouble saying Mary and Joseph and I would say Mary and Jovith.

8 October 2003, Wednesday

My earplugs worked well last night. The moment I removed them, I could hear Thunderlung's dulcet tones.

She soon calmed down when I cuddled her. I took the time to rock her off to sleep before having my own breakfast.

I obviously have the knack with babies. I just wish I had the knack with the other variety of babe. No offence to Mandy, but she hardly falls into the category of babe. At the moment, though, she could hold the key to the magic jar that is currently holding my cherry. That was a reference to the magic jar in Disney's *Beauty and the Beast*, which held a dying rose. I imagine my cherry in place of the rose and, unlike the rose in the story, my cherry is not deteriorating.

Bill asked me to mind the till at work today, while he nipped to the loo. My heart rose for a few moments until he called out, 'Don't touch anything, though. If anybody wants to buy anything, just tell them I'll be back in a mo.'

This put me in a bad mood for the rest of the day. This evening's trip to the pub was a welcome diversion from my grumpiness and soon the lads had me in stitches of laughter.

It was Jason 'Entertainment' Dwyer who provided the moment of the evening when he ordered some pub grub, which was a bowl of chips.

'Do you want a fork?' asked Maxine, the barmaid. She is a rather buxom woman who is around my mum's age.

'I'm not that bloody desperate, thanks,' said Jason.

Maxine just laughed. He was lucky she saw it as a joke and didn't think that he was being serious. The fact that she found it amusing set all of us off in fits of giggles.

I went to the toilet to check for condoms and, as I was peering through the window on the front of the machine, Karl walked in.

'That's always empty,' he said as he unzipped his flies. 'Let's move on to the Fountain. You might get some there.'

So we all went to the Fountain and I got a two-pack from their toilet.

This was my first ever pub crawl, even if it was just two pubs.

9 October 2003, Thursday

I seem to have earned the job of giving Angelina her breakfast. It makes me feel quite contented watching her sucking the teat on the bottle and making gulping noises while still maintaining steady breathing. I didn't realise that babies could drink and breathe at the same time.

There is no point in my mentioning anything about work.

Spud and Annicka told us all tonight that they would be taking next week off, as Annicka won't be needed anyway.

So I will be home alone next week. Wicked!

Maybe I will arrange a quiet little gathering. If I pick a midweek day it should cut down on gatecrashers.

10 October 2003, Friday

Mum and Dad left before I headed off for work. Annicka was already out at Spud's house, so I had a small taste of being master of the house before going to work.

I spent the whole day fretting about the possibility of a shag tonight - how I would perform, et cetera. I thought that if I put both condoms on my penis at the same time it would numb it enough for me not to climax at the first contact with bare female flesh.

Mandy phoned during the day to confirm that she would arrive at six o'clock. This just heightened my anxiety.

Walkers are doing a 'buy an Indian meal and get one free' offer and I had a voucher, which I redeemed from Cowes Tandori on my way home.

Mandy arrived, bang on time, and we ate the Indian over a glass of Cabernet Sauvignon, which she had brought with her in a carton.

We sat for a couple of hours drinking the wine, which was disgusting at first, but tasted nicer the more you drank.

We talked about sex and she said that she thinks she is allergic to condoms because she always gets a green discharge after she has had sex with a man who has worn one.

The thought of this green discharge turned my stomach and put me off my Indian meal.

It must have been gone midnight when we decided it was time to go to bed. She went to bed wearing her jeans, which seemed to me a bit like going to bed wearing a chastity belt.

We snogged for hours. I even plucked up the courage to fondle her bare breasts, which, I have to say, felt perfect. They were smooth and firm, with no sign of flaky skin.

My Dad's advice of no sex on the first night kept coming into my head and she ended up going to sleep, leaving me with a throbbing pain in my scrotum yet again.

11 October 2003, Saturday

It is a shame that I had to work today. I told Mandy that she could stay in our house all day and make herself at home, but she elected to go home. However, she did agree to meet me this evening so that we could go to the cinema together.

I threw my condoms away. I slipped them into the postbox opposite the entrance to Battery Lane - a little gift for the postman.

After work I watched England qualify for the European Championships by drawing nil-nil in Turkey. I had a bath at half-time and got Karl to give me a lift to Newport. It took us five minutes from my house to the cinema car park. That included a slowdown as we passed the speed cameras at the bottom of Horsebridge Hill.

Mandy was waiting at the door of Pizza Hut where we had a very pleasant meal. Then we went to watch *Calendar Girls*. For a woman's film, it was really good.

I had hoped that, afterwards, Mandy would be coming home with me, but her Dad was waiting outside to give her a lift home.

Gutted!

I had left my phone at home all day, charging. I switched it on and a message appeared from Spud: CALL ME

So I did. Annicka answered.

'Hello Troy! Mrs Hudd here.'

'What?'

Spud then came on. 'Hello little brother,' he slurred. 'You are speaking to a married man.'

'What the bloody hell are you on about?'

'We're in Gretna, fella! We are married! I wanted you to be the first to know, but if you don't mind we have got some consummating to do.'

12 October 2003, Sunday

Old Woottonians were the visitors to Northwood Rec this morning. Our two absentees made no difference to the side as we romped to a four-nil victory. We are top of the league and Pitbull is ecstatic. I had my best game of the season so far. I scored two and made two. Even Vernon was singing my praises.

When I got home I phoned Mandy. She invited me over to Ryde as she was going to a friend's party tonight.

So I caught the bus and met up with her and her friend Amy at Yelf's in Union Street.

After a few drinks, all of them alcoholic, we went to the party. The moment we entered the house was the last time I saw Mandy.

I spent the evening getting drunk on free cider and chatting to Amy, who is very nice but has a boyfriend.

The other people at the party were very hospitable towards me and everyone was very sympathetic when word broke out that Mandy had been having sex with some lad in the bathroom.

I didn't feel the slightest bit bothered by this news and thanked the host and Amy and caught the bus home.

On the bus I received a text message from Mandy: 'I THINK WE'ED BETTER CALL IT A DAY'.

I texted back: 'OK "SUNDAY" AND GOODBYE'.

What a relief! I am still a bloody virgin, though.

13 October 2003, Monday

A weekend of great promise is over, but Spud and his new bride arrived back today and came to see me in the shop to ask about arranging a party.

I had promised not to have one, but I am sure that all parents who leave their teenage kids at home alone must half expect them to ignore this instruction.

I told Spud to sort things out, as I would be providing the venue for the piss-up.

This turned out to be an incorrect assumption. Spud arranged the shindig at his parents' house in Arctic Road.

The whole of our year at school seemed to be crammed into that little house. Spud had bought countless crates of alcohol and everyone got wrecked, apart from me. I had to work the next morning, so I limited myself to one bottle of Woodpecker Cider.

Being sober didn't prevent me from having a great evening, the highlight for me being when Karl, Tom, me and Ed pinned a virtually unconscious Meat down while Jason Dwyer shaved off one side of Meat's black bum-fluff moustache.

Spud apologised to me for not having me as his best man. I said that if he wanted me to be his best man that was good enough for me. Even if I wasn't present at the wedding I was best man in spirit.

Just before I left, I went upstairs to go to the loo and lost my bearings. I opened what I thought was the toilet door and was greeted by someone's arse flashing up and down between some girl's bare legs.

'Oops! Sorry,' I said.

I told Ed what I had seen and he said that it was Paul Squires and Hayley Knight.

Bloody hell! Does that girl get staff discount on birth control or something? It used to be Katie Wallace that had that sort of reputation.

I also keep getting text messages from Saints fans that are going to Bucharest asking me if I am going.

It's a long way to go to see your team get knocked out. Besides I haven't got three hundred quid or enough holiday entitlement to cover it.

14 October 2003, Tuesday

I nearly overslept this morning. It was only Griz barking at the postman that woke me up. I had to eat my toast as I walked down the road, a recipe for indigestion.

I had a lunchtime visit from various bleary-eyed sixth formers and it serves them right. I had to suppress my laughter when I saw how baby-faced Meat looked without his moustache. He has, not surprisingly, evened it up by shaving off the other side.

This evening was spent down the pub. I played darts with Meat, Ed, Karl and Tom. We played a game called Killer, which I still don't completely understand but enjoyed, even though Ed won.

I wasn't tired when I got home so I went on the computer. I thought that I would have a look to see how Dad's novel was getting on and the passage I read really upset me. He set the scene in which the main character had taken his daughter to shop at the Disney Store, which was hit by a terrorist attack.

'He struggled to his little girl, desperate and helpless. Blood was pumping fast from a gash in her side. She was crying. It was a fearful, harrowing cry.
He too was crying. He held her in his arms. He felt her warm blood soak into his clothes.
'Am I going to die, Daddy?' she asked, her crystal blue eyes swimming in tears.
He smiled at her. 'Yes, darling' he said.
'I'm scared, Daddy.'
'It's all right. Daddy's here. Daddy loves you.'
'I love you too, Daddy.'
He held her and caressed her as the life he had given her slowly ebbed away.'

I never knew he could have such morbid thoughts. It made me think that his inspiration was Angelina, as I thought of her when I read it. That's what upset me, imagining that the little girl was her.

15 October 2003, Wednesday

I overslept this morning. I didn't get to work until a quarter to ten.
'What time do you call this?' was Bill's predictable remark.
'Nine forty-five. What time do you call it?'
I spent the day helping Jean.
Spud and Annicka came in to see me on their way to London for a couple of days, on a shopping trip.
If he doesn't leave school he's going to end up getting kicked out anyway at this rate.
When I got home from work I went on the computer to find a website that was showing Saints away UEFA Cup leg against Staeua Bucharest, as it wasn't being shown on television. I eventually found one and watched the match on a small, poorly rendered window.
We lost one-nil.
Pissed off and hungry, I went out to get a Chinese.

When I got back I ate the rather lukewarm meal and watched *Teen Big Brother*, which included the first ever shag in the *Big Brother* house. Although it was all hidden under a duvet and less graphic than a sex scene from a BBC2 drama, it was mildly historic, in a television sense.

16 October 2003, Thursday

I managed to get to work on time this morning after setting the alarm.

I was listening to Vernon's radio at lunchtime and there were lots of complaints about the event on *Teen Big Brother* last night.

IF YOU DON'T LIKE IT, DON'T WATCH IT!

Why do people watch a programme that they don't like just so that they can complain about it? Besides Channel Four has shown clips of sex that has happened in versions of the show from other countries.

When I got home there was a woman sitting on our doorstep. I could hear Griz going mad inside.

The woman had dishevelled mousy hair and a big rucksack with her. It was my Auntie Cathy back from her round-the-world trek.

My Auntie Cathy is slightly older than my mum and decided not to indulge in having babies and therefore has kept her teenage looks and figure and, even with unkempt hair, looks mighty fine.

I hope that it isn't perverted to fancy your Aunt but she has something. It is that sexy-older-woman thing, like Kylie Minogue has.

'Haven't you grown,' she said as she gave me a slobbery kiss and a bear hug.

Where my mum hasn't inherited her parents' attributes, Auntie Cathy has.

I invited her in and she offered to cook me some dinner after I explained that Mum and Dad were away in Penarth and that they would be back tomorrow.

She invited herself to stay and I had to stay in and play host.

I did phone Mum and Dad to let them know, and they said that they would leave early tomorrow.

She has been away for two years and wasn't in a hurry to get home until she got the news that Mum had had a baby.

I had to sit and listen to her tales and adventures for two hours, knowing that I would have to relive them several more times in the near future.

It was a relief when she announced that jetlag had caught up with her and she went to bed.

17 October 2003, Friday

I was awakened at one o'clock in the morning by an argument just outside my bedroom between Annicka and Auntie Cathy.

Auntie Cathy had decided to sleep in Annicka's bed and she wasn't happy. Spud was there trying to calm the irate Swede down.

Cathy was being equally awkward and, not knowing anything of Spud or Annicka, thought that we were being burgled.

'It's all right. This is their room, Auntie Cathy,' I explained. 'I wasn't expecting them back tonight.'

'We decided to go to see The Lion King show,' Spud explained. 'That's why we are so late.'

Spud persuaded Annicka to go to his parents' house with him and they would return after a night's sleep.

We went back to bed and I explained all to Cathy over breakfast.

Mum, Dad and Angelina came in to see me at work when they arrived back on the island. Angelina smiled when she saw me. It gave me a huge buzz.

'Is that wind?' I asked, but I knew it was a real smile because her mouth opened revealing her gums. Mum told me that she gave her first real smile to Grandad while they were away. I gave my first ever smile to him as well.

When I got home the house was full - Mum, Dad, Spud, Annicka, Auntie Cathy and Angelina. They were all sat around the dining table apparently waiting for me.

'Sit down, Troy,' Dad said. So I did as I was told.

I first met Spud at the old Denmark Road Primary School playgroup. He had been there for six months already and was assigned to be my partner. He made me very welcome and looked after me, which was the foundation of our friendship.

It is weird when you think that my mother used to pick me up and greet Spud, totally unaware that he was her son. She only became aware of the possibility when I was invited to his fourth birthday and she got talking to his mum and found out that he had been adopted.

They kept it all quiet for years.

Spud and I remained exclusive friends until we entered the brand new Cowes Primary School. There we met up with Ed and Meat. I didn't meet Jason Dwyer until I went to Solent Middle School, which is down our road, and the rest of the lads came up to Cowes High from Somerton Middle School. I didn't see as much of Spud for four years as he went to Somerton.

So all our history was about to merge at this moment with all of us gathered around the dining table and Dad about to speak.

'What the hell did you think you were doing?'

'What?' I said.

'Be quiet, Troy, I'm talking to Stuart.'

'Der Getting m-a-r-r-i-e-d,' Spud mocked.

'You are too young to get married.'

'Apparently not, if you'd like to see the licence.'

'You shouldn't marry someone on the spur of the moment. Where are you going to live?'

'Er in a house? Anyway, what's it to you? With respect, you're just my biological mother's husband.'

'You need money coming in and somewhere to live as a basis for a marriage.'

Had Dad gone mad? We all knew that Spud was coming into money. What was he worried about? Spud looked as if he was thinking the same thing as me.

'Mr Brown. Kevin. The other day I paid a cheque for five hundred and fifty thousand pounds into my bank account. I think that I am solvent enough at the moment to support my beautiful wife and myself. I have also made an offer on a house, so we will shortly have somewhere permanent to live. I appreciate your concern but we are quite happy, thank you very much.'

'You said that you had to submit a blood test before everything could be finalised,' Dad said, looking like someone had injected his face with muscle relaxant. Auntie Cathy had a smirk on her face as if she was enjoying a theatre production.

'I was only joking about that. God, there's no need for that malarkey. We all know who my dad was.'

There was a rather long, pregnant pause as all the faces in the room stared at Dad, waiting for his response.

Mum broke the silence. 'No offence, Annie, but Stuart, don't you think she might be marrying you for your money?'

'Annie was in love with me before all this happened, so I know I can trust her.'

There was another long pause.

What Dad said next changed our family for ever. 'Stuart. I am your dad.'

'Are you having a breakdown or something? All those sleepless nights must be affecting you.'

There was a murmur of agreement from all of us. Even Angelina seemed to make a noise that sounded like 'mmmmmm'.

'Let me explain,' Dad said.

'Please do!' Mum and Spud said together.

'Alison, what blood group are you?'

'O positive.'

'Stuart, what blood group are you?'

'AB.'

'I am AB.'

'So! That proves nothing,' Spud said.

There was another murmur of agreement.

'You cannot have a baby with AB blood if both parents are O positive.'

'So! Kinsella must have been AB as well.'

'He was O.'

'How do you know?'

'I met him at a donation in the summer. He showed me the free key ring they had just given him. He remarked that he had no use for a key ring and offered it to me. I looked at it. It was blue and had the words 'Group O+ Blood Donor' printed on it.'

The few moments of stunned silence were broken by Spud. 'Shit!' he groaned.

'You see?' Dad continued. 'You can't possibly be his son and I am the only other man your Mum has been with.'

'Yes, I get the picture.'

I looked at Mum. Her eyes were filling with tears. She stood up and sobbed the words, 'I'm so sorry, Stuart.' Then she left the room followed immediately by Cathy who handed Angelina to me.

Dad continued talking to Spud. 'I'm sorry, Stuart. If we'd known we'd never'

'Have given me away. I know. But you did, didn't you?'

'Yes.' Dad hung his head.

'Don't worry *Dad*. I don't hold it against you. Things haven't worked out too bad for me have they?'

'You're keeping the money?'

'Of course! It didn't say in the will that the money should go to his son. It just named the benefactor as Alison Stenning's firstborn. That's me!'

Six months ago I was my mum's firstborn. If the adoption agency had adopted Spud out to Scotland or something, I would now be rolling in cash. Never mind. Six months ago I didn't want a sister or a brother. Now I am delighted that I have full-blood siblings.

A little later, Cathy returned with Mum who hugged Spud, emotionally.

When she had eventually let him go, Annicka spoke. 'Zere was anuzzer sing. I will not need to be working for you any more.'

'Don't worry!' interrupted Cathy. 'I'll take on that job, if you'll have me?'

Spud said that they were nipping over to Sweden for the weekend to break the news to her parents. What a jet-set life he leads!

When everything had finally subsided and Spud and Annicka had left, I settled down to watch the new series of *Superstars* and the final episode of *Teen Big Brother*. Meanwhile, Dad was having a very serious talk with Mum in their bedroom and Cathy was on the computer, sending e-mails to all the friends she'd met on her trip.

18 October 2003, Saturday

I was glad to go to work this morning as Thunderlungs, Mum and Dad were going at one another, hammer and tongs.

I hoped that a day at work would mean that when I got home they would have sorted things out. They hadn't.

I sat eating my dinner in the front room with Cathy while Mum and Dad were in their bedroom discussing things.

Cathy told me that Mum was finding it very difficult coming to terms with the guilt of giving Spud up for no reason. She has been crying a lot.

The disappointing thing this evening was that I couldn't go down to the pub because Karl was going to Chicago Rock Café in Newport.

Cathy asked Dad if she could borrow his car and she took me to Newport so that we could go and watch *Finding Nemo* at the cinema.

Although I enjoyed the film, I wished I could have been next door at the Chicago Rock Café.

19 October 2003, Sunday

Pitbull was gloating this morning because Portsmouth beat Liverpool yesterday and he knew that if we, Southampton, lost to Everton today, they would go above us in the league.

Dad joined the team today to play at right back in place of Spud. The game turned out to be a welcome excursion from his problems and he ended up man of the match' in our nil-nil draw with Ventnor.

Karl said that he had had a great day yesterday. He drove to Loftus Road to watch the nil-nil bore draw between Fulham and Wolverhampton Wanderers and got home with enough time to get to the Chicago Rock Café just after nine. So that means that he will be confident he can get us to the Fulham versus Southampton game on Boxing Day. All I need now is the match tickets.

Nan and Grandad came round for lunch and were told the news about Spud. They took it in their stride. Mum cried again and was comforted by Nan.

Grandad has had another appointment for his operation cancelled, but he still seemed upbeat.

Me, Dad, Cathy and Grandad watched the Everton versus Southampton match live on Sky this afternoon.

Saints played really well but seem to have lost the ability to score goals. We drew nil-nil.

Spud and Annicka arrived back this evening and Mum became emotional again. Spud hugged her and said, 'Don't be silly. I'm happy.'

'But I feel like I've missed out on sixteen years of your life,' Mum sobbed.

'I feel privileged. A wonderful couple that I am proud to call Mum and Dad have brought me up and I have been reunited with my true family. Look to the future. You have a new daughter and daughter-in-law.'

They hugged for a while and I think that helped as Mum stayed in the front room for the rest of the evening, even after Spud and Annicka had left.

David Blaine came out of his box tonight. I know I went to London to take the piss out of him, but I have got to admit, he's an amazing man - A self-inflicted ill and painfully thin man, but still amazing.

20 October 2003, Monday

I am finding that my weekends are far too short. It is very demoralising to have to return to work after just one day's rest.

Spud and the sixth-form gang came to see me at lunchtime and we went to see Vernon.

Kinsella's old bench has a new resident, or should I say residents. Four loud mouthed year ten girls dish out heckles and swear words to passers-by.

We avoided looking at them, otherwise we would have heard, 'What are you lookin' at, innit!' squawked back at us. God, the youth of today!

I wish Barry Whitticker had claimed it. Apparently he tried, but the girls scared him off by calling him a half-witted idiot.

I think that the residents of Cowes will soon look back on the Ricky Kinsella era as the good old days.

These girls are sober. God knows what grief we will have to put up with when they start drinking.

When I got home I had hardly got through the door when I was crushed into a bear hug and soaked in greetings from my Stenning grandparents. They had come down to see Cathy, and Grandad wanted to see Spud.

Spud and Annicka dutifully turned up in the evening after Spud had finished a driving lesson.

Grandad attempted to greet him with a bear hug but Spud backed off.

'What are you doing?' Spud said.

'Welcoming you to the family, son.'

'Oh you are, are you? Well, that's interesting isn't it.'

'I'm sorry about the way I behaved towards you.'

'You're sorry and that makes everything all right does it?'

'I hope so.'

'Well, I'm afraid that I can't forget the dirty looks, the snide comments, the sneers'

'I know, I'm...'

'All because you thought that I was Ricky Kinsella's son.'

'Yes.'

'But I'm not.'

'No.'

'Everybody else accepted me when we all thought I was Kinsella's son.'

'Yes.'

'But not you.'

'No.'

'So why should I just suddenly accept you as my grandfather, just because you have decided that I am worthy?'

'I don't know.'

'Well I can't. I'm sorry but you are just a massive hypocrite.' Spud turned to Nan. 'I'm sorry, Mrs Stenning. It's nothing against you. You've always been very kind, but he always made me feel like a worthless piece of shit and I will never forget that.'

Pieces of shit aren't always worthless. In horticultural circles they can be worth a fortune. I didn't mention that notion.

Spud headed for the door with Annicka and Mum, who was trying to talk him round. It didn't work and, after they had left, Mum and Cathy spent the evening trying to cheer Grandad up.

It was nice not to be the centre of a dramatic event in my house. I wish I'd had a portion of popcorn to eat while I was watching. It was all very entertaining.

21 October 2003, Tuesday

It was so cold this morning that, on the way to work, this old bloke that was walking ahead of me farted and you could see steam issuing from his trousers. It was a shame that nobody else saw it. You look a bit daft laughing when you are alone.

Spud came to see me at lunchtime, without his sixth-form cronies, to apologise for yesterday evening. I told him that he was fully justified in what he said.

Spud said that he'd passed his driving test theory exam yesterday.

Wicked!

This evening was spent in the Union, playing darts and bar football. We had a great time.

22 October 2003, Wednesday

There was a hell of an atmosphere in the house this morning. So work was an unlikely island of peace and the day seemed to pass quicker than normal.

When I got home from work I found that Nan and Grandad had left. They could have come and seen me!

I stayed in and watched the Champions League while having a very pleasant cuddle with darling little Angelina, who is really getting the hang of this smiling business.

When Mum took the slumbering little angel away to put her in her cot for the first time, as she had finally outgrown her Moses basket, Griz jumped up to take her place. The poor little bugger must be feeling a bit left out since Angelina's arrival.

I fell asleep, lying on my back, on the settee with the dog lying, legs outstretched, on my chest.

23 October 2003, Thursday

It is an illustration of how bland my life is when the most dramatic event of the day was when Bill, at work, proudly showed me this horrendous and stomach churning blood-bogey that he had painstakingly extracted from his left nostril with his right little finger.

His pride in the disgusting act soon backfired, however, when his nose started bleeding. It started quite undramatically but, after constant irritation from the tissues he kept poking up there, it started bleeding like a tap and whatever he and Jean did to try to stem the flow it seemed to get worse.

It was all I could do to try not to laugh. It was to my great pleasure when it became obvious that Colin was going to have to take him to A and E.

I longed to go with them, just for the chance to see the expressions of amusement on the faces of the doctors and nurses, but I had to stay in the shop with Jean as we were now understaffed.

Jean minded the till and I ran the back of the shop, quite comfortably, for the rest of the day. I left Jean there at five-thirty. She had to wait for the return of Colin, who had the keys to the shop with him.

I enjoyed recounting this story with the lads down the pub this evening.

Sweet!

24 October 2003, Friday

Bill was back at work this morning. He described the process of cauterisation in sickening detail several times during the day, turning various people's stomachs.

This evening I went down the pub and Karl was high on excitement because he had managed to get two tickets to the Manchester United versus Fulham game tomorrow.

He is going with his dad who is a Man U fan. They will be in the Fulham end, so Mr Sibley will have to kerb himself if United score.

They got the tickets off eBay. I was under the impression that you were not allowed to sell tickets on eBay. The fools paid two hundred pounds for them.

Karl was moaning a bit because his dad has insisted that he will be driving.

'I wanted to get in some practice on the motorway, ready for our trip,' he said.

25 October 2003, Saturday

Southampton have not played a home match for a month, so today's half day was most welcome.

Dad and I caught the twelve-thirty, but there was no bus to pick us up at the other side so we had to walk.

There was a sale on at the Saints megastore and I bought a model of The Dell, our old ground, for ten quid. They were originally sixty and Dad always refused to buy me one. I was very happy to get one for a tenner.

We also took a stroll into St Mary's town, past the King Alfred pub with its aqua-coloured paintwork, overflowing with drunk but well-behaved Southampton fans.

This pub was the target of a Pompey thug attack when England played Macedonia at St Mary's last year. The pub's wrecking was pre-arranged and common knowledge, but that didn't prevent it from happening. I am expecting a similar thing to happen when we play Portsmouth in the league, but on a larger scale.

We walked to this little memorabilia shop to have a browse. We didn't buy anything there, but I purchased a small Saints badge from a northern bloke who had set up opposite the King Alfred pub.

I was expecting a scoreline that would include a zero from us and anything from zero to three from Blackburn, especially at half-time when we all settled down to listen to the other half-time scores.

The dour mood of the fans seemed to lift when we heard that Portsmouth were losing two-nil at Newcastle and this upturn in the stadium's mood seemed to get across to the Southampton players and we won two-nil.

To make things even better, Pompey lost three-nil and I could hardly believe it when I heard that Fulham had beaten Manchester United at Old Trafford. Karl must be over the moon.

Something quite rare happened this evening. Ed called to see if I would like to go round to his to help celebrate his sister's fourteenth birthday. So I did.

Zoe had some of her friends there and you would be forgiven for not believing that a couple of them were as young as fourteen, especially Zoe, who is challenging Lara hard for the most-beautiful-girl-I-have-ever-seen title. She didn't want to speak to me though. She kept giggling with her friends. They must think that I am some sort of idiot or something.

The only thing this little gathering lacked was alcohol but it was quite a good laugh. It was nice to be able to spend some time with Ed for a change.

26 October 2003, Sunday

We had an excellent match this morning against St Helens. Excellent because Dad scored a goal in open play. They had just had an attack that our keeper had comfortably gathered. He threw the ball out to Vernon, who ran past the halfway line with it before playing it out to Karl on the left wing. Karl floated an under-hit cross that was meant for me. I was running towards the far post. The ball dipped right in front of Dad who, without having to jump, nodded it past the floundering St Helens goalkeeper. We won one-nil and it felt better watching the joy on Dad's face than it has ever felt scoring myself. He'd played crap up to that point.

Karl's high spirits helped him earn the man of the match award from Pitbull.

Of course we will have to relive Dad's goal in our house for years to come, but I will be leaving home within the next couple of years, I hope.

The first reliving was over lunch, when Grandad announced that Spud had paid for him to have his operation privately.

Now we can all worry about whether he gets through the operation or not.

I phoned Spud this evening, in my room, to thank him.

'He's my grandfather too you know?' he said.

'So's Grandad Stenning,' I remarked.

'Yes, but to Grandad Brown it didn't matter when he thought I was only his step-grandson. He was still kind and respectful to me.'

Fair enough, I thought.

After all today's Premiership games had concluded, Southampton are now sixth in the league, four points above Pompey. And next week Pompey are playing Manchester United at Old Trafford. Will they be able to emulate Fulham's achievement? I hope not.

27 October 2003, Monday

Spud came to see me this lunchtime, along with the usual crowd. It must be a sixth-form thing because nearly all of them were smoking. That included Ed, Lara, Tom (surprise, surprise) and Meat. Spud abstained, but I don't know if he had already smoked one.

He handed me a small box wrapped in red and white striped paper with a tag attached. The tag read, 'To my biological family'.

'You are not to open it until our father comes home from work,' he ordered. 'Now you have got to swear on the thing that means most to you in the world.'

I had to think very carefully about that.

'All right. I swear on Southampton's Premiership status.'

'You shallow git!'

He was then quite confident that I wouldn't open the box and, superstitious as I am, I didn't.

When I got home there was a brand new, slick black Volkswagen Sharan parked in our driveway. I asked Mum whose it was and she didn't know as she had been out all day shopping in Southampton with Cathy. She thought that someone next door had parked it there because they couldn't fit it into their driveway.

Dad came home and I handed him Spud's package. Inside were a set of car keys and a note:

To my beloved biological family

I am happy to be able to buy you this gift as a thank you for coming into my life and giving me my identity.

With deep love and regards

Your Stuart

We all ran out to the car and admired it, overcome with emotion. Our first trip in it was to Spud's parents' house where Spud was thanked. We did notice, though, a brand new BMW parked outside which turned out to be his gift to his parents.

He is holding back on buying himself one until he passes his driving test.

Then we went back home and had dinner.

I wonder if he will buy me a car when I pass my test?

28 October 2003, Tuesday

It absolutely chucked it down today. The people that came into the shop had obviously had to dig out their old, stale-smelling, wet-weather gear, so most people stank.

The bad weather had evidently generated bad moods in everyone because I don't remember seeing one cheerful face.

This evening I stayed in and watched the *National Television Awards*. This was mainly so that I could avoid hearing the score of Southampton's Carling Cup match against Bristol City.

The highlights were shown after the *News at Ten* and we won three-nil.

29 October 2003, Wednesday

More rain this morning meant more smelly raincoats to put up with, but the weather improved this afternoon.

I stayed in again this evening and watched Blackburn lose at home to

Liverpool in their Carling Cup game.

After that came the draw for the fourth round, and Dad and I cheered when Southampton were drawn at home. We then waited in anticipation to find out who we would be playing against. We half cheered and half gasped when Portsmouth were drawn out.

That game is going to be massive.

The news reports were going on and on about the departure of the Conservative leader who has been called in the papers 'IDS'. This stands for Ian Duncan-Smith. I can't say that I have ever heard of him.

Mum said that IDS sounds like some sort of modern designer disease.

30 October 2003, Thursday

My life is so bland at the moment. Nothing worth mentioning ever happens at work, and most evenings I spend at home watching television.

I am turning into a couch potato. How the hell am I supposed to find a girlfriend with a life like this?

I did go out this evening, though. I went down the town with Tom, Karl and Meat. We had to run the gauntlet of the loud-mouthed girls as we passed Kinsella's seat: 'Ooo! Nice arse' 'My mate fancies you' 'Oi I fink you're horny' 'Don't smile, mate, or you'll crack you're face!'

I suspect that the last jibe was directed at me.

We ended up in the Union as usual. We played darts and bar football until eleven-twenty, when we were kicked out.

I think, perhaps, that I stayed out too late, but I have to try to reclaim my social life somehow.

1 November 2003, Saturday

Today was an utter let-down. I look forward to my afternoons off and the football that accompanies them. This afternoon, however, I had to sit through the worst Southampton performance I have ever seen. We lost two-nil to Manchester City, and it is the first time that I can remember cheering the away team's second goal. The goal allowed us all to leave the match with five minutes still to play. What a waste of an afternoon! Pompey's defeat at the hands of the other Manchester club hardly cushioned the blow as we were all so pissed off.

I went out for a drive with Karl this evening. Tom, Stevie and Jason Dwyer also came.

First, we went to Newport where we managed to get in to watch *The Texas Chainsaw Massacre*, which is the first eighteen-certificate film I have ever seen at a cinema. I must look older now.

The film was excellent. Really gory! Jason Dwyer kept on making chainsaw noises and trying to look demented in the car on the way to Sandown.

'You don't have to put much effort into looking mad, Jase!' Meat remarked. Jason just carried on.

We hovered outside Colonel Bogey's and admired the talent on view. Then we went to Ryde and hung around the icafé, flirting with Ryde's equivalent of Cowes' loud-mouthed girls. This ended when their boyfriends arrived smarting for a fight. The chase back to the car put an end to our original plan of a round of bowling.

Then we went to Cowes and arrived at the Union just before last orders. It was so busy that Karl was able to get all of us pints of lager without anyone noticing that we were underage.

Spud was down there. He has paid for a lad's holiday in a villa in Ibiza, starting next week. I hope that I can persuade Colin to let me go. Everybody else is going!

2 November 2003, Sunday

With Cowes Park Rangers having a free weekend, which was just as well with the weather being so bad, I had a lie-in until ten-thirty. I sat on the settee with Dad, eating breakfast, while Cathy sat opposite in the armchair, clad in her dressing gown.

I wondered if she had anything on under it as she crossed her legs and the split in the gown revealed nearly all of her amazing pins. She glanced over and noticed that I was looking, but instead of covering up she uncrossed and re-crossed her legs the other way, giving me such an erotic display of flesh that I had to make a quick exit to the bathroom.

I feel so perverted. You can't have erotic thoughts about your mother's sister, even if she is amazingly nice looking. What did she think she was doing, teasing me like that? I wish we had been alone. Maybe she might have flashed me a nipple or something even better.

That sounds awful. She's my auntie, however horny she is. This is all down to severe sexual frustration on my part. The only cure - I need a bird - NOW!

Nan, Grandad, Spud and Annicka came round for lunch. Grandad is going into Southampton General for a private heart bypass operation tomorrow. We all wished him good luck

The weather cleared up this afternoon, but I stayed in and watched both Sky football matches followed by a film on Sky Box Office, which was surprisingly good despite having Leonardo Di Caprio in it.

3 November 2003, Monday

Disaster! Colin refused to let me have next week off, unpaid or not. He said that if I wanted to go he would have to sack me as I will have broken our agreement re. football et cetera.

Now I have a dilemma: either a one-off holiday with my mates that I will regret missing for the rest of my life or a job in a crap shop that I will resent for ever because it made me miss out on this experience.

With the kids back at school, I took the opportunity to seek Vernon's advice. All he said was, 'You're only young once. You will regret missing out on opportunities like this when you get older. There are plenty of jobs out there.'

Yes, but I will have the word 'sacked' printed on my CV, which is hardly going to stand me in good stead when seeking a new job.

I have until Saturday to decide. It's so unfair.

I had a terrible day at work, and as a result and I didn't feel like doing anything tonight, except seeing Ed for an evening of moaning which Lara must have hated being in on.

They didn't have any answers for me either.

4 November 2003, Tuesday

I still had the dilemma on my mind at work.

Spud and Annicka met me at lunchtime. They had borrowed the key to their house from the estate agent, bought me a bacon baguette from Tiffins and decided to give me a personal viewing of their new home. It took just under ten minutes to get there.

You open the front door and you are immediately in the living room, which has a stone fireplace, encasing a gas fire. The stairs run up to your left as you pass through to the dining room and adjoining kitchen, which is partitioned by an open archway.

Upstairs is a front bedroom and a back bedroom with an en suite bathroom, which Spud says will be their bedroom. There is also an attic bedroom, which is accessed by a very narrow stairwell.

The house is very small but cosy and homely. They are both very happy with it.

They also showed me the back garden, which is all patioed and rises up in a series of ever-increasing steps. The top step is a platform that has a small shed on it, which is reached by climbing a small flight of rickety wooden steps.

The most impressive thing for me was a stadium seat that has been mounted onto a wooden frame. Spud told me that the estate agent is sure that the seat originated from Southampton's old ground, The Dell.

After the viewing, Spud said that I was welcome to stay there at any time, and when they have settled in properly they are thinking of having a lodger and I would have first refusal.

Then I explained about my dilemma. I could not lodge there without a job.

'I hope you do come, fella,' Spud said, 'It wouldn't be the same without you.'

That didn't help my state of indecision.

I even had a quiet talk with Bill who, for once, seemed to offer some sound advice.

'The decision you make will provide the answer as to whether you are a man or not.'

'How?'

'Responsibility, mate. The more responsibility you take on in life, the more you are ready for manhood.'

It appears that Spud is already there and he is less than a year older than I am. I haven't even had sex yet so I am well behind. If I go, then at least I might get over that enormous hurdle and move up one rung of the ladder towards being a man.

Grandad's operation went well today. He is in a stable condition. Dad is spending as much time with him as possible at the moment.

5 November 2003, Wednesday

Bill kept pulling my leg today.

'Holiday or P45? What will he choose?' he kept saying.

'Hey, Troy. DOLE us all out a cup of tea, will ya?'

'Troy. UB40 in twenty-four years time. That's a long time signing on.'

Bastard!

When I got home, Cathy showed me The Dell seat that Spud had got her to pick up from his house today. He had given her and Mum a guided tour this lunchtime.

We didn't have to bother going to any firework displays tonight. They were on all evening, all over the place. All you had to do was walk onto the golf course and there were hundreds of them hitting the night sky.

After I had got bored I went inside and watched the Arsenal versus Dynamo Kiev match. The Gunners won one-nil.

Grandad is doing really well. Dad said that he sat up today and moaned about the salad he was given for dinner.

6 November 2003, Thursday

Decision time is approaching fast and I still can't make my mind up. Work is awful because of the constant jibes from Bill.

The only highlight of the day was being able to watch *Superstars* with Angelina cooing and blowing bubbles in my arms.

7 November 2003, Friday

Decision made! Although I know that I will regret it for the rest of my life, I cannot have the blot of the sack on my record. I will also hate Colin for the rest of my life for depriving me of this opportunity.

The other reason for my staying is that Grandad is still recovering in hospital. If anything did go wrong, I couldn't live with myself if I was out there when it happened.

'Good lad, Troy' is all Colin said.

'You've surprised me, mate,' Bill said. 'I would have gone!'

I heard on the news, as I had my lunch in the back room where Colin has a radio (one rule for him a different one for me - hypocrite), that a new strain of killer flu has killed five kids in this country. It is called the Fijian Flu. Here we go again. I had almost forgotten about SARS, and then another bug arrives and it's closer to home this time.

I decided to take the day off tomorrow so that I can go and visit Grandad.

I went down the pub tonight with Karl and Tom. It was quite quiet for a Friday night, apart from the extraordinary amount of fireworks going off in the neighbourhood.

Some of the bangs were so loud that the pub shook.

Spud and Annicka arrived just after we did. She got pissed, but underage Spud did not. By the time the bell rang she was completely wasted and Spud had to call a cab.

She was so drunk that we weren't sure whether she was speaking in English or Swedish. It was the best laugh I have had for ages.

Someone else in the pub, who was also enjoying the spectacle, asked Karl who the drunken girl was.

Karl pointed at me and said, 'His sister-in-law.'

I hadn't realised, until then, that I had a sister-in-law. Can I really be that much of an idiot?

8 November 2003, Saturday

Cathy was clad in her dressing gown at breakfast again this morning, but this time she was sat on the settee with her legs tucked underneath her. She had obviously noticed me ogling at her last time.

Visiting time at the hospital wasn't until two-thirty so I took the opportunity to window shop around Southampton.

West Quay shopping centre was buzzing with the highest concentration of the country's most beautiful women, as it usually is.

I love the upper floor eating area because you can buy a McDonald's or a KFC and sit in the communal seating area. Today I had a KFC.

I had to get a taxi to the hospital because I hadn't got a clue where it was.

Grandad looked very well and was full of spirits. He flirted with the nurses blatantly. I took him a bag of Starburst. I remembered that when I was in hospital, at the age of six, having my tonsils out, he brought me a bag of Opal Fruits, which was the original name of the sweets.

In his private room he had *Sky Sport News* on, so me, Dad and Grandad, watched as Southampton put on yet another poor display at Bolton

Wanderers. Nil-nil was very unfortunate for Bolton who more than deserved to win.

Saints are playing so badly at the moment that I am seriously considering asking Colin if we can go back to the standard working week, which would give me a most welcome day off during the week.

Dad and I left at seven. We were famished so Dad treated me to chicken fried fice, chicken chow mein and sweet and sour chicken balls. It was wonderful.

I went down the pub again this evening. I am not the only person who regularly goes, but they keep calling me Pub Troy.

Karl was there as our chaperone, but was grumpy because Charlton had beaten Fulham.

Spud and Annicka were there again, but Annicka behaved herself this time.

I got teased because of my absence from the holiday boys, but Spud stood up for me. 'You do realise that Troy is going to be here, alone, with all the girls at his disposal.'

Excellent! I hadn't thought of that. Maybe my staying here will turn out to be a blessing in disguise?

9 November 2003, Sunday

I had to miss England's Rugby World Cup quarter-final victory against Wales this morning because of football.

I haven't been able to see any of the competition because it is in Australia and the matches are always on in the morning.

Pitbull was not impressed when we told him that most of his team would be unavailable next week.

We won our game this morning, against The Horseshoe, three-nil. I got our second goal.

Pitbull asked all of the players that will be available to ask any mates that might be interested in playing to come along. He was delighted that I will be available.

'You will be my skipper for the day,' he said.

Excellent!

Nan came round for lunch and we all trooped over the water to visit Grandad, who loves the attention.

Dad and I missed both of the live games on Sky this afternoon as a result.

I stayed in and watched the television tonight. *Prime Suspect* was good.

10 November 2003, Monday

The lads came in to see me at work this morning, on their way to Ibiza.

Spud has rented a villa in a town called Portinaxt. He found it on the Internet as it isn't really the holiday season.

The fact that Manumission and all the other nightclubs are likely to be closed made me feel a lot better. I don't expect the weather will be that good either, but they are going there to get pissed up and will probably set up parties at their villa.

Lara came to see me at lunchtime. She wasn't very happy.

'I'm free tonight if you want to come round for a chat,' she said.

I joyfully accepted her offer.

After dinner, Thunderlungs was causing havoc. Dad said that he would take her out in the pram for a walk to calm her down. I offered to take her with me to Lara's.

She was fast asleep by the time I got there and Lara and her Mum were fussing over her as soon as I lifted the pram over their threshold.

'You haven't been around here for ages,' Lara remarked as we sat down on her bed, each with cup of tea in our hands.

'Well you have been busy with your boyfriends who I haven't seen much of either.'

'You'll be in that situation soon.'

'Yeah, right!'

'You will!'

'Whatever!'

She placed her cup of tea on her bedside table and turned to face me. 'Troy, I gave Ed an ultimatum before he left.'

'Did you? What was that?'

'If he chose to go on this trip then I would consider our relationship to be over.'

'Oh.'

'He was very flippant about it.'

'Was he?'

'Yes. He said that we'd talk about it when he gets back.'

'Yeah?'

'Yes, but my mind's made up.' She put her hand on my knee, causing an unwanted reaction in my pants, which I tried to conceal by holding my mug there. 'Why can't he be more like you?'

'I don't know, but it doesn't make any difference because you would never go out with me anyway.' I tried not to sound stroppy while saying it, and thankfully my pants returned to their normal state, which was a relief because the mug was starting to burn me.

'That's because you are my friend.'

'Yes, but Ed was your friend before you went out with him.'

'Yes, but not like you. You are like a sort of brother friend.'

These clichés were starting to annoy me, so when Thunderlungs burst back into action I was grateful to have the excuse to leave.

11 November 2003, Tuesday

Mundane! That is the best word to describe my working life which, today, was highlighted when the till played up for the whole day.

Bill and Colin were both prodding at it with screwdrivers as they attempted to get the drawer to shut properly.

At one point I was asked to keep an eye on it while Bill phoned the engineer. It popped open and when Bill returned he gave it an almighty slam and that seemed to cure the problem.

'That was technical,' I remarked.

'That's what they advised me to do,' Bill said.

I thought that, with the lads being away, I would have access to girls but I can't bring myself to call on any of them for fear that I would be accused of sniffing around them. So I spent the evening in watching television - AGAIN!

12 November 2003, Wednesday

I was hardly through the door this morning when I was called into Colin's office.

'Troy? Can I have chat?' he said, ominously. I followed him in. 'Sit down.' I sat down.

'Now, I'll get straight to the point. Twenty pounds has gone missing from yesterday's takings. I appreciate that you might have borrowed it and intended to put it back before we noticed, so you are not in trouble, as long as that is what happened. I would appreciate it, though if, in future you would ask before taking money out of the till.'

'But I haven't taken any money out of the till,' I pleaded.

'Troy, it's all right. You are not in trouble.'

'I don't care. I didn't take any money out of the till.'

'There was nobody else, other than me and Bill, that had access to it yesterday.'

'I don't even know how to use the bloody till.' I was getting rather annoyed now.

'There's no need to swear and you are not doing yourself any favours at the moment. Just own up, pay back the money and we'll forget all about it.'

'NO! I'm not paying back money that I don't owe.'

Colin folded his arms. 'You don't want me to get the police involved, do you?'

I started wondering, 'This is a wind-up isn't it?'

'Troy. I'll give you one more chance. It is pay day on Friday. If the takings are up twenty pounds then the matter is closed and we will forget that this conversation ever took place.'

'I won't forget it. I'll be twenty quid down!'

There the matter was dropped, but I was fuming inside for the rest of the day. How does he know that Bill or Jean didn't take it? Now I know how Charity Tate must be feeling in *Emmerdale*, accused of a crime she didn't commit.

I told Mum, Dad and Cathy about it this evening and, to my relief, they didn't once question my integrity. Dad even threatened to go down and have a word with Colin. I told him not to.

The trouble is, even if I did put twenty pounds of my own money into the takings, I don't know how to open up the till to do it.

13 November 2003, Thursday

I got a postcard from the lads this morning:

> *Troy*
>
> *The weather is a bit naff but we are drowning in alcohol and women. Don't tell the girls. Wish you were here. See you soon.*

It was signed by all of them.

At work the twenty-quid-gate scandal was overly deliberately avoided. I felt as though all of the other staff members were speaking to me less, and when they did there was a strain of awkwardness about the conversation.

I risked seeing Lara tonight, hoping for a bit of emotional support from someone who wasn't a biased family member, but she blew it when she asked the question, 'Did you take it?'

I'm starting to think that she might be a bit of an idiot.

14 November 2003, Friday

Again, it was the same strained atmosphere at work. I got my usual wage packet, half expecting to have twenty pounds less in it. I felt that I was being watched as I left at the end of the day, having not donated money to the firm out of my own wages.

I was naturally asked, over dinner, what had happened, but I suspect that that question will be resolved tomorrow.

Dad took me to the cricket club tonight for an evening of pool and to cheer me up. It didn't work.

15 November 2003, Saturday

Once again, as I walked into the shop, Colin said those immortal words, 'Troy, can I have a chat?' I again followed, this time with trepidation.

'As the takings were up twenty pounds yesterday, as promised, the matter is now closed. However, if there is any repeat of this then I'm afraid I will have to let you go.'

I was a bit baffled by this, so I didn't ask the obvious question, but I suspected that one of them had donated twenty pounds of their own money to the takings to cover for me. This notion was confirmed later when Bill winked at me and whispered, 'You can pay me back when you can afford it, okay?'

'Whatever,' I said.

'Well, I thought you might be a bit more grateful about it.'

'Either way, I am still out of pocket.'

'Oh forget about the bloody money. Let's just get on with our work, shall we?'

What right has he got to be pissed off with me?

So it was yet another terrible day at work. I should have gone with the lads after all.

Dad told me that he has heard that some of his mates have already received their Pompey Carling Cup tickets so, in a panic, he phoned the club and ordered ours, even though he still had over a week to reserve our seats.

Amazingly, Scotland beat Holland in the first leg of their Euro 2004 play-off. We should have watched that game but plumped for Wales' nil-nil draw in Russia.

16 November 2003, Sunday

I was watching England win the Rugby World Cup semi-final against France this morning but had to leave at half-time to go up to Northwood Rec for our football match.

Nine players turned up for today's game. Pitbull persuaded a bloke that was walking his dog around the park to sign up and play in goal, and also roped in someone who had turned up to be a sub for another team on another pitch only to find that he was surplus to their requirements. He bribed his older son to run the line, so we had just scraped eleven players.

We played against Shorewell and drew three-three, partly because the bloke Pitbull had persuaded to play in goal was absolute rubbish.

I led by example, proud to be wearing the captain's armband for the first time, and scored our first from a free kick. Roberto Carlos eat your heart out! The lad Pitbull poached from the other match got our second from my Beckhamesque cross and Vernon got our third after a knock down from Dad. Of course Dad went on about his assist for the rest of the day.

The most amazing thing about the game was that Pitbull managed to get through the whole game without getting booked.

After the match we had a quick lunch and went over to visit Grandad in hospital. We watched the England versus Denmark football match with him. James Beattie played the whole of the second half but hardly received a pass. It must have felt like playing for Southampton.

Grandad was just as appalled as the rest of the family when he was told about twenty-quid-gate. He changed the subject by announcing that he would be going home tomorrow.

When I got home it was obvious that the lads had returned from Ibiza. There was a huge crate of wine on the back doorstep and a parcel for me that turned out to be a big donkey wearing a sombrero. A tag read 'My name is Campo.'

17 November 2003, Monday

At work this morning I was introduced to our new shop assistant, Mark - the same Mark that I had to put up with at MP Graphics all those months ago, and he is no less annoying now than he was then.

I had to show him the ropes and put up with his reminiscences of Stan and what a good mate he was, knowing full well that Stan couldn't stand him. He didn't call me Troy Tempestuous today though.

Colin called me into his office around halfway through the day, which was a bit worrying, but he was only asking me what I thought of Mark.

'I've worked with him before and he's an annoying twat,' I rather unwisely stated.

'You need to sort out your attitude young man,' Colin replied. 'I expect better from you now, especially after recent events.'

What a wanker!

I was in a right mood for the rest of the day.

When I went to the pub this evening with all the holiday lads, I was treated to the various tales of their exploits. The one that stands out in my mind was when they paid for Jason Dwyer to lose his virginity to a prostitute in Ibiza Town, only to find out that it was a transvestite. They had more success the following evening when they asked before parting with their money.

I was surprised when I heard that Jason was a virgin. With all his bravado I thought he would have blagged a shag a long time ago. Kelly must have refused to let him shag her and that's obviously why they split up.

Ed knows that Lara has dumped him and he didn't seem too bothered. We all had a great laugh, which helped me forget about my troubles at work.

18 November 2003, Tuesday

Things are going from bad to worse. Bill spent the day training Mark how to use the till. This is the ultimate humiliation. It is even worse than the fact that Mark has resumed his unwanted nickname-calling and he and Bill are getting on like a house on fire, giggling and joking like a couple of girls, usually at my expense.

When a delivery lorry arrived I expected some help from the new boy, but he got excused because of till training.

I don't know how much more of this I can put up with.

When I told Dad about it he said that it sounded like they were trying to get me to leave so that they don't have to sack me or make me redundant.

Well, if that is true they are succeeding big time.

I watched a programme on Channel Four tonight that said that the government are going to try enforcing the age of consent so that any sexual contact under the age of sixteen will be regarded as indecent assault, punishable by up to four years in prison. Even kiss-chase will be illegal!

Convicts will also be put on the sex offenders' register.

I hope that they don't decide to backdate this law, otherwise most of the country will end up in prison!

At least I will be innocent worst luck!

19 November 2003, Wednesday

Bill and Mark are really hitting it off now, so much so that Bill confided in Mark about twenty-quid-gate. What an absolute wanker! Both of them! Mark has even come up with a new annoying nickname for me.

'Did you take it, Woody? You can tell me. I won't say anything.' (Woody as from the film *Toy Story*. Bill asked Mark, 'Do you believe Troy's story?' Mark misheard and said, 'No it's only a computer animation.' From that conversation came my new nickname.)

Highly irritated I said, sarcastically, 'Yes, I had my hand in the till every week but this time was the only time they spotted that they were short.'

I was so close to punching him I really don't know how I didn't.

Mark has now got the hang of the till. He was operating it all afternoon as Bill took a half-day's holiday.

I went around to Ed's tonight and played his new Quidditch World Cup game. He also has the new Sugababes album. It is brilliant!

I missed Scotland and Wales' failure to qualify for Euro 2004, thank goodness.

20 November 2003, Thursday

It was Mark's day off today but there was no respite for me. Colin had me in his office, yet again.

'This is the final time that I am going to bring the subject up, Troy. I am glad that you have finally admitted your guilt. I just wish that you could have admitted it to Bill or me. It's all about trust.'

'And I suppose you trust Mark do you?'

'Well he has done nothing to suggest that he isn't trustworthy.'

'Well nor had I, but I never got a chance to work the till.'

'It's just as well isn't it?'

'I give up!'

'What? You're quitting?'

'That's what you want isn't it? You're trying to hound me out.'

'What has happened to you? You started so well and things have just gone downhill, and after all the favours we have done for you.'

'Favours?'

'Football. Flexitime. Time off. Et cetera, et cetera. Maybe it would be best if we called it quits? I'll give you a good reference. It won't go down on your record as a sacking.'

I felt the emotion building up inside me and the tears began to well up in my eyes. I didn't say a thing. I just got up and walked out, throwing my overall jacket down on the floor on my way out.

I went home and straight to bed where I burst into tears. I was howling like a baby, uncontrollably. Mum came in and hugged me tenderly.

'Shhhh, it's all right sweetheart,' she kept saying. I needed her so much.

When I eventually stopped crying, I crashed out and went to sleep. It was only five in the afternoon but I was shattered.

21 November 2003, Friday

My day at home was ruined by the news that Southampton's manager, Gordon Strachan, might be joining lowly and penniless Leeds United at the earliest available opportunity.

So tomorrow we face second-placed moneybags team, Chelsea, with our soon-to-be ex-manager in charge.

We are so obviously going to lose, I don't think I can be bothered to go.

I feel so pissed off at the moment. I spent the day watching *Sky Sports News* in bed and Mum left me to it, popping in occasionally with a cup of tea or a bite to eat.

I did come out of my pit when Dad arrived home from work. He said that they need a lad at his work place to look after all the processors et cetera. A general dogsbody, again!

'Will you come with me on Monday and give it a try?' he asked me. I could tell, by the expression on his face, that he was expecting me to say no, and I didn't want to let him down so I agreed.

He did say, though, that there would be plenty of opportunity to climb the ladder of promotion there.

22 November 2003, Saturday

Being unemployed today meant I was able to enjoy, along with the rest of the country, England's historic victory in the Rugby World Cup Final in Sydney against Australia. It was a tense two hours, but England sealed victory with a Jonny Wilkinson drop goal in the last seconds of extra time. If only our footballers could emulate their achievement.

After the match, Dad and I braved the drizzle to go to St Mary's Stadium to watch yet another ninety minutes of our team failing to score a goal. Even though Saints played well, Chelsea got the very thing that any team needs to win against Saints, a goal.

I was feeling a bit depressed on the way back to the ferry. Then a wave of optimism swept over me, along with the rain. I have a feeling that, despite the absence for the next five weeks of James Beattie, that will be the last game that we fail to score in for a while.

The rain continued into the evening as we headed to The Bargeman's Rest for a meal to celebrate Nan Brown's sixty-first birthday. Grandad Brown came along as well but he had to have salad. He is looking very well now.

Nan wore a low-cut blouse that displayed her saggy, leather-skinned cleavage. It nearly put me off my fillet steak. Her short skirt showed off her awful varicose vein clad legs, which were also covered in leathery skin, and I can't understand why she can't see for herself how revolting it looks.

After dinner we all went to the cinema to watch *Love Actually*. The place was packed. There wasn't a spare seat. I don't ever remember being in a full house for a film before. It was good, though.

23 November 2003, Sunday

We were back to full strength for our away trip to Seaclose Park where we were supposed to be playing against The Vine, but persistent rain had turned the pitch into a quagmire. The match was therefore called off.

I went home where I had lunch with the family. Spud and Annicka, who were absent last night, came along, and Grandad presented Dad with a cheque. It turned out to be the original money that Dad had raised for Grandad's operation. He had never needed to use it because Spud paid for it.

The gesture led to a very emotional moment between Dad and Grandad, which everyone found quite embarrassing to watch.

The rain continued for the rest of the day and so we all stayed in.

After Nan and Grandad were taken home and Spud and Annicka left, we had a snack tea and watched a film on Sky Box Office.

I had an early night to prepare myself for tomorrow.

24 November 2003, Monday

I got up at the same time as Dad this morning - Five forty-five a.m. We had breakfast and walked down to catch the seven-twenty Red Jet. Thankfully, it wasn't raining.

I had a doze on the ferry and when I woke up we were docking. We caught the free bus to the railway station. Dad used a free ticket for me, which he had been given as a gold ticket holder, and we caught the seven fifty-nine train to Fareham.

Diamond Kingsland is very new and pleasant, and Frank who, like most people there, is a Pompey supporter, quickly showed me the ropes of processor care.

Frank is a portly fellow, balding with a grey beard that goes all the way down his neck and disappears under his collar. He was very friendly and helpful. He made me several cups of tea throughout the day.

I spent the day cleaning the five processors they have. It was dirty and tiring work, but it shouldn't always be as bad as that as the machines don't need cleaning every day. It is just my responsibility to keep them in good working order.

I was also trained in calibrating the image setters, which is a doddle.

I had lunch with Dad and his best workmate, Bernie, in the kitchen. They let me join in their card game.

After lunch the boss, Gerry, called me into his office and talked to me about the position. He asked about my last job and I told him what had happened. He said that he would have to contact them to get their angle on the story.

He must have seen the disappointed expression on my face.

'Don't worry. I won't take their word for it. I'll judge you on what you do for me. I'll see you again at the end of the week.'

'So I'm on a week's trial?' I said.

'That's right.'

If Colin and Bill slag me off I have got no chance.

We finished work at four forty-five and caught the delayed four fifty-six train to Southampton Central. We just missed the free bus that would have got us on the six o'clock Red Jet and therefore caught the six-thirty one. We didn't get home until seven-fifteen. What a long day! Twelve hours off the island!

After we had finished dinner we sat down and watched Pompey get beaten by Fulham. Sweet!

25 November 2003, Tuesday

With little work coming through at the moment, Darren, the production manager, sat me down with Dad and I was given some training in what is called Mac Repro. It looks quite interesting.

I was given a dummy job to work on during the afternoon.

We managed to catch the six o'clock tonight, so that was much better.

Later, I went down to the Union with Karl, Tom, Jason Dwyer, Ed and Meat. Jason has been unsuccessfully trying to get back with Kelly, which reminds me that she is single. I had forgotten about that. I could have asked her out ages ago.

Karl and I had a laugh at Pompey's expense. He had watched his team's glorious victory last night and loved it as much as I did.

I texted Kelly when I got home: 'HI KEL. D U FAN C GOIN 2 DA FLIX WIV ME SOON?'

I didn't get a reply.

26 November 2003, Wednesday

We were quite busy today. I spent the morning training on the Mac and the afternoon helping Frank to clear a problem with the large image setter where the film kept jamming in the bridge.

You have to thump the machine in a specific place in a special way to solve the problem. Very high tech!

I got a text from Kelly: 'HEY TROY. SORRY MY PHONE WAS OFF. YES ID LIKE THAT. JUST LET ME KNOW WHEN AND WHERE.'

I noticed, on the way home, that you can see St Mary's Stadium from the train, across the Itchen River, as the train leaves Woolston Station at five-eighteen. You don't get to Southampton Central until five-thirty. I reckon that if you get off at Woolston you might be able to catch the five-thirty ferry. Dad said that it was worth a try. So we will give it a go tomorrow.

We didn't get home until seven-fifteen again.

I phoned Kelly and suggested that we go out on Saturday night. She agreed. Excellent!

27 November 2003, Thursday

We were still having problems with the large image setter this morning, but I was able to sort out the problem myself, as I now know how to hit the machine the correct way.

I had to change the chemicals in the small image setter this afternoon. It stank. I had to put the developer in the fix container and vice versa. I got bollocked by Darren, and it took all afternoon to clean it thoroughly to remove the contamination and get the machine up-and-running again.

On the way home we got off at Woolston and there is a bus station right across the bridge. We jumped straight on a number eight bus and caught the five-thirty ferry. I felt quite pleased with myself that my plan had worked.

I went down to the pub again with the lads. Jason was a bit off with me.

'What's the matter with you?' I asked, half knowing the answer.

'You're trying to poach my bird,' he said.

'Sorry, I thought that you had been blown out. If you want me to steer clear of her I will.'

His attitude changed slightly. 'Nah nah. It's all right. You go ahead. It's just me being stupid. I still like her, you know? It's just hard coming to terms with the split.'

'Okay, if you are sure.'

'Yes. You're all right.'

I think I handled that one rather well.

28 November 2003, Friday

After yesterday's shenanigans with the processor, I half expected that my meeting with Gerry would result in a thanks-but-no-thanks. But, to my relief, he was away for the day. So today was a bit of a skive for everyone. We even had an hour-and-a-half lunch break down the pub.

I called Kelly tonight to confirm our date tomorrow and went down the pub with Karl, Ed and Jason D.

29 November 2003, Saturday

It was wonderful this morning. I had a lie-in. I didn't get up until gone eleven. After brunch I went to Newport with Dad. He was shopping for a hands-free kit for the car. We got one from the VW garage. We tested it out on Mum and it works brilliantly. It just plugs into the cassette deck.

We popped into Nan's for a cup of tea and to watch *Football Focus*. It was nice of the BBC to pay tribute to Ted Bates, Southampton's Club President and longest serving member. He died the other day at the age of eighty-five. If it wasn't for his efforts as a player and a manager, Southampton would still be in the lower leagues.

Dad discussed a surprise get-together for Mum's birthday, which is in a couple of weeks' time. Nan said that she would arrange everything as it is difficult for Dad, seeing as he works on the mainland.

We got home in time to watch *Gillette Soccer Saturday* but Saints were just as crap as usual and lost one-nil at Aston Villa.

Kelly called off our date this evening, so I decided to compile a CD of my favourite tracks for my journeys to work, but I couldn't find my Sugababes CD. Then I remembered that Ed had borrowed it so I went round to his house. Zoe let me in, saying, 'You know where to go.'

So I went downstairs, yes downstairs, to his bedroom. I knocked on the door. I heard Ed call in a comedy deep voice, 'Enter' and went in.

He was lying on his bed. My CD was playing on his sound system. I walked over and removed the disc without asking.

'Oi! What are you doing?' he screeched.

'Reclaiming my property,' I replied.

'You c***!'

'I can.'

I packed the disc into its mistreated case and gave him a clip around the back of the head. 'Naughty boy.'

'Don't touch what you can't afford,' he said.

'Loose change in my pocket, mate,' I retorted. 'I emphasise the word loose.'

I heard him say 'cheeky bastard' as I shut his bedroom door behind me and quickly left.

30 November 2003, Sunday

I received a call from Pitbull this morning. Our match had been called off because of a waterlogged pitch, so I went with Mum, Dad, Cathy and Angelina to pick up Nan and Grandad.

Dad showed off his new hands-free kit by phoning Nan to let her know that we were on our way. Everybody in the car could hear the conversation:

'Hello Mum,' said Dad.

'Hello love,' replied Nan.

'We're on our way.'

'Good, I'll get my coat. Oh, by the way, I have booked the Eight Bells function room for Alison's surprise party.'

Dad tried coughing to drown out what Nan had said but it was too late.

'What surprise party is that then, Mum?' asked Mum.

There was silence at the other end.

'What's going on?' asked Nan.

'It's all right Mum,' Said Dad. 'You are talking to everyone in the car on my new hands-free kit.'

'HELLO!!!' We all chimed.

'Oh shit!' said Nan.

'Mother! Angelina's in the car.'

'Sorry! Oh no, I've spoilt everything now!'

Nan was quite upset when we met her. I heard Grandad growl, 'Stupid bitch!' into her ear as he got into the car. They must have had a row about it. She was very quiet for the rest of the day and there was a definite atmosphere between them.

Spud and Annicka came around this evening. They are expecting to exchange contracts for their house tomorrow. It must be very exciting for them. I wish I could have my own house or flat.

1 December 2003, Monday

Gerry called me into his office and I expected bad news.

'Now then, Troy. What are we going to do with you?' he said.

'Give me a job?' I suggested, trying to be funny.

'I have spoken to your previous employers.' My heart sank.

'Oh!' I said.

'It appears that you were treated very poorly by them.'

'Was I er I was?'

'Yes, Carl told me that you had left after being accused of theft.'

'Colin,' I corrected.

'Sorry, yes. Colin told me that their till broke down a few days ago and the engineer found the missing twenty pound note in the drawer mechanism.'

'Oh!' I said, feeling surprised, relieved and satisfied all at the same time.

'He has asked me to offer you your old job back.'

My heart sank again, 'Oh!'

'What do you think?'

'I don't know.'

'Do you want to go back and work there?'

'Not really, but if I haven't got a job here, I guess I will have to.'

'Well, you have got a job here if you want it.'

My jaw dropped and an uncontrollable smile beamed across my face. 'Yes please!' I said.

I am going to be earning the same wages as before but the company is going to subsidise my travel. Superb! I wanted to do a victory run but I had to control my excitement.

I have got a career. Now all I need is a girl.

The one negative thing is that I am going to be paid monthly and in arrears, so I won't get any money until the end of the month. Dad said that he would help me out.

I went down the pub tonight with Karl, Tom, Meat, Kylie, Lara and Ed to celebrate.

What an excellent day, apart from the rain!

2 December 2003, Tuesday

The day was dominated by today's Carling Cup fourth-round tie between Southampton and Portsmouth. The Pompey fans at work kept asking me if I was nervous. I told them that I wasn't because I knew that we were going to lose.

'We didn't score a goal in the whole of November,' I argued when I was accused of being negative.

It wasn't a good day for Dad. He had a huge range of jobs to work on that had to go out by ten o'clock tomorrow morning. He knew that he was going to miss the match. I offered to stay with him, but he insisted that I go to the game without him. He even arranged for me to leave an hour early to avoid meeting too many drunken Pompey fans on the train.

It worked. I had no aggravation at all on the way to the stadium. I had a burger outside the ground and bought a couple of programmes.

The atmosphere inside the stadium was worth turning up for and the result was just what I had wished for. Southampton two, Portsmouth nil. My greatest footballing dreams were realised. We had won against Pompey and I can hold my head up at work tomorrow.

James Beattie scored a penalty right on the final whistle. I, stupidly, decided to walk back to the ferry terminal instead of catching the bus. I picked a quiet road for my route and got cornered by three annoyed and burly Pompey thugs who obviously had travelled to the city without tickets and brains.

'Hello Scummer!' one of them snarled at me. I said nothing. I was frozen with fear.

'Which leg shall we break?' Another one of them asked the first one as he slapped a baseball bat into the palm of his hand.

'How about both of them?' Said the other one. They all laughed loudly and menacingly.

'You touch him and you'll regret it,' Said a girl's voice from the shadows.

'Hello Snowy. You know this Scummer, then?' asked the first thug.

The girl came into view. It was Donna Bull.

'Yes, we are old friends. Hello Troy!'

'Hi!' I said.

'You pick your friends well, Scummer. It's your lucky day!' They all wandered off laughing and singing choruses of 'Play Up Pompey, Pompey Play Up.' I hate that song.

'Heading for the ferry?' asked Donna.

'Yes,' I replied.

'May I join you?'

'Yes,' I said. Please, I thought.

In the clearer light of the ferry terminal I could see her face. She is so beautiful. How could I have ever considered her to be ugly? We chatted constantly for the whole time that we were together. She laughed at my attempts to be funny as well. In no time at all we were back in Cowes and she had to go.

The words came out of my mouth almost without any control from me. 'Can I see you again?'

'Yes please,' she called back.

I think I am in love.

3 December 2003, Wednesday

I wore my Saints shirt under my jumper to work and expected to be able to enjoy a day of unrivalled gloating, but the Pompey fans were all very gracious in defeat.

It wasn't until late in the afternoon, when egged on by Grant, one of Dad's fellow Mac Ops, that I took the opportunity to strut around the place with my shirt in full view.

'What are you like?' said Cindy from the admin office.

I also received a text from Donna: 'HI SEXY. WHAT R U DOIN 2NITE?'

I texted back: 'DUNNO. CAN I C U?'

She replied: 'YES PLS. CALL ME WEN U GET HOME.'

So I did and we met up at Newport Bus Station. We walked around the town chatting and she grabbed my hand. It felt like touching a piece of heaven. Girls' hands are so soft, small and cold.

Mine was all hot and clammy. I apologised but she said that my hand was warming hers up. We teased each other about the Pompey match last night.

'How did you get out so early when they kept the Pompey fans back for ten minutes after full time?' I asked her.

'I showed a steward my Red Funnel ticket and fluttered my eyelashes at him,' she said, fluttering her eyelashes at me in demonstration.

'What about those idiots?'

'They must have travelled there without tickets, hoping for a punch-up.'

'They nearly got one. How do you know them?'

'They're mates of my dad's.'

'I'd hate to meet your dad's enemies.'

'You probably already have. They're all Scummers like you.'

We walked down to the Quay where she stopped me by stepping in front of me and placing her hand on my chest.

'Am I going to have to make all the first moves?' she asked, beaming up at me with her glittering peridot-green eyes.

I thought that she might be suggesting that I should kiss her, but in my unconfident frame of mind I said, 'What do you mean?'

She grabbed the front of my coat and pulled me down to her. The roughness of that action was a contrast to the tender way in which she kissed me. From that moment there was no stopping us.

The deep pleasure and emotion involved in our embrace were entrancing and I knew too that it was completely mutual.

When we had finally finished, which was so much later that I could not believe what the time was, I asked her, 'Will you go out with me?'

'You don't have to ask me that, silly. If you want an answer, though, I'll give you one.' She tiptoed so that she could whisper into my ear. Her hot breath tickled as she whispered, 'Yes'.

She told me that all her friends called her Snowy and that I was to do the same.

I asked her why, even though I already knew the answer. She looked at me with a knowing, playful frown. 'It's something to do with the Abominable Snowgirl. I am the Snowgirl, hence Snowy.'

'How on earth do they connect the Abominable Snowgirl to you?'

'The Abominable Donna Bull Troy, everybody that knows me knows that and I'm sure that you do to. Tom is bound to have mentioned it.'

'I just wanted to make sure, in case I put my foot in it one day.'

I arranged to meet her on Friday night, this time in Cowes where she is staying for the weekend with her father.

I travelled home on the bus knowing the true meaning of the phrase 'being on cloud nine'.

I have got a girlfriend and a beautiful one at that.

I am completely happy for the first time this year.

4 December 2003, Thursday

There is a lot of talk, in the media, regarding the Fijian Flu that has killed more than ten children in this country.

In contrast to my SARS fears earlier this year, I am anxious that my baby sister is very vulnerable to this bug. I don't know how I would cope if we lost her. We all love her so much. Her smile can cure the worst of bad moods.

It was very quiet at work. I spent the whole day calibrating the image setters. It was all right, though, because I was able to have various chats about football with whoever came into my vicinity.

When we got home, Mum told us that Spud had finally got the keys to his new house. They are going to decorate it while it is empty, over the weekend. Spud's dad is going to help. I said that I might pop my head around the door on Saturday.

I had an hour's chat with my dear Snowy. We actually started saying goodbye after half an hour, but neither of us wanted to be the first person to put the phone down. The call eventually ended when her credit ran out.

I went round to Ed's to tell him all about my sudden love life. Lara was there. They were really happy for me.

'I had a funny feeling you might end up with her,' Lara remarked.

'Yeah right!' I said, disbelievingly.

'I did! You told me she was ugly when she was quite the opposite. It was obvious to me that you secretly fancied her, and the fact that she was always teasing you showed that she felt the same way.'

'That women's intuition thing is utter bollocks, isn't it?'

Before I left, Ed gave me a DVD of the Saints v. Pompey game. He had recorded it just in case we won. That was excellent of him. He also told me that he had got back together with Lara.

After a phone call from Karl, who was at the pub with Tom, we went down to join them.

Karl handed me twenty-six pounds for his ticket to the Fulham away match on Boxing Day. I will buy the tickets on Sunday when I go to our game against Charlton.

5 December 2003, Friday

I had a laugh at work today. Dad put the DVD of the Saints v. Pompey match on his Mac and whenever a Pompey fan came near he would play the injury time penalty with the commentator announcing, 'Southampton's hero it had to be James Beattie!'

I went to the pub at lunchtime with Dad and a few colleagues. Dad bought me a beef lasagne and chips. The unusual thing about it was that there was more bacon in it than beef. I didn't complain though, because it was delicious.

I went down to see Snowy at her weekend home in Arctic Road. Her Dad, stepmother and brothers were out, so we took the opportunity to indulge in some very heavy petting.

She is fantastic. She knew that I had a terrible throbbing in my nether regions and relieved the problem by giving me a handjob. When the moment of relief came (excuse the pun) it actually hurt. I moaned with the pain and she thought I was moaning with pleasure.

I tried to gain access to her knickers, but access was denied because of the usual reason. 'I'm on, sorry!' she said.

I did get to see and fondle her gorgeous boobs though.

I told her that she was the first girl ever to touch my willy and she seemed surprised that I was still a virgin.

I told her about my relationship with that ugly Mandy and she said, 'Love finds beauty.'

'What do you mean by that?'

'If you loved her you would have found her beautiful.'

'I thought you were beautiful before I fell in love with you,' I blurted out, without thinking. I cringed, anticipating an awkward reaction.

'Do you love me then?' she asked shyly.

'Yes. I know it's not long that' She put her finger across my lips to stop me rambling and then planted a wonderful lingering kiss there and, considering she had just taken a long drag on her cigarette, it was as sweet as custard.

'Beauty is not necessarily confined to the handsome or pretty,' she said, 'but in your case it is.'

'That is the nicest thing that anybody has ever said to me,' I said.

'That is sad, Troy. I'll tell you something else that I hope you think is nice.'

'Oh yes. What's that then?'

'I love you too.'

What a magical collection of words they are.

We decided to go for a walk before it was time for me to go home. We went to Spud's house. He was busy decorating with his dad and Annicka. He didn't know about Snowy and me and seemed overjoyed by the news. He had a kettle and some biscuits in the kitchen so we stayed for a cuppa. Afterwards I walked my beloved home. The lights of her house were on. Her family were in so we said our goodbyes at her gateway.

I can't believe how much my love for her is intensifying every moment I am with her and even more so when I am not.

I'm in love and I love it.

6 December 2003, Saturday

I didn't waste any time in leaving the house this morning, in my quest to see Snowy. As soon as it was nine o'clock I texted her to see if it was all right for me to come around and she replied to the affirmative.

When I got there I knocked on the door and I heard two little boys bickering about which one would answer it. Then I heard one slapping noise, one of them shout 'Ow!', and a man growl, 'Get out of the f***in' way you little arsehole', before the door opened.

''Ello Troy! What're you after?'

'Pitbull!' I exclaimed. 'What are you doing here?'

'Der! I live 'ere. My house,' he said, doing a poor impersonation of Goofy.

'I've come to see Sn - Donna.'

'No Snerdonna livin' 'ere! Oh! You're the new mug oi mean boyfriend.'

'DAD!' Snowy called as she appeared at the top of the stairs. 'Let him in.'

Pitbull moved aside and I was invited up to the haven of Snowy's bedroom.

'So Pitbull's your dad then?'

'Yes. Is there a problem with that?'

'Not at all. I'm just surprised. You are so beautiful and erm he isn't!'

'You smoothy! I get my looks from my mother.'

'Obviously!'

Why didn't I guess? Peter Bull Donna Bull. There is an obvious connection there. I am going to have to ask Tom why he didn't mention this little detail.

It is just as well that me and Pitbull sorted out our problems.

I spent a couple of hours kissing and cuddling and fooling around with Snowy, then we went out for a walk. It was bitterly cold, so she wrapped up in several layers of fake fur. We went to see how Spud was getting on with his decorating and got roped into painting his front room. It was quite a good laugh. Spud told us that he has a date for his driving test. It is on Monday. I hope he passes, then I will have another chauffeur as well as Dad and Karl.

At half past four we left. I walked Snowy home and we took a good half an hour saying goodbye on her doorstep.

I got home and had my dinner, then I went back to Snowy's and we walked back to my house where I introduced her to my family.

Unlike the carefree attitude of Pitbull, my parents were obviously uneasy about us spending time alone in my bedroom. They didn't tell us not to go there but you could tell by the expressions on their faces that they weren't happy about it.

Cathy grinned though. She obviously found it all quite amusing.

Griz took to Snowy. We had him in the room with us while we cuddled up for the evening and watched television.

'You must be all right if Griz likes you,' I told her. 'He's a very perceptive dog.'

7 December 2003, Sunday

This morning we played away at Southern Vectis at Seaclose Park. Snowy was there to watch me. This gave me a huge lift and I don't just mean in my pants.

A full-strength side meant an absolute trouncing for Southern Vectis. We were six-nil up at half-time and I had scored two. I got lots of stick from the lads who said that I was showing off for my girlfriend.

'Bloody hell, Troy!' gasped Jamie, our recent signing. 'How did you pull her? She's well worth a shag!'

All of our faces turned to stony fear as we all turned to look at Pitbull who walked over to Jamie. 'Nice isn't she, nipper?'

'Yeah, she's gorgeous.'

'Yes she is. She's also my daughter.'

Jamie's face turned white and he started to splutter apologies. Then he got substituted and Dad came on.

In the second half I completed my hat-trick and was showboating when I turned awkwardly and strained my groin and had to be substituted.

We finished up nine-nil winners, and when we got back to the changing room Vernon asked me what the matter was.

'I've got a stiff groin,' I replied.

'I bet you bloody have, you dirty little bugger,' Jason Dwyer added, to predictably raucous laughter.

After the laughter had died down, Jamie piped up. 'Excuse me, Pete, but will Jason now be dropped to the sub's bench because of that comment?'

'Why should 'e be, nipper?'

'Well, I was taken off for what I said at half-time.'

'Nah, you were taken off because you were shit, nipper!'

I had a shower and bid an all-too-brief farewell to Snowy, before heading back to Cowes for a quick roast dinner. Today it was just Mum, Dad, Angelina, Cathy and me for Sunday lunch because Dad and I had to head off for Southampton for our Premiership game against Charlton Athletic.

I bought Karl's ticket and mine to the Fulham away match before going in. Dad bought me a pint! I was well chuffed about that.

It was a brilliant match. We won three-two but we were two-nil up at half-time. Charlton got the score back to two-two before Brett Ormerod got a late winner.

I didn't see Snowy tonight. She went back to her mum's after our match at Seaclose. I stayed in and watched the recording I had made of the Charlton match.

8 December 2003, Monday

My groin was so bad this morning that I could hardly walk. I struggled to work though, and thankfully was put on Mac training for the day.

I got a phone call from Spud before lunch. He has passed his test. Brilliant!

Dad and I went to West Quay on the way home where we met Mum, Cathy and Angelina. We went upstairs for a KFC and I saw Chris there. The wanker was signing autographs.

I ignored him.

When I got home I spent an hour on the phone (landline) to Snowy. I miss her desperately.

I went down to the Union where I gave Karl his Fulham ticket. Ed was there, so were Tom and Meat. We played bar football and had a great laugh.

Vernon came in a bit later. He had been to London to watch the parade of the England Rugby team with the World Cup. He said that it was an awesome experience.

9 December 2003, Tuesday

I thought that my groin injury was getting better until I tried running up the stairs at work. I appear to have aggravated the problem.

It was a quiet day at work. I just did Mac training again.

I phoned Snowy hoping that I could see her tonight, but she put our meeting off until tomorrow so I went down to the icafé for a while. The noisy girls on the bench were being so annoying that I decided to see how Spud was getting on with his decorating. When I arrived I found Mum there drinking a cup of tea and chatting to Annicka in the kitchen.

Upstairs, Spud and his adopted and biological fathers were stripping the carpet out of the front bedroom. I gave them a hand and got covered in dirt.

Before I left he showed me the brochure for the car he is picking up tomorrow, a VW Beetle Convertible. It is lovely.

I missed all the Champions League games because of helping Spud.

10 December 2003, Wednesday

I spent the day in the plate room at work being shown how flexographic printing plates are made. I had a long chat about football with Matt, the plate maker (a Pompey fan). It helped the day pass quicker.

After dinner I got Spud to give me a lift in his gorgeous new car to Snowy's house and we spent ages kissing and cuddling, just in saying hello to each other. I met her mum who is very nice looking for her age. How on Earth did an ugly sod like Pitbull ever pull a beauty like that?

In Snowy's room we indulged in some very heavy petting. She let me put my hand down her knickers. It was the most wonderful experience of my life so far. She offered to relieve my frustrations but there was no need. My pants were already in a sorry state.

Spud picked me up at eleven o'clock and teased me by asking if I had done it with her yet.

'I'm in no hurry,' I said.

'Get in there, fella. Now's your big chance. Tom's been there, so there's no reason why you shouldn't.'

I hadn't really thought about her relationship with Tom up to that point, but now that I was thinking of it, I felt quite jealous.

I kept imagining the two of them together, having sex, and I just got more and more jealous.

11 December 2003, Thursday

It was back to Mac training today, after cleaning the two big image setters. The day went quite slowly because I just wanted to see Snowy.

After dinner I went to her house, unannounced, but she didn't mind. We began where we left off last night, but it all went a bit sour when I asked her, 'Did you do it with Tom?'

'Yes I did. Why? Does that bother you?'

'Yes it does. I know it shouldn't but it does.'

'You have no need to be jealous. I love you now much more than I ever loved him.'

'So when do you think that we might do it?'

'I don't know. Is that all you are interested in? Is that all you want me for? Sex?'

'No, of course not! But I am your boyfriend and you have done it before.'

'It was three weeks before we even discussed it. Tom was very patient.'

That statement filled me with rage and I stormed off.

I am sure that Tom told me that they did it almost straight away. That's why he dumped Lara.

We have had our first row and I just hope that I haven't lost her.

12 December 2003, Friday

I tried all day to phone Snowy and her mobile was turned off. I thought that I had blown it until after dinner when she turned up on my doorstep.

'I'm so sorry,' she said as she wrapped her arms around my neck.

'So am I. I didn't mean to act like an idiot. I just really love you and want to show you in the most intimate way possible.'

'I understand that, but I don't want to rush into it yet.'

'That's Okay. When you are ready.'

She gave me a wonderful kiss and we went to my room where we did everything but have full sex. I finally got to see her naked. I am so lucky that the first woman I have seen naked (not counting my mother or my grandmother) is the most beautiful I have ever seen.

I had to wedge a chair in front of my bedroom door, in case any of my nosy parents decided to barge in.

Dad gave Snowy a lift to her father's house and I went with them.

I am so glad that I didn't lose her.

13 December 2003, Saturday

I spent the morning with Snowy, in her room, frolicking around. We didn't do anything sexual, just played Monopoly.

She left, just before lunch, so that she could go to Fratton Park. She has to go on her own because Pitball is banned from all English football grounds. I wondered why she was on her own when I met her in Southampton.

I spent the afternoon watching *Gillette Soccer Saturday* on Sky. To my amazement and delight, Southampton won two-one at Liverpool, and to Snowy's disgust, Pompey lost two-one at home to Everton.

She was a bit down about it when I met her at seven o'clock at her house. I didn't say anything about our good result as we headed down to the Union to meet up with Karl, Tom, Jason, Ed, Meat, Kylie and Lara. It is the first time I have been out with my mates with Snowy on my arm. I felt very proud.

At one stage Snowy had a chat with her old boyfriend, Tom. I know it was stupid but I felt really jealous. I tried not to let it show, but as we walked home she teased me by saying that I was making it obvious I was jealous because I couldn't keep my hands off her.

I walked her home, kissed her goodnight, and went home myself.

Dad was away at his work's Christmas Party in Southsea. He had an all-expenses-paid night in a hotel. I would have gone but I was taken on too late in the year.

14 December 2003, Sunday

I couldn't play this morning because my groin still hasn't fully recovered. Dad couldn't play because he didn't get back from Southsea until ten-thirty.

I got a text from Tom, saying that they drew two-two.

After lunch with Nan and Grandad, I went to see Snowy for an afternoon of everything but sex. I am beginning to feel confident in her seeing me naked and I think she feels the same way because she is more than happy for me to undress her. I just wish that I could make love to her. It is so tantalising, but I have to show patience and restraint. If I don't complain, she might be impressed enough to bring the date of our consummation forward.

She had to go back to Newport after dinner, a dinner I attended at her house with Pitbull, her stepmother and her two brothers - a noisy affair that stopped just short of becoming a food fight.

I went with Pitbull as he took Snowy back to Newport. He then dropped me off at home.

I spent the evening watching Jonny Wilkinson win the BBC Sports Personality of the Year award, then I went to bed.

15 December 2003, Monday

The news this morning was dominated by the fact that the US has found Saddam Hussein. The scruffy, bearded tyrant was found in a tiny, dark hole only just big enough to lie in.

The Americans announced the news in their usual Hollywood style in a quote that will become as legendary as Churchill's We-will-fight-them-on-the-beaches speech.

'Ladies and Gentlemen, we got 'im!' was their announcement.

Yesterday's Premiership results have left Pompey in the relegation zone and all the Pompey fans at work fear the worst. Us Saints fans, however, can bask in the fact that we are currently lying in sixth position.

I hope they stay up though, as long as we beat them on the way. I know that a lot of Saints fans would prefer it if they went down, but it is good for the region to have two Premiership clubs.

There were lots of stories and pictures being bandied around about the goings-on at the Christmas party. There was a funny picture in which Dad looked like he was ogling at some girl's tits.

After work I did some Christmas shopping and bought my mum's birthday present.

I got Mum some earrings for her birthday and a necklace for Christmas.

I got Dad a book from the Saints Megastore called *In That Number*. It contains all of the club's statistics since the war.

I got Spud and Annicka a joke book called *How To Make Marriage Work.*

I got Angelina a customised teddy bear from The Bear Factory.

I got Snowy a locket that I am going to put my picture in.

I got Grandad Brown a Parker pen and Nan Brown a naked woman apron.

I got Grandad Stenning a Parker pen and Nan Stenning a naked man apron. They had run out of naked woman ones.

I got Ed a Manchester United calendar. He's the only mate I buy a present for as he is my oldest and best friend.

16 December 2003, Tuesday

Mum loved her birthday present. Dad made her cry with his present. It was a folding set of five silver frames with a picture of Dad, Spud, Angelina, Griz and me in it.

It was frosty on the way to work. Red Funnel had sprinkled salt onto their walkway in Southampton, presumably to stop people slipping on the ice. Instead, people were slipping on the salt. It was like walking on marbles. Highly dangerous!

I spent the day cleaning the processors.

Mum's party was at Murray's Restaurant in Cowes. All her old friends were there. The surprise guests were Nan and Grandad Stenning. They only came down for the evening and stayed in the Fountain Hotel. They are heading back to Wales first thing tomorrow morning.

Spud and Grandad continued to avoid each other.

I did have a short conversation with my beloved before the party. We are seeing each other tomorrow at the cinema. I can hardly wait.

17 December 2003, Wednesday

It was quite busy at work today. The Christmas rush seems to have finally arrived. This gave me the opportunity to watch Dad at work and learn from him.

News came over the radio that Ian Huntley had been convicted of murdering Holly Wells and Jessica Chapman, ending over a year of speculation. Hopefully he will get his comeuppance in prison.

Spud and Annicka were there when I arrived home. Their house is ready and we have been invited around for a family house-warming on Saturday night. I can bring Snowy.

Talking of my darling girlfriend, Spud gave me a lift to meet her at Cineworld this evening and we watched *The Lord of the Rings Return of the King*. It lasted three hours and twenty minutes. We couldn't get up to any shenanigans because the theatre was packed.

Spud kindly picked me up when the film had finished. He dropped Snowy off at her mum's and took me to see his finished house. He's got a great entertainment system - surround sound, big plasma screen, DVD recorder, Sky Plus, the lot. It is superb. I stayed there with him until gone two, playing X-Box games on his massive TV.

18 December 2003, Thursday

I was absolutely knackered at work today. I had a nap on the train on the way in and on the way home, but in the evening my weariness disappeared.

I phoned Snowy and she has managed to get a ticket for Sunday's match so that we can go to it together. Excellent!

This evening I went down to the pub and Karl told me that we would be catching the nine-thirty car ferry from Fishbourne on Boxing Day. We can't use Red Funnel because they stop running at five o'clock that day. He asked me to give him thirty quid towards travelling expenses. When I got home I asked Dad if he could help me out. He agreed to do so, rather begrudgingly.

19 December 2003, Friday

It was quiet at work again today. I struggled to keep my eyes open during my training session, but as soon as we went to the pub for lunch, I woke up again. Then I became drowsy a few minutes after returning to my desk.

It was a long day.

After dinner and a nice hot bath I waited for Snowy to call. Her dad dropped her off and we spent the evening messing around in my room.

I asked her if she loved me enough to give up smoking. She said, 'Yes I do, but do you love me enough to let me carry on?'

It was an excellent response and, of course I do.

After she left I wondered to myself, how can she do all the sexual things she does to me and not let me shag her? Why is the penis in the vagina thing such a big deal? I've had my tongue and my fingers in there and she had mine in her mouth this evening. And very wonderful it was too.

Also, why, after a passionate session, does she always need to pop outside my bedroom patio doors for a cigarette? All I seem to want to do is go to sleep.

20 December 2003, Saturday

I had a long lie-in this morning. I didn't get up until gone midday. I had a couple of slices of toast for lunch then I went round to see Snowy.

She wanted to do some Christmas shopping so, I phoned Spud to see if he could give us a lift to Newport. He was on his way to Ryde anyway.

I can't believe how knackering it is following somebody around clothes shops all day.

We caught the bus home and she went to her house to change for our evening at Spud's.

Annicka cooked a lovely dinner of chicken curry and then Spud and his wife stood up and we knew that an announcement was imminent.

He handed Mum and Dad an envelope, which they proceeded to open. Inside was an ultrasound image.

'We have been dying to tell you this news for weeks, but it's bad luck,' Spud said. 'We want you to be the first to know that we are going to have a baby.'

We all congratulated them, but Mum was mortified. 'I'm too young to be a grandmother!' she whined.

'Apparently not!' Dad said.

Annicka is already three months pregnant. The baby is due on June the twenty-sixth. So it could be born on my birthday.

I can't believe what an amazing year Spud has had. I wish *my* life were that interesting.

21 December 2003, Sunday

Snowy arrived during breakfast, bravely or stupidly (depending on your own personal opinion) wearing her Pompey shirt over several jumpers.

I wore my Saints stuff with confidence because of the lack of trouble at the last game.

We must have looked strange walking down the road hand in hand, and an ideal advert for the clubs' combined efforts to establish a friendly rivalry.

We had to part company at twelve when she headed for the Pompey end and I headed for my seat, where I met Dad who was really looking forward to the match because he had missed the Cup game.

We won three-nil and enjoyed joining in the Saints songs of the day:

'You're shit and you smell of fish.'

'You're going down with Harry and Jim.'

'F*** off Pompey Pompey f*** off.'

(To Teddy Sheringham) 'Old man You're just a f***ing old man.'

(To Pompey's number-one fan John Westwood) 'Have you ever have you ever have you ever had a shag?'

(When the score was two-nil) 'Westwood what's the score? Westwood Westwood what's the score?'

'Westwood takes it up the arse.'

(To John Westwood again) 'Who's the wanker who's the wanker who's the wanker with the bell?'

'Premier league? You're havin' a laugh.'

'You'll never play here again.'

Good, clean, offensive banter. Well, perhaps not clean.

The Pompey fans were kept back for ten minutes and Snowy phoned me to say that she didn't manage to blag her way out early this time. I went home with Dad and had dinner before heading around to her house where the atmosphere was very subdued.

'You're a very special Scummer to survive comin' in vis house on a day like vis,' Pitbull moaned.

Snowy was a bit moody about the football, so I made sure that I didn't make any reference to it, despite being overjoyed.

We didn't do anything tonight, just kissed and cuddled.

As I left she thanked me for not mentioning the football. Brownie points for me there I think.

She is spending the days leading up to Christmas with her dad and Christmas Day with her mum so she gets to open some of her presents on Christmas Eve. I will give her my present then.

When I got home, Dad and I relived Marian Pahars' wonderful second goal over and over again until bedtime.

22 December 2003, Monday

Our penultimate day at work this year was a panic, with people trying to get all remaining jobs out of the door on time. Dad and I left half an hour later than normal and picked up a Chinese meal on the way home. It was absolutely delicious.

Snowy was in a much better mood this evening and we met up with Karl and the lads down the pub.

Karl told us that he was very excited about our trip to the game on Boxing Day.

When he had gone off to speak to some of the others, Snowy turned to me and said, 'You never told me that you weren't here for Boxing Day!'

'Sorry, I kept forgetting.'

'That's a shame. I had something special planned for that day.'

'What?'

'I can't say. It's part of your Christmas present.'

'I should be back between nine and ten.'

'Good. You won't want to miss out.'

She must mean that she wants to shag me! I wish I wasn't going now.

23 December 2003, Tuesday

I spent the morning cleaning and emptying the processors, ready for the Christmas holidays. Dad and a couple of his mates gave me a hand.

At lunchtime the whole firm went down to the pub for a free Christmas dinner with all the trimmings. Free drinks as well, although I was only allowed to have Coke.

Dad got pissed and was a nightmare on the way home. He dozed off and snored ridiculously loudly on the train.

When we got home he went to bed and I went round to see Snowy.

We got down to some passion for the evening. I tried to tickle out of her the answer to the question, 'What have you got me for Christmas', she isn't very ticklish.

24 December 2003, Wednesday

I had a long lie-in. I got up at around midday, had a quick lunch and went round to all my friends' houses to drop off their cards and, in Ed's case, his present.

I dropped in at Spud's and they were making a hasty getaway. They had decided that they wanted to guarantee a white Christmas by spending it with Annicka's parents. He gave me my, Mum's, Dad's and Angelina's presents and climbed into a taxi with his wife.

I then went to Snowy's and it was like walking into Christmas Day. They were already sat around the dinner table, dolled out in Christmas hats, and I took my place next to my beloved.

We pulled a cracker each. I got a small puzzle game and she got a clip-on moustache.

After a delicious Christmas dinner with all the trimmings (for the second day running, now) I went upstairs with Snowy and gave her her present. She had a tear in her eye when she saw it.

She gave me a present from Pitbull and the family. It was a Pompey shirt with 'Brown 16' on the back. What a waste of money! She made me put in on and parade in front of them. It delighted them all.

Then she gave me my presents from her. First she handed me a package that turned out to be a St Christopher with the words 'I love you' engraved on the back. The second one was a condom with a tag sellotaped to it reading 'Boxing Night X.'

I knew it!

I gave her the longest kiss ever as I left. I tried to phone Karl to cancel my trip with him but I couldn't get through to him. I texted him and I hope to get a call from him tomorrow.

25 December 2003, Thursday

Today was the first Christmas Day that I'd slept in. I was awakened by Dad, Mum, Cathy, Griz and Angelina, who all brought presents in for me to open in bed.

From Mum and Dad I got a new Saints reversible jacket, a big book called *In That Number* (the same one that I'd bought Dad), a large selection of DVDs and the Busted CD.

From Cathy I got a Kylie Minogue calendar and a huge bar of Cadbury's Fruit and Nut.

From Angelina I got a mug with 'Big Brother' on it. Inside was a big bag of Cadbury's Buttons.

I checked my phone and there was a reply from Karl. 'DON'T LET ME DOWN M8'

I texted him back to say Happy Christmas and to say that I will go with him.

I got up and had a bath before heading for the front room in time for the arrival of Nan and Grandad Brown.

From them I got a new diary (that will come in handy), something called Geomac, which is made up of magnetic sticks and ball bearings, and some new socks.

We all sat down for the traditional Christmas dinner with all the trimmings, and Lambrusco Bianco, and after we had crammed the Christmas pudding down our necks and were adorned with paper hats, Dad and Grandad were soon snoring at the table.

While Mum and Cathy washed up, I phoned Snowy. She told me that I should encourage Karl to get back as soon as possible tomorrow night.

I wish I wasn't going. We are bound to lose. But I have committed myself now. I don't want to let Karl down. He has been looking forward to this for months.

After the women had washed up, we all gathered around the table for a game of Scrabble. Dad won.

Then it was time for dinner, which consisted of various party snacks that Mum and Dad had bought while they were on offer at Tesco - turkey sandwiches, cheese and pineapple sticks, mini sausage rolls and crisps.

The pudding buffet of mince pies, trifle and chocolate fingers were the limit for me, and I had dozed off by the time *Eastenders* came on.

I might have to pay a visit to the doctor very soon - I actually like Victoria Beckham's new single!

My last day as a virgin ended as it started, with me in bed, thinking erotic thoughts about my beautiful girlfriend.

26th December 2003, Friday

Kevin Brown here, writing for Troy who is in a coma.

My worst nightmare began when I received a visit from two police officers at ten-fifteen. We hadn't received a call from you all day and we were getting a bit worried. The visit from those officers gave us the news that we dreaded.

It could have been worse, though. We should be thankful that you are still alive, but the doctors can't be sure that you will remain that way.

All we can do is hope and pray.

All the information that we have been given is that the car in which you and Karl Sibley were travelling overturned at high speed along the M3, heading towards Southampton at around seven o'clock this evening. The awful weather conditions must have had a bearing on it. Driving at high speed in torrential rain is very dangerous, especially to a relatively inexperienced driver like Karl.

Karl is also in the hospital with a broken leg and a broken arm but he is conscious. I have spoken to him but I am sure he is being cagey. He must have been speeding. I have seen the way he drives. He was always an accident waiting to happen. How I let you go with him I'll never know, and I will never forgive myself if you don't pull through.

So here we are in the Intensive Care Unit of Southampton General Hospital. Your mother and I are beside ourselves with worry. You are our very reason for living, you and Angelina and, of course, Stuart.

I am sitting here, totally helpless, and all we can do is keep you company and hope that the power of our love will help you on a spiritual level, not that I have ever believed in that malarkey, but you grab hold of anything when you are desperate.

The hospital chaplain has helped us, given us hope, but I think what have I done to deserve God's help? I haven't ever asked for his help in all my life so I haven't earned it.

Oh my boy, my beautiful, precious boy. Stay with us, please. We love you so much.

27th December 2003, Saturday

A CT scan this morning revealed severe bruising on your brain. It means that it's up to you whether you can fight against the injuries your brain has received or not.

Tom Sibley popped in to see you this morning. He told me that his brother admitted to him that he was trying to get back home as fast as he could. His wheels locked at very high speed and the car skidded and overturned into a ditch.

I didn't tell Tom that, if you don't pull through, I will probably kill his brother.

Donna spent most of the day at your bedside. I asked her to write a message for you:

Hi, my handsome man. I know we haven't had much time together but I want you to know that I love you so much.
I have been holding your hand all day, praying that you would squeeze mine, but you didn't. Maybe tomorrow, eh?

Your Mum wanted to write something:

Hello baby. I don't deserve my children, but nevertheless, I have been blessed with you all, especially you sweetheart.
You have always been there for me. Whenever I have been down you have always said or done something funny to make me realise how lucky I am.
I am worried that I have been too lucky and maybe God is going to take you away from me to even things up.
Then I think that maybe he is just trying to remind me of how precious you are, just so that I will appreciate you more.
Well, there has never been a day when I haven't looked at you and thought how amazing you are, considering that I made you
From the moment I first saw you I knew that you were special. You must pull through. You are my baby boy.
Please darling, I long to see your smile again, to hear your voice, your laugh. 'I love you' is only three words but it's a pinprick in the universe of the way I feel about you.

Stuart also paid you a visit as soon as he and Annicka returned from Sweden:

Hey fella! What have you gone and done now? You are always getting yourself into predicaments aren't you?
*I have had a brother for too short a time to lose him now, so get your arse into gear and get f***ing better!*
By the way I love you too, and so does Annicka.
She has put a pair of her knickers under your pillow, for luck. Her knickers have been very lucky for me when they have been off her body.

28 December 2003, Wednesday

Your mother and Cathy sat with you today. The lack of improvement is very worrying. We hold your hand, talk to you almost non-stop, but there is no response. The doctors assure us that these things take time, but time means worry and stress.

We have kept Angelina away until now, but maybe the sound of her voice will trigger a response from you.

Here is a message from Cathy:

Hi sweetheart. I don't know what I can say that hasn't already been said by everybody else. We all love you and miss you.

All the grandparents are her now. First of all Grandad Stenning:

I just wish I could write a big hug because it is killing me not being able to give you one. You will be pleased to know that Stuart and I have gone someway towards patching up our differences. It is events like this that help to put things into perspective. Hang in there, son.

Nan Stenning:

A big kiss from me. At least I was able to plant one on your forehead. We are all so worried and are praying for you. The chaplain has been a great comfort. We'll be staying here until you get better, so hurry up.

29 December 2003, Monday

We brought Angelina in today. I hope you could hear her. She doesn't cry as much as she used to but she did have one wailing session that meant we had to take her out of the ward for the sake of the other patients.

They are limiting your visitors to family only, but all your friends have been sending in cards and good wishes - Edward Case, Nathan Edge, Jason Dwyer, Lara Mathews,Terry Smith (by telegrame), Jason Ince, Peter Bull, Vernon, Colin and Bill from your old work place, Kylie, Kelly, Katie, Hannah, Rachel. We have put the cards up round your bed.

Grandad Brown wanted to say something:

My boy. It just isn't the same without your mischief and shenanigans. My dodgy heart aches to hear your voice again, to compliment your flatulence again and to hear you laugh at my toilet humour. Please get better. We can't function properly, as a family, without you.

Nan Brown:

It has been a hard year for you. It would all be so pointless if you don't come through this. You wouldn't believe how worried everybody is. All of your grandparents went to church yesterday to pray for you. I am wearing a necklace made of wooden beads that I got from the Quay Arts Centre, so that I am always touching wood for luck.

30 December 2003, Tuesday

The doctors assure us that you are making progress, but we see nothing to support this theory.` We feel that they are just trying to keep our hopes up.

Vernon has been trying to set up a special visit from a Southampton legend for you tomorrow. Fingers crossed. That would be a wonderful thing, especially on New Year's Eve.

31 December 2003, Wednesday

James Beattie popped in to see you today. The doctors bent their rule about family members only to let him in. He spent an hour here, giving you his personal recollections of the matches you have missed. What a top bloke! He has promised you a VIP trip to St Mary's as his guest when you are better.

The year is nearly over for everybody else, but for us the celebrations are in limbo until we get our boy back. We can't begin to have a Happy New Year without you.

11.59 p.m.: I came around to find my face full of tubes and things and my dad writing in my diary. It will not be a Happy New Year for him if I find out that he has read any of it. I can't believe I missed James Beattie. Typical of my luck!

1 January 2004, Thursday

I have read all the goodwill messages that were written in my diary of last year and, although touched by them, I am paranoid about how many people have been reading about my private life. Dad is the main focus of my suspicions as he was the person writing in the days when I was out of it.

I will have to use some better form of security this year.

I woke up this morning in my own private room paid for my older brother, Spud. A pretty, petite young Asian nurse came in and introduced herself to me as Lakshmi. She gave me a bed bath and I was so scared that I was going to get a hard-on but I didn't.

She seems very nice and friendly.

Nan and Grandad Stenning, Mum, Dad, Cathy and my baby sister, Angelina, turned up while I was being checked over by the doctor. He explained a few things to me in a broad foreign accent and I pretended that I knew what he was on about, to be polite.

Spud and Annicka arrived soon afterwards with flowers, chocolate and grapes. Then, at proper visiting time, Snowy turned up. She started crying and sobbed, 'I was frightened that I was going to lose you.' She stayed for the rest of visiting time, holding my hand.

During her time at my bedside Ed, Lara, Meat and Kylie came to see me, but I was feeling so tired that I had to tell them, 'It's all right, I am listening. I just need to close my eyes for a while.'

When I woke up, at nine-twenty, I was alone. I pressed the buzzer and another nurse came in - a rather abrupt older nurse who moaned about me pressing the buzzer when there was nothing wrong with me.

2 January 2004, Friday

This morning I had to undergo some tests. I tried standing up, but I was far too dizzy and had to lie down again. They think that my head injury has damaged an area of my inner ear (the area that controls balance). I asked when I could go home and they said that they didn't know.

I was asked questions about the accident. I can remember talking to Karl about wanting to get back home as soon as possible as I was on a promise with Snowy, but I don't remember anything about the crash.

Lakshmi stayed in and chatted with me after my bed bath. She said that she is leaving the hospital soon. She is moving to London.

The family turned up again, then Snowy appeared and Nan and Grandad

Brown. Nan and Grandad Stenning are considering leaving their home in Penarth and moving to Australia after Grandad retires in April.

Snowy came for the whole of visiting time and, when we were eventually alone, teased me by telling me that the first thing she is going to do to me when I get out is f*** the living daylights out of me. The mere thought created a pointy lump in the bedclothes, which she attended to.

At least that part of me is still working properly.

3 January 2004, Saturday

I had a lovely chat with Lakshmi this morning. I feel that I can talk to her about everything and, since she is leaving soon, I might as well do so. No one else will ever find out. I told her about by terrible bad luck in my efforts to lose my virginity. She seemed very sympathetic.

I managed to stagger to the toilet this morning. It is like I am pissed up whenever I stand.

Being stuck in hospital meant that I could not go to Southampton's FA Cup third round match against Newcastle. We lost, so it didn't matter.

Snowy spent every available minute with me, and whenever we had an extended period of time alone, she performed the usual sexual favour for me. I am aching to make love to her.

I am not going to list the people who visited me today, but it seemed like everyone I knew came to see me. The worst part of the day was when Snowy's dad, Pitbull, and the boys came in. The boys were a complete nightmare. They kept touching things and getting told off. In the end Pitbull knocked their heads together, which produced a hollow sound. Or maybe that was just my imagination.

I had to watch *Match of the Day* on my own tonight.

4 January 2004, Sunday

The Sunday lunch I was given today was a sore reminder of what I am missing at home.

Sunday television is crap, so I was just bored all day.

I did get a visit from Mum, Dad, Nan and Grandad Brown but Snowy couldn't come.

This evening was rather more pleasant. Nurse Lakshmi had finished work and decided to spend a couple of hours in my company.

We talked about sex and stuff and she was quite happy to tell me about all the things that she liked to have done to her in the sack and what she likes, to do to her men. The conversation created a duvet hillock that I hid by rolling onto my side.

I hope she didn't notice.

It was really nice of her to keep me company.

5 January 2004, Monday

I spent the whole day alone as Dad went back to work and Snowy went back to school.

I struggled to the communal television room for a bit of company and chatted to this old bloke called Bob who was recovering from a heart attack.

He was telling me how much he was dying for a cigarette. I told him that if he had one he would be dying, literally.

He has been a Saints season ticket holder for forty years, and we spent a pleasant day reminiscing about our Saints memories. It was fascinating hearing all the old stories he had to tell.

I saw a doctor today and he said that they would like to keep me in for observation until the weekend. They also said that if everything was all right by then I could go home.

Hooray!

It was Lakshmi's day off today, so I spent the evening watching TV in the room with Bob and his mate Hubert.

6 January 2004, Tuesday

Today was spent in much the same way as yesterday, vegging out in front of the TV and chatting about football with the old fellows.

Dad came in to see me this evening on his way home from work. He had picked up a KFC from a local drive-through and gave some to me. I can't tell you how wonderful it was. He stayed for about an hour.

Lakshmi had been to see me several times during the day, in line with her job, but after she had knocked off I was delighted that she decided to spend a couple of hours with me again.

I told her that I might be able to go home on Saturday and she said that she finishes on Friday.

The conversation soon returned to an erotic subject and my sexual frustration is now at bursting point. I can't wait for the weekend and Snowy.

7 January 2004, Wednesday

Mum came over to see me today with Auntie Cathy and darling Angelina. They bought some nibbles with them, thank God! They stayed from two until four, then Dad arrived to keep me company until he was ready to go to the Southampton versus Leicester City game this evening.

I listened to the game on the radio, which was weird as I am always usually at the match when they play at St Mary's. It was a dour nil-nil draw, so I didn't miss much.

I can't believe how slow time is passing at the moment!

Lakshmi was going to sit with me tonight, but when she saw that I was listening to the match she decided to go home.

8 January 2004, Thursday

I had a bit of a nasty shock this morning. I asked one of the nurses, Michelle, if she had seen anything of Bob and she told me that he had passed away on Tuesday night in his sleep.

I was only chatting with him that afternoon! I can't believe he's dead! It was all I could think of all day.

No family visitors today, but Lakshmi stayed with me after she knocked off work and was great company.

She talked to me about death and things, and she helped me when she climbed onto my bed and gave me a lovely cuddle.

I hope she didn't notice my penis pressing into her, unwanted by me, through the bedclothes.

I found out that she is giving up nursing, when she finishes tomorrow. She has got a job as a social worker.

That's a great loss to the nursing profession, as she is a terrific nurse.

9 January 2004, Friday

I had a visit from the doctor this morning and he told me that I should be able to go home tomorrow.

When Dad visited me after work I told him and he said that he would arrive at the hospital early to be ready to take me home.

Lakshmi worked her last day today and, to my surprise and delight, decided to spend her last evening with me. She was wearing a short skirt and I did think that it was unusual attire for the time of year.

After a short chat she went to the door and put the 'Do Not Disturb' sign on the door handle.

'What are you doing?' I asked her.

'I won't ever see you again after tonight and I wanted to leave you with a lasting memory of me.'

With that, she whipped off the bedclothes and straddled me as she bent down to kiss me. Shocked, I just went along with it. I could feel her bare genitals, hot and moist against my throbbing and ready to explode willy.

As she passionately kissed me she slid up and down over my penis. I couldn't say anything or stop the inevitable.

'Sorry!' I murmured to her.

'Shhh!' she replied as she grabbed my still erect member and eased it into her.

Then we just, well, shagged. It was only about two minutes before I had come again and she made some moaning and panting noises before she climbed off me and offered me a bed bath.

'Thank you,' she said.

'That's all right!' I said, still not believing what had just happened.

'You are so gorgeous, I just couldn't resist you!'

'No?'

'No,' she said as she bent over and gave me another passionate kiss.

Then she got a pair of knickers out of her handbag and slipped them on. She kissed me again and left, leaving me with some very erotic memories and the massive fact that I was no longer a virgin.

It soon began to sink in that I could not share my amazing story with anybody, then I thought of Snowy, my love, and I started to feel very guilty, but those feelings of guilt were outweighed by the wonder of the experience that I had just had.

Somehow I am going to have to pretend to still be a virgin when the opportunity arrives to make love to her.

Having said all that, I would not have changed this event. It was fantastic.

At last I am a virgin no more, and in a way that I would never have dreamed of.

10 January 2004, Saturday

As expected, Dad arrived at about eleven o'clock this morning. The doctor had given me the all-clear to go home and I was happily dressed and packed. I thanked all the ward staff before Dad chaperoned me to the car that he had brought over on one of his free passage tickets that he had got from Red

Funnel.

Dad wouldn't let me have anything to eat on the ferry, but I did have a cup of delicious hot chocolate.

I was overwhelmed when we arrived home. As I entered the house I was mobbed by Mum, Cathy, all my grandparents, Spud, Annicka, Ed, Meat, Pitbull and the boys, Lara, Kylie, and most wonderful of all, my beloved Snowy. I could not resist giving her a huge kiss and cuddle in front of everyone, which was greeted with choruses of 'Aw' from all the onlookers.

There was a huge banner in the front room that read 'Welcome Home Troy' and Mum had laid on a large buffet with all my favourite nibbles. I stuffed myself with as much food as I could while I caught up with what had been going on since I had become incapacitated.

My Sunday league football team have had a lull in form but are still top of the league, so that was good news.

Terry Smith came home on leave and upset Jason Ince with the news that he has got a boyfriend at his barracks.

Spud and Annicka excitedly showed me the latest indecipherable picture of their future child.

Ed and Lara are still very much an item, which must be the longest relationship that Ed has ever had. I wished Lara a belated 'Happy Sixteenth Birthday. Her birthday had been on Tuesday. She was having her party tonight but I couldn't go.

My baby sister, Angelina, has grown so much since I was last at home, nearly three weeks ago. I really enjoyed cuddling her but I noticed how much heavier she is. She is now on solids, as I discovered when I offered to change her nappy, and I couldn't believe that awful smell that accompanied the event.

As dinner time approached, people began to leave. Finally, and at last, I had a chance to have some private time with Snowy. We lay on my bed for a while, kissing and cuddling, but I was so shattered that I must have dozed off. When I woke up she had gone and there was a note on my bedside table.

Sweetheart,

See you in the morning.
Sleep tight.
I love you.

Snowy.

It was eight o'clock and I couldn't get back off to sleep for thinking of my shag with Lakshmi, so I got up and watched television, including Saints' defeat at Birmingham.

11 January 2004, Sunday

I met Snowy at Northwood Recreation Ground to watch Cowes Park Rangers play Shorewell in the Isle of Wight Junior A Cup quarter-final.

I, of course, am sidelined until the doctor says that I can play again, and it was difficult watching when I was itching to get out there and do my stuff.

Snowy hugged my arm as we cheered the boys on. Shorewell scored first and, with one minute to go, they were about to go two-nil up before my Dad made a goal-saving tackle. The ball squirmed out to Vernon on the edge of the area and he hit a long but perfect pass to Tom. We waited with baited breath as Tom ran across the halfway line and caught up with the ball. The Shorewell defence had pushed up to the halfway line and Tom had beaten the offside trap. He had the keeper to beat and we went mad when he calmly lobbed the marauding goalkeeper to send the match to a replay.

I can't wait to play again!

After the match I had a chat with Tom as he helped to take the nets down. He asked me to go to his birthday party tonight. He and Lara had agreed to have their parties on different days this weekend. I told him that I would see how I felt at the time.

Snowy and I parted for lunch but she came round to my house at just past two o'clock and we went to my bedroom.

We moved my cupboard to the door to stop it from being opened by any unwanted visitors. Then we started to frantically undress each other. We climbed into bed and being able to hold her beautiful naked body next to me and knowing full well that the end result would be sex was exhilarating. I was turned on too quickly and she looked after that problem with her mouth. I didn't lose any libido after that, and in no time at all I was having sex with her.

Again, like Lakshmi, she went on top. We had to keep the noise down but I now know what an orgasm is. It is different from ejaculation and it is fantastic.

During our fourth session, Snowy told me that she had come.

'You're fantastic!' she puffed, 'Are you sure you haven't done this before?'

'I think I would remember if I had,' I fibbed. But in a way I hadn't done it before. My sex with Lakshmi was nothing compared with this love making with Snowy. It was so brief that it was like a dream. I have decided to pretend that it was a dream. Now I can tell people that I have lost my virginity.

We weren't disturbed during the afternoon, and just before dinner Snowy was picked up by her dad and left for Newport. I was on a high and was well up for Tom's party. I was desperate to tell somebody about my day, so I had a bath, got changed and went to Tom's house.

All the usual crowd were there. I wasn't allowed to drink, worst luck, but I got chatting to Meat and told him about my steamy session with Snowy. He shook my hand and said, 'About time!'

Ed and Lara had some sort of disagreement during the party, which resulted in Ed storming off in a huff. Lara attached herself to me for the evening. She was very drunk and finally passed out and lay her head on my lap.

'Bloody hell, mate!' said Meat 'They can't leave you alone now, can they?'

I tried to look uncomfortable. Karl hobbled over and had a chat with me. It was the first real chat that we had had since the accident. He told me he was sorry, again. He said that I was so keen to get back as soon as possible because I was on a promise with Snowy. He was determined to help me and nearly killed us as a result. I told him that Snowy's promise had been fulfilled and he was delighted.

I was a bit disappointed that Spud wasn't there. I really wanted to tell him my news.

At about half eleven, Tom and Karl's parents arrived home and the party was broken up. Lara was awakened and was just about able to walk, so I allowed her to lean on me as I walked her home. When we got to her house she tried to kiss me goodnight. I offered my cheek but she grabbed my face and planted her lips on mine. Then she kissed me again and pushed her tongue into my mouth. It tasted of Pernod. I didn't know what to do. I had always wanted to know what it was like to kiss her, but I didn't want to risk my relationship with Snowy. I went along with it for a few delicious seconds. I thought that she was so drunk that she didn't know what she was doing. She had her arms locked around the back of my neck and pulled me into another lingering snog. Yum yum! I relaxed a bit and relished the moment.

After she finally came up for air she dribbled into my ear, 'I really fancy you Troy!'

'You're drunk!' I said. 'You'll regret this in the morning and deny it if you remember it.'

She giggled and hiccoughed and tried to kiss me again, but I managed to struggle free. 'Think about Ed,' I said.

'We're finished,' she slurred. 'He f***ed off with Katie's cousin, Hannah!'
'Think about Snowy, then.'
'I couldn't hic give a toss about her! She took Tom off me once, so why can't I have my revenge?'
'Lara! Go to bed and sleep on it. Everything will make more sense in the morning.'
'Just one more kiss,' she pleaded.
'Goodnight!' I called as I left her on her doorstep.
It has been quite a good day today. I have had sex with Snowy and had a lovely snog with a girl who has been a heartthrob of mine for ages.

12 January 2004, Monday

I went to the doctor this morning to get a sick note. The note covers me until Friday. Spud's adoptive mother works at the clinic as a receptionist and she asked me how I was, which was very nice. Mum and Angelina came with me and Mum and Spud's mum chatted as if there had never been a problem that Spud is my Mum's natural son and that he has somewhat turned his back on her and her husband.

Dr Flux examined me. Why I had to be virtually naked for this I don't know. She is a rather sexy female doctor in her mid-thirties. She got me to lie on her couch with just my underpants on while she prodded me. As her prodding reached my private regions I got an unwanted hard-on. I was very embarrassed and said, 'Sorry about that!'

'Not to worry,' she said. 'At least we know that's working properly. Right, okay, clothes back on!'

I asked her when I could start playing football again. She said whenever I felt like it. I was delighted.

Mum and I went down to Tiffins where I enjoyed a bacon baguette and a pot of tea.

I texted Snowy with the news and she said she was really pleased.

I spent the rest of the day, up until dinner time, playing Scrabble with Auntie Cathy. The games ended just before Dad came through the door. She won three-nil, but I think that she put me off by taking about fifteen minutes on each go.

I gave Dad my sick note so that he could pass it on to Gerry tomorrow morning.

We had our dinner and I phoned Snowy. She talked dirty to me. It really turned me on. Afterwards I went to Ed's house. I hadn't seen Ed's little sister

Zoe for weeks. Phwoah! She's fourteen and is becoming a perfect ten. She ran and hid when I said hello to her though!

Ed told me that he had finished with Lara because of the simple fact that Hannah is amazing in bed.

'Nurses certainly know their anatomy!' he remarked.

I felt like saying 'I know they do', but I didn't. He said that the only drawback was Hannah's shifts at the hospital. She is on lates this week, so he won't see her until the weekend. I know how that feels!

When I got home, Mum told me that Lara had called for me. I texted her to see what was up and she just texted back with the words: 'JUST WANTED TO C U'.

13 January 2004, Tuesday

This morning Cathy and I had another three-game match of Scrabble. This time I imposed a five-minute time limit on taking your go. I won as a result, but she just said that it wasn't fair.

There was a report on *Sky Sports News* that Southampton's manager Gordon Strachan will be quitting at the end of the season to have a break from football. Shit! This upheaval might end with our relegation. We haven't won a game since December the twenty-first!

There have also been reports about a new killer strain of flu. It is called Bird Flu and has been transmitted by chickens in Thailand. Scientists think that it will mutate and be passed on by humans soon. Christ! We get past SARS and the Fijian Flu and another one, more deadly, comes along!

I went to Newport tonight to see Snowy. Her mum was very nice and considerate towards me.

Snowy and I stayed in and, of course, had sex several times. I can hardly believe that after all this waiting I am now getting so much of it. I am very pleased about it though. I now need to buy some condoms.

Dad came and picked me up at half past ten.

14 January 2004, Wednesday

Mum and Cathy went out to Tesco to do some shopping. They took Angelina with them, so that left me at home with the dog, Griz.

I walked him down the town and went into Boots. My old busty classmate, Hayley Knight, was serving but, unlike last time, I was not too embarrassed to ask her for some condoms. In fact it was she who went bright red at the request. This left me with a sensation of perverted satisfaction.

I went to see Vernon at the Icafé to tell him that I would be available for Sunday's match. He introduced me to his friend, Brad, a flash, smug-looking bloke who spoke like an old-fashioned yuppie. He used to be Vernon's agent when Vernon was playing in Crystal Palace Reserves. A real tosspot! He told us that he has three Nationwide League Division One players on his books but hasn't yet managed to bag a Premiership player.

Spud came down with Tom, Ed, Meat, Lara, Kylie and Kelly for their lunch.

'I thought you were going to leave school?' I said to him.

'I've got nothin' better to do at the mo, fella. I might as well see it out!'

This was the first time I had managed to speak to my older brother since Snowy and I did it. I took him aside and told him.

'I'm really happy for yer, fella!' he said. 'Aye, come round tonight for a chat and a beer. Annie's off out at some pregnancy group thing. Then you can tell me all the details.'

I was really pleased to get the opportunity to sit down and chat about things. So after dinner I got my old bike out and rode around there.

It was great. We slouched on his settee and watched a porn film while I told him about Snowy. Then I told him about Lakshmi and apologised for my past criticism of his similar exploits.

'Don't worry, fella!' he said 'On a plate or what? You lucky bastard!'

'I haven't told anybody else! Only you, Lakshmi and I know about it and she has gone to London. Other than that I don't know where she is. I won't ever see her again. I do love Snowy so I have decided to try to forget about it.'

'Best way. Did she provide the condom?'

'No she didn't, she just jumped on top of me.'

'That's a bit dodgy! You don't know if she was shagging all the patients in the hospital! You'd better get yer todger checked out. Have you been using one with your bird?'

'Yes!'

'That's all right then!'

I hadn't expected that from Spud and I left his house feeling decidedly paranoid.

15 January 2004, Thursday

I went to see the doctor first thing this morning. I had to wait until all the scheduled patients had been in.

'Hello Mr Brown,' said Dr Flux in her sexy voice. 'That's twice in a week! What can I do for you today?'

'Erm, I have had unprotected sex quite recently with a relative stranger.'

'I see! Pop into my examination room and slip off your clothes. I'll be just a moment.'

I did as I was told and I was lying on her couch as she came in, donning rubber gloves. She was wearing a low-cut top that clearly revealed a youthful looking cleavage. I felt a stirring. As soon as she grabbed my penis that stirring became a throbbing hard-on.

'I am so sorry!' I said.

'I am quite used to this sort of thing,' she said softly. 'Don't worry!'

She also knew how to put an end to my embarrassing arousal. She stuck a swab deep into the end of it. It didn't hurt but it was quite uncomfortable.

'It looks fine to me, but this swab should tell us if there is any infection.'

'How long will it take for the results?'

'Call me next week.'

A whole week! Shit! I wish Spud hadn't said anything now! How can I face Snowy this weekend with this on my mind?

I have been an ex-virgin for less than a week and I have already been examined for suspected VD!

I went home after that and played on my computer for the rest of the afternoon.

I didn't feel like going out and seeing anyone so, for once, the unexpected visit I had from Lara this evening wasn't as welcome as it would normally have been.

She stayed for a couple of hours. We chatted about various things. Then she left. I got the impression that she is feeling lonely.

16 January 2004, Friday

I had an awful dream last night. I dreamt that I had gone to see Dr Flux for the results of the tests and that I was lying on her couch with a huge erection as she told me that she had got the results and that the only treatment was immediate removal of the infected area. She then produced a huge machete, grabbed my penis and swung the blade at it. At that point I woke up in a terrible sweat.

I tried to put this nightmare to the back of my mind and look forward to seeing Snowy. I played two games of Monopoly with Auntie Cathy. I won both of them despite her attempts to cheat by stealing money from the bank when I went to the toilet.

Soon after I had finished my dinner, Snowy arrived and seeing her made me forget about all my troubles. We went to my room and indulged in some bodily pleasures. Everything was all right except for the moment when I became a bit anxious when she was giving me a blow job and I lost my erection.

'That's never happened before!' she said in a surprised voice.

17 January 2004, Saturday

At long last a football match to go to! I went over to Southampton in the morning so that I could enjoy the beautiful women of West Quay and a KFC lunch.

Dad met me at KFC and we went to the match together. After recent results we were half expecting to lose, even though our opponents, Leeds United, are in a terrible state both on and off the pitch, with financial difficulties.

In a good performance, but not outstanding, we won two-one, and that was with James Beattie on the bench.

The player that usually misses easy chances to score, so much so that he hasn't scored a league goal since the first game of the season, Kevin Phillips, actually scored today.

After dinner, Snowy came around and we spent another evening in bed. I love sex.

18 January 2004, Sunday

I was quite excited about the prospect of being able to play football again this morning. We had our cup replay against Shorewell. It was an away match and Dad gave Ed, Meat and me a lift out there.

Pitbull was dubious about my fitness, so he put me on the bench. I was very disappointed, but early on Jamie, our young striker, took a knock and had to come off. I took my opportunity to play with great enthusiasm, and even if I say so myself, I was instrumental in our two-nil victory. I made our first with an away swinging corner that was nodded in by Vernon, and I scored our second with an overhead kick after Tom had sliced his cross behind me. So we are in the semi-finals. I haven't enjoyed playing so much for ages.

Snowy came back with us to join us for Sunday lunch. Meat and Ed got a lift with Spud, who joined us for lunch without Annicka who wasn't feeling very well.

With all the guests in the house, Snowy and I felt a bit awkward about leaving for a bit of privacy and so we didn't, and I didn't get a shag this afternoon as a result.

Spud gave Snowy a lift home but later this evening he phoned us with worrying news. When he'd got home he found Annicka had been bleeding and he had to rush her to hospital. Mum and Dad immediately left to join him.

They returned hours later with the awful news that Annicka had lost the baby.

What am I going to say to them when I see them next?

19 January 2004, Monday

Dad and I were both feeling down on our way to work this morning. Poor Spud, he was so happy to be a prospective father.

I was mortified when I arrived at work to find that they hadn't given the processors a proper clean while I'd been away. So I had to spend the whole day cleaning them. The complete bastards!

We caught the five-thirty Red Jet, and after dinner we went around to see Spud and Annicka. Annicka was in bed, crying. I gave her a sympathetic kiss and a hug and Mum stayed in with her. We left Angelina at home, in case her being there might rub salt in the wound, but Spud said that we should have brought her round and perhaps a cuddle with her would have helped Annicka.

Dad, Spud and I went to the kitchen to make a round of teas and coffees. Spud was trying to put on a brave face but all of a sudden he just burst into tears. Dad hugged him. I didn't know what to do. He was bawling. I felt so bad for him.

When he had calmed down a bit we sat down in his living room. He said that he just doesn't know what to say or do to help Annicka. He is just as destroyed as she is.

'It'll take time, but the pain will go away,' Dad advised. 'Just hang in there. If you need anything you know where we are. Just call. Any time, okay?'

We stayed there until around ten and then we left, with Mum promising to spend the whole of tomorrow there.

With all that stuff going on, I forgot to phone Snowy. I hope she doesn't get funny about it.

20 January 2004, Tuesday

I got a text from Snowy this morning: 'WHAT HAPPND 2 U LAST NITE?'

I texted back: 'ANNICKA LOST HER BABY.'

A few moments later my phone rang and Snowy was crying on the other end. 'Why couldn't you have told me with a phone call? That's a horrible thing to find out by text!'

I felt really bad. She was upset now and I could do nothing about it. I just wanted to hold her. As a result of these recent events I had a terrible day at work.

When I got home I phoned Snowy. She said that she was on the bus and coming to Cowes. She told me to meet her at Spud and Annicka's house.

When I arrived, Spud's adoptive parents were there and Snowy was upstairs with Annicka. I hardly saw anything of her.

When it was time to leave I just walked her to the bus stop where we had a short snogging session before the bus took her back to Newport.

21 January 2004, Wednesday

I spent the day doing my first ever, real repro job. It was only a simple job, but I needed to know that I was doing everything right. I was expecting QC (Quality Control), to find something wrong with it but it went through all right.

I felt very pleased with myself.

When I got home, Mum had a huge bouquet of flowers and a card for Dad and me to sign. It was for Annicka, and she headed around there with Cathy and Angelina while Dad and I washed up the dinner things.

We spent the rest of the evening watching the Carling Cup semi-final on Sky.

During the match I got a call from Ed. Hannah is having her twentieth birthday party on Friday night. I can't wait!

I phoned Snowy, but she can't come, as it's her mum's birthday that night. Shit! Will I never be able to go to a party with a bird on my arm? I'll be just playing gooseberry as usual.

22 January 2004, Thursday

I was anxious today as the time approached nine-thirty and I was able to phone the doctor's for the results of my VD test. The result, thank God, was negative. Now I can completely forget about the whole thing.

I did another successful repro job on the Mac today. I'm well pleased with myself.

I went around to Ed's tonight. We had a laugh teasing Zoe and her friends who were camped in Zoe's room. We kept on trying to get in.

It was nice to be able to enjoy a good laugh after recent events.

Ed confided in me about his feelings for Hannah. He said that he is besotted. She is amazing in bed, apparently - very adventurous. But he wouldn't go into details, unfortunately, but then I couldn't go into the details of my sex life with Snowy. That is strange because, in the past, when I tried to imagine what it would be like to have a sex life, I always thought that I wouldn't be able to help myself and would tell everyone all about what I got up to between the sheets.

Tomorrow night's party will be at Hannah and Katie's house, which will be nice because I haven't seen Katie for ages.

23 January 2004, Friday

I enjoyed my day at work today. I spent the day doing repro and Gerry called me into his office to tell me how pleased he was with my progress.

After dinner I phoned Snowy briefly and she told me not to go off with anyone at the party.

The party was the usual type of thing. Spud was the only absentee that I noticed. There were a few older girls and women that Hannah knows from work. We all got drunk fairly quickly, especially me as I haven't had a drink for a month.

Katie spent ages chatting to me. Lara came along and tried to butt in. Then Katie went to the toilet and Lara started telling me how much she fancied me! I told her she was drunk. Katie came back from the loo and I told her what Lara had said and she said, 'I'm not surprised. You have turned into quite the hunk.'

'Don't take the piss!' I said.

'I'm not! A lot of the girls I have spoken to tell me that you are gorgeous.'

'But I couldn't get a girlfriend last year!'

'You have matured, Troy!'

I was quite stunned by what she said, but she was drunk so I put it to the back of my mind.

At some stage in the evening I went to the toilet. I was just about to shut the door behind me when Lara stuck her foot in the door and barged in. 'I am bustin', she slurred.

I offered to wait outside but she just locked the door, pulled down her knickers and sat on the toilet. I didn't see anything because I turned my head away. I could hear her going and then she said, 'Your turn!'

I didn't feel very comfortable going in front of her, but she turned her back on me so I went. When I turned around she was standing as close as she possibly could without touching me.

'Erm! What's the matter?' I nervously asked.

'You are standing on my knickers!'

I bent down to pick them up, and as I went to stand up again she lifted her skirt over my head. My face was inches away from the one thing I have longed to gaze at for years, and it was just as amazing as I had imagined it to be, if not more. I thought to myself, I can't do this, she is drunk, so I got my head out from there.

'Lara, that was very nice but you are drunk.'

'Only a little bit! Don't worry Troy, I know exactly what I am doing and what I want!'

With that she grabbed my left hand and thrust it into her crotch, put her right hand around the back of my head and snogged my tongue almost out of my head.

It was a total dream come true. I got to see her naked, yes, but that two minutes of passion was something I have wanted with her for longer than I can remember.

She must have planned it because she had equipped herself with a packet of condoms. But, unfortunately, it was only a three pack.

Maybe I was still lying in that hospital bed in a coma. This must be an hallucination. We didn't even hear people knocking on the door as went about each other in a frenzy.

We did leave the bathroom to strange looks from Hannah's friends. I was going to head downstairs, but Lara yanked me into a bedroom where we did it again.

Thank you, God. This is the most wonderful moment in my life. I have just had the most wonderful sex with the most beautiful girl in the world.

24 January 2004, Saturday

I awoke this morning with Lara next to me in a bed at Hannah and Katie's house. Lara stirred soon after I did.

I tested the water, 'Morning!'

'Morning!' she groaned.

‘You all right about last night?’

‘Yes, it was great!’

I thought to myself, thank God for that. Not because I was worried about my sexual performance, but because she might have thought that I had taken advantage of her.

It was gone ten and I had to get home and freshen up.

Snowy was at Pompey’s FA Cup game against Scunthorpe, so I watched Sky Sports all afternoon. This gave me plenty of time to think.

What if Lara tells Snowy and she complains to her dad and he turns nasty towards me again?

Shit! What have I done?

Lara texted me while I was churning things over in my mind: ‘AM I CING U 2NITE?’

I texted back: ‘SORRY IM CING SNOWY.’

‘RU DUMPING HER?’

‘I DON’T KNOW.’

‘OK, TALK LATER.’

I bloody knew it. I’m right in the shit now!

When I saw Snowy this evening I found it difficult disguising my angst. I just told her that I was still tired from last night. She decided that the best cure for my condition was sex. That was a nice thought and it did take my mind off Lara for a while.

I walked her home and thought long and hard about who I wanted. Lara was always a dream. I am not sure that mixing dreams and reality is a good thing. I do love Snowy, so how could I be unfaithful to her? If I went out with Lara I could see her every day, but as a person she is not as nice as Snowy.

What am I going to do?

25 January 2004, Sunday

We played a home league game this morning against Pan. I was put in the starting line-up. I was horrified when I noticed Lara watching the game. She was standing next to Snowy. I had a shit game as a result. Pitbull was moaning at me at the end of our one-nil defeat, but I didn’t take any of it in.

When I left the changing room, Snowy was waiting for me and there was no sign of Lara. I was greeted in her usual affectionate way so I knew that Lara hadn’t said anything. The relief helped to cheer me up a bit and we got on all right for the rest of the day. Snowy joined us for lunch, as did Spud and Annicka. They were very quiet and the atmosphere was tense. They left soon after the meal was finished. Annicka hardly touched hers.

Snowy and I spent the last couple of hours of our weekend together, doing what lovers do. She left at around four-thirty and, only a few minutes after she left, Lara called. I invited her to my room.

She naturally asked me what was happening with us.

'You know what I think of you, Lara,' I said. 'You are exquisitely beautiful.'

'And I'm yours if you'll have me!"

'If you had come to me three months ago, things would be so simple, but the trouble is I love Snowy.'

'How can you love her when the other night you were making love to me?'

'I know. I feel bad about that. You have been a fantasy of mine for so long. I was drunk. Maybe, in a way, I thought that I was dreaming. I wish I could have you both but I can't.'

'So you still want her?'

'Yes. Sorry!'

Tears started to well up in her eyes so I tried to put my arm around her to comfort her. She just shrugged me off and sobbed, 'I thought you were different! But you are just like your brother!' Then she left.

I am assuming that she won't mention anything to Snowy. I will just have to make sure that they are kept apart.

I went down to the pub this evening, after an invitation from Tom. Karl and I hardly exchanged words. I think he still feels guilty about the accident.

26 January 2004, Monday

I spent the whole of the working day in the Cromalin proofing room learning the technique. It was quite boring.

Dad and I got off at Woolston Station on the way home from work, and picked up a Chinese takeaway. We then caught the bus over the Itchen Bridge and walked up to St Mary's Stadium. We went into the Dell Supporters Club and cheekily ate our Chinese meal. It was cheeky because they serve food there. Nobody told us off though, and the meal was delicious.

Southampton played a friendly, tonight, in memory of the late club President, Ted Bates, who died last year. German champions Bayern Munich were the visitors and the match finished as a one all draw.

27 January 2004, Tuesday

I felt terrible today at work. The job I was doing was bounced by QC and therefore didn't go out tonight. Gerry, the boss, can't stand jobs going out late. I was expecting a bollocking but he didn't say anything.

When I got home, Spud was there. He told us that Annicka had gone to Sweden to spend some time with her parents, so Mum had invited him around for dinner. He is still very down about recent events. It's amazing how, when things are going so well for you, life can just turn around and kick you in the stomach. He has got all that inheritance money but it can't help him sort out his current problems.

He didn't stay for long after his meal. He said that he wanted to get home and speak to Annicka on the phone.

I went down to the Union again tonight and played darts and bar football with the lads (Jason Dwyer, Tom and Meat).

28 January 2004, Wednesday

I was called into Gerry's office this morning. I was expecting to be read the riot act but instead he told me that I was to spend all of next week in the retouching department. I don't know if that is a punishment or not. Dad says that it's all part of my training.

I was given my first payslip today. We get them the day before our wages go into the bank. I was absolutely delighted when I saw that the net pay amount was £911.72. To make things even better, Dad let me off all the money I had borrowed from him over the last couple of months. My annual salary in £15,300. I might be able to afford to rent my own place! I will look into it when the *Isle of Wight County Press* comes out on Friday.

Spud came around tonight. He was still miserable. He was asking us if we thought that he should follow Annicka to Sweden. Mum and Dad advised him to give it time. The poor sod. He is lost without her.

29 January 2004, Thursday

At lunchtime today I went to the nearest bank and drew out nine hundred pounds in twenty-pound notes. My wallet bulged and strained with its newly acquired filling.

The day dragged because I couldn't wait to spend some of it.

After work I went into Southampton to buy Snowy a present. I got her some Ysatis perfume. It cost thirty quid! I hope she appreciates it.

My new monthly keep-bill lightened the load in my wallet by two hundred and fifteen pounds. I have still got six hundred and fifty-five pounds left though.

I went down the pub tonight and gave Karl thirty pounds to buy a round. It felt great! He told me that Lara is going out with Stevie Perry on the rebound from a one night stand with a bloke called Corben!

What have I done to her?

30 January 2004, Friday

We went to the pub as usual for a Friday lunchtime. I bought a lovely sirloin steak and chips for fifteen pounds. It was absolutely delicious.

This evening I saw Snowy and the predictable follow-up to the presentation of her gift was a rampant sex session. Thirty quid well spent in my book!

I persuaded her to come shopping with me in Southampton before she goes to her Portsmouth versus Wolverhampton Wanderers game tomorrow.

31 January 2004, Saturday

I got up early this morning and met up with Snowy at the Red Funnel terminal. We caught the eight-thirty Red Jet and I paid for Snowy. I hadn't bargained on having to follow her around all of her shops all morning. It was exhausting!

I spent one hundred pounds on buying her some new clothes, some of which was for my benefit as she bought a sexy negligee from Ann Summers.

We broke for lunch at West Quay's KFC, then I walked her to the railway station and bought her a one-way ticket to Fratton.

Then I was able to go back into the city and go around my shops. I went to Dixons and bought myself an excellent new personal DAB radio. Then I bought myself some new Etnies, some YSL jeans and an Armani shirt. I set off for home so that I could get there in time for dinner.

I showed my parents what I had bought and received a lecture. They think that I should have saved my money.

I assured them that it was a novelty and that I would start saving next month.

Snowy came back from her Pompey match slightly disappointed. She had expected a win but they drew.

I apparently missed a cracking game on Sky, as Saints were very unlucky to lose three-two at Old Trafford to Manchester United.

Snowy and I soon forgot about football. It was the moment she put on her new negligee. It didn't stay on her for long!

1 February 2004, Sunday

I got myself and Snowy excused from our normal Sunday lunch today, before setting off for our match.

We beat Medina two-one and I scored both goals, the second with an overhead kick. Medina's manager was gracious enough to shake my hand after the game. I thought that was really nice of him.

After showering and changing, I bummed a lift to Newport for Snowy and me from Nathan. I took Snowy to the Bargeman's Rest for lunch. We both enjoyed roast beef. Then we went to her mother's house, which is on the same road.

We messed around in her room for the rest of the day. The hours passed as though they were minutes and I left at ten-thirty and caught the bus home.

As the bus stopped at Parkhurst, Lara got on. I hoped that she wouldn't spot me but she did and came over and sat next to me.

'Where have you been?' I asked.

'At my boyfriend's house!'

There was an uncomfortable silence, then she spoke again. 'Are you not talking to me or something?'

'I just did!'

'Wow! That's really making conversation isn't it?'

'I don't know what to say!'

'You've never had a problem talking to me before!'

'I know! It's just'

'Just what?'

'I feel uneasy about the way you feel towards me.'

'I still fancy you if that's what you mean, but you blew me out big time!'

'Yes, I'm sorry.'

'Have you changed your mind then?'

'No, not at all!'

'That's a shame! Well, you know where I am if you do!'

There was another awkward silence.

'Look Troy! Shall we just forget about what happened and return to being just friends?'

'I'd like that.'

'Good! That's sorted then!'

Our conversation improved slightly for the rest of the journey and I walked her home, but there will always be a nagging worry in my mind that she might drop me in it one day.

I should enjoy Snowy's special visit on Tuesday night. Mum has invited her around for dinner, to give me a chance to see her midweek.

2 February 2004, Monday

I spent the morning cleaning the processors and the afternoon doing Cromalins, so it was a pretty crappy day at work.

While we were eating our dinner, a car drew up. It was Spud. He popped in for a few minutes and asked us to look after his car for a while. He has decided to go to Sweden to be with Annicka. He doesn't know when or if he will be back.

He has asked me to look after his house. I can live there while he is away, rent free!

'We'll discuss this later!' Dad snorted.

We quickly finished our meal and drove him down to the ferry terminal. He gave each of us an extra big hug before departing. Poor Spud!

When we got home we had a heated discussion about me living at Spud's. Basically Dad put his foot down and said no. I am not happy. It's up to Spud not him.

Shit! I really want to move out now.

3 February 2004, Tuesday

Dad and I didn't speak much on the way to work this morning. I did some simple repro jobs on the Mac today. We are starting to get busy, thank God. Everybody was starting to get a bit worried about the quiet spell we have had for the past few weeks.

Things were still quiet on the way home.

Snowy was already there when I got home. I had a bath and we settled down for dinner.

Mum got a little tipsy on Lambrusco Bianco and started talking about the events that led up to my running away to Wales. The word 'diary' got mentioned and that ignited Snowy's curiosity, or should I call it, nosiness!

She wanted to have a look at my diary. I told her that I didn't write a diary any more. Then a big argument ensued when I refused to show her last year's diary.

'It's personal,' I explained.

'What are you hiding?' she said.

'Nothing!'

'Let me read it then!'

I refused and she left in a terrible mood after shouting, 'If you keep secrets from me we have no future!'

She didn't even accept Dad's offer of a lift as she slammed the front door behind her.

Mum apologised to me. I ignored her.

4 February 2004, Wednesday

There was a knocking on my patio window at three o'clock this morning. It was a cold and upset Snowy. She threw her arms around me and tearfully apologised. I hadn't been able to sleep anyway. I had been flicking through my diary for last year, trying to see if there was anything bad about her in it. I had found nothing too bad in recent weeks.

She noticed it open on my bedside table.

'Go on, take a look.' I said.

'No, it's all right.' she sniffed. 'You're right, it's private.'

'If you're sure.'

'Well, perhaps just a peek!'

After she had read a few pages she said, 'What about this year?'

'I got out of the habit of writing when I was in hospital, so I stopped writing one,' I lied.

She swallowed it, thank God. She left at four-fifteen.

With that near miss in mind, I have decided that this diary-writing malarkey has caused me all sorts of trouble over the last few months. I nearly lost my girlfriend because of my diary. There is no way that a diary can really be private when there is a chance that somebody can find it and read it. It is too dangerous.

You can't be totally honest if you think that somebody else might read what you have written.

That in mind, I really can't be arsed to write any more.